£2

THE SHADOW OF A SORCERER

Mrs. Lambert, an elderly widow, had brought her daughter to Austria to learn German. Meg was pretty and attractive, but so irresponsible at nineteen that her mother looked forward to the day when she could see her happily married. Her friendship with Robin, a fellow-student, was one which would never have bothered Mrs. Lambert, but Esmé Scarron, the rich and mysterious man who lived in the house across the lake, was quite a different matter. Strange and sinister was the power he exerted over Meg—as undesirable as the curious guests he entertained in his secluded villa

Stella Gibbons

THE SHADOW OF A SORCERER

. . . in the green and cloudy Austrian land . . .

LONDON
HODDER AND STOUGHTON

First Printed 1955

MADE AND PRINTED IN GREAT BRITAIN FOR
HODDER AND STOUGHTON LTD., LONDON, BY
HAZELL, WATSON AND VINEY LTD., AYLESBURY AND LONDON

Contents

CHAPTER ONE

Arrival

ON their first evening at Martinsdorf Mrs Lambert and her only child, Meg, ate their supper slowly and in a daze of fatigue. The mother hardly glanced at the other people in the dining-room, not even at those seated with them at the same table, although her first hasty glance on coming late to the meal had given her an impression, which remained with her beneath her exhaustion, that there were no other English people present, and that all the faces bent over the fried liver and dumplings were what she thought of as "interesting" —but too alive, too demanding of attention, to be welcome this evening, when she was so dreadfully tired.

Meg's weariness expressed itself in a flush on cheeks usually pale, an unwonted sparkle in eyes usually dreamy, and in restless glances in the direction of their neighbours. Introductions had been made when the Lamberts entered the room; Frau Schacht had preceded them, walking with the upright and gracefully springy carriage that Mrs Lambert so well remembered after ten years, and she had presented them to the diners already seated. The men—Mrs Lambert had seen with mingled resignation and satisfaction that they outnumbered the women—had risen, and made those little military bows which seemed to pull their muscles flatteringly to attention in the presence of females, while the women had smiled and pleasantly murmured.

Frau Schacht's presentation of her English guests had been brief. As she took her place, and became aware of a sparse, faintly odorous steam wavering up from the soup-bowl set before her, Mrs Lambert had a number of confused thoughts: that she must get into the habit of addressing Hansi as "Frau Schacht"; that thank goodness Hansi had not repeated publicly, in front of the whole School of Languages, the emotional speech of gratitude for three years'

sanctuary in England which she had made to the Lamberts on welcoming them privately half an hour ago; and finally, that that man
in the corner, the young one with the square head, was already
looking at Meg.

Meg was looking at him, too, but only in the intervals of eating
liver and dumplings and glancing at everyone else; and it lay within
the boundary of decorum to look, because after all they had been
introduced. All the same, Mrs Lambert experienced the familiar
sensation of a sinking heart, and wished, for the several thousandth
time, that her life and the life of her surprisingly attractive daughter
were still sturdily cushioned by the presence of a husband and a
father. Harry would have known how to deal with all the men,
young, middle-aged and old, whatever the shape of their heads. But
Harry was dead; had been dead, now, for nine years. "Now" was
still the word, though. At any moment, his widow was liable to be
assailed by memories.

It is always surprising to find how reviving hot food is. After
some ten minutes passed in passively moving her knife and fork between her plate and her mouth, Mrs Lambert's incipient tearfulness
had receded. It would not have been indulged, if it had persisted; it
hardly ever was; but there was comfort in feeling complete control
once more of her throat and eye muscles. She glanced, a little more
observantly, about the large, dim room whose only light was the
fast-fading one of a spring evening.

The wooden walls were varnished dark brown; there were
flourishing hyacinths and daffodils and some plants with bright
green trailing sprays growing in a box before the open window and
making a frieze against the motionless clear air. Beyond this frieze,
growing on the downward slope of the alp on which the house was
built, there were apricot and plum trees in blossom, the tops of
whose branches alone were visible. Beyond them, the green-blue of
the lake. Beyond that, the blue-green of pine forests fledging the
farther shore, and over all the pale orange of the after-sunset sky.
The tall tiled stove, taller than Frau Schacht where it stood in its important position against the longest wall, warmed the cold spring
air even as it blew faintly into the room. There was an old wooden

chest thickly painted with dim foliage, a shining bare floor, a shabby wooden sideboard where salt and bread were kept. The half-darkness was grateful to Mrs Lambert's tired eyes, and, beneath the chatter of voices and the subdued din of knives and forks at play, she could hear the running of a stream through the deep grass outside; a detached, secret reminder of wild Nature.

Yes, it was a nice place; restful; there were some things that she liked already about Hansi's home, although she had not yet been in it an hour, but she hoped that she was not going to feel as exhausted as this all the time, or it would be difficult to summon up the energy to help Hansi run the place.

"Mummy, are you awfully tired?"

It was the beloved voice; so pretty, so musical.

"I am rather, darling. I shall go to bed as soon after supper as Hansi will let me."

"I thought you must be. You keep on not hearing what I say. I want to get down to the lake. And didn't you notice on the way up?—there was a beer-house with paintings on the walls . . . rather exciting. And two girls in Austrian dress. And the maid wears it, too. I thought no one did now, except in Ivor Novello's plays. . . . Do you think they might have dancing at the beer-house? Hansi will know; I'll ask her after supper. It's marvellous her speaking such good English, or we should be utterly sunk. . . . I've forgotten all the German I ever knew. Oh *no*, thank you. I simply loathe stewed fruit," and with a wide smile but a decided gesture she waved away the small dish which the Austrian serving-girl, in bodice and apron, was about to set before her.

Mrs Lambert happened at this moment to glance across the room, more from an involuntary nervous flutter caused by Meg's action than from any wish to see what their fellow-diners were doing, and the object upon which her eyes fell was Frau Schacht. That lady's own small clever eyes, with their expression of intellect that was untouched by meditation, were fixed steadily upon Meg, and it was plain that the lofty waving away of the dessert had been marked.

In an instant she had crossed the room and was beside them.

"You find Austrian cooking strange at first, no?" she said, addressing Meg, and again Mrs Lambert caught the waft of scent; French undoubtedly, and expensive, and not in keeping with Frau Schacht's neat and almost prim exterior. It was the exotic presence of this scent which had helped to confuse Mrs Lambert on her meeting with Hansi, the altered Hansi, earlier in the evening. And yet— was she so greatly altered?

"Oh no—it is delicious," Mrs Lambert now said hastily.

"I shall get used to it, I expect," Meg answered, "but I must say it tastes awfully queer at first. Perhaps it's having lived on sandwiches for the last two days. But I always loathe stewed fruit wherever I am."

"I am sorry that your dessert does not please you, Meg. Perhaps we could find something else that you would like better. A cake? Or there is some *apfelstrudel*, I think, left from lunch?" And Frau Schacht turned to the maid who stood by the table with her eyes moving from Meg's face to that of her mistress, and spoke to her in German.

"Oh no, thank you. I can't eat cake, I'm on a diet. I'm slimming." Meg's tone, at first as firm as when she had dealt with the stewed fruit, wavered slightly. She had remembered that Austria, even as Scotland, was famed for its cakes. And Frau Schacht nodded.

"You will have a nice Austrian *torte*," she said calmly, her gaze just touching the well-filled outline of Meg's cherry-pink jersey and then moving aside. "As for the slimming—do not. You are very well as you are," and she went smiling away.

"I shan't eat it. Even if she brings it, I shan't eat it. She treats me like a baby. She always did. It was all very well, I suppose, when I was nine, but now I'm nineteen."

"Nearly nineteen, dearest. And I think Hansi meant it kindly."

"She tries to boss me. I do *dislike* that so."

"Yes, well, do eat it when it comes, dear. You have had so little to eat for the last two days that it surely can't put any weight on you."

This young lady, thought the elderly Austrian gentleman seated opposite to the Lamberts and slowly savouring his stewed apricots, *has nineteen years, so her mother has said, but she talks like a child, and her face is a child's also in the way that it shows all she feels. Not so are most young English girls, so I have heard and read. Already young Müller is looking at her. Soon after supper, I think, he will approach her and talk to her. It is a pity that I go home to-morrow, for I should much like to see if there is to be a romance.*

Then, because he intended to wring the utmost benefit from his stay at the School of Languages, he bent towards the English lady and stiffly inclined his head with a polite smile.

"Have you a goot churney, *gnädige frau?*"

"Oh—very tiring, thank you." Mrs Lambert smiled fleetingly and looked down at her plate; the firmly introductory note in his voice caused her a sensation almost of despair. I cannot, I simply cannot, talk to foreigners to-night, she thought. Hansi is sure to want a long discussion about business arrangements with me presently, and that will mean being careful. . . . I am not going to be put upon by Hansi, or have Meg done out of anything, either. And I don't think she is going to like Meg now Meg's grown up. How I wish I were safely in bed and asleep.

But the elderly Austrian gentleman was saying—"*Ach, zo?* Then you must wish to rest in peace, and I will not talk to you again," and with this unexpected display of perceptiveness he lit a small and cheap cigar (having first waved it at her enquiringly and received silent permission) and relapsed into unembarrassed silence. Mrs Lambert, though relieved, felt slightly ashamed of herself.

Dear God, the mother shows her feelings as plainly as the daughter, the Austrian was thinking. *They are easily to be wounded, these two. Where is the famous English reserve? Or perhaps the war has changed the English character?*

Meanwhile, some of the guests, having finished dining, were helping the sturdy maid to move the small tables to one end of the room, while others arranged chairs in a circle about the stove. Someone turned on the electric light, so that the evening suddenly appeared to have become twilight. Nevertheless, outside it was not yet dark. Young Müller lingered by the window, only moving away with a mutter, a bow and a blush when someone officiously closed it. He continued to glance covertly at Meg. Would she come out for a walk? What hair! It was the brightest thing in the room.

"As yet, so far, I have no *salon* in which my guests may sit," Frau Schacht said, pausing at Mrs Lambert's side, "so we have to do as you see, and make a cosy little circle about the stove. In the summer when the stove is not used we sit about the window. That is——" She hesitated and frowned, then muttered something about Martinsdorf being full of unreasonable souls, and gripped the edge of the table at which Mrs Lambert and the Austrian were sitting. "Come, lazy people, you have sat long enough. Help me to move this table."

Mrs Lambert was slightly disconcerted; the Austrian gentleman —perhaps supported by the knowledge that to-morrow evening he would be beyond Frau Schacht's reach—rose with a bow and obeyed. When after some manipulation the table was arranged to her satisfaction she stood for a moment looking critically about the room, where a talkative circle had already gathered round the stove, and other guests, more studious or less sociable, lingered with books or knitting in their hands and exchanged gossip before retiring to their rooms. The apartment wore an interim air, as if between its earlier and later rôles of dining-room and sitting-room.

"Mummy," said Meg, materialising at Mrs Lambert's side with young Müller so close to her that he appeared to be attached to her belt like a fob, "you don't mind if we go for a walk, do you?"

We! And they could not have exchanged more than five sentences under cover of the table-moving and other bustle. But Mrs Lambert was used to this sort of thing. She looked a little more closely at the boy, whose unalarming appearance she had already automatically noted while she sat at dinner, and smiled.

"Don't be too late, darling, will you? Can you find your way back here, do you think?"

"Oh yes. There's a moon."

"Yess, there iss a moon," smiled and bowed young Müller. He thought of adding that the gracious lady need not be alarmed, because he would take good care of the young fräulein, but his English was not equal to it. Frau Schacht suddenly struck in decidedly.

"If Meg is here to learn German she must *not* talk English. Now,

Hermann, remember—you are to *talk German* to Fräulein Lambert. No English. Do you understand?" and she kept them waiting while she repeated the command in his own language.

When they had gone—after the young man had assured her that he would not utter one word of English to the fräulein, and refrained from pointing out that although the fräulein might be here to learn German, he was here to learn English—Frau Schacht turned to Mrs Lambert.

"We will go into my room," she said, "and then at last, my dear Eve, we can have a good talk. It is downstairs, opening upon the garden. Shall I lead the way?"

It occurred to Mrs Lambert, as they passed a small lobby where growing plants were arranged on shelves against the wooden walls, and went down a flight of stone steps into what appeared to be the basement, that this question was superfluous and had a double meaning. What else had Hansi been doing, since their meeting two hours ago? And Mrs Lambert suppressed a sigh.

She had a personal peculiarity; when confronted by a stronger will than her own—which was of average strength—she felt a sense of bodily oppression, an impulse to smile weakly while she fought for breath. She had occasionally experienced this during struggles with the infant Meg, although Meg's will had been passionate and wayward rather than strong, and had been less so—oh, much less so —since the death of her father. And now, following Hansi's small, broad back down the stairs, hearing Hansi chattering about her plan to build a sitting-room on to the house next summer—"Franz owns the land and I shall find the money"—she felt once again the disagreeable sensation of helplessness. However, it was not as if she had to deal with a stranger. She and Hansi had lived for three years in the same house, and she knew Hansi well . . . or had known her.

"There! This is my own little room—where I come to be quiet and get away from my worries. I shut the window—it is still cold at this time of year. Sit in that chair, Eve, it is the most comfortable. So. A cigarette? No? I shall smoke, I think. I allow myself five a day. Now, how do you like my room?"

Mrs Lambert, thus encouraged, permitted herself that frank look at her surroundings which good manners usually forbids, but was prevented from at once expressing admiration by the fact that the small, stone-floored, whitewashed apartment with its thick plain rugs and curtains of chintz in a modern design contained twin beds.

"Oh, you are wondering where Franz is," said Hansi, interpreting the hesitation. "He has a job in Salzburg, not a very good job, I am sorry to say, but all he could get. You know, he was in a camp——"

"I do know, Hansi. We were so glad when you wrote to say that he was home again."

"Yes, I had your kind letters. But he was made very ill there. He has tuberculosis."

Mrs Lambert was silent, looking at her with an expression which, because she was not a sentimental woman, she felt to be both sentimental and inadequate to Hansi's grief. Hansi was staring at the eiderdown, buttoned to the sheet beneath it, that covered the bed.

"Yes, poor Franz. The journey would of course be impossible for him to make every day. So he has a room there in the house of a friend, a war comrade, and he comes home here at week-ends—where there is always a bed and a welcome for him, of course, and where I am always at work, building up the Language School and the guest-house so that one day he will be able to live in comfort."

Mrs Lambert made a murmur of sympathy and admiration.

"I am always making plans for this place. Everything is sacrificed to it, you might almost say," and Hansi laughed. "That's why I cannot spare one room each for Franz and for me. We have had to make the best of this little cellar that leads out into the garden. But I have tried to make it pretty. You like it, *nicht wahr?*"

"Very much." But in fact Mrs Lambert found the room curiously disagreeable; perhaps the impression came from the contrast between rough walls and floor and almost luxurious furnishings. It was as if an anchorite should have had his cell done up by Heal's or Maple's.

"And now," continued Hansi, "we must arrange how we are to work together during the next six months. I said in my letter, didn't I, that you should pay me one pound a week for you and for Meg."

"Yes, that was it." Mrs Lambert was now sitting upright in the most comfortable chair with a flush on either cheek. "A pound each."

"But of course, Eve! I could not give you three good meals a day, and your rooms, and all the little extras, for only *ten shillings* a week each."

"Yes, that was what I meant. A pound *each*."

"So. And in return, I am to give Meg German lessons."

"That was what was arranged, yes."

"So. And you, my dear Eve, in return should help me to manage the pension; to talk English with my German pupils, and sometimes to go into Villach to make the shopping and to arrange the tables sometimes. I do not ask you to make the beds or to do the dirty work. I have two maids for that work. Last year I had only one. But this year (always hoping that Frau Trauber at the *weinstube* in the village does not get her away from me by offering her more money than I can afford) I have Trudi also; Trudi as well as Maria. So I'm sure you will be very happy here, and Meg too. It should be a grand holiday for Meg. She will work at her German in the mornings with the others, of course, but in the afternoons they are all free to go on excursions. Did she want to come here?"

Her eyes were fixed intently upon Mrs Lambert; their greyish hue was lightened by the contrast with a row of stiff golden curls arranged above her lined and sallow forehead. Mrs Lambert answered readily:

"Yes, indeed, she has always longed to travel. Last year, as you know, I managed to get her into a French family after she had finished her secretarial training, and now her French is quite good. I want her German to be good too, then she can be sure of a first-class job. She had a lovely time with the Lebruns; they took her to the *Opéra* and to concerts, and they spent a fortnight at Chartres and she really got to *know* the Cathedral. She loved France . . . she is so fond of music and poetry, you know. Do you remember how she used to recite to us?"

Frau Schacht nodded, her eyes dwelling upon the face in which personality, and what was left of personal life, had become submerged in the calm passion of maternity.

"She plays the piano well, now," Mrs Lambert went on.

"I remember how she would practise," Frau Schacht said.

"And she sings. Her voice is a contralto; so pretty. I wish that you could hear her. Perhaps——"

"There is no piano here. But sometimes our young people have what you call a 'sing-song' with our southern Austrian zither. I shall hope to hear her sing then. And how about the men? Is she attractive to them?"

Mrs Lambert was not quite the typical Englishwoman, but this did take her a little by surprise. Such frankness. . . .

However, now that the slightly embarrassing subject of arrangements had been dealt with and apparently dismissed, she felt relieved, and even welcomed a little gossip with Hansi. There was no one else in her family or social circle with whom she could, or cared to, discuss the subject of Meg and men, and yet she sometimes felt the need of a confidante; even, sometimes, of advice. And about Hansi, even when she had been an unusually shabby refugee of twenty-eight, with cheeks hollowed by hunger and eyes full of fear, there had always been an atmosphere of knowing the secrets of sex. In her more critical moments Mrs Lambert used to think that it was sex as distinct from love.

But Hansi's expression was interested and benevolent. Mrs Lambert gave a little laugh, looking down at her shoes.

"Yes, very attractive. I am sometimes surprised at *how* attractive. Oh, that sounds so unkind——"

"Not at all. We must see all things objectively, even our children. And Meg is not exactly pretty, no? Her face is still the face of a baby. Her nose—now that is really a shame, her nose. It is undignified and without character or shape."

"Hansi—it's a dear little nose!" Mrs Lambert enjoyed nothing so much as talking about Meg, except being with Meg, but she did not enjoy Hansi's tone, and she was uncertain about the precise meaning of "objectively", which she always confused with the other word meaning the exact opposite.

Hansi shook her head with decision. "And she has many admirers, you say?" Mrs Lambert had not said so, but her expression was unmistakably complacent.

"Oh yes, but nothing serious so far, because she is not easily attracted. I don't mean that she's hard to please, for she seems to enjoy the simplest outings if she likes the boy she is with, but she is— Meg is romantic, you know. Not in that silly way that the pictures seem to make worse, but *really* romantic. I think she actually prefers older men. (Well, girls so often do at that age, of course.) She often comes home after an evening out saying this boy or the other is so *young*. Of course, in Tormouth the young men aren't interested in music or poetry or the theatre—it's all cars and sailing. And the older men are all married. Not that I should *like* her to marry an older man—not much older, that is; six or seven years would be all right, or even ten, but——"

She was looking full at Frau Schacht while she talked but, as always when she spoke of Meg, her hearer might not have been there; was no more than a listening-machine; and now her own weariness, the result of two days of unbroken travelling and an almost sleepless night, was forgotten, and she did not notice that Frau Schacht's face had suddenly become more sallow, while black shadows had gradually, mysteriously, painted themselves under her eyes. Suddenly, abruptly, she stood up and yawned.

"My dear Eve, I am going to bed. I need much rest, I work so hard all day and I am up each morning at six o'clock. But you need not get up until a quarter-past seven, you are so much older than I am, and also I do not mean to make you work too hard. You must enjoy our beautiful Austria and benefit from your stay with us. Meg need not get up until eight o'clock; I do not like the pupils about in the house while Trudi and Maria are making the breakfast and I am arranging the work of the day. So good night, Eve. Can you find your way through the garden? Yes? So. Sleep well."

It seemed to Mrs Lambert rather as if she had been elbowed on to a steep chute and propelled out into the chill, delicious-smelling darkness. There she stood, surrounded by small white blurs and glimmers that were flowers, with the stars overhead and the black mountains faintly outlined by the young moon, having barely had time to return Hansi's "good night", while already the door of

Hansi's room was shut and its windows, protected by an outer pair against the winter's cold, were being banged to.

She made her way carefully up the dark stairs, thinking irrelevantly about a comment always made by her mother, dead these twenty years, upon the many stray cats which Eve's pleadings had so often persuaded the family to adopt: *they begin by asking your kind permission to breathe, and end by having kittens in your best hat.*

Hansi had been not unlike a stray cat; arriving in Tormouth in the middle of the war after experiences at which she had only hinted; thin, grateful, making herself useful in the happy Lambert household in many ways (catching mice, so to speak, in return for scraps and a bed): charming them all with her Austrian alternations of gaiety and gloom (waving tail or somnolent brooding eyes) which were so different from their own English placidity and amiability. Perhaps they had not all been completely charmed by her. Mr Lambert had frequently said that she was ambitious, and would do you a bad turn if it served her purpose, and Mrs Lambert had not entirely disagreed. But they had become fond of her, as people do in England of foreigners who share their home.

It was particularly annoying that Hansi should have adopted a tone implying that the Lamberts were paupers, because they were by no means the poverty-stricken pair that her condescending manner suggested; they possessed an income from investments left to them by Mr Lambert, and rents from two excellent houses which he had owned in Tormouth Bay, and at this time they also had the rent paid by an old married pair who had taken Mrs Lambert's house for six months, while their own house, an ancient manor, was being made fit for habitation and the Lamberts were in Austria. Had it been permitted, Mrs Lambert could have brought with her enough money to live in Martinsdorf with Meg in comfort, with none of this getting up at seven-fifteen and making the shopping. But currency regulations made it impossible, and the Lamberts must make their money last during the six months of study which, Mrs Lambert and Hansi agreed, would be necessary to make Meg fluent in German.

It had not occurred to Mrs Lambert to ask Hansi to let them stay there for nothing, as her guests, and if it had occurred to Hansi she had suppressed the impulse.

Mrs Lambert, wishing that Hansi had not suddenly taken to addressing her by her Christian name, stepped on to the balcony of her room and looked out across the dimness. Below were the white tops of the flowering fruit trees, scentless in the spring night, and beyond them the soft blurred shapes and shadows of the descending alp, with dew-wet roofs gleaming dimly out of the foliage. The lake was invisible, but its farther wooded shores were steep and dark against the moonlight, and as Mrs Lambert stood idly gazing, resting her hands upon the balcony rail and wishing that Meg would come in, she seemed to see a white house slowly emerging from the shadows there. But when she looked full at it, trying to discern if it were really there or were merely a trick of the failing moonlight, she saw it no longer; she saw only blackness, and above it the pointed fir trees outlined against the starlit sky, and, suddenly overcome by weariness, yawning, she turned back into her room and shut the balcony doors.

CHAPTER TWO

Charmer

OF course, neither Meg nor young Müller attempted to speak any German after he had nervously uttered his opening enquiry about how long she was staying in Martinsdorf, and had been sweetly answered in quick English. But this defiance of Frau Schacht's *diktat* rather disturbed the good, serious, round-shouldered boy; he walked back to the *gasthaus* beside the lovely and mysterious creature after half an hour's wandering beside the lake convinced that if he had to stay on here, under the same roof with her, his studies would be fatally disturbed, those studies so necessary to him in the task of supporting his widowed mother and his sisters.

Romantically, as if all the songs of Wolf and Schubert were chiming in his heart, he thought that any sacrifice of study and philosophy would be worth while for her, but then he thought of his little family, so meek and grateful to him, so upward-looking to his superior masculine brain and strength, and put temptation away.

As for Meg, she thought him nice but a bore and did not notice, until she was half-way through her breakfast the next morning, that he had already left the *gasthaus*.

The morning following their arrival was so warm that Frau Schacht decided to hold the German class under the tall nut tree already shading with freshly budded boughs the garden stream, and here they all sat; some eight young people from three or four countries of Europe, and read Schiller by turns under her strict eye, which often dwelt upon Meg because the latter could not help staring at the pale distant mountains instead of at her book. They were in Italy!

But she never looked at them long enough to draw down upon herself a spoken reproof. She truly intended to work; she was eager to learn; she said so to her mother. She wanted to equip herself for a really first-class job: in the Foreign Office or as secretary to a famous and *useful* M.P.; and although, she knew, she was not unusually bright, her success in learning French had encouraged her to believe that in six months she could become equally proficient in German. She knew that her mother had made a sacrifice in letting her home and coming to live for six months as a kind of lady-help in southern Austria; at Mrs Lambert's time of life—she had married late and was nearing sixty—it is no pleasure to exchange familiar habits and old friends for ruined castles and glaciers.

Meg *knew* all this. But she did not *realise* it. Martinsdorf was delightful, the distant mountains of Italy were thrillingly beautiful, and she sat under the light shadows of the nut tree, with the stream singing freshly in her ears and the still-wild alp, covered with spring flowers, spread all around her; placidly aware that the two Danish young men were trying not to look at her in the intervals of their reading; and not once wondering what her mother was doing. But then it is not normal at nineteen to wonder what one's mother is doing.

"Mummy," she said, when they were sitting in Mrs Lambert's room that day after lunch, "I absolutely must get started with my sketching; I keep on seeing things that I long to paint. I suppose you didn't notice any art shops in Villach last night?"

"No, I did not. What with trying to find the Customs for our trunks, and trying to find someone who spoke English to ask how far Martinsdorf was from Villach, and then trying to find a taxi, and then arranging with him to bring us here, I didn't think to look for art shops, strange as it may seem."

"Didn't Villach look wonderful when we arrived? I thought we'd *never* get there," Meg said dreamily, "and then, when we did, all those white streets and towers under that peach-coloured sky . . . it looked so *foreign* . . . do you think it's too cold to bathe?"

"I'm quite sure it is. But Hansi says it may be warm enough in a month's time."

The lavish suggestion of a long procession of days and weeks to be spent in this peacefully romantic place caused Meg's eyes to assume their characteristic dreaming expression; she slowly turned her head, as she sat curled upon her mother's bed, and looked silently out at the mountains.

Mrs Lambert looked at her.

The mother's limbs still ached from the rattling and cramping of the long crowded journey across Europe which the need for economy and fear of accident had prevailed upon her to make by rail rather than by air, and the banging and bumping of the short crowded bus journey into a nearby village on a shopping excursion that morning had bruised her. She was finding Hansi's dictatorial tone and Hansi's commissions increasingly irritating—the more so because she was becoming sure that Hansi was unhappy, and one should not, justly, be irritated by an unhappy person. She missed England, her neighbours and her home, and, try as she would, could not help wondering whether her two ancient tenants would not, by dropping lighted matches upon it from their shaking hands, set it on fire. Yet it was all worth while; none of the anxieties she had endured and the sacrifices she had made mattered, if only Meg could learn enough German to secure for herself a really good job with a really good salary. Then, if she did not marry—but it was almost Mrs Lambert's dearest hope that she would, happily and well—she could at least be sure of a useful, dignified and modestly comfortable life.

But she would marry; oh yes, she would certainly marry. Gentle reader, we have said that this was almost Mrs Lambert's dearest hope. Her dearest was that whether she married or remained a spinster, Meg should be happy.

She looked at the bright, full hair lifting itself slightly from the forehead like the crest of some young bird, at the surprising dark brown eyes set amidst pallor and gold, at the nose deplored by Frau Schacht, the mouth drawn by the illustrator of a woman's magazine story, and the form too plump, too Victorian, to please its readers. Meg wore a cotton frock of commonplace design; the outcome of that prolonged and earnest thought which she bestowed upon buying the wrong clothes, and Mrs Lambert, who wore a more subdued version of the same type of dress, thought how well the child's frocks always suited her. At the same time, rising suddenly from beneath the warm current of love like a cold rock out of a summer sea, there came an unexpected thought—*I'll be glad when she's safe and I'm free. It's too much, the responsibility and the love. When she's quite grown up or married and being taken care of by someone better able to do it, it will almost be a relief.*

Meg slowly turned her head, and looked at her. They exchanged a silent smile. Then Meg said with a touch of impatience:

"Mummy, you've got a wisp of hair. Not there; on the other side. Here, let me do it for you."

*　*　*　*　*

The first week passed. Montag, Diesentag and Mittewoch went by slowly, but with increasing speed, and Donnerstag, Freitag and Samstag went almost as quickly as days in England but in a more interesting manner. Mrs Lambert remarked more than once to Meg that there was nothing like a routine for making the time pass

quickly and Meg implored not to be reminded that time was passing at all; she was so happy; she was having such a marvellous time.

Indeed, for all the young pupils at the house, life was agreeable.
Because Frau Schacht's writing-paper was headed *School of Languages and Gasthaus Venedig*, the ordinary tourist demanding luxury
and a round of gaieties tended to be scared away by the threat of
brainy types, and those who came to her were usually young, poor
and intelligent. Often they were morose as well, for they came from
countries only now beginning to recover from war's worst miseries,
but usually there was a cheerful flow and stir of youthful life through
the rooms and up and down the staircases, accompanied by mild flirt-
ation, and unnecessary laughter, and small attention to early hours.

The quiet countryside, curiously melancholy for all its loveliness,
provided many excursions to some ruined monastery or famed
castle crowning its limestone crag, that neatly filled in the long
afternoons after the half-past twelve luncheon; one could go with
the party and practise one's German on the officials during the
pleasantly cheap train or bus journey; or one could take an English
or German book down to the shore of the lake, which every day
grew warmer and more clear, and lie under the acacia trees, pre-
tending to read, until it was half-past four and time to stroll up to
the *weinstube* for a drink of apple-juice and—if money would run
to it—a cake coated with nuts and chocolate.

Mrs Lambert soon learned, however, that the shabby furnishing
and cheerful studentish atmosphere at the *Gasthaus Venedig* did not
satisfy Frau Schacht. She had re-started her School of Languages
immediately after the war because she had been trained to teach and,
having greatly improved her knowledge of English during her four
years' stay in England, had felt that she possessed a means of making
a living in a country where livings were not easy to make, but what
she really wanted—as she often told Mrs Lambert—was to run
two separate establishments: a well-equipped school with resident
teachers and domestic staff for her pupils, and a small hotel luxurious
enough to attract rich tourists.

Her husband owned the large, old wooden house standing in
about an acre of fertile mountain pasture, and she made enough

money from it to enable her to put away each autumn a sum large enough to keep them both throughout the dead season, but the house, she knew, would have to be pulled down, and two new buildings erected in its place; the stream must be diverted, the land terraced and the old nut tree sacrificed. On the long silent evenings of winter week-ends, when the big stove warmed the air of the room to a drowsy heat and Franz sat dozing and coughing in his chair, Frau Schacht passed the hours with sheets of figures and little sketches of houses and gardens, and pored over leaflets advertising refrigerators, vacuum cleaners and electric mixers.

The Lamberts frequently discussed poor Franz. Meg, who drew her ideas about people who had been in camps from the cinema, had a definite conception of how he would look; Mrs Lambert, upon whom time had bestowed caution, attempted no guesses but merely hoped that he was not infectious.

He was expected home on the afternoon of Samstag; one of the few advantages of his job was that sometimes it permitted him to catch a train bringing him into Martinsdorf at about what, in England, would have been tea-time. Meg and her mother were returning homewards along the path that led to the small white Protestant church when they saw, coming up the hillside path with frequent pauses for breath, a smallish man who had evidently just alighted from the train now moving off beside the lake. His skeleton thinness was covered by a grey woollen cloak and his be-feathered hat was too large for him. He carried a brown-paper parcel.

They exchanged smiles, after he had passed them, because he was such a perky-looking little man; and that evening, when guests and students took their places in the dining-room, Frau Schacht presented him as her husband. He was observed by Meg to eat three helpings of *Wiener schnitzel*; he took no part in the general conversation; and they saw nothing of him during the week-end except his red face bent over his plate at meals. Mrs Lambert thought it rather shocking to see one who presumably was head of the household seated silently amidst noisy young people, with no distinction of place, or deference, but then there never was any understanding other people's marriages.

CHAPTER THREE

Portrait

THE social life at the *gasthaus* exactly suited Meg, who liked company, and easily made friends, but who also enjoyed solitude and its pleasures. The guests stayed in the house perhaps three days, perhaps fourteen, and while there was always the opportunity for a pleasant acquaintanceship to be struck up, if anybody proved less agreeable than usual or if one of the young men wanted more of her company than she cared to bestow, the winding shady paths of Martinsdorf alp and the woods higher up afforded places in which to hide—or, if this sounds too dramatic—to loiter, until he had gone off elsewhere.

Usually she accompanied the afternoon party to some local place of interest, but occasionally she took book and knitting down to the lake or up into the woods alone, while her mother rested or made the shopping in Villach.

One afternoon, when they had been there three weeks, she set out thus by herself under a softly clouded sky whose grey light deepened the blue of the distant forests. She went through the orchard, whose fading blossom drifted down on her hair, and on her way studied the lake, calculating how to fix that peculiar colour upon paper and trying to remember how much she had left in her paint-box of certain greens and blues, for she was eager to begin.

Sketching was her newest pleasure, to which she had been led, first by inclination, and then by the example, encouragement and advice of Sir Winston Churchill.

But when she had chosen her point of view, and arranged herself where an opening in the woods overlooked the lake, she found to her irritation that the supply of necessary colours was even less varied than she had supposed; in fact, there were only two almost empty porcelain containers.

She was in that mood—most common, perhaps, to youth but

found in enthusiasts of all ages, when only the one, the first-desired, thing will serve; she had come out full of eagerness to sketch the lake, and it was no use to think of sketching the far-off mountains or the sky; she felt violently impatient at the mere idea. She looked at her watch and realised that if she hurried there was time to catch the afternoon bus into Villach.

A little crowd of women in village dress and one or two elderly men, as well as an early holiday-maker or so, was waiting outside the post office where the buses stopped, and she joined them, warm and panting from her hasty descent but glad, now, that she had come. She decided to see something of Villach after she had bought the paints; there had been talk at the pension of a fine view from the bridge, and of mediæval courtyards, and this would be her first visit to the town since the night of her arrival: there had always seemed to be more interesting places to go to.

The large bus arrived; the passengers crammed themselves into an interior already packed to bursting; and away it rushed. The passengers were flung up to the roof and from side to side despite the excellence of the chalky surface over which they were travelling; they went between the beeches and acacias of *gasthaus* gardens and the thin reed-fringes of the lake's shore; past old wooden bathing-cabins, and landing-stages projecting into the water, and new houses, small and square and made of white concrete, which lacked all the pretty, Hänsel-and-Gretel grace of the older ones. The small neat fields flew past, where young maize was springing, and Meg peered through the window at the mountains; the low-ish, rounded, wooded mountains that always, even in sunlight, wore the thin haze of dark blue—"blue-aired Carinthia"—that gave them mystery on the clearest day.

The bus finally bumped into the spacious square in front of the railway station, and the passengers, bruised and hot, climbed out and strolled—Austrians may sometimes hurry, but Meg had yet to see them at it—off on their various errands.

She stood in the clear cloudy light, looking about; she was not fond of hurrying, either, and presently she set off at a leisurely pace towards the centre of the town. The outskirts did not appear so romantic in full daylight as they had on the evening of the Lamberts' arrival. Much damage had been done there during the war, and rebuilding, in the square, white, Continental style, was still going on. Inevitably, it was the fragile ancient buildings that had suffered most heavily.

But on the bridge that spans the broad Drau, Meg paused and went off into a dream. This was glacier water, running down pale and green and icy from the mist-curtained heights of Grosse Glockner or Hohe Tauern; racing along between its banks where a few substantial old hotels stood in the thick foliage of their gardens, and the booths of a little market were arranged on the flag-stones of the farther shore. She lifted her eyes, and there were the mountains again, shutting in the horizon with their indigo serrations, setting off the white houses and milky torrent. The Austrian crowd moved past her across the bridge, and she stood watching; small boys with legs thin as a bird's in breeches of pale grimy leather, young girls whose cheek bones betrayed Jugoslav blood and convinced the observant Saxon that an eye can be truly black; elderly men wearing flowing cloaks of grey frieze and be-feathered hats, and stout old women wearing the unexpectedly becoming full skirt, sleeveless bodice, and blouse with short sleeves and square neck edged by coarse, snowy lace. The faces were alive; often full of grief, or wrinkled and exhausted by years of cruelly hard work and war; yet always *responsive*, in a way that English and American faces seldom are. *They don't pretend*, Meg thought vaguely as she walked on into the town, sometimes catching a few words or a sentence in German that she understood, but more often hearing a bewildering, distorted patois.

When she had found a shop that sold artists' materials and made her purchases—greatly to her satisfaction without having to use one word of her native tongue—she came out into the crowded yet peaceful high street once more. It was a little wider than that of an English country town, lined on either side by large, amply-proportioned houses faced with cream plaster and often having a square opening large enough to admit a coach and horses between the shop-fronts. The thick walls were often pierced by the arched entrance to

some small courtyard or alley, where a green-trellised plant waved
in the shadows or steps led down to a beer-cellar. Meg wandered
along in the warm grey air, absorbing sights and smells and sounds
with a satisfaction uncomplicated by the artist's desire to transmute
and reproduce; and presently, having loitered looking up at a great
church of dark grey stone whose lower walls were hung with
baskets of spring flowers, and explored the narrow ways lying behind the main street, she found herself standing in it once more, and
looking dreamily about her.

Her glance fell upon a house on her left.

There was a passage hollowed in it; narrow, white and very old;
even fresh plastering could not conceal the feeling of age, the
crumbling quality, breathed forth by that long, slender, humble-
seeming entrance of stone. There were some letters painted above
the doorway; for some reason they had not received a share of the
attention given to the stones, and were faded and worn; it could be
seen that they curved in a half-circle to follow the line of the arch
but they could not all be read. Was the sentence in German or was
it in Latin? Meg stood looking up at it, while the unheeding crowds
drifted by. A faint cold air, a breath from age-soaked masonry,
floated out from the doorway into the warm noon. She could make
out one word clearly—a name?

PARACELSUS.

She repeated it below her breath, and it hissed softly, with its
many sibilants, between her teeth and on her tongue. Paracelsus. It
struck no chord of memory; she had never heard it, she thought,
before this moment. She turned aside from the street, full of curiosity, and went down the dim, cool, arched passage.

It led into a courtyard; not enclosed, although the houses surrounding it were close-set and high, for it ran on to meet a narrow
alley at the far end. But the first thing Meg noticed there was a
house; a lofty and graceful house whose lower front and colonnaded
upper storeys supported by short pillars had been freshly coated with
white plaster, while piles of mortar and broken bricks lying nearby
suggested that the beautiful sturdy building had recently been
treated for war damage. It seemed to be empty.

She stood there, looking up at the blanched shell, for a little while. Then, glancing downwards, her eyes fell upon a plaque set in the wall, which was carved with the weird and forceful head of a man.

Meg's first impression was of intellectual power, expressed in a massive bald cranium and the forehead's splendid lift and in the projections above the brows. But a delicate upper lip and sensitive flaring nostrils gave quite another character to the face—and then the full lips curving downwards looked at once passionate and bitter—and lastly came the jutting chin of a fighter. This head was set on a bull's throat and fringed with the tonsure of a monk. There encircled it some raised letters, in which occurred again the name—if name it were—PARACELSUS.

Half attracted and yet half repelled, Meg moved forward and studied it more closely. She looked up at the bleached and vacant house which, despite a design that appeared unfitted to survive the onslaughts of time and war, had in fact withstood both; then down again at the plaque. It was not a modern face by, surely, three hundred years. It was a face in a dark old painting or older yet, a face from some mediæval wood-engraving. It was not possible to imagine communicating with that face out of the past, and yet, thought Meg, it is so alive and so wise. No, wise is not quite the word. It is too full of strong feelings to be wise. It's the strangest face I have ever seen.

The courtyard in which she stood was quiet but not deserted. Occasionally someone turned aside from the street and came down the passage towards the small shops and the beer-cellar at the far end, and she felt no sensation of loneliness as she lingered there. Sunlight had now broken through the mass of the clouds and shone down warm and clear into the courtyard, and it threw the shadows of the passers-by upon the stones as they crossed behind her. Sometimes the steps were quick, and once they loitered for a moment while the shadow accompanying them glided across her own, but she did not turn round, and steps and shadow passed on. She turned away at last, determined to question Frau Schacht about the house, and found that if she was to catch the bus she must hurry.

*   *   *   *   *

"Oh, that *is* good, darling; you *are* improving," said her mother, when, after supper, she saw the sketch made hastily in the light of late afternoon. Meg studied it for a minute, then put it back in her portfolio. "I should like to do one of Paracelsus's house," she said.

"I heard you asking Frau Schacht about some house, didn't I, and then she corrected your pronunciation." Mrs Lambert had remained at the side table for meals when Meg joined the group of students at the larger one, because Frau Schacht complained that she and her mother talked English together.

"Yes; she loved doing that, of course. It's Paraselsus; I pronounced the *c* like a *k*."

"I wish you didn't rub one another up the wrong way so often, dear. Who was Paracelsus?"

"Oh, he lived about five hundred years ago . . . he was all sorts of things . . . a doctor and an astrologer as well . . . but I don't think Hansi really knows much about him. That's why she was cross, and so pleased when I pronounced him wrongly."

"An astrologer? Like Lord Luck in the *Daily Express*, and Naylor —but you wouldn't remember Naylor, that was during the war."

"I expect Paracelsus took his astrologising a bit more seriously." Meg laughed, and came to rest her chin on Mrs Lambert's shoulder where she stood at the window. "What are you rubber-necking at? The mountains?" Her eyes followed the direction of her mother's gaze. But it was not towards the peaks that Mrs Lambert was gazing.

"What is that house on the other side of the lake, the white one? An hotel?" Meg asked idly.

"I don't know. I'm always meaning to ask Hansi and always forgetting. I shouldn't think it's an hotel, there are so few villages on that side. There never seems to be anything happening there. No, I was just looking at it . . . I always notice it when I look out of the window. Sometimes you can hardly see it's there; it depends on where the light is."

"It's so hidden by trees."

"Yes, but sometimes that makes it show up all the plainer. It's a funny house. . . ."

"Hasn't everything got thick and green suddenly?"

"Yes. It's the middle of May; really summer. Next week we shall have been here five weeks."

"Don't want to think about it. Can't bear the idea of going home." Meg had crossed to the mirror and was tweaking at her hair with the absorbed expression and inept gestures in which girls of her age waste minutes and minutes of every day.

"I'd like to find out some more about Paracelsus," she said, "he's got a fascinating face. Mummy, why don't you come down to the *weinstube* this evening?"

That night, when Mrs Lambert went on to the balcony before going to bed to take her customary last look round, she saw for the first time a light shining out from the house across the lake.

CHAPTER FOUR

Nostalgic

So far, the life of Martinsdorf had seemed to be centred upon the large courtyard of the *weinstube*, where the buses stopped, and the cars of passing holidaymakers paused for an hour while their owners sat under the drooping chestnut-boughs to drink *apfelsaft*, or beer, or the almost milkless coffee which Austrians take at all hours of the day. But with the coming of hot weather, social activity moved to the lake.

The same family that owned the *weinstube* owned a rough wooden enclosure on the most accessible part of the shore, fitted up with small bathing cabins which they hired out to the public for a *schilling* or so, and a long wooden building where the bathers, for a few more *schillings*, might refresh themselves on coming out of the water with the unpleasant drink, bright orange in colour and nebulous in flavour, which passes in Austria for orangeade. The most agreeable part of all this was the lake-water. Perhaps the English, who own plenty of sea-coast, do not as a race enjoy freshwater bathing with its usual accompaniments of thin mud, reeds and sun-bathing on grass accompanied by a feeling that one should not be sitting half-naked on twigs and beetles and dead leaves, but even Mrs Lambert, who was fastidious about slime and gritty grass, conceded that the water of the Saint Martinsee was agreeable to swim in.

But she did not get much chance to swim, for her afternoons, like her mornings, were usually spent in the kitchen helping Frau Schacht with the ritual entombment of the apricot crop, or waiting for the bus in the glaring white station *platz* at Villach, laden with a heavy basket.

She had grown very tired, during the past weeks, of that bus journey into Villach and of the town itself; even the view from the bridge over the racing Drau, which had at first refreshed her, had ceased to do so because she saw it so often, and usually when she was in a hurry.

Austrians who travelled with her on the same bus, two or three times a week and at the same hour, came to know her by sight, and would give her a smiling *"Grüss Gott."* There were not many English people in Villach that summer, and the peasants from outlying villages would study with interest the tall woman with greying hair dressed in a roll about her head, who must once have been slim and now was thin, dressed in a frock patterned with ugly bright flowers and a large straw hat. Her nose was large, her thin lips sweetly curved, she had a clear, fine complexion and blue eyes like an anxious child's. Most of those who studied her, being unfamiliar with the lore of wedding-rings in any country outside their own, assumed that she was a Mees.

Mrs Lambert, in her turn, thought about the Austrians. As she sat in the stifling bus with these plump women in peasant bodices and men in leather breeches and braces, and they all crashed their way back to Martinsdorf between fields now smiling with what would soon be tall tasselled maize, she thought how strange it was thus to be travelling with people who eight years ago were her enemies. These were the subjects of "that wicked man over there", and this was "over there", and here was she, Eve Lambert, bouncing along it in a bus.

She could not fully realise—she told herself—the strangeness. It had been easier to realise as they travelled across Germany; when the rolling uplands, and the vast lifted hills of Bavaria going off into Wotan-only-knew what Wagnerian hinterlands of tremendous mountains and dark mist, had convinced her that Hitler had been talking nonsense when he demanded *lebensraum*. The place looked as if it went on for ever. Why could he not have been satisfied with his two vast, beautiful, tidy, very slightly melancholy countries?

Then she thought how surprised her Harry would be if he could see her here, and then she wondered if perhaps he did see her, but she turned her mind from this fancy because it, and others like it, led on to puzzling and disturbing thoughts. It was best, she had found, to remember Harry as she had known him during their eleven years together, and to keep her wonderings strictly within the few beautiful phases sanctioned by the Anglican Church: the many mansions, the purification from stain of earthly conversation, the place of refreshment and light.

Harry—her thoughts wandered on, as the bus careered round the western limit of the lake—most people would have said that he never did any harm to anybody; he had been a merry elderly man when he was killed; the inheritor from his father of an old, prosperous estate-agent's business in Tormouth, and she had known him all her life: they had grown up together on the fringe of the same group of young people, the 1895–1900 vintage; had been to the same dances and read the local paper and heard the local gossip. She had been away for three years, training to be a teacher, and then she had taught in several schools up and down the country—with some little success, to the surprise of her friends and relations, because she was gentle, and rather shy, and did not possess the authority of personality deemed necessary for a teacher. But she had patience, and she loved the young, and she was interested in learning and in life.

She was in her middle thirties when she came back to live and teach in Tormouth. She had made up her mind, very sadly, because she loved children deeply, that she would never marry now . . . and she was making the best of it with dignity when she met Harry Lambert again, at a concert given for charity at the Town

Hall. Within a month they were engaged. Within three they were married.

It had been the most popular match of that year, in spite of its autumnal character, and when Meg was born, and later played and went to school in the town, it was generally though tacitly agreed that more than a merely "sensible" relationship must have gone to the making of such a lovely and lively child. The three had been happy together for ten years, and then Harry was killed in a five-minute attack by a sneak-raider. The town's angry verdict was that it had to be Harry, who had never harmed anyone in his life, but the widow had always felt with pride that there were some people whom he had harmed a good deal: the Nazi leaders. For he had been a Home Guard, an organiser of savings and salvage drives, a skilful partner in the running of a war-time home, and as grimly cheerful in the bad early days as Mr Churchill himself.

It was queer, Mrs Lambert thought, looking vacantly at meadows spinning by; no one was kinder than Harry, and yet about the Germans he had been adamant: he had disliked them; at times he had even said so. When Hansi had arrived in Tormouth, recommended to the Lamberts' care and interest by some busy friend of Eve's in London, he had helped his wife to find her a teaching post in the school where Eve had formerly taught, but he had shaken his head. He had shaken it still more when Hansi had insinuated herself into their spare bedroom—one of the few empty ones in the overcrowded town—and proceeded to live with them as family. But he had ended, against his judgment and his prejudice, by becoming fond of her; they all three had.

Remembering her husband's opinion of Germans and Austrians, Mrs Lambert occasionally felt guilty over her mild liking for the young people of both races who came to the *gasthaus*, and had to remind herself that on the only occasion when Harry had come in daily contact with an Austrian, he had been even kinder than usual and had never betrayed his feelings; she reminded herself also— though this was hardly necessary—that she was here for Meg's sake, to help Meg secure a well-paid post, and that putting up with her fellow house-members was part of her task.

At this moment the bus lurched to a standstill outside the *wein-stube*, and the passengers alighted.

Mrs Lambert walked slowly up the road skirting the foot of the alp, with the early summer sun blazing down on her back. The villas and pensions on the slope were reached by a series of steep paths ascending from this road, each winding away under beech and fruit trees and over streams amidst the orchards and past the saw-mill and the waterfalls; Mrs Lambert remembered how bewildering this had seemed on the evening of their arrival, and now it was all as familiar as their road at home; only prettier, of course.

She reached the gate, pushed it open with her knee because she knew that if she put down her two shopping bags she would not have strength to pick them up again, and toiled on up the garden, past the fading garden flowers in the beds and the fresh ones on the alpine lawns. She went on, past the house of Hansi's nearest neighbour.

Suddenly she looked up. A deep, fierce droning, louder by many decibels than the noise of wasps, was coming from the shadows of an eave jutting overhead, and there—oh, horror—crawling in and out of their nest, revived by the first day of summer heat, was a horde of hornets. Each was twice as large as its English counterpart; they were almost two inches long; they launched themselves into the hot shady air like dive bombers; their fine black and yellow glowed as they crawled against the black weather-boarding of their runway; and it was terrifying to see so many of these creatures, usually seen as solitary invaders, together. Mrs Lambert, like most human beings, had a worst insect: it was hornets; and here, within fifty yards of her bedroom window, was something she had pic-tured all her life with shudders: a hornets' nest.

She staggered on as fast as she could for the weight of her baskets, feeling sick. She felt herself deserted and wretched; Meg cared for nothing but daydreaming and pleasure and Harry was dead; her head ached; she ached all over, and at any minute one of those huge winged horrors would—would . . .

"Eve! What on earth is the matter? Here, give me the bags. Do not run up the hill like that, you must be mad in this heat."

Frau Schacht's small hard hands had gripped her own and jerked the shopping bags away; she was being hustled into coolness and dimness, and pushed into a chair, a cup of water was being held to her lips, and she thirstily drank.

"Oh—thank you—that was lovely—I'm sorry to be such a fool," she gasped in a moment, "but it was the hornets. . . ."

Frau Schacht's expression, which to begin with had not been sweet, grew even more louring. She nodded with compressed lips.

"I know. I have seen and heard them. This is the time of year when they first come out. When you just came, I am standing at the door here, thinking about them and cursing."

"Cursing?"

"Certainly I am cursing, Eve. They are a problem, these hornets. Each year when summer comes I send a polite message to Herr Zeller asking may I have them poisoned or killed with smoke. I do not ask him to pay for this; I offer to pay myself. You would think, wouldn't you, that he would be glad? To get rid of the hornets in his roof and someone else to pay for it? No, he is not glad. He says no. Every year—one, two, three, *four* years, now"—Hansi banged her dwarf's fist on the kitchen table—"he says *no*, so every summer when my guests would like to sit after supper with the window open and then switch on the light and have some music, we cannot do so because of the hornets. They come in attracted by the light. And I can do *nodding*—nothing, I mean, nothing at all. Herr Zeller is a most unreasonable man."

"He must be. I don't know how he can bear to have them there himself. I should be terrified."

"He does not care, he says. He says it would damage his roof to have them killed with the smoke. Of course he does not care; why should he care; he is seventy years old and he has always lived in that house and the hornets have always lived there too and by this time he is half a hornet himself."

Mrs Lambert, who was feeling better, laughed.

"Oh, it is very well to laugh. But how shall I have my hotel and my school of languages while there are those hornets? You know what guests expect nowadays. . . ."

She paused. Footsteps were passing the top of the stairs.

"Robin," called Frau Schacht, "is that you? Have you read your Schiller? Are you going down to the lake?"

"Yes. Yes. Yes, Frau Schacht," replied a male voice, languid and young, down the staircase well.

"Good, then. Go and wait under the nut tree and Mrs Lambert will come to you. You can go down to the lake together."

"Love-lee," said the voice on a more reserved note, and footsteps were heard receding.

"Really, Hansi—poor boy. He won't want to be saddled with me, though I am Meg's mother." Mrs Lambert stood up, feeling almost too tired to move again.

"Never mind," was the dampingly realistic answer, "it will be good for him. He is a nice boy, no?" following her out of the kitchen and up the stairs.

"He's very amusing. How old is he, do you know?"

"Twenty-two, I think. Yes, twenty-two certainly, because he mentioned that he has had a party for his twenty-first. He is of very good family, that boy," she added complacently, "his father is somehow connected with the Duke of Davenham."

"Yes. . . . Of course, he seems very young to Meg . . . such a pity. He's just the type . . . but not quite serious enough, perhaps. . . ."

"Meg's verbs are still weak; she must work harder at them, much harder, or she will never talk fluent German by the end of the summer. You must speak to her about them," said Frau Schacht as she mounted the stairs to her own room, there to resume the siesta which the droning of a stray hornet (they did not usually invade the *gasthaus* during the day) had disagreeably interrupted.

Ten minutes later poor Mrs Lambert joined Robin Gascoine with a pensive face. If there was anything she disliked worse than hornets, it was Speaking To Meg.

CHAPTER FIVE

Exterior

WHEN they came along the raised wooden platform bordering the bathing-huts, they saw Meg sitting under a plane tree, gazing out over the lake and looking rather noticeably alone amidst plump Austrian matrons with attendant husbands and their hopping, munching children, who were seated in groups all about the grassy enclosure. The windless air was cooled by the presence of four miles of water, and all the sounds were softened: the harsh German tongue, the noise of the motor-boat engine towing would-be water-skiers along in showers of foam, and the slap of the waves made by their passing, the cries and splashing of the bathers.

The grass was occupied by some of the forty or so visitors who patronised the public swimming-place because it was cheap and convenient; they were mostly young, or married with small children; people belong to the middle and lower-middle Austrian classes, with little money (though almost every class in Austria has little money now) who liked a quiet holiday near open water. They sprawled with closed eyes and fast-reddening limbs under the glare of the white spring sun, or stared dreamily up at the mountains robed in green pines and azure air, while the drops dried on their smarting shoulders, until they should be ready to swim again.

"Missy Meg, honey chile," began Robin Gascoine, sitting down beside her and assuming the voice and supposed manner of an elderly negress, "how many times Mammy Gascoine done tell yo not 'xpose yo pretty white skin to dat bad ole sun? Put on yo hat," handing her an enormous plaited straw shaped like those formerly worn by Roman shepherds.

"I was just wondering," Meg said to her mother, giving him a fleeting smile, "if we could get a boat and go over to the other side? It looks so exciting and lonely. Mummy, will you come?"

Mrs Lambert hesitated; Meg had been shut away studying Goethe all the morning, and she herself had been in Villach most of the afternoon; they no longer sat together at meals, and in the evenings after supper Meg usually went down to the *weinstube* with Robin and the other young people from the house and danced there with the locals until midnight. Meg's society, Meg's chatter and confidence, were the chief pleasure of her mother's life, and Mrs Lambert felt that lately she had not had enough of them, but the waters of the lake, far out, shimmered in the fierce heat and her head still ached.

"I don't think so, darling, I'll stay here in the shade and rest."

"All right. Coming, Robin?" Meg scrambled up, brushing twigs from the seat of her bathing-dress. "Mummy, ought I to put on a skirt?"

Mrs Lambert nodded decidedly, being unable, like many people born before 1914, to get accustomed to the practice of wearing a bathing-dress anywhere but in the water.

Presently she saw them launch off into the almost rippleless lake, Gascoine at the oars, and Meg, now wearing her skirt and hat and a jacket as protection from the sun, at the steering rope, while the youngest daughter of the boat-owners, a stout maiden with slant gipsy eyes, stood up to her knees in the water to give the clumsy small craft a final push. Outward they glided, and in a few moments were fifty yards from the shore. Mrs Lambert, leaning back against the trunk of the plane tree, thought how unaccommodating it was, then thankfully shut her eyes.

The boat slid on over the clear deep water, accompanied by a soft splash and ripple, and gradually, even while the sounds from the shore still came clearly, Meg began to feel shut away from the rest of the world. The mountains stood close about the lake clothed in mysterious blue forest; a haze crept and shimmered over the water on a level with her heavy eyes, and the inhabited shore fell from them until it became small and unreal. She sighed, and turned away from it.

"Yo is awake den, honey? Mammy tink yo done take a doze."

Even Robin's voice, usually so distinct, sounded drowsy to-day. His pale, well-bred and rather boneless face, with the shelf of brown hair falling over the brow, smiled at her with drooping eyelids.

"Won't you get sunstroke? We ought to have brought you a hat."

"Ob all de words ob tongue or pen
De saddest am dese: it might hab been.

Nebber mind. Mammy Gascoine glad get sunstroke rowing missy Meg."

Meg studied him for a moment, then let her eyes rest peacefully upon a farther shore, to which they were now slowly drawing near. Reeds crowded right down to the edge of the water, concealing the place where it met the strand, and after an expanse of shingle the pines began; tall and crowding, strangely-shaped presences filled with a gentle dark green life, they looked out across the approach and seemed to be silently delivering a message to those who thought of landing there. Meg's thoughts were lingering upon Robin; she had never been sure, since his arrival a week ago, whether he really admired her or whether she really liked him, for his manner was never serious, and he irritated her by making frivolous comments upon the poetry of Christopher Fry and Laurie Lee and disparaging remarks about the local scenery. But he liked to hold her hand, and his kisses were gentle; he told her she had a skin like privet-blossom, and at the *gasthaus* he made them all laugh a great deal. On the whole, he was a pleasant addition to the party.

She twisted herself about once more, the better to watch the approaching land. Now Martinsdorf was a pensive picture across the lake, a tiny village lying at the foot of wooded mountains, a strange place, and this strand they were approaching, with their prow already brushed and whispered along by the reeds, was the near shore. She stared up into the woods.

"I can't see our house now. How funny, when it's so much nearer."

"Miss Meg, yo want *drown* yo'self and poor old Mammy? Pull yo *left* line, honey—LEFT, I said—oh, you dumb cluck."

The boat rammed itself slowly into a bed of reeds and stopped. Meg looked at him, a little surprised, smiling. Around them the

tufted brown heads stood up motionless in the light, there was a
scent of water-plants and of freshly-churned mud.

"Come on," she said, casting aside the steering rope and beginning to make her way forward, "look, there's a landing-stage."

With a man's greater respect for a boat or a car or even a pair of
skis, Robin lingered to inspect their craft before he followed her on to
the single broad plank which led, over the water and through the reed
clumps, to the shore. She was already gazing eagerly up into the woods.

"The boat, you will be relieved to hear, is not damaged, nor can
it float away," he said.

"Good," Meg answered absently. "Look, there's a path."

She almost ran across the pebble-strewn, grassy shore, and he
followed. The shore was very still; there were no distant voices, no
houses—except those in the mirage across the lake—in sight, and
yet the place did not appear entirely wild, for a rough wooden
railing followed the path winding upwards through the woods
which they were now climbing; and Robin pointed out to her a
small summerhouse, painted white and ornately carved, but fallen
into decay, standing upon a hillock amidst the trees.

"I wonder if we're trespassing?" she said.

"Almost certainly, I should think. At any moment some large
kraut with a gun will appear."

"Never mind—I'm enjoying it."

He glanced with raised eyebrows at the trees, which were less
green here than elsewhere in this country of fresh, moist-floored
forests; boughs so dark as to be almost black drooped lifelessly
earthwards, sometimes patched with silvery decay. No breezes
from the lake could penetrate their aisles and thickets, and the shafts
of sunlight piercing them increased the airless heat.

Robin had relieved his boredom by walking quickly and un-
gallantly ahead of her. Presently, when he was almost out of sight
at the turn of the path, she saw him pause, turn back, and begin to
gesticulate elaborately, pointing downwards.

She quickened her pace and soon came level with him. Then they
stood, side by side, looking down at a small alp of greenest grass,
filled with flowers. It was surrounded on three sides by the forest,

but on the fourth it overlooked the lake. Standing in it was an old Austrian house; a miniature mansion once painted white but now faded to a ghostly grey, with a great heart-shaped eave cut back to reveal a balcony on the topmost storey; with other balconies projecting from every floor, all screened by fragile trellis-work of almost Moorish style and every balcony blazing with hanging baskets of flowers. It was surrounded by a small garden, planted with sheltering shrubs and having a space levelled off and covered in chalk pebbles, where garden chairs and a table were arranged. All was in noticeably perfect order; the little lawn newly scythed, the iron furniture freshly painted white, and the monster umbrella that lolled above the table glowing in red and yellow as if an hour ago delivered from Harrods.

"It must be the house Mummy and I always look at from our balcony," Meg breathed at last. "Isn't it lovely?"

They stood looking down at the silent, beautiful, luxurious place. There were no signs of life. The windows stood wide, with their shutters folded back to admit the summer, and in the dim rooms they caught glimpses of books, and gilt screens, and great Chinese vases holding stiff clouds of flowers.

Meg touched her companion's arm. "There's a newspaper and cigarette-case on the table——"

"The Beast is evidently at home. You'd better watch out."

A harsh voice speaking German suddenly exploding behind them startled both.

"What are you doing here? It is private and visitors are forbidden. Get out at once."

They turned quickly and saw a man standing on the edge of the pines and looking at them angrily. He wore Austrian dress, and held by its massive collar a big yellow dog, which was silently straining forwards with scarred and shredded ears laid back and savage eyes fixed upon them.

"(The kraut—what did I tell you?)—I am sorry," Robin went on, speaking now to the man in faulty but fluent German, "we've just rowed over from Martinsdorf and were taking a walk."

The man stared without answering.

"We didn't see any notices, so we came up the path and through the forest. Our boat's down on the shore——"

"It is forbidden to land. All this is private property—the shore, the forest, the path—all is private and forbidden."

"I'm sorry," Robin said politely. "You'd like us to go, I expect. Come on, Meg," in English, turning to her, "we'd better beat it."

"Oh, why? We weren't doing any harm. I want to have a really good look at the house so that I can describe it to Mummy." She turned to the man, who was watching out of little black eyes. "Who does the house belong to?" she asked in slow German, pointing.

He did not answer, but continued to stare at her, and Robin, who had already gone back towards the forest, turned and called to her.

"Whose is that house?" repeated Meg, "who does it belong to?"

But again he made no answer, and suddenly the dog strained forward, growling fiercely, and startled Meg into hurrying away. She turned back as she reached the trees; the man was still standing there, his hand on the dog's thick throat, steadily watching them.

"An unpleasant type," Robin began, as they went quickly and in silence down the path. "Jugoslav, I should think."

Meg did not answer. She was annoyed because he had hurried her away before she could take a long look at the house, and felt contemptuous of him because he had been afraid of the dog, but she was thinking more of the house than of him; it lingered in her mind's eye as the coloured circle does after the physical eye has been staring at a light.

He glanced at her, then said with a faint ruffling of his cool manner:

"Did you expect me to challenge him to a duel? You don't know these people; that Englishman we met at the *weinstube* last night told me that only two years ago the Jugs. shot some poor devil who was picking blackberries a few yards over their side of border. This part of the world isn't like Eastbourne, you know."

"No, thank heaven," Meg said fervently.

"And we were in the wrong."

"We weren't doing any harm. He made such a fuss."

"That's being a foreigner. Oh, good, the boat hasn't budged," as they came in sight of the shore and saw the little craft still resting in the reeds. He took her hand, which remained cool and plump and unresponsive, in his, and gently swung it. "Missy Meg come wid ole Mammy Gascoine eat watermelon at de *weinstube*?"

"I wish we could get some tea. I miss tea *frightfully* and so does Mummy. Don't you get awfully browned off with that beastly *apfelsaft*?"

"There's always beer and it's cheap enough. If you want tea shops everywhere you should have *gone* to Eastbourne."

When they were once more afloat, Meg insisted upon taking the oars while he steered, so that she could look up at the receding shore, but the woods revealed no gap in their terraces—dark blue, as soon as a quarter-mile of air lay between them and the human eye—and of the house there was not a glimpse.

Slowly the silent, and now forbidden, shore receded. Meg's hands began to smart under pressure of the clumsy, heavy oars; the rowlocks were smaller than those she was accustomed to on Tormouth river and would not allow the oars to turn in the smart feathering merited by such smooth water; she felt tired and cross, and was relieved when they reached the middle of the lake and, after much cautious manœuvring and advice, Robin reversed their positions.

She described the house at length to her mother later that afternoon, while they sat on the terrace drinking the despised *apfelsaft* under the chestnut trees; Robin, having treated them to their first round of the sickly beverage, had gone off to bathe.

"Robin's a coward, you know," Meg suddenly interrupted herself to say, "he was scared stiff of that dog."

"Everyone is scared of something, dearest" (Mrs Lambert was thinking of hornets), "and a fierce dog *is* very alarming, you know."

"All the same, boys oughtn't to be. It's most—it's—I can't explain it, but I feel they oughtn't to be. It's bad enough for *us*, having to pretend we aren't scared of anything, without having *them* scared as well."

She paused, and reflected. The long evening sunrays, falling across the distant peaks of Italy, made their way between the great chestnut leaves to gild her hair.

"Robin's only a little boy, really. You're always wondering why I don't get serious about any of the people I go out with, Mummy —well, that's the answer. They aren't properly grown up. A man of about forty wouldn't be afraid of a dog."

Mrs Lambert thought it less fatiguing to let sleeping illusions lie and made no comment; and Meg returned to the subject of the house, which she was determined to see again: she would ask Hansi that evening who was the owner.

*   *   *   *   *

"That house?" answered Frau Schacht, taking from Trudi a bowl of sliced cucumbers swimming in oil and water and beginning to serve it, as they sat at supper, "how did you get there? It is forbidden to land on that shore. He"—she ladled with steady hand the vegetable on to Meg's plate—"he forbids it: the shore, for half a kilometre, belongs to him. Who? The owner of the house, of course—Mr Scarron. Mr Esmé Scarron; he lives there alone with his servants for a few months in each summer. No, he is English, but his mother was Austrian. She left him the house. But, my dear, you won't see *him*, I can tell you; he never comes over to this side of the lake." She paused, and ate a mouthful with the muscles of her sallow cheeks moving steadily as if she relished the food. "It is many years since he honoured us with a visit. We are not grand enough for him. He is rich, you see; very rich. And very, very clever."

CHAPTER SIX

Zither

"I wish it were possible to arrange for Meg to see that house again, Hansi. She talks about nothing else. . . ."

"She should talk about her German verbs—and in German. Really, Eve, how young she is for her age. You must not mind my saying this—that is correct, 'my saying'?—yes, thank you, but I do not think you have brought her up properly or well."

Mrs Lambert swallowed an impulse to retort "Thank you."

"No, not at all well." Frau Schacht dropped some potatoes, which she and Mrs Lambert were slicing for luncheon, into a pan of water. "She is too romantic. She believes life to be a novel by Vicki Baum. One day there will be for her a terrible awakening—well—perhaps not terrible," irritably, as Mrs Lambert stared at her open-mouthed, "perhaps I spoke too strongly. But she will find life harder than most of us do, because you have brought her up so soft."

"Softly," Mrs Lambert corrected, rather pleased to be able to do so.

"Softly, then"—Frau Schacht decimated a very small potato with energy—"because you have brought her up so *softly*. Have you read a book by Gustav Flaubert, the French writer, about a woman whose life was ruined by reading novels?"

"*Madame Bovary*? But Meg doesn't read many novels: she prefers poetry. Besides, Emma Bovary"—here Mrs Lambert made her second score; if Hansi was in a literary mood this morning she should be shown that other people could remember names and plots in books—"was bad to begin with; the novels didn't start her off; they only made her worse."

"And they will make Meg worse."

"Oh, I don't think so. . . ." Mrs Lambert had learned that a vague tone could be useful when one wished to abandon a topic. ". . . But don't you know anyone round here, Hansi, who could get permission for Robin to take her over to that house again? She wants to sketch it. What about the man who owns it——"

But here an angry deep droning, fatally familiar to the ladies but nowhere near breeding contempt, caused both to leap to their feet. Mrs Lambert ran out of the kitchen, while Frau Schacht, shouting "Maria! *Eine hornisse!*" darted into a cupboard and slammed the door upon herself. Then, summoned by the alarm and bearing aloft a fish-slice, snatched from the wall in passing, as if it were her lance, Maria the sturdy cook marched in from the garden where she had been picking peas and darted her eyes round the kitchen in search of the raider. After much flapping, panting and slapping it was knocked to earth and squashed; Frau Schacht emerged from the cupboard and sombrely congratulated Maria upon her victory, with many head-shakings over the devilish pig-headedness of Herr Zeller, and Mrs Lambert crept back into the kitchen in the mood of the poet—

Mother, is the battle over? Am I numbered 'midst the slain?

and the excitement had quite effaced her impression that Hansi did not want to discuss the owner of the house on the opposite shore.

This happened several times a day since the hornets had awoken to another summer. No one else at the *gasthaus* was so frightened of hornets as Mrs Lambert, but no one regarded their arrival with indifference, and Maria was the only person who was roused by them to a splendid crusading fury in which she swung the fish-slice like a berserk Valkyrie. The cry "Maria! *Eine hornisse!*" rang through the house, interrupting harmless conversations and the diligent preparation of German grammar, and Robin said that it reminded him of some passage from a book that his father was fond of quoting, but he could not remember what.

At this time, the middle of June, there were only four young people staying at the *gasthaus* to learn German; Robin was, as he put it, "going in for the Diplomatic" and was faced with the prospect of mastering a working knowledge of Russian after he had got his quota of German, and the Danish girls, Kristin and Helga, were going to teach. They all worked hard . . . or tried to . . . but when it was said previously that Meg Lambert was eager to learn, perhaps it should have been said that she was eager *to have* learned; to read Heine and Rilke in their originals, with all the drudgery and hours of steady concentration put away behind her for ever. And now that alps and lake and distant mountains were clothed in the light of summer, when there was young society, and dancing with picturesquely dressed youths in quaint surroundings every evening, and when her head was full of Italy, and Paracelsus the astrologer, and the house across the lake, it was difficult indeed to stick to her book.

Robin was naturally lazy—which Meg was not—but he came from a family which regarded intellectual sloth with polite surprise; and his father had warned him that the posts in the Diplomatic Service which had fallen more or less naturally to Robin's uncles and great-uncles in their youth because of their connections and birth, would now have to be *won*; by exceedingly hard work. So Robin worked, and only led Meg astray from her tasks when he had thoroughly completed his own.

The guests who were not learning German came and went; and every Saturday afternoon Poor Franz, as the Lamberts now called him, toiled up the hill carrying his brown-paper parcel, with drops rolling off his forehead under his too-big hat, and when he happened to meet them he would stop, and lift the hat, and make each lady a precise bow, while he enquired after their health and their opinion of the past week's weather. His manner was faintly flirtatious—gallant, perhaps, best describes it—and was not made more attractive by the permanently uneasy expression in his eyes; but Meg and her mother excused that; that was natural, after what he had been through; and they were almost relieved to detect in him some outward sign of his sufferings. It was plain that he greatly admired his wife. Sometimes he would get into conversation with one of the guests, and sooner or later a reference to Frau Schacht's intellect and learning would be introduced. Very occasionally, they would be seen out strolling together on the paths above the lake. He never talked about his job in Salzburg. In that little town, thronged with tourists, there were no doubt many humble and ill-paid posts connected indirectly with the tourist trade—and hundreds of applicants for them. Once, when conversation at the supper table had turned on the appalling post-war unemployment in Italy, he had observed with a slight laugh that he was lucky; he had work; and Frau Schacht was remarked to look annoyed and change the subject. Poor Franz dug in the garden, picked vegetables, and repaired the railings, and Frau Schacht was once overheard preventing him in a fierce whisper from carrying a departing visitor's cases down to the bus-stop. On the whole he had a mildly depressing effect upon the Lamberts, and they were always guiltily pleased when early on Sunday evenings he came to say good-bye before catching the train which would get him into Salzburg at midnight.

Mrs Lambert was now pretty sure that Frau Schacht did not want to discuss the owner of the house across the lake. She was not always so fortunate as to have this topic interrupted by a hornet, but she made interruptions of her own, and her tone whenever house or owner came up in conversation was curt and dismissory. Was she envious of his riches? or was he another Herr Zeller, obstinate about something that Frau Schacht wanted done away with or changed? Perhaps she disliked the subject because it distracted Meg from her grammar. It was not easy to guess what went on behind those dyed curls, faintly smelling of French toilet-wash, arranged on Hansi's lined forehead, and Mrs Lambert had no intention of trying. She was not very inquisitive by nature, and preferred to leave small mysteries unsolved; solved, they might prove to be disturbing.

She was already wondering if the plan to come to Martinsdorf had been wise. Was Meg really learning any German?

"Where are you off to, darling?"

"Out, Mummy," in the mild tone which hardly conceals raging impatience. It was after luncheon; Mrs Lambert was, for once, on her way upstairs to rest.

"With the others or by yourself?"

"Oh, by *myself*. Mummy, don't *fuss*."

"I am not fussing, Meg . . . but have you done your verbs to-day?"

"Yes, before breakfast." Her tone was slightly softer owing to guilt, as she remembered half an hour spent with open book and her eyes fixed upon the house across the lake.

"Well . . . where are you going, dear?"

"Up into the woods—by the waterfall—read——" Her voice died away as, blowing a kiss, she went down the wooden stairs at a pace that would inevitably have tripped up someone older, and darted across the garden. Her mother went slowly up to her room; before she dozed off she had convinced herself that Meg was so en-

joying being at Martinsdorf, and storing up such reserves of sun-
shine and health, that perhaps it did not matter if she were not
learning as much German as had been hoped . . . if only everyone
at home were not so critical . . . expecting such great results . . .
saying Meg . . . spoilt. . . .

But an hour or so later Meg was found by the Danish friends,
Kristin and Helga, wandering disconsolately by the lake.

"Hullo, Meg," said the elder, carefully, and beaming.

"Hullo, I *am* glad to see you. Where are you off to?"

"Nowhere. We are readink our German." Helga, whose fair
braid encircled a head mistakenly supposed by Mrs Lambert to be
filled with placid thoughts, held up her book. Kristin, whose
equally fair hair floated about a calm moon-face belying the passions
raging behind it, nodded and held up hers.

"All right . . . I've got mine. Let's go and sit on the shore. I've
been up in the woods, but—I don't know—usually I adore it up
there but to-day it was horrid."

Helga nodded sedately, as they paced under the acacias along the
road leading to the shore; her tone contained no hint of questioning. She knew what the English "horrid" meant, and was not surprised to hear that the woods were so: her temperament had prepared her to hear anything.

"Yes . . . I felt as if I were being watched."

"Please?" Kristin turned grave interested eyes, "someone stea
your watch?"

"No." Meg did not laugh. "I felt as if someone were watching
me; someone I couldn't see, hiding among the trees."

"Ah. It was a murderer, no?"

This time Meg did laugh, as the eager question escaped Helga's
primly shaped lips.

"Oh no, nothing so . . . so ordinary. It wasn't like that at all. It
was . . . oh, I can't explain it. Never mind. Here's a nice place; let's
sit down here."

And for an hour or so they actually managed to do some work,
interrupted only by their refusal to acknowledge the admiring
salutes of a passing boatload of holidaying Austrian males; and their

own admiration of a large, powerful and fast motor-boat, painted white and flying a green flag, which they all agreed was a newcomer to the St Martinsee; it quite eclipsed the motor-boat which towed the water-skiers; and it threw up such impressive waves against the shore that Kristin's shoes were wetted by the spray.

*   *   *   *   *

That evening, someone suggested that they should go down to dance at the *weinstube*; so Robin Gascoine and Meg, and the Danish pair escorted by two young Austrians who had arrived on the previous day, set off about nine o'clock through the soft summer dusk.

"Same old *weinstube*, same old beer, same old bun-faces varied by an occasional *pretzel*-face. Who wants to give the *weinstube* a rest?"

"You know there's nowhere else to go, Robin—at least, we can't afford to go anywhere else."

"Mammy Gascoine used to de best dance-places—best melons, best bands, best high-yaller gals. Mammy Gascoine hab had de *weinstube*."

"Do be careful," Meg said in a whisper, "those boys understand more English than you think. . . . Moritz looked at you very queerly when you said '*pretzel*-faces'."

"Mammy Gascoine not afraid ob anyone, black or white. Fight 'um all, arm tied behind back. Look here, how much money have we got between us?"

They halted under the trees, half-way down the lane, and counted their *schillings* and calculated how much it would cost to visit the famous restaurant in a ruined castle, high on a mountain overlooking the lake, which was frequented by the wealthier English visitors and American Army officers with their women folk.

"That is a bad place, no?" Helga's tone was hopeful.

"No such luck. But it's a better place than the dear old *weinstube*. Rudi, how much have you got?" in German.

But the Austrian boys either did not understand or did not want to join in the scheme, and after some minutes, during which Robin tried to explain it and they listened with smiles and occasional shakes of the head, he said grumpily, "Oh, for Pete's sake—I give up," and they resumed their walk down the alp.

Broad yellow light shone out from the open door of the *weinstube* and the large black shadows of chestnut leaves swayed gently on the white road. The brash, twanging music of a zither drifted out steadily into the night. Meg's spirits rose; she was easily pleased, and the novelty of dancing with the opposite numbers of the policeman, the postman and the greengrocer at home had not yet worn off. Besides, these young men were so much better-looking than their English equivalents; and what could be more picturesque than their *lederhosen*?

The strong light in the low, warm room dazzled them all at first, and then they began to make out who was there and who was not: groups of cheerful elder people sitting over their wine at tables near the wall, who nodded a "*guten abend*" while the few old men and women muttered the "*Grüss Gott*" of a simpler age; there were the curly oiled hair and beaming face of Georg the young postmaster; Klara, the gipsy belle from the bathing-station, sat—rather reluctantly, judging by her expression—under the wing of her mother; there were Ida and Maria, in fresh lacy blouses displaying their sunburnt arms, and Rudolf and Josef in shirts worn outside, American fashion; in the inner dining-room there was a group of boys drawn-faced and drowsy from a day and a night on the Hochalmspitz, eating their first hot food for fifty hours and blinking at the company like deported eaglets; and that was Frau Trauber the proprietor's wife, with a black sateen scarf bound Italian fashion round her head, sitting behind the little bar and soberly observing the company. Every now and again she circulated among the tables to bring more beer or wine; and in the corner two enthusiasts, who did not care for talk or drink, plucked out the music.

The *gasthaus* party settled themselves near the musicians where they could influence the choice of tunes. Their table was a large solid, shapely piece of furniture, made entirely by hand from pine-wood and varnished a clear red-brown, decorated with a few graceful scrolls, and calculated, war risk apart, to be in use when the great-grandchildren of those present were dancing, drinking and chatting in the same room. The doors and window frames had the same satisfying solidity. The walls were painted cream and decorated with murals; an ibex and its hunter upon a mountain peak, a wreath of alpine flowers, a little steamer on a green lake. It's so *pretty*, Meg thought passionately; it's all so romantic and different from ghastly Tormouth, and I never want to go home.

Presently they were all dancing except Kristin, who sat alone at the table looking placid.

"She's awfully miserable: her boy has dropped her," Meg explained to Robin, as they circled cheerfully to a Viennese tune, "she had a letter this morning."

Robin said "Dear, dear" in his airiest voice. He refused to listen to anyone's troubles, saying that Mammy Gascoine, with her piccaninnies, had enough of her own.

"Well, you might be a bit more sympathetic; how would you like it?"

"Not at all, I have no doubt. So far, it has always been me who has done the dropping. I have seen to that, and I intend to go on as I have begun."

Meg listened with the inscrutable expression that gave to her face a kind of false maturity; all expression—and usually her face was exceedingly expressive, changeful and varying—was banished, and she presented to the world a smooth little Sphinx's mask. In fact, what Robin had just said seemed to her one of those remarks which enlighten one about the young male, and she went away within herself to think it over.

So, while she was moving slowly through the crowd of dancers, in the arms of a young man, with her thick eyelashes lowered and her face looking secret and calm, Esmé Scarron saw her close at hand and for the third time.

A few moments previously there had been a bustle and confusion of arrival near the door at the far end of the room; and Frau Trauber had come round from her seat behind the bar to see what was the matter, advancing with her usual placid manner and slight smile that was far from being servile.

But when she had seen who it was that stood there, slightly in advance of the group of people in the doorway, her smile had died. She lifted her head, then bowed it.

"*Guten abend*, Herr Scarron."

"Good evening," he answered, and came forward, followed by his three or four friends, into the room. He seemed to make up his mind to come at that instant, for he had been, as it were, poised in the doorway, looking among the tables and at the dancers. One of the women following him, a tall American in a red dress, said something and he looked back over his shoulder and laughed.

Frau Trauber led the party to the only unoccupied table, and they sat down. The dancers did not stop, but everyone was covertly looking at them.

"Laura—Handford—Bessie—what will you have?" Esmé Scarron spoke in English, "there's nothing here worth drinking, of course, but since you've insisted on slumming——"

"I like that—'we' insisted," interrupted the tall American.

"We'd better drink the local wine." He turned to Frau Trauber, who stood stiffly near with her eyes fixed on the wall opposite, and gave the order. She turned, and walked heavily away.

CHAPTER SEVEN

Pick-up

"BITTE," said the Austrian youth who was now Meg's partner, "I tread on your foot."

"It's quite all right, it was my fault, I'm afraid—I wasn't—I'm sorry."

She had been staring at the newcomers. At first, the clothes of the women fascinated her, and their hair, and their jewellery. Obviously they were rich, yet they were not opulently dressed; their wealth was betrayed by exquisite finish in all details and in their manner; only a complete detachment from worldly cares, due to spirituality or to an exceedingly large income, could have supported that manner. And it was anything but spiritual. Then Meg began to notice the men who were with them, and one in particular; how alive he was; that was her first thought; not his age, nor his looks, nor the elegance of his appearance, but his aliveness came straight across the room to her where she danced in Rudi's arms.

"You are very interested in those people," Rudi said stiffly at last, "they are friends of yours, yes?"

"No, I never saw them before. But I do think they look interesting. Don't you?"

Rudi, who was attracted to her and suffering from jealousy, shrugged and smiled and did not answer.

"They're English, too," Meg said presently, as if in excuse, "at least, some of them are."

Their progress down the long room had by now brought them near to the newcomers' table, and as they danced past it the man who seemed so alive, the one in the white evening jacket, turned swiftly —he had been sitting with his arms on the table, talking—and looked straight at her and smiled.

She smiled in return. Her heart glowed: the room seemed brighter and the music sweeter. She saw that he had a big head and an oddly shaped nose and unusually bright eyes. His complexion was exceedingly brown and made his thick hair appear a bright silver. Then, before she had time to observe him further, he got up and came quickly over to them. He touched Rudi's shoulder.

"May I cut in?" he said.

Meg stopped dancing, and hesitated, looking smilingly from the man's face to the boy's sulky one; then, as Rudi barely nodded, the other clasped her and bore her away.

She was conscious of heads inclining towards one another, of people whispering and watching. She saw Robin, looking surprisingly sour, and Kristin and Helga staring. The people at the stranger's own table—and that annoyed her slightly—were not looking at them at all.

Then she discovered that he did not dance well; his style was too springy. He breathed a little faster, as if dancing were an effort; and the dry heat of his hand was faintly disagreeable to the touch. There was the faint fresh odour from his jacket—it was made not of linen but of some stiff material with a sheen—and of strong American cigarettes. How ugly he was, and he reminded her of someone, but she could not remember whom. Then, just for a fraction of an instant, for so fleeting a space of time that it left no surviving impression upon her mind during the many quick impressions following—she wanted to be back with Rudi or Robin— it did not matter which. She was afraid.

"I do hope you don't mind my doing this? None of my friends over there care for dancing. Are you staying in Martinsdorf or at St Lorenz?" His voice was light in timbre and pleasant to hear.

"At Martinsdorf, at the *Gasthaus Venedig*. Are you staying here?"

She thought that he might be a guest at the luxurious hotel near the western end of the lake.

"No," he answered, looking down at her, "I live here. That is, I am living here for part of the summer. My house is on the other side of the lake."

He was given a view of pretty teeth as she opened her mouth in surprise.

"*Oh!* Is it that perfectly beautiful house we can see from our bedroom windows?"

"I haven't the honour of knowing which are your bedroom windows, but my house is visible from most parts of Martinsdorf."

She was beginning to speak again when he interrupted abruptly.

"You are not married, are you?"

Meg laughed loudly, screwing up her face in delight.

"Of *course* not. Why, I am not nineteen yet. Oh, I must tell my mother—she *will* be so amused."

He looked at her, smiling in sympathy. If he thought that the idea of marriage was not quite so exquisitely amusing as all that, he did not say so.

"It is the loveliest house I've ever seen," Meg went on in a moment, a little sobered by seeing, out of the corner of her eye, four observant faces boding comment and criticism to come as she passed the table where her friends were sitting, "and—oh, but of course, we ought not to have been there but we didn't know——"

"Were you trespassing?" he asked teasingly, and when she nodded he observed that he must have the *Verboten* notices replaced; the Germans had taken them down during the war.

"I expect Lorenz and Melchior frightened you, didn't they?" he went on, "they are rather alarming, taken in conjunction, but they are both dears, really." Suddenly he glanced impatiently towards the two musicians.

"Those two are well—er—in—in the groove, aren't they? and seemed likely to stay there. You must be tired; shall we sit down?"

Meg was not tired, but, now knowing that this was the rich and clever Mr Ismay Scarron named by Frau Schacht, she went willingly. She was so eager to win from him permission to sketch his house that she felt only slightly disappointed when, murmuring that she would not find his friends interesting, he led her to an unoccupied table near the door. She had never spoken to such people in her life, and the party was now sitting in silence and looking sulky, but she would have liked to have a nearer view of the bracelets, the bags and gloves, in order to describe them to her mother.

"Then you are Mr Ismay Scarron," she said distinctly, when they were settled in their chairs; she had a feeling that their relationship ought to be given a more conventional colouring. "My name is Meg Lambert."

He was silent for a moment, and she had the curious conviction that he was thinking about her name. When he looked up, he smiled.

"Esmé, not Ismay."

"I beg your pardon—Frau Schacht—we are staying with her— she is Austrian and perhaps she didn't pronounce it properly—she never heard it before, I expect. It—it's an unusual name, isn't it?"

"It was my mother's; she was Esmée, with two e's, and I am named after her. Would you like something to drink?"

"Well—no, thank you. The wine here is so sour and beer makes me sleepy."

"Coffee? Orangeade? *Apfelsaft?*"

She shook her head, laughing.

"I would like tea, really; proper English tea, with enough milk. I know all English tourists long for tea when they are abroad and it's supposed to be awful of them, but Mummy and I always have tea about this time in the evening when we're at home and I miss it."

"Will you bring your mother to tea with me? on—not to-morrow—Wednesday—no, Thursday afternoon, and I shall be happy to give you real English tea with enough milk."

The friendliness of his tone was now touched with a respectfulness that soothed Meg's misgivings which, after all, had some grounds. He had picked her up in the *weinstube*. She was on holiday, this was care-free Austria, he was known and presumably respected by most of the people in the room, yet they had not been introduced, and she had had a disturbing conviction that things were moving too fast.

"Thank you very much. I will ask my mother, and if we are not engaged on that afternoon of course we shall *absolutely love* to come," she said, and could not help ending on a squeak of excitement.

A deep dimple suddenly appeared in his cheek, then vanished.

"You are not going home just yet—home to England—I hope?"

"Oh no, not for a long time. I am here to try and learn German in six months. . . ."

They sat there for the next half-hour, while she told him about herself and her mother and their plans and hopes, and he listened attentively, occasionally making a comment that made her laugh, when his brilliant little eyes shone in sympathy. Meg was enjoying the occasion immensely, none the less because Rudi and Robin glided at intervals past the table where she sat with her new friend, piloting Helga or Kristin, and all four looking positively funereal. But when at last she said that she must go back to them, and he rose at once to say good night, she did feel slightly apprehensive. She had to live with the other four; Mr Scarron, however charming, was only an interlude.

After she had rejoined her friends, he left almost at once, accompanied by his own. The quietly opulent dresses of red and grey, the shining carefully casual heads of hair, followed him down the room between the dancers, and the two men in the party, one with a red thick neck and long nose, the other tall and with a clever, ravaged face, followed the women. Once or twice Mr Scarron paused to exchange a word with people seated at the tables or to lift a hand in salute to someone across the room. Sometimes the person thus singled out looked uneasy or sullen; sometimes they responded effusively. It was not possible for Meg to tell whether he really were "known and respected" or not.

Soon after this the *Venedig* party decided to go home. They were all rather quiet as they walked up the shadowy lane, where stars were glittering between the leaves.

"Ah well," observed Robin at last—who, like one of Jane Austen's characters, *would sooner be quarrelling than silent*—"now at last I know what my father meant."

"Bitte?" Moritz was always eager for English conversation; Rudi and the girls continued to trudge up the slope without speaking.

"He uses old-fashioned expressions; he calls a certain type of man a bounder. I've never known what he meant, but he always said that I would when I met one. Now I have, and I do. It's Pal Scarron," turning to Meg, who started indignantly, "Mammy Gascoine don't like dat baby at all."

"Don't be silly, he's very nice," Meg said dreamily, her indignation subsiding as she thought of the treat which would be hers on Thursday, "but even if he hadn't been, I should have encouraged him because of wanting to see his house. It was the most marvellous luck, getting invited without having to ask."

"All right. I don't grudge you your pleasures. I only wonder at your liking to sit for hours with a bounder old enough to be your grandfather."

"Is he? I didn't think about his age."

"Is he! Rudi, Moritz"—turning to the Austrians and breaking into German—"how old would you say that chap was?"

Followed much contemptuous laughter and speculation, while Meg gazed sleepily at the dim path and Kristin gazed tranquilly up at the stars with eyes full of tears, leaning the while upon the faithful arm of Helga without which she would have stumbled.

Unfortunately, Mrs Lambert was in bed and asleep, so she could not be told the news and made to swear to keep Thursday afternoon free, but Meg could lean long over her balcony, staring across the lake at the lights shining forth from every window of the house on the farther shore: shining so freely and so strongly, with an effect of triumph.

CHAPTER EIGHT

Interior

"WHERE on earth have you been?" she said rather crossly, meeting her mother coming slowly up the garden just before luncheon on the following day. "Trudi said something about going into Villach with Hansi, but I couldn't understand her extraordinary dialect . . . and rushing off like that before I came down to breakfast. . . . Mummy, you do look tired. Let me have those," and she masterfully took over the two laden baskets. "Really, she is an old brute, making you slave like this . . . where is she, anyway?"

"Seeing her bank-manager, and some man whom she hopes to get to design her new houses . . . I don't know . . . late last night she suddenly said that we mustn't miss the chance of getting some huge cabbages very cheap in Villach, so we'd go in together by the first bus this morning——"

"Have you had any breakfast?"

"Yes, thank you, dearest; horrible coffee. Oh, how I would love some tea," with an exhausted sigh. Meg turned, her face alight with pleasure amidst the dancing sunrays and leaf-shadows and the bright pink phlox.

"Well! That's just what you're going to have. Oh . . . not now, poor pet . . . next Thursday. Who do you think has asked us to tea? and he sent a special message to you, that it will be real *English* tea with enough milk."

"I can't possibly guess. I'm too tired." A faint smile, the reflection of Meg's own, came on Mrs Lambert's face.

"Mr Esmé Scarron. Yes," nodding in reply to a satisfyingly incredulous look, "truly. He was at the *weinstube* last night and I picked him up."

"Oh, Meg! Was that . . . I do wish you would be——"

"It's quite all right, darling; everyone there seemed to know him and no one thought it was peculiar—except Robin; he was rather lofty about it, but who minds him? and——"

"Robin comes of a very good family, you know; his father is some relation to the Duke of Davenham, Hansi was telling me. In fact, I don't know quite how she got hold of him——"

"Oh, he knew some ghastly deb. who strayed in here and she recommended it and Robin's father was only too glad to hear of somewhere good *and* cheap; they're awfully poor; his sister's working in some institute in London and can't afford nylons, so she goes without any stockings at all, and last year she got pneumonia and had to go to a State hospital and that saved them *pounds*; they were *frightfully* pleased. But never mind Robin . . . Isn't it marvellous about Mr Scarron? By the way, it's Esmé, not Ismay, and—oh! I know who he reminds me of."

"Who, darling?" her mother asked in a moment, as Meg was silent. They had reached the kitchen door and Mrs Lambert had thankfully sunk down on the wooden bench outside it.

"Paracelsus."

"The astrologer-man whose house you saw in Villach? (I haven't seen it yet; I'm always meaning to, but if I'm alone I have so many things to see to and Hansi drags me along when we go in together as if she were permanently trying to catch a last train. . . .) But wasn't your Paracelsus very ugly?"

"Yes. At least . . . not exactly ugly. More . . . more strange-looking, and clever. And Mr Scarron isn't exactly ugly and he doesn't really *look* like Paracelsus, it's just that it's the same type of face."

"Oh! Interesting," Mrs Lambert said languidly; now that the bargain-cabbages were safely home, her arms were recording, through all their strained muscles, how enormous those vegetables were.

"Well, on Thursday you'll see him. We can go, can't we?" darting at her mother a sudden glance which had in it all a child's suspicion of the grown-ups; be they never so loving, they are always capable of stopping you going to the circus.

But Mrs Lambert answered heartily, "Of course, dear. I shall enjoy it; it's very kind of him." And out of her gratitude, looking at Meg's happy face, she added, "He must be a nice man."

But, if he were a nice man—and of course, the fact that he had included the mother of an unusually attractive girl in an invitation to tea did not prove that he was a nice man, because he might be anxious to secure Meg's company at any price—why did Hansi not want to talk about him?

Frau Schacht returned hot and irritable and silent late in the afternoon from her excursion to Villach. She went at once to her room to rest, and it was not until the preparation, and the consumption, of supper were over, that Mrs Lambert thought it prudent to start pumping her.

"Hansi," she began, when they were sitting in the dining-room in the dusk.

"I know just what you are going to say, my dear Eve. It is about the cabbages. Why did I have to go into Villach when here in Martinsdorf there is more than one excellent cabbage-field owned by my neighbours where I might buy them? Well, it is because these particularly large and good cabbages are grown by Rudolf Schmidt who lives out at Judenburg and does not bring his cabbages any nearer to Martinsdorf than Villach, and every now and then I will buy my salad-cabbages from him, although it means going into town and to pay the fare on the bus as well as the price of the cabbages. Yet in the end—I have calculated it carefully, over some years—I do save money by doing this."

"Yes, I am sure it is well worth while," mechanically. "Hansi, you know that man who lives on the other side of the lake, the one with the peculiar name, Meg—er—she met him at the *weinstube* last night, and he has asked us both over there to tea on Thursday."

"I heard that he has been at the *weinstube* for the last few evenings; he was there on Sunday and on Monday also. With his friends, the Americans."

"You don't like him, do you?"

Mrs Lambert had decided to have this matter out. Hansi's opinion of Mr Scarron did not matter while he was unknown to the Lamberts, but if he had made friendly advances to Meg her mother must put aside her own shrinking from possible awkwardnesses and try to find out whether he was the kind of person with whom they should associate. Mrs Lambert possessed the quiet respect for virtue of the middle-class Englishwoman, and to do her justice the fact of Mr Scarron's riches did not weigh heavily with her.

"No, I do not like him much," Frau Schacht answered readily. "I think you have seen that I don't want to speak about him, no? You see, in the war . . . at first he was very friendly with the German commanders here and then, before the Americans came into the war—just in time—he got away to America himself."

She was looking straight at Mrs Lambert as she spoke, but the air was now so dusky that it was difficult to see her expression.

"The war—yes, of course, I can understand that the village wouldn't like him collaborating and then running away" (why did every Austrian and German talk as if they had all been strongly pro-Ally throughout the conflict?), "but I really meant more personal things—what type of man is he? Is there a Mrs Scarron?"

"She lives in Venice. They are divorced."

"Divorced? Oh dear."

"Why 'Oh dear'? In England is no one ever divorced?"

"Of course, Hansi, don't be silly; I only meant that it would be nice if they weren't."

"No doubt. But life is not often nice. That is a word you have only in England, I think."

"But perhaps it wasn't his fault . . . did he divorce her or did she divorce him?"

"I do not know. He doesn't tell us, here at Martinsdorf, the story of his life. That house is only one of his homes, you know; he has also a house in Savoy and a palace in Venice, and although we are interested in him because we live here all the time, to him, I know, this is only a small place where dull people live." Frau Schacht had turned aside and was looking down at the pale lake shining between the trees.

"He must be immensely rich," said Mrs Lambert, her lower nature for the moment taking command.

"Ah. But not quite so rich as once, I think. Americans are often staying with him—having parties—going in that motor-boat up and down the lake—wasting money. And he knows many of the Occupation people who bring their own drink and have their food sent from America in tins because they imagine that our Austrian food is full of microbes, so they are not even good for the tourist trade, his parties. Now, I have told you about his being friends with the Nazis and about his running away and about his divorced wife and his three homes and his parties . . . what more do you wish to know?"

"Well, *don't* sound so cross, *please*, Hansi. And you haven't really told me anything at all. I wanted to know what kind of a man he is; he, himself."

"He is very charming." Hansi's voice sounded toneless again as she stood up, a white blur in the dusk, smoothing her dress over her hips, "everyone says this. And no doubt you will find him kind . . . he is immensely clever. There is a library over there, full of great books . . . he speaks nine languages, I believe."

"Then you think we shall like him?" was Mrs Lambert's last attempt to obtain definite information.

"I expect so. But really, Eve, I don't wish to speak of him, I have said this before. I don't like how he behaved during the war. Now shall we switch on the light and risk the hornets? I will sit here and keep you company while I add up my accounts."

The next two days passed rather drearily, being regarded—by Meg at least—as mere obstructions to be lived through before the splendours of Thursday. Helga devoted herself to Kristin, who irritated Frau Schacht by placidly refusing to eat anything at all ("she will make herself ill, the wretched child, and it will reflect upon my school"), Meg increased the irritation by neglecting her studies, and Robin, who had been brought up in a family whose older members played and sang, went about whistling *Silver Threads Among The Gold*; occasionally Mammy Gascoine besought Missy Meg not to let de white boss at de Big House steal her little heart away. Meg was annoyed, but could not help laughing, which annoyed her the more.

And then on Thursday morning Mrs Lambert was aroused at seven by a voice saying dolefully, "Mummy, what shall we do? It's pouring with rain," and lifted a dazed head to see through the window swathes of white cloud lying so low along the mountains as almost to conceal the lake, while the air was full of musical drippings and tinklings.

"Really, Meg, sometimes you go on as if you were six. I was in the most heavenly sleep . . . I don't know what we shall do. It may have cleared up by this afternoon."

Meg went back to bed after blowing a penitent kiss, and her mother, being unable to get to sleep again and having in any case to get up in fifteen minutes, got up.

After lunch, however, rain was still teeming down. They stood at the door of the *gasthaus* in their waterproofs, looking hopelessly at the sky and wondering how they were to reach the opposite shore—now hidden in wet mist—and whether Mr Scarron would, in such weather, expect them?

"Well, what shall we do? It's twenty to four . . . shall we chance walking round by the road? Or shall I go down and see if there's anyone there *now* who would take a boat out?" said Meg.

"The road doesn't lead anywhere near the house; I asked Hansi this morning; it goes off to Velden behind those mountains we can see from here, and we should only get soaked to the skin and perhaps lost. We'd better go down and see if we can bribe somebody."

"It's very suspicious, how everyone vanished about eleven this morning when we started making enquiries about getting across, and now again after lunch . . . I thought Robin might have volunteered, but what a hope. It's simply maddeningly disappointing. I may never get this chance again."

But they had not gone more than a few yards through the down-pour when Mrs Lambert exclaimed, "Here comes somebody," and they saw plodding up the slope towards them a sunburnt sulky face above an ancient Army gas-cape.

"It's Georg, the postmaster—perhaps he's got a message," and Meg splashed forward.

Yes, he had a message for the ladies, sent over the lake by tele-phone. With the compliments of Herr Scarron, would they please come down to the nearest landing-stage immediately.

"The motor launch! He's sent it for us!" and Meg's sulky ex-pression vanished, and she hurried down the alp after Georg, whose sulky expression had not vanished; it was difficult to realise that only last night they had been cheerfully waltzing together. He dis-liked walking half a kilometre to the *Venedig* and back in such weather.

But there, racing towards them across the grey water in an im-posing arrow of foam, was the launch, with a figure in oilskins at the wheel which—Meg hastily explained to her mother as they waited sheltering as best they could under the trees—must be Mr Scarron's servant Lorenz. Mrs Lambert, whose enthusiasm for this adventure was dead and cold, wondered if the launch possessed any-where she might creep underneath and at least not get any wetter.

The engine cut off suddenly and the vessel swept slowly in to the landing-stage. The figure at the wheel snatched off an oilskin hat, revealing a head covered in silver hair, and waved.

"Hullo! how do you do, Mrs Lambert? Come along, I've got oilskins and boots and everything here."

Mr Scarron himself, their host in person. How flattering, thought Mrs Lambert, feeling, however, rather an Old Thing as she picked her way along the slippery planks of the landing-stage and out over the slapping little waves. Meg had run on ahead and was already shaking Mr Scarron's hand, and then Mrs Lambert was doing likewise, and receiving from its warmth and strength a strong im-pression of vitality while brilliant, laughing little eyes looked steadily into her own. What a strange man; how masterful, she thought confusedly as she sat in the shelter of the small cabin, warm and dry in ample oilskins; how wet Meg will get out there, the spray is going all over them—oh! what a bounce! I had no idea these things could go so fast.

Suddenly the engine stopped. In a hush broken by the tinkling of rain, they glided to a stop by a landing-stage in an expanse of water from which the reeds had been cleared for a hundred yards. The pine trees half-way up the slope were hidden in cloud. Down out of it advanced a figure in oilskins, holding an outsize umbrella, and accompanied by a large yellow dog.

"Is that Lorenz?" Meg said eagerly.

"Yes" turning from where he bent over the engine to smile at her, "and Melchior too. Lorenz," he shouted in German, "why weren't you waiting here, you fool, to meet the ladies? Hurry up, now."

The dog ran down the slope among the rivulets until it reached the water's edge, then sat down and looked at Meg with its tongue hanging out.

"He manages to look dignified all the time; I suppose it's because he's so marvellously poised," and she held out a hand to him, which he ignored.

Mr Scarron looked at her for a moment, then said, "Yes, I suppose so . . . can you put these boots on?"

He gave Mrs Lambert his arm up the wet slippery path and through the woods, while Meg led the party, and Lorenz and the dog brought up the rear; when they arrived at the house, and the women exclaimed on seeing its delicate grey wooden traceries and green shrubs under the veil of rain, Mrs Lambert had an impression of having been wafted there as if by magic, for the sticky paths, the steep ascent and the dreary sameness of the dripping pines, all of which would have been deplored by most men, their host had simply ignored. How he does charge ahead; those wide nostrils look as if they enjoyed snuffing up the rain, she thought—and certainly everything smells delicious. I wonder how old he is? Not more than forty-five—perhaps not that.

As soon as they entered a small panelled anteroom, he gave them into the care of a dark plump woman with her hair bound in a coloured scarf, who led them to a bedroom on the second floor, where Meg had to be prevented from elaborately re-designing and painting her mouth.

"Don't be long, dear, we mustn't keep him waiting, I'm sure he hates it. Oh, Meg, that will *do* . . . you look perfectly all right. . . ."

"What a heavenly room," Meg said, rolling one eye round as she leaned earnestly towards the mirror, "what's that wood? It looks like silk."

"I have no idea," Mrs Lambert said, examining the light grey panelling—"and the carpet—what a charming design—all those green bows and yellow roses—is it an Aubusson, do you think?"

The air in the room smelled faintly of spice; it floated out, perhaps, from the Chinese cabinets and nests of drawers in black, red and gold lacquer or from the pale plum-coloured draperies of the tester bed. Mrs Lambert could not resist wandering round, looking, while the attendant stood near Meg, occasionally offering her a comb or a hairpin, without a smile. Mrs Lambert had just come to the satisfactory conclusion that although the room was exquisite she would not want to live in it, when Meg, turning reluctantly from her reflection, announced that she was ready.

CHAPTER NINE

English Tea

THEY followed the woman downstairs. The scent of spices went with them; the house was brimming with it, as if it were a box from the East, and Mrs Lambert decided that many of the woods, unfamiliar in appearance as they were to her, must be from scented trees. The entire inside of the place was panelled and floored with the shining grey wood they had already seen in the bedroom, transforming what must originally have been the country villa of a rich Austrian merchant into a dim, exotic dwelling where daylight hardly penetrated between curtains of brocade and the gilt knees of seated Bonzes were faintly reflected along gleaming floors. The blending of grey and gold throughout the rooms was strikingly rich and depressing; Mrs Lambert thought of museums, and she also felt, less decidedly, that it showed bad taste to set such furnishings amidst the fresh mountain landscape. But then she reflected that just here it was not particularly fresh; those pines seemed to muffle everything. Glancing at Meg's face, however, she knew that she must keep these criticisms to herself.

The dark attendant was opening a door in front of them.

"Ah . . . now you must have your tea . . . I am sure you haven't had a decent cup since you came to Austria . . . but first may I present——"

Their host, coming forward to meet them as they stood hesitating on the threshold, smilingly indicated a number of people seated about the long, dark, lofty room, and Mrs Lambert, who was not one of those who hear people's names when introduced, caught a musical prolonged speech in which *principes* and *principessas* and *duces* appeared with rather alarming frequency. She saw smiling dark faces, small smart white hats, light suits and shoes. In a moment she was seated on a *papier mâché* and mother-of-pearl chair and drinking perfect tea while trying not to look too obviously at the room and its occupants.

Books . . . bound in olive leather and maroon and clay-colour and black, reaching from floor to ceiling . . . how dark they made the room, and the french windows at the far end opened only into a dim conservatory filled with the blotched leaves of tropical plants. The air was too hot; not stifling, but too hot for normal English lungs. She decided that the lady sitting near her in the darkest corner of the room, the one wearing that wonderful dress of white embroidery, must be an American and accustomed to central heating. She was quite silent. She sat still, with transparent fingers wrapped about her transparent Japanese cup, and did not move. Mrs Lambert had to try not to let her eyes wander in that direction; how ill she looked, poor thing; the rims of her dark glasses were no bluer and thicker than the veins on her arms and brow, and that long lustreless silver hair—was it ash-blonde or was she old? It was impossible to tell.

She was thankful that the rest of the party, the four women and three men who seemed to be Italians, were talking animatedly among themselves and that Meg had been drawn by their host into the conversation. Their English was faultless; they must be very highly born as well as very rich and, as sometimes happens to the highly born outside England, also highly educated; their clothes were light and gay and unexpected as clothes in the top-flight fashion magazines; and she did not want to talk to them at all. She felt that she was being gauche and stupid, but she could not help it. She felt utterly out of it. The conversation was flippant and turned every subject into a joke. There was no comfortable small talk. Meg, bless her, turned laughing bright eyes from one face to another and spoke little; but her admiring expression must flatter, and her mere presence must give pleasure.

The Italian manservant in a white jacket who presided over the wide silver-gilt tray and its brilliant load of fragile china looked sulky. So had the woman who had waited on them upstairs. Mrs Lambert's thoughtful inspection of her host, who was talking animatedly to Meg, and her efforts not to glance again at the silent figure in the dark corner, were interrupted by a hoarse cry which might have been uttered by a depraved baby, sounding at her knee. Startled, she looked down and met the turquoise eyes of a Siamese cat which was steadily regarding her.

Mr Scarron had glanced round at the sound of the creature's voice. He now came across the room and took the chair at Mrs Lambert's side.

"Iliaster, you jealous little beast, behave yourself." He put out short strong fingers and caressed the cat's head and she mewed again. "Iliaster, the hidden power in Nature by which all things grow. Isn't it a lovely name? And don't you agree that she looks like the spirit of Nature, so deft and yet so savage?"

Mrs Lambert, who thought that she looked sulky, like everyone else in a subordinate position in this house, answered only by a nervous smile.

"Perhaps you don't like cats, Mrs Lambert?"

"Well, I do prefer dogs. While my husband was alive we had such a dear old dog, called Johnno, and we were quite devoted to him."

I am talking like a fool, she thought, her feeling of being a stranger, an outsider far from home, increased by what she had just said; and for some reason she felt it was important that she should not seem a fool in the eyes of Mr Scarron. She felt suddenly helpless.

"Your husband . . . you are a widow, then, Mrs Lambert?"

"My husband died about nine years ago, when Meg—my daughter—was ten."

How irritating, that second utterance of her name. How absurd to find it irritating. Was there something faintly mocking in the repetition? He said nothing in reply to her statement. He was looking down at the cat, motionless under the slow caressing sweep of his fingers.

"Is your tea good?" he asked in a moment, looking up with such sudden sly gaiety that to her own surprise she laughed.

"It's delicious," she said emphatically.

"It's scarce and dear over here; my housekeeper gets a supply from Twinings at the beginning of every summer when I'm expected; we never buy it locally."

"Do you come here every summer? How lovely for you."

"Is it? Yes, I suppose it is. I'm fond of this valley and the house, because I spent so much time here as a child—my mother was born here in Carinthia and her father gave her this place as a wedding present—but I like my home in Savoy much better. I love mountains." He turned and looked down the long room and through the french windows, where a dark shoulder heaved itself out of the white low-hanging clouds. "I'm only really happy in the mountains. My parents also left me a little *palazzo* in Venice, but I'm hardly ever there, I hate the crowded feeling of a city; I go down for three weeks or so every autumn for the international film contest—festival—whatever they call it, but I get away as soon as I can."

"It must be difficult to choose where to live, having houses in three such lovely places." Mrs Lambert impatiently repulsed a passing thought about the housing shortage in England: must one always be hounded by one's social conscience: could one never revel vicariously in another's good fortune?

"We hope to go down to Venice for a fortnight at the end of our stay," she went on, "the friend we are staying with at Martinsdorf, Frau Schacht——"

"Yes," he said quickly, "your daughter told me you were staying there. I'm sure she makes you very comfortable."

"Oh yes, very." Now Mrs Lambert suppressed an impulse to mention hornets. "She knows somewhere cheap and clean where we can stay."

Cheap and clean! How dreary I'm being, she thought, and finished her tea at a gulp. But he doesn't look bored. His manners are charming . . . but I don't like charming manners. I like kindness. I wish I could decide whether I like *him*.

Mr Scarron now smilingly excused himself and went to the tea table, where he poured some milk into a bowl. The Siamese, which had been sitting in front of the stove covered in turquoise tiles modelled with white swans and lilies, now rose and walked slowly towards her master, and he set the bowl down on the floor in front of her. Mrs Lambert became aware that the room had grown quiet. She looked round, and saw all the dark, lined, lively faces stilled. They were all watching Iliaster, as she daintily lapped her drink. But Meg was glancing, rather nervously, at the motionless lady in the fairylike dress.

Mr Scarron looked up from his contemplation of his pet, smiling.

"Are you ready to see the house?" he asked, and with murmurs of assent (prompted on Mrs Lambert's part by genuine gratitude) they rose and followed him to the door. The other guests did not move. In their light, rich clothes, seen against the dark setting of the room, they oddly resembled puppets; things assembled and arranged; and their faces were curiously alike, as if the sharing of some common interest had bestowed a general expression.

As Mrs Lambert followed their host out of the room, she heard, or thought she heard, a faint remark—or it might have been a call; it had a wailing, protesting quality—which could have come from that dark corner where sat the woman in the notable dress, or it might even have been a note in the unfamiliar range belonging to Iliaster. She naturally didn't turn back to see. But when they were out in the long narrow hallway her host, turning to Meg and herself, said gently:

"I must apologise for poor Rosalba—that's our friend in the striking costume—she has been ill and has come here to rest."

Then it had been she who was responsible—except that "responsible" was hardly the word to associate with such an appearance.

"She does look shockingly ill. I hope she is getting better," Mrs Lambert said, with one of those sudden bluntnesses which compel gentle people when they have had enough of whatever it is they are enduring. She wanted to walk straight out of that house.

"This is the China room," said Mr Scarron, opening a door into a room filled with tall cabinets, "oh yes, thank you, she is much better than she has been."

There was an obvious remark to be made, but Mrs Lambert did not make it. She looked at the miniature china prettinesses, the girls with flower baskets and the curly dogs and cupids and languishing shepherds, half without seeing them because her thoughts were busy with poor Rosalba, and half-wistfully, because Dresden and Meissen and Saxe work invariably made her wistful. Its sensuous prettiness belonged to that world towards which she was naturally drawn: the sweet world of musical comedy, wherein most people were good and none were truly evil. She would willingly have believed that Heaven has just that atmosphere. It was a low view of the place, of course.

Now they were upstairs. And he, their host, Mr Scarron, was talking to Meg.

"Yes, he was a doctor but a most unorthodox one, so unorthodox that he was always in hot water with the medical profession of those days. He believed in the empirical method of studying medicine, you see, on the battlefield and in the house where plague had been. . . . But it's quite wonderful that you should have heard of him."

"I hadn't—until I saw that house in Villach where he used to live with his father. And then Frau Schacht told me a little about him, but she doesn't know much, and when she told me that *you* were very clever," laughing up at him, "and knew nine languages and had a houseful of books, I thought you would be just the person to ask about Paracelsus."

"And I am, my dear child—I probably know more than anyone else living about Paracelsus—his work and his philosophy have been my chief interest all my life. But do come in—this is my study—not my favourite one, that's in the house at Savoy—but all my reference books are here and my notes—but I'll tell you about that later on. To think that you should have heard of Paracelsus. What an astonishing child you are."

Brilliant rays from a clearing sky poured through the windows of the room into which he was ushering them; they saw the lake lying below, a deep, ghostly and exhausted green, beneath clouds shredded and snarled by hours of ceaseless rain, and above the clouds the firmament, bleached to its palest blue as if drained dry. Mr Scarron swept papers off chairs; he made Mrs Lambert sit down and entertain herself with the oddments lying on his great desk while he showed Meg book after book, and presently, through the dazzling haze of evening, the mother glanced up from her unenthusiastic inspection of an African image and counted six chimes drifting across the lake.

She looked at the other two. He was holding a book in such a way that she could see the ancient woodcut upon its opened page, and she was looking, not at it, but up into his face, with her own so candidly filled with admiration that her mother's heart contracted in surprise and dismay. The next instant showed her no more than Meg's usual delight in a romance, a legend, or a character in history.

"Meg, do you know the time?"

Meg slowly turned a bright, blank face.

"Darling, it's six o'clock. We must be going; you know how cross Hansi gets if we are late for meals," and Mrs Lambert rose.

"But you haven't seen more than a quarter of the house! Won't you stay for a drink—stay to dinner—we can telephone to the post office at Martinsdorf and they'll get a message up to your pension—do, please, stay?"

Meg's eyes were pleading, but Mrs Lambert pleasantly refused. Her reasons were commonplace, even petty, compared with the treats he was offering; she did not want to annoy Hansi; she did not want Georg of the post office to trudge a second time up to the *Venedig*; and she did not want to eat her evening meal with those Italians and poor Rosalba. She just smiled and said that it was tempting but they really must go.

"Then you must come again; you must come again *soon*, and see the rest of the house and hear some more—that is, Miss Lambert must—about Paracelsus. You can't possibly know how much I have enjoyed having you here; I love seeing English people; I usually have English friends over here in July, but this year, alas, they can't come. Now I am going to hand you over to Janka again, and then Lorenz will bring you down to the shore and I'll take you across . . . no, of course not . . . it's a pleasure. If you won't change your minds and stay, then I want as much of your company as possible."

They saw no more of their fellow guests, but when they came downstairs into the shining and silent vestibule, preceded by Janka, they saw Iliaster sitting beside the front door gazing out into the evening. Meg went towards her, calling, and the cat slowly turned and looked past her and up the stairs.

"Iliaster, lovely puss. . . ." Meg bent to stroke the narrow plushy head, then snatched away her hand, exclaiming.

"What is it, darling? Did she scratch you?"

"Yes . . . never mind . . . it isn't bad. It's my own fault; Siamese hate being patronised; they're one-man cats; they're more like dogs."

Mrs Lambert thought that they were not half so nice, but this opinion was not confirmed by the sight of Melchior, waiting beside Lorenz to lead the guests down to the landing-stage and wearing an expression several shades more disagreeable than his master's; did no one on this estate, she wondered, ever look cheerful except its owner?

CHAPTER TEN

Duologue

THE pleasures of the afternoon did not seem to have inclined Meg towards a quiet evening; she was full of them, but immediately supper was over she hurried off with Robin and the Austrians and Danes to some new dancing-place they had found in a village two or three miles away. Mrs Lambert was left to some hours of welcome solitude. She retired to her room and sat by the window in the afterglow, looking sometimes at the darkening mountains, sometimes at the book open on her lap, while reflecting, as had become habitual with her now that she no longer had Harry to talk things over with.

Frau Schacht had also retired to her room, with a fiercely intellectual French novel; presumably to fortify herself by improving her mind before the arrival of a new pupil for her German classes whom she described as "a scientist, *ein Schottländer*—a Scotchman—and so clever! *Wunderbar!*"

Mrs Lambert, feeling certain that she would not want to discuss their visit and respecting, to some extent, the foibles of one who had suffered bitterly through the war, had briefly described the main events of the afternoon and said that she had found Mr Scarron, as Hansi had predicted, charming. Then Hansi had nodded, with tight lips, and snatched up her French masterpiece and retreated, without commenting or asking if they were to see him again.

They were to see him again, and soon; when Mrs Lambert emerged from the cabin where she had been sheltering from the spray on the homeward crossing, she had heard Meg delightedly repeating the arrangements made for a visit, in two days' time, to that restaurant in a castle already mentioned as being too expensive for the purses of students. It was understood that Mr Scarron was to be responsible for transport, the booking of tables and in short the entire expedition. Robin happened to be lounging along the shore road, taking the air after the day of unrelenting rain, as the launch drew in to the landing-stage, and he was instantly included in the party as Meg's friend (a position which he did not altogether relish). Then, on hearing that Kristin and Helga and Rudi and Moritz would be green with envy, Mr Scarron extended his invitation to them. It would all be tremendous fun. He would see them on Thursday evening at half-past eight. But of course he would see Meg before then. Her German classes were in the morning, weren't they? But he himself was usually about in the afternoon, swimming, or cruising in the *Lorelei*, and he would see her down at the shore.

"Now *isn't* he a pet, Mummy?" Meg said, almost as though she had won a point in an argument, the moment after *Lorelei* had gone off in a bounce and a shower of spray. "Don't you like him?"

"I'm not sure, Meg. I shall have to see more of him before I can make up my mind. You know I always——"

"Oh!" Meg turned away impatiently. "Robin, you like him, don't you?"

"If you care to hear the truth, I'm rather embarrassed. I can't take back any of my remarks about his grey hairs (all right, silver, then) and his bounding, but I've allowed myself to be hustled into accepting an invitation from him."

"You need not go."

"You don't ask much, sweetie, do you? Martinsdorf isn't so madly exciting that one can afford to refuse invitations. Nor can I afford to take you and me to the Rittersaal."

Meg smiled and did not reply; she was pleased that he had wanted to take her there. She was also pleased by the thought that he might be a little jealous.

"Well, Mummy," turning again to her other victim, "even you must admit that he's kind."

"His *manner* is kind, Meg. I don't know whether *he* is. And——"

"And what?" aggressively.

"I can't imagine what he sees in us. No—darling"—as Meg broke into indignant laughter—"of course I see that it's natural for him to admire *you* and like your company. But he is very rich and learned and his world is *so* utterly different from ours. I should think he would be bored by an old lady and a nineteen-year-old girl coming from a country town."

"He may be yet," Robin said pleasantly. "Actually, Mrs Lambert, *you* aren't boring. You never put on an act and you don't talk too much. Some of us do not ask more from our older acquaintances."

Mrs Lambert tried to look indignant and had to laugh; in fact she was a little flattered.

"Oh, my hair—I'm going to fly ahead and do it . . . and my nails . . ." Meg muttered, and rushed away.

"Has she become infatuated with him?" Robin asked in a cool tone, when they had walked on a little way in silence. He *was* slightly jealous; he knew that Mrs Lambert liked him, and had not been overwhelmed by her first taste of the charms of Mr Scarron; and he thought that he would get a line on Meg's state of mind which might be useful in his future dealings with her.

"Oh no," Mrs Lambert's tone and headshake were decided. "When Meg is in love she gets dreamy and quiet and pale, not pink and talkative. . . . Robin?"

He turned towards her attentively, and before she spoke again she had a fleeting thought about the desirability of good manners, a good school, breeding. . . .

"You don't think he's . . . pursuing . . . her in . . . an unpleasant way, do you?"

"No," Robin answered, after a pause in which he gave the question unusually serious thought, "I do him the justice to think it isn't like that. But I do think he is pursuing her, Mrs Lambert" (he was careful not to set the verb in inverted commas), "and I think you had better make up your mind to a rather hectic time for the next few months."

"*Months!*"

"You are going to be here for another three months, aren't you? If I were you, I would try not to worry too much, and just let Meg have a wonderful time. He'll give it her . . . he can afford to."

Mrs Lambert glanced at him, and decided to say nothing about that.

"Even if she doesn't like him?" she said presently.

"I think she does like him. That's going to be the trouble," Robin said.

But there was not going to be any trouble in it for him, he decided, while they were climbing the last slope to the *gasthaus*. Meg was *a sweet little middle-class piece*, as he had described her in a letter to his sister, but she was not sweet enough to upset the tenor of the Gascoine life; Mammy G. would, from now on, gently withdraw her devotion from Missy Meg and be prepared to lay it down elsewhere.

That did not mean he would bear her malice. These things happened. It hadn't been serious. And if she really preferred leaping about with an old goat who might be her grandfather, Mammy Gascoine was well quit of her.

Mrs Lambert was thinking over her conversation with him while she sat in her room after supper that evening.

She felt relieved that Robin, the well-connected, had not referred to the fact that Meg had picked Mr Scarron up. But probably he had not been shocked by it. Well-connected people, or so one heard, were less easily shocked than ill-, or unconnected ones. And this was free-and-easy Austria, where one danced with the village policeman, and no one in Tormouth need ever know how the two had met. It was pleasant to think that Meg now had the chance of enjoying a very good time, as good as that enjoyed by those ghastly debs. so often discussed by herself and her friends. Now their limited supply of currency need not be hoarded so strictly; Mr Scarron would probably pay for most of Meg's gaieties. And their friendship (Mrs Lambert supposed she might call it that) was not entirely frivolous, for not one person in a thousand had heard of Paracelsus; the name had been vaguely familiar to herself when Meg had mentioned it some weeks ago, but she had not connected it with a personality or a history. A mutual interest in a mediæval alchemist gave a covering of respectability, a high-brow tinge, even to a pick-up. And his behaviour that afternoon had been almost irreproachable.

Almost . . . yet she was certain he had been mocking, under that caressing manner, at herself; and she did not like his house or his servants or his dog or his cat or anything that therein was; and as for his friends, the word for them was—and it jumped into her mind without any reason—sinister. Which was absurd, of course; they were probably only too rich, and spoiled. But that poor thing in the white embroidery had given her the creeps. And then there were Hansi's hints about his having been a collaborator . . . not that the term could be correctly applied in Austria, which had been anxious to join itself to Hitler's Germany some years before war came. Hansi spoke as a refugee, who had seen what was coming and fled to a free country. Most people would not have accused Mr Scarron, who after all was half-Austrian, of collaborating at all.

It was good of him to have that silent skeleton of a woman under his roof to rest, and recover.

Perhaps he was the type that was unworthy of, and exploited by, his friends.

But somehow Mrs Lambert did not think so, and try as she would she could not feel at ease about him, and she hoped that Meg would be reasonable about not going too often alone to the house across the lake. Following on a pick-up, such visits would be bad for her reputation.

But on the whole, Mrs Lambert decided, the advantages of this new acquaintanceship outweighed the disadvantages.

*   *   *   *   *

"I won't, I won't. You promised I could stay here; you promised."

"I said you could stay if you behaved yourself. You promised, too—perhaps you don't remember? You made enough of a scene at the time."

"No, I don't remember . . . don't remember anything properly since you started giving me that stuff. . . . I can't even remember coming here properly, except the noise of the engines, and the hostess asking me if I were ill—and—then you in the car——"

"*Primum Ens Melissæ* grew your hair again for you, anyhow, after you'd been to every so-called beauty doctor in Paris and New York . . . as I promised you it would."

"It was starting to grow before I began taking it . . . oh God, I

was so sick with it . . . I don't want any more. I won't take it—I
won't—I won't."

"Don't be such a fool—drink it; go on—drink it. It's only
brandy. As for the other stuff, I told you it was only an experiment
and it hasn't done you any harm; it doesn't hurt you to be sick, it
will get some of the nicotine and alcohol poisons out of you."

"I'll never be really well again."

"Yes, you will—if you do what I tell you. But I can't cure you
if you go on like this: you behave like a mad child. I could have
killed you this afternoon, when you made that noise as we went
out of the room."

"I only said 'Don't go'. I didn't mean to make you angry. You
won't send me down to the palace, will you? Please. I do hate it
there so, it's so dark, and I can't get that smell from the canal out of
my throat; you know it gave me a terrible throat the last time we
were there and I hate being with Constanza and Andrea——"

"If you're going to say they're 'cruel' you can save yourself the
trouble."

"I didn't mean they're cruel, truly, but they don't like me and
they leave me alone so much and I'm so weak now I sometimes
can't sit up in bed to ring for them, and they're always downstairs
anyway, 'way down at the back by the *calle*, they can't hear even if
I shout. I was there a whole day without food. . . . If you send me
back there again I'll just die; that's what I'll do; I'll die."

"Shut up, you fool."

"I used to think Charles would come back. I know he won't, now,
of course, because the divorce is through. He's had me. I did try,
truly I did, but it wasn't any use. Will you let me have the money
to telephone him, just once, from a public box in Venice, so no one
can hear what I'm saying?"

"You know you can telephone from here to New York any day,
every hour, if you want to. Can you, *please*, try not to behave like
a maniac?"

"You say that because you know he won't come to the telephone
when he knows who it is. Oh, what shall I do? Listen—can I go
back to my mother?"

"No. She's been too ill; she can't have you yet. Later on, perhaps. But meanwhile you're driving down to Venice to-morrow, and you'll stay there until I tell you to clear out. I don't want you here for the next three months."

"Because of that girl? Why? I've never seen two women like that before; the mother talked like a parody of something . . . what can you possibly see in that girl? She's too fat, she wears awful clothes; awful clothes; she isn't even feminine . . . why do you like her?"

"I want to try a new way of life. I suppose even you can understand that? Now be quiet; go and get ready to go down to Venice. Get out of here, anyway. . . . I want to work."

"Oh . . . oh . . . oh . . ."

CHAPTER ELEVEN

Social

It was early July and very hot. Visitors to the *gasthaus* went down to spend a few days in Venice, at the small hotel recommended by Frau Schacht, and returned with awe-inspiring tales of the fierce heat and the city's astounding, sleepless beauty, and at Martinsdorf *gasthaus* and school were now both filled to capacity—or would be when Humphrey Scott, described by Frau Schacht as so clever, arrived—and Mrs Lambert found her share of the work heavy indeed. Accounts, linen, mending, shopping, tidying, soothing, translating, table-laying, entertaining, and walking with the lonelier and less interesting visitors all came within her duties, and she found herself more and more tired, her limpness contrasting with the energy of Frau Schacht which only increased as the heat became greater . . . *like the hornets*, Mrs Lambert would think muzzily, as she crept into bed at the end of her seventeen-hour day, *the hotter it is the livelier they are.* She could imagine them stowing away honey or wax or whatever it was they did stow, with the same fierce satisfaction that was displayed on Hansi's face after her weekly visit to the Reichbank to deposit the week's takings. She was saving money hard and fast.

She said nothing about the growing intimacy between the Lamberts and Esmé Scarron, but Mrs Lambert knew that she strongly disapproved. Sometimes when Meg had dashed out of the house in the afternoon with the other young people, calling back as she went that Mr Scarron was taking them all out in *Lorelei*, Frau Schacht would pull in her thin lips until they were almost invisible, but she made no comment, and Mrs Lambert did not invite any by asking her opinion or her advice. Meg was so happy, she was having such a good time, that her mother did not see any reason for requesting either.

The excursion to the Rittersaal had taken place; the climb up the moonlit mountain in two cars packed with cheerful young people (for Mr Scarron had added two Americans and their wives to the party)—the dinner in the raftered hall, at a long table where fifty candles burned and hardly penetrated with their light the shadows overhead where dim banners hung—the dancing amidst armour whose gleaming snouts added a salt of harmless terror to the gaiety— all had been delightful until, at the evening's end, Mrs Lambert had heard Meg say, as she paused at her bedroom door—

"Esmé waltzes beautifully, rather a surprise, because——"

"Darling, do you call him that?"

"Of course," yawning.

"Did he ask you to?"

"Oh, Mummy, of *course*. But if he hadn't I should have asked if I could. He's such a pet."

"I wish you'd said no. He's so much older and cleverer; it simply sounds impertinent. I never can get used to this habit of Christian-naming everyone; I am always expecting Robin to 'Eve' me. Well, don't let Hansi hear you, that's all."

"What's it got to do with her? She's a blight, and so *dreary* nowadays. What's biting her?"

"I don't know. She doesn't like your friend."

"She'd better not say so to me," said Meg, pushing out her jaw in a most peculiar manner. "Mummy, did you have a good time? Wasn't he nice to you! What did you talk about?"

"Oh . . . all kinds of things." Mrs Lambert was wondering whether an account of the bomb damage at Tormouth, into which she seemed to have been lured by Mr Scarron, had really been as lengthy, and as tactless, as she now feared. "The peasants round here . . . not that he seems to know much about them. And I warned him that you had *got* to stick to your German. I wish he wouldn't call me Mrs Lambert so often. It makes me feel . . . unreal, somehow, and it's irritating."

Meg laughed and said good night and went to her own room, and her mother composed herself for sleep on the thought that, although she liked Mr Scarron no better, it might be her fault rather than his.

During the next ten days she found herself continually refusing his invitations, simply because she disliked him so much. She made the excuse that her duties at the *gasthaus* could not be neglected, though in fact Hansi had surprised her by saying earnestly, when the first invitation arrived, that she must not let the work prevent her from accepting; she must feel free to go sailing or motoring or dining with him and with Meg and the other youngsters whenever she liked. "And you should go, Eve," Hansi had concluded, "it's your duty."

"I'm afraid I can't see why. Meg's old enough now to take care of herself—and he seems to take good care of her anyway—and I do dislike him so. Doesn't matter how oily he makes himself, I can't stand him. And besides, I feel a fish out of water, or an old ewe among the lambs, with all those children. I don't know why he keeps on asking me."

"So that later on you shall not be able to complain to Meg," Frau Schacht said, and Mrs Lambert laughed and told her not to be mysterious.

Soon, within less than a week, he was seeing Meg every afternoon; swimming with her, and afterwards sitting under the lime trees over a book of poems and tea brought across in *Lorelei*; or driving her, with Robin and the others, in his Cadillac to some village where the church or the beer had an interesting reputation.

And where reputations were concerned . . . Mrs Lambert was relieved that "the others" so often went along with them. In a small place like this there was certain to be gossip about a rich middle-aged man and a young girl who spent much of their time together, but it would be less spiteful if they were often accompanied by a crowd.

She was also relieved that he had not again invited Meg to his house, either with her friends or alone. He made the excuse that he must devote regular hours each day to the writing of his Life of Paracelsus, which had already occupied him for seven years and which he hoped might become the standard work of reference about the alchemist-astrologer; but Mrs Lambert suspected that that first tea-party had demonstrated to him that his old friends and his new would not mix, and that he preferred to keep open house for people of his own type.

She still did not know why he liked running around with all these simple young creatures. And, in spite of her dislike, she did not suspect him of gross designs upon Meg. If she had, she would have told Meg to end the friendship.

For now a friendship it was.

Meg was delighted to discover that Esmé liked poetry; and surprised to find that he had read no poets later than Valéry, Mallarmé and Cocteau in French, and Yeats, Henley, Dowson and someone called Stephen Phillips, of whom she had never heard, in English; and of course she was flattered to introduce him to the work of Eliot, Dylan Thomas and Laurie Lee. He ordered the books from Vienna, and they undid the parcels together, sitting in the car or on some alp open to the sun while the other young people lay about making irreverent or respectful comments.

"One day," Robin observed to Meg in private, "Missy Meg find out dat Mus' Scarron got a black heart. Also, him bery camp. But Mammy Gascoine nebber say 'Ah done tole yo so'."

Robin admitted to himself, with amusement, that he was just a little jealous. He stood by his verdict of *the sweet little middle-class piece*, and when the thought came upon him that in fact Meg was more like a bad but irresistible poem, *Annabel Lee*, or something of Thomas Brown's, he banished it. Yet he missed their dawdling, wandering, lazy arguments, he missed the clasp of her soft child's hand and the occasional sweet contact with her cheek, and if he did not decline Scarron's invitations, it was partly because he loved pleasure and found Martinsdorf mildly dull, but also because, half-unwillingly, he could thus keep a cousinly eye on Meg.

Meanwhile, Kristin had consoled herself for her boy's defection by having an affair with Rudi, while Helga and Moritz, not finding one another kissable, indulged in long conversations about social reform in their two countries. Robin found this so tedious that he fell back upon studying his German, and soon found it growing fluent, colloquial and authoritative.

Meg was absorbed by her new friend and did not miss silly little Robin at all. She had not so much enjoyed those prolonged arguments about poetry, which he had punctuated with parodies of her favourite lines, because, to her, poetry was not a subject for humour; she preferred Esmé's serious interest in the contemporary poets to which she introduced him, and his deference to her greater knowledge of their work.

She, in her turn, was getting on more familiar terms with mighty Paracelsus, under the tuition of one who wore his learning as lightly as Paracelsus had worn his massive sword Azoth. She felt her mind expanding under the influence, and, if she found a difficulty in remembering the titles and subjects of the alchemists' books, there was the excuse (readily given her by Esmé himself) of their great number and wide range of subjects—*Explanation of the First Section of Hippocrates's Aphorisms* and *Two Tracts on Turpentine and Honey*, for example. Anyone who was not a scholar might be excused if such widely differing works slipped from the memory.

And if some of the titles and subjects did so, there were others that touched her imagination and lingered there. Paracelsus's works on Magic, Esmé told her, were perhaps the most interesting of all his books. When, on that first day, he had shown her the list of them lying on his desk, the vaguely recognised and half-familiar words in mediæval Latin and German had echoed through her mind like far-off, heavily tolling bells . . . divinibus . . . monstris . . . mortem . . . occulta . . . each possessed and followed by its solemn associative echo. The names of the works on Magic, too, were easier to remember: *Sorcerers and Witches and their Arts, Devils and Obsessions.* . . .

She saw, with the lay awe of the scholar's selfless labours, the thick pile of manuscript that was Esmé's life work, and pored with a respectful lack of comprehension over the packed and learned paragraphs.

She enjoyed his company, too, on their more frivolous occasions. He possessed tireless energy and youthful power of enjoyment, yet his vitality did not exhaust his companions, and when he fell silent, as he did frequently on the few occasions when he and Meg were alone, he became so still that it was possible to forget his presence there. "You make yourself like a—a stone or a tree," she said to him once, with an unconscious memory of Wordsworth's poem, "how do you manage it? I don't notice you," and he had laughed as he answered, "How rude of you—your host! Ah, I am a follower of Paracelsus Bombastes, you see, and I am linked to all the stones and trees by one universal force; no wonder I can become like them."

Meg was flattered by the playful yet intellectual note of their conversations. He never condescended to her. He implied that he was in her debt, benefiting from the contact of her fresh young mind, and this was delicious to her vanity, for her secret ambition was to be thought interesting, rather than admired for her looks and charm.

Then, too, he was the most interesting companion she had ever known; his mind was stored with the history of Carinthia's past and the folk-legends of her plants and herbs and metals; he knew all their anciently reputed properties and could tell her, with a grave face suddenly dissolving into laughter, what ailments of soul or body they could cure. He was an ardent herbalist and alchemist; she had heard of the two rooms in his house used as still-room and furnace, where he rendered down the vital ingredients of herbs into decoctions and burnt out the souls of minerals. For it was proper, he told her, to speak of these properties as souls, and as he spoke of them his eyes looked luminous and large. Often they were so sunk within their sockets that it was difficult to see their colour, and on those days she knew that he had been working late over his heaps of dried plants and his little mounds of finely ground, richly coloured powders. He was absorbed by this hobby, it seemed; the ocean-bed, so to speak, of his mind was always busy with it, and every now and then he dropped some remark that brought the abiding interest to the surface.

"You know what that chap is like?" said Rudi, one evening after the party had been entertained by Mr Scarron, "he's like a woman. He is not interested by anything in the world-politics or war or the newspapers, but only by his—his—*alchimie*—what's the English, please?"

"Alchemy—same word, different spelling," said Robin.

"*Alchemie* and his *herbs*. Yes, herbs. Now this is like Meg and Kristin, who are not interested by anything but arts and music and dresses—yes, yes, we know Helga is interested by politics"—waving a hand at the protesting bespectacled face of Moritz—"I'm speaking around Herr Scarron, not speaking around your girl-friend—this is like a woman, I'm saying."

"He gave us all a smashing dinner, anyway." This was Meg.

"So, and I thank him. It was very good. I do not mean to say bad things around him. Nevertheless, not to be interested by world-politics is like a woman."

"I think it makes a blessed relief. If only you knew how bored I get with world-politics and all that sort of thing."

"That is exactly how I am saying." Rudi ended the discussion with a bland smile.

"What was the former Mrs S. like?" Robin asked idly. "Any snaps of her in his watch? Any photographs on the piano that afternoon you went across to tea?"

"That's like a woman, anyway. Who cares what she was like?"

"I do. I burn to know what sort of a female could have taken on Pal Scarron for life."

"He never mentions her," Meg said with dignity, after a pause in which the foreigners, who naturally found Robin's English very difficult, moved their eyes from his face to hers, translating diligently as they went, "and of course I never do either."

"Frau S. knows all about her, I will wager."

"She doesn't like talking about him and his affairs."

"Ha! More in this than meets the private-eye. Mammy Gascoine, lovable black detective, smells out another mystery."

Meg smiled haughtily and changed the subject. She liked Esmé so much now that she was annoyed when her friends made fun of him, however good-naturedly, and she also felt, in a way difficult to explain, that he and his life were not matters for mockery. It was not that his circumstances were tragic. Indeed, they seemed unusually fortunate. He had money, health and congenial hobbies, and if the breaking-up of his marriage had grieved him, he seemed to have recovered from the hurt. If ever a man's circumstances should be able to stand up to a little youthful teasing, his should. And yet, to Meg, there was some quality in himself, his house, his work, his whole life, before which mockery, however slight and harmless, faltered and died away, and not once, during those weeks in which the wit of his young guests played about him like summer lightning, did she find herself amused by it or tempted to laugh at him. Indeed, though there was so much laughter amongst them when they were all in his company, when she was alone with him she usually found herself listening gravely to the incantatory spell of his voice while he instructed her.

But they were not often alone. He seemed to like the society of the five whom she often passionately thought of as ungrateful pigs, and he took them round Carinthia as if—as if he were the Pied Piper and were also calling a delightfully luxurious tune. She was usually at his side on these occasions, and became more and more accustomed to her position there; she was the favourite; the pet scholar; perhaps the neophyte who was being initiated into Carinthian folk-lore and the philosophy of Paracelsus.

But the best time of all had been a day when he took her, with Lorenz to propel their heavy old craft, on a lingering voyage along the far western shores of the lake, where the cliffs dropped to the narrow white sand and the rushes and plants and ferns for which he sought grew in moist clefts of the woods. The sun blazed in a faint blue sky, and shadows of tiny fish darted over the sand beneath the creeping prow. Lorenz sat with slack arms, and small jet eyes staring steadily while she and Esmé scaled the low banks or waded in the shallows, tearing up the knotted brown roots and pulling lush white stems from the mud. Slowly the stern grew heaped with a green, rustling, aromatic cargo. Strange scents wavered up from it, sharp and wild and faint, and presently his master made Lorenz spread a protecting canopy over it against the heat and glare. The lake was deserted; the sun slowly sloped westward in yellow light. When at last he said to her, "That will do, we have enough," she stared at him as if he had broken a spell; it seemed to her, so soaked in air and drenched with fresh water and odours of green plants was she, that she had never lived in a house and would never return to one. On the journey back to Martinsdorf he did not speak, and she forgot, as she so often did, his presence. The loveliness of the evening oppressed her spirit.

CHAPTER TWELVE

Fairy-tale

ONE Saturday afternoon, the train from Salzburg was as usual insufferably crowded; with Austrians going home for the week-end or visiting friends in the country, with peasants who piled themselves in at the small stations on their way to or from the week's marketing, and with a sprinkling of tourists, although this part of Austria was too far, and too remote, to attract the large crowds. They sat on their luggage in the corridors, thirsty as cattle and more patient, and crammed the carriages, blinking through windows open to the blazing evening while the train made its way—much too fast, in the eyes of the elderly and nervous—along a track

scooped in the side of a mountain with only a stone wall between
it and a two thousand-foot drop into the valley. Roads, forests, river
and villages below were all seen in fascinating miniature, like those
tiny metal images sold in toyshops, and the tremendous hollow
filled to its brim with light attracted even the Austrians, who knew
it well, to stare and point and exclaim.

Humphrey Scott had begun resenting the scenery again almost as
soon as Salzburg was left behind. He had resented the Rhine at
dawn, with stormy mountains wreathed in mist pierced by the
dramatic gold of sunrise, and the mighty river rushing pale and
broad below; it was magnificent, he supposed, but he had never
cared for Wagner. He hung out of the window, letting the cool
wind blow in his face while he watched the little towns beside the
river, each with its soaring Gothic spire, going past. Birds flew
round the red and grey steeples, in dark showers against the pale
sky, slowly flapping down to rest on corbel and parapet. He had a
feeling of having seen this country before. Where? In a film? In
dreams?

Then he remembered a book of fairy-tales, given to a little Scottish boy by an English aunt-by-marriage who secretly condemned
his severe and sensible upbringing. It had had coloured pictures.
After nineteen years, he still felt slightly ashamed of the passion of
delight they had aroused in him; he must have been a soft sort of
kid. Home-work and house-duties—his family had been poor—
had left him only a few stolen moments late at night in which to
look at the pictures and read the stories, but he had kept the book
hidden in his attic room until his mother had found and burnt it.
He must pass his examinations and win a scholarship, otherwise he
could not have that long, solid, extensive education which the
family regarded as more necessary than enough food and clothing;
there was no time to waste on idle reading.

His mother had made him watch while the pictures shrivelled
and turned black in the flames, holding his hand in hers while the
set expression of her pale face was illumined by the firelight. She
loved his soul, she had said, too dearly to see it softened and made
weak by lies. So that night he lay face downwards on his pillow,

tearless, seeing in his mind's eye the pictures that he would never see in truth again. Presently, as time went on, they faded. He won his scholarship, the first of many, and earned the education that his family wanted for him; and he had not thought of the pictures in the burned book of fairy-tales until this moment, nineteen years later, when he saw them going by outside the window of the train, with their gay yet soft colours glowing in the sunrise, and their towers and turrets and piebald houses looking as if they sheltered no ordinary people, but princesses and witches and Youngest Sons.

But presently he began to feel irritated by this landscape, so simple and bright yet carrying an invisible haze, an undernote, of sadness and mystery, and drew his long, gaunt, young Scots mask, with the straight sandy lashes over the dark blue eye, in from the sweet air of dawn. He returned to his corner in the carriage and went to sleep.

Going through Bavaria, it had been impossible not to be interested in such good grazing and arable land and what use the Germans were making of it; but when once the train was over the Austrian frontier the fairy-tale appearance intruded itself again, with frowning mountains—though not so startlingly Wagnerian as the German ones—thrown in for good measure; and by the time the train was trundling down the broad valley towards Villach he was putting up a strong sales-resistance to the picturesque. Refreshed, however, by a glimpse of some industrial chimneys, he stepped out again into the corridor to take a closer look at the place near which he was to stay for the next few months.

"A long way from Scotland, no?" said, in German, an undersized man with a red face who was also standing by the window; he had been in the same carriage with Humphrey and had joined occasionally in the general conversation by which the travellers had learned something about one another.

"Yes."

"It seems a long way to you? How long have you been travelling? Two days?"

"Three."

"From Scotland to England and then to France and then through

Belgium? Why didn't you fly? It's much more comfortable . . . so they say. I've never flown. Never had the money. Dear God! it's an expensive way of getting about, that is, and besides, I don't like aeroplanes, I saw too much of them—or it would perhaps be truer to say I heard too much—ten years ago. Is there much damage from bombs in Scotland? Do the Scottish people still hate the Germans? Down here in Carinthia nobody ever talks about them."

"Good," said Humphrey, unsmiling.

"Ah, you don't like them? That's because you aren't an Englishman. The English are forgetting already, and besides, they're so afraid of . . ." he jerked his head towards the East, where the mountains of Jugoslavia caught the light of the sinking sun, "so they're giving them all guns again. Well, I don't know . . . no one can know, really, can they? With some of us it's all right if we can only have a job and a home and a wife. I'm very lucky, I've got all three. I've got a good steady job in Salzburg where they don't mind me being not so young as I was; it isn't making my fortune, you'll understand, but it buys my food and my clothes and every 'week-end' I can take something home to my wife. This 'week-end' I've bought her a sausage. I make a change every week, running it on a system, you'll understand; one week it's something to eat, next it's something for her to wear, then it's something for the home. Were you fighting in the war?"

Humphrey shook his head. He did not like to talk, nor was he fond of listening, preferring to read or think.

"No? You were lucky. How old are you, if I may ask?"

There was no reply, and he peered into the young man's face and repeated the question.

"Twenty-eight." Humphrey controlled the impulse to ask what the hell it had to do with him.

"Weren't you in the war at all?"

"Yes, I was. At the very end, in Germany, but I didn't see any fighting. Here, do you smoke?" and he held out a packet of Gaulois bought on the platform at Brussels.

"Thank you, now that's really kind of you, cigarettes are a luxury to me, I have to cut down my smoking to work out my little system of weekly presents. You don't mind me asking you all these questions, do you? I——" His expression changed. "You see, I was in a camp. Just at first, we always used to ask each other where we came from and that kind of thing, and I suppose I got into the habit."

"That's all right," Humphrey was inhaling the pungent smoke with conscious enjoyment. He was poor and his pleasures were few and he never hurried over any of them. "I have seen some fighting, actually. In Malaya: I was in the Malayan police. I came home last year; invalided out."

"It's a long way off," the man said vaguely, looking out of the window, "there's always some kind of a little war going on some-where, isn't there? . . . excuse me, it's always interesting to hear about other people's lives, only sometimes, you know, if you hear about so many, hundreds of them, and all only a little different, you get muddled. I was listening to what you said, but I always look to see if my wife is on the platform when the train gets in; she comes down sometimes to meet people who are coming to stay at our Guest House and School of Languages."

"I'm going to stay at a School of Languages in Martinsdorf."

"Yes, that's our School. It's the only one in Martinsdorf. And you're one of our guests? Well, isn't that surprising. And I was talking to you and never dreaming . . . well, Hansi—that is my wife, her name is Joanna, but we call her Hansi—she doesn't seem to be here, so we'll get out and go across to the local train. It's lucky we met, I can show you the ropes and save you a lot of bother. Come on."

Humphrey got his case from the carriage, and followed the little man out of the train and down the platform. The light under the station roof was dim and the air hot and still. Outside, there was a white street and white buildings under a yellow sky. He heard German being spoken all round him, and suddenly this place seemed as far from everything familiar as if it were at the world's end, farther away than Germany, than Malaya even, and he thought of his betrothed, Ruth, and hoped there might be a letter from her awaiting him at the *gasthaus*.

Presently he was sitting opposite Herr Schacht on a hard wooden seat in a local train, watching fields go slowly past in the summer twilight. There were only a few people in the carriage, a young mother with an infant, two old women with their market baskets, and a young man who had fallen asleep; the women talked ceaselessly, but their light quick voices sounded subduedly through the rattling of the wheels, and as the air became increasingly dark the atmosphere grew more dreamlike. Humphrey yawned, and yawned again; he had not slept unbrokenly for three nights. He kept his heavy eyes fixed upon the sloping meadows, each with what looked like a procession of sinister dark manikins of different heights strung across it: this was the hay harvest, draped upon poles of pine to dry. These goblin-like effigies, with their half-human, half-monstrous appearance, gave a most singular look to the valley in the growing dusk; there was none of the placid peace bestowed by English haycocks; and the word "outlandish" came into Humphrey's head.

He was favourably impressed by the first sight of Martinsdorf, climbing among thick orchards above the motionless gleaming lake. As he and Herr Schacht plodded slowly along the road which, his companion said, would bring them in a few minutes to their destination, a car's horn sounded behind them, and they drew aside to allow a Cadillac to pass. It was not travelling fast, and Humphrey was able to see clearly the face of the girl sitting beside the driver; it imprinted itself, like the images transferred by the atomic flash, instantly and permanently upon his mind's eye. She turned to wave and smile at Herr Schacht, who returned the salute, but the man beside her—an odd-looking type wearing youthful sports clothes in spite of having longish silver hair—did not look round. The car turned a corner and disappeared.

"I hope you like young society, I expect you do, being youngish yourself," Herr Schacht said presently as they passed along the side of a brown wooden house, between beds of flowers and under windows open to the garden. "We have a houseful here, all learning from my wife's classes. (You'll meet my wife soon, any minute now.) Our Danish young ladies, Helga and Kristin, are learning German; they are twenty-two and twenty-three; then Mr Robin

Gascoine, our other English gentleman, is twenty-two. We have two Austrian boys, Moritz and Rudi, who are both twenty, and then there is Miss Meg Lambert, she is the young lady we passed just now in the car, she is eighteen—eighteen and ten months. She is the youngest."

"Quite a kindergarten," Humphrey said shortly, hoping this nurseryful would not be noisy and talkative. "I don't like girls under twenty; they're always so full of themselves."

When he was given Miss Meg Lambert's hand in greeting half an hour later, before the company sat down to supper, he wondered why it was taken away so quickly and why her manner was so cool.

CHAPTER THIRTEEN

Fiancé

SOME days later, Humphrey wrote to his betrothed.

MY DEAR OLD RUTH,

Thanks for your letter, which was waiting when I got here after a very long but on the whole good journey. I'm glad you've got it all fixed up to come out in August. It's a pretty place and I think you will like it. The gasthaus is comfortable but not at all smart, so don't bother to bring anything extra smart to wear. But do bring my old favourite, the blue! I am taking things quietly so far. Later on, when I've settled down a bit, I hope to get some swimming and rowing. No sign of tennis-courts in the village; nothing but table-tennis at the swimming-place, but bring your things if you like, as there may be courts at some of the hotels where you could get a game.

My German is already coming back satisfactorily, though I haven't spoken any for five years. I am in the junior class (rather amusing, as I'm the oldest pupil here) run by one Fräulein Keller, a friend of Frau Schacht's from Vienna. We work from 9.30 to 12.30 every morning, in the garden if fine, indoors if raining—which it hasn't done so far. The senior class run by Frau Schacht herself works just round the corner of the house, under a big nut tree, and makes such a row laughing and fooling about that I find it hard to concentrate—and you know that isn't usually my difficulty. There's a chap here called Robin Gascoine who seems to keep Frau S. perpetually in stitches—he is quite amusing but there's too much of it for my taste—they're all under twenty-five and very noisy. So far I haven't talked much to anyone, though don't get the idea I don't like it here. I'm just getting my bearings. It seems a long time since I had a chance to be quiet and think. I usually go for an exploring walk in the afternoon—the country is very pretty—then get in in time for supper at 7.30, do an hour's work afterwards, go for another walk, then bed about ten. The gang usually go down to the local dance hall in the evenings, but so far I haven't honoured it with a visit. There don't seem to be many people staying in the village. I suppose there isn't much to do. The local millionaire who lives on the other side of the lake sometimes livens us up with a sight of his motor-boat. The crowd staying in the house go out in it with him and you can hear the girls laughing across half a mile of water. There is a nice elderly Englishwoman staying here, another friend of Frau Schacht's, whom I know you would like. She has been particularly nice to me—I expect she thinks I'm lonely! She little knows. I have read about half of Bertrand Russell's book—will tell you later what I think of it. I want to see some of the mining work in Klagenfurt, but so far haven't managed it. Have not been up a mountain yet, either. I shall be very glad to see you, so don't let anything stop you coming, sweetheart.

Good-bye for now,
Your
CAT.

At the end of ten days, by which time, of course, he seemed to have been at the *Gasthaus Venedig* ever since he could remember, Humphrey Scott was on friendly terms with everyone there except the Lambert kid. He spoke to her no less than to anyone else, and with an identical manner, but hers towards him was cool, even occasionally pettish, and at last he concluded that she must have overheard his remark about girls under twenty being full of themselves. Then he was amused, but he was also slightly irritated. He had no sisters, his family consisting of three clever brothers; his only woman friend was Ruth Courtney, and she had been as frank, cheerful and sensible at eighteen as she was now at twenty-six, and offered him no clue to read Meg by. When he thought about this behaviour—and he did think about it, quite often—he used to himself words like silliness, bee in her bonnet, little fathead; sometimes, even, little drip. Why couldn't she be sensible, like Ruth?

He would look at her across the length of the *speisesaal*, or over the pink and yellow flowers of the garden, even across that half-mile of water where she laughed beside her friend in his launch, and wonder why she could not be like Ruth?

Apart from this small irritation, he liked life at the *gasthaus*. His German was progressing well; he found the food palatable and only slightly too Austrian for his taste; and he had taken a liking to Herr Schacht, whom he was pleased to welcome at the week-ends as additional masculine company, for he found Robin Gascoine a little too young and a little too fantastic to be congenial. Frau Schacht he did not like so well, but there was something about her which commanded his respect; he thought of it as character; she had character; and he got on well with Mrs Lambert, in whose eye he sometimes surprised a twinkle when Meg was being cool.

Mrs Lambert had precisely that mixture of self-effacement and strength which he liked a woman to have, and which the two women he knew well, Ruth and his mother, both possessed. He liked Mrs Lambert the more because he could tell that she was naturally nervous and a worrier. If that little idiot—otherwise Miss Meg—were late in returning from a solitary stroll or sneezed at breakfast or complained of a pain anywhere in her person, such a look of anxiety as amounted to terror would strike the mother's face, to be instantly effaced by an expression of common sense, and she would make some calm comment. Once, on one of these occasions, Humphrey thought that it must be a burden to love someone so much.

But apart from himself, Herr Schacht and Robin, no one at the *gasthaus* could be described as appearing unburdened. Those Danish girls were always getting letters from their boys which cast them into fresh states of placid despair; while Moritz and Rudi (whom Humphrey suspected of hankering after silly little Meg) supported identically opposing political parties and could be heard arguing in their room far into the night, so that hopeless disagreement and prolonged sleeplessness marred their breakfast-faces; while Frau Schacht . . . Humphrey was sometimes a little disturbed about Frau Schacht. Austrians, he knew, were notoriously emotional, and it might all be caused by next to nothing, but certainly she sometimes did look almost desperate with grief. He reminded himself that her husband was victim to a deadly disease and that her country had been occupied in the war.

His greatest lack at Martinsdorf continued to be congenial male society. He enjoyed shop, and would have relished a discussion about mining, but when he introduced the subject during his first stroll with Robin Gascoine a few days after his arrival, he was met with an airy—

"*Need* we talk about mines? So repellent, I always think. Of course, you know Keats's line about the scientists who have *emptied the gnomèd mine.* They must be *worse still* now they are gnomeless. Gnomes in *gardens*, needless to say, I abhor."

Humphrey came back at him, inferring from his remark a whole-sale dislike of science, with the dry reminder that Shelley's interest in the discoveries of his day had indirectly inspired some fine poetry. "Do you admire Shelley? How odd," said Robin, concealing his surprise, and Humphrey was left wondering (but not for long, because the subject bored him) whether it was odd that anyone should admire Shelley or only odd that he should.

He did not suggest any more strolls, although he decided that Robin was less of an ass than he seemed and bright enough in his own line, which was languages and European history. But he made Humphrey, with his harsh upbringing, his arduous and prolonged studies, his term of service in Germany and his fighting in Malaya, feel about sixty years old.

The other possible companion was Mr Scarron. That is to say, he remained possible while he was still unmet by Humphrey, but described to him by the others as clever and pleasant and middle-aged, but as soon as they had been introduced, one evening in the *weinstube*, Humphrey took such a dislike to him that he did not want to see him again, much less talk to him. The way he hung round that girl was sickening; it might be understandable, but it was undignified and sickening, and although Mrs Lambert might talk about Mr Scarron's kindness, Humphrey gave it quite another name.

So, surrounded by people too young to talk to and without male companionship, he fell back, as so often before, upon reading, walking and his thoughts. His early poverty and loneliness had encouraged a mind naturally serious to seek entertainment in the cheapest of pastimes, the relaxation that costs nothing, and now he had plenty to think about. He had to make up his mind, for instance, whether he should try for a job that would take him into remote and wild country, or for one that would keep him either at home, or in some pleasanter and more accessible part of the world. He knew that Ruth was so devoted to her people, and so relied upon by them in the crises of family life, that it would be demanding a great sacrifice of her to ask her to leave them all for perhaps years at a time, perhaps indefinitely, and although she did not complain at the prospect, he intended to think things out thoroughly before he decided to ask it of her. She was domesticated and home-loving; there would be a second and smaller sacrifice required if he asked her to live in a squalid mining camp or some dull South American settlement. Yet he felt a strong disinclination for the peaceful life of research. On his return to England after being invalided out, he had been attracted by the accounts of the work being done at Cambridge on the production of alloys to endure the terrific speeds of contemporary air travel. A group of highly gifted metallurgists was at work on the problems and he had thought of trying to join them, but later, almost without his consciously making the decision, he knew that he did not want to. He was still sick of books and four walls and a lamp, just as he had been sick of them when he entered the Army, and what he still wanted, although he had not completely shaken off the effects of hardship and combat, was to work with his hands and his acquired skills in lonely, wild and remote regions of the world.

He had spent his later convalescence in catching up with the developments in metallurgy that had occurred during his active service. This holiday was intended to improve the German that would always be useful to him in his work, and he hoped it would be his last spell of idleness for a long time. He called it idle, although he did read German four hours each day and philosophy (he had the Scot's love of that, and of argument) for two. Martinsdorf seemed to him a drowsy, lazy little backwater of a place, in which it would be easy to become bored, and he looked forward increasingly to the coming of Ruth.

"Mr Scott, you are by yourself, you are alone again," Frau Schacht said, pausing with a worried expression as she met him as he set out one evening for his walk after supper, "now why didn't you go with the others this afternoon? They had a delightful excursion. I know you would have enjoyed it."

"Thanks, but I'm all right, really."

"But are you sure? You are always alone."

"Oh no. I went down to the *weinstube* with them all last night. And I like being alone. Don't worry about me, please."

"But I do worry, I must worry. What will your *fiancée* say when she comes here and learns how we have all neglected you?"

"Laugh, I expect. She's known me since I was fifteen and she knows what I'm like."

"Yes. . . ." Frau Schacht's expression became dry; English girls, it seemed to say, laughing at things not in the least amusing, things likely to lead to all sorts of trouble, like lonely *fiancés*, yes, we know what English girls are.

"Oh well, if you prefer it so . . . but often I think about you."

"It's kind of you but you mustn't. I'm planning how to smoke out your hornet friends. When Ruth—that's my girl—comes, we'll have a grand massacre. She loves that sort of thing."

"Indeed . . ." said Frau Schacht. Her extremely expressive face suddenly became merely polite: what sort of a girl was this? To laugh at a *fiancé's* loneliness was only to be expected of an English girl; they were so sure of themselves in all the wrong ways; look at that little fool, Meg; but to admit that one enjoyed massacring, even hornets. . . .

"It is very kind, but Herr Zeller will never give permission."

"Then we'll do it first and ask him afterwards," said Humphrey, moving off.

"It would be impossible," Frau Schacht said longingly, "but thank you for the kindly thought."

A few days after this conversation, when Humphrey's stay at the *Venedig* had lasted a fortnight, he heard with some dismay the Danish girls announce that they must go home the day after to-morrow, and Moritz and Rudi loudly regretting the fact that their own stay must come to an end on the day following. Robin told everybody not to become hysterical; *he* was not going home; *he* would still be there, a graceful enigmatic figure sipping its *apfelsaft* in the yard of the *weinstube* and putting the new lot who were arriving on Saturday into the picture; and while Mammy Gascoine lingered on, Martinsdorf would keep its old flavour.

Humphrey was surprised to find that he would miss the noise and laughter. He also did not relish being left to face Meg Lambert at meal-times without the protective covering afforded by the crowd. The coolness she showed towards him would be more noticeable and might even be embarrassing.

But when they had gone, and the laughing sunburnt faces and waving hands and big boots and battered rucksacks had vanished down amidst the orchard trees and were seen no more, while the house seemed dolefully quiet now that himself and the Lamberts, Robin and Fräulein Keller, were the only guests, he found that he would not have to put up with Meg's company at luncheon for to-day, at least.

"That naughty child cut her class," Mrs Lambert said in what Louisa Alcott would have called a "mortified" tone, as she arranged the sadly reduced places for lunch, "she went off to meet Mr Scarron and won't be back until this evening."

Humphrey contrived to look interrogative and sympathetic; he was trying to get the news from England on Frau Schacht's ancient wireless.

"Yes. It's the first time she's done it. I'm rather worried."

"It's a bad habit to get into," he said austerely, with the poor clever scholar's dislike of truant idleness.

"Oh, I hope she won't make it a *habit*. I expect she just couldn't face the class this morning without the others. It *will* be dull, of course. . . ."

"She should get more individual attention now."

"I'm afraid Meg wouldn't see it like that. . . . I'm afraid she'll be seeing much more of him, too, now that they've gone, and alone."

He said nothing. He was concentrating upon the faint voice crackling across Europe.

"Unless of course Robin goes about with them as usual. I wouldn't mind so much, then. . . ."

But that evening, when she said to Robin with clumsy casualness, "You and Meg will miss the crowd, won't you, when you're out with Mr Scarron?", he answered in his smuggest voice: "You don't imagine *I* shall acccompany them on their junketings *now*, do you, Mrs Lambert? Mammy Gascoine am *much* too tactful," and when she said sharply that there was nothing to be tactful about, he shook his head, saying that he was sure he hoped so.

CHAPTER FOURTEEN

Expedition

A FEW days later, Meg having persuaded Esmé Scarron to take her to the summit of an overrun and overrated mountain which she had formerly visited on a cloudy morning that had prevented her from seeing the view, they set out for the village where the funicular station was.

The day was excessively hot, but every tourist staying in the valley seemed to have come to the station, and the cage was full. As it climbed steadily upwards, and the pine forests fell away below, the keen wind that began to sigh through its windows was welcomed with exclamations of pleasure. Meg kept her eyes fixed upon the floor, partly because she did not like heights, and partly to avoid looking at Scarron, whose expression lacked its usual gaiety.

"Are you cross?" she asked bluntly at last, when they were climbing the path leading up to the chair-lift that carried on the ascent.

"No. But you know I dislike crowds."

"Do you call this a crowd?" glancing back at the ten or fifteen people on their way down from the summit, then forwards at the five or so who were toiling ahead of them.

"Certainly. It wouldn't be in Paris; it is here, where one expects solitude."

"I like people," Meg said with a touch of defiance.

She was not completely sure of herself; she realised now that he had been reluctant to come, and felt irritated with herself for having persuaded him.

"I know that, my child. You are no exception to the rest of your sex. And I like 'people', too, when they are also persons—individuals—but not these. . . ." And his slight nod indicated the bare thick legs of a woman in shorts who was plodding immediately ahead of them. "They have nothing to give me; and usually I neither see them nor think about them nor remember that they exist; I suppose they are what the newspapers mean when they speak of 'the people', but fortunately my life doesn't touch theirs at any point; when I am staying in London or New York I come into contact with them as servants but otherwise never. Lorenz and Janka are servants, too, but they are also individuals. I don't think of them as 'people'. "

"It's so queer, your never having been in the tube . . . like the Queen. When I wrote to my friend Rosemary about it she wouldn't believe it."

"She must be lacking in imagination. Don't you realise that there are men and women, living in Spain, for example, who are not necessarily of Royal blood, children born into ancient families which are still very rich, who have never ridden in a public vehicle?"

"Yes, I suppose there are." Meg's subdued tone was caused by an impulse to defend Rosemary, but this could only be done by protesting that although she might be lacking in imagination, she had been awfully kind last year when Meg was in such a state about Derek Jones. And, glancing at Esmé walking beside her, she felt that both Rosemary and Derek belonged to another world, which was far away.

She continued to look pensive, and presently he said: "I suppose you will want to go to that dreadful place on the summit where everybody collects to eat . . . but surely you are not hungry yet? Already?" as Meg nodded, laughing, "but it is only two hours since you had breakfast. Oh well, perhaps we can get some bread and cheese. We will sit outside to eat it, away from the crowd, and then we can come down again in two of these horrible contraptions and I will show you the woods. They haven't been spoilt yet. But wait until you see my mountains in Savoy—and better still, the alps above Arolla in the Valais—you will be able to imagine Paracelsus wandering there and gathering his medicinal herbs as we did beside the lake—not that he ever did wander there, so far as we know, but as he wandered from England to Tartary he may well have gone to the Valais . . . he's like Jesus Christ in at least one respect—there are a great many years of his life about which we know nothing . . . that dreadful noise is the chairs . . . look at them, coming down like angels designed by Dali. . . . I could kill the people who did this to an ugly but inoffensive mountainside, kill them cheerfully. Are you quite sure you don't want to walk up?"

Meg shook her head, and they made their way towards the shed, built on a stone platform, where the machinery controlling the chair-lift was housed.

They stood side by side watching the chairs ascending and descending in an unbroken procession along cables slung above the steep grassy slope. Three hundred feet higher up, the receiving station, at which passengers embarked for the descent, appeared small and ugly against the turquoise sky. Scarron turned away, with an exclamation of disgust, to look at the labyrinth of pale crags and crests winding away into Italy; but Meg continued to watch the chairs, although she was not seeing them. *Wait until you see my mountains in Savoy . . . you'll be able to imagine. . . .* Was he going to invite her mother and herself to stay with him in Savoy? or had he meant something else, about which she did not want to think because it was too alarming? Yet at the same time she was flattered, excited and pleased.

She went quickly across to him, and he turned to her with the dimple showing in his cheek.

"Do let's come—I long to get to the top," she said.

It was fascinating, it took her mind off what she found disturbing, to see how precisely the attendant at the embarking station timed himself to swing away from the descending passenger, whom he helped alight, to the ascending passenger whom he must assist into the moving chair. It must be the result of *months* of experience, Meg thought, settling into the swaying carrier, and feeling herself beginning to float onwards, over the rocks and tangled grass and matted bushes below. Delicious airy motion! and Esmé might scorn them, but she liked the light metal chairs painted a gay scarlet; they reminded her of the air-boats and swings at a fair.

At the summit, reached after a second chair-lift, a wind of ice crept over the stunted grass, and tourists were sheltering behind the unbeautiful walls of a solid little restaurant whose windows were obscured by steam. There were notices outside, illustrated with feeble coloured drawings of chefs and girls in peasant dress, and announcing the delicacies on sale within. The chair-lift kept up its ceaseless clanking, and a group of boys wearing cheap and ill-fitting clothes, more suitable for a city, greeted Meg with delighted whistles.

"They are English," she said, turning a primmish face to her companion: it became primmer still when she saw his expression.

"So I gathered. If you will stay here out of the wind I'll bring you some cake and fruit."

"That would be lovely, but couldn't we go into the restaurant? It says *hot soup* on that notice, and I'm so cold and absolutely starving."

"All right," he said, after a moment's pause, "all right, child."

While she drank her soup, he sat opposite her in silence, looking about the low, long room whose air was dim with the smoke of cigarettes and noisy with the sounds of people talking and eating. His expression was cold and forbidding, and people stared at him so openly and long that Meg became embarrassed. The boys who had whistled at her had come into the place soon after themselves and were now trying to attract her attention from their corner, and their grimaces of commiseration, and miming of long beards and general decrepitude behind Esmé's back, so increased her discomfiture that she swallowed the soup in scalding gulps. She was also very conscious of the difference between Esmé's face and theirs —for all six were so young, irregularly featured, crop-haired and wide-mouthed that they could be said to enjoy a collective face— she had not realised until now how un-English he looked.

"Do those louts worry you?" he said suddenly—to her surprise, for she had supposed he could not see what was going on.

She shook her head, hoping that he had not noticed the miming.

"Because if they do I can easily find out their regiment and lodge a complaint to their commanding officer; I probably know him, anyway."

"Oh, please don't. They're only silly little boys. Are they soldiers? I thought they were tourists but rather unusual ones; I was wondering about them."

"Yes, they are soldiers. Are you ready? I don't want to hurry you, but the air in here is impossible, and I want to show you the woods."

As Meg left the table on her way to the cloakroom, she saw him turn round and look quickly into the corner where the boys were sitting. Perhaps he thought that a dignified glance of reproof would have some effect. Evidently he did not know the modern English working-class youth. It must be years, she supposed, since he had spoken to one—if indeed he ever had.

When she emerged he was waiting for her by the door.

"Has there been a fight?" she asked, as they went out, "the waitresses and the proprietor and some other people were all round the table where those boys were sitting—didn't you see?"

He shook his head, and they went down the path towards the chair-lift.

Later, as they walked slowly along a path in the heart of the woods, it seemed to Meg as if the bare and ugly summit of the mountain and the restaurant with its greedy noisy diners might never have existed, so fresh and silent were the glades. Sunlight fell between the bounteous branches and the long calls of birds pierced the pine-scented air from near and far; every dell, every hollow beneath a bush, was mantled with cool green leaves, and stems of which the very thorns looked moist. How rich the earth must be that gave life to this sappy, leafy, springing coverlet. The boughs of pine and fir and larch drooped until they almost swept the emerald grass. There was nothing sinister here. It was the wood of a happy fairy-tale.

Yet Meg was not enjoying it. Her companion was silent, walking with dragging step, and he was so pale that once or twice she glanced at him, apprehensively. The hand lightly clasping hers— and this added to her uneasiness, for it was the first time that he had held her hand—was cold and moist, and he gazed at the ground as they walked along. Deep melancholy stole over her, amidst the sunlight and the delicate fresh scents and the calling of birds; the wood was sad in spite of its loveliness, and she was afraid to ask her friend what the matter was. She wondered if he were feeling ill, yet somehow his appearance prevented her from believing that he was, and in spite of his pallor and silence he did not appear to be suffering.

She began to dislike intensely the clasp of his hand, and was on the verge of withdrawing hers when she felt the chill begin to leave it; rapidly it grew warmer until her own fingers were glowing within it, and soon he turned to her smilingly and asked if she were ready to go down into the valley? or would she prefer to walk on to the hotel near the funicular, and there have tea?

"Oh, tea at the hotel, please. I'm not hungry for once, only walking has made me thirsty. But are you sure you don't mind? You looked so pale when we were coming down in the chair-lift, I thought the air in that place might have made you ill. You don't want to go into *another* hotel."

He shook his head, laughing.

"I'm perfectly all right and the *Florence* is a much better hotel."

"But . . . I'm afraid you were feeling ill." Meg was driven to pursue the subject by a curious sense of duty. She did not want to think about his pallor, his silence, the chill of his hand, yet felt that she must persist.

"No, no, I'm all right. Now let's collect some plants and you can tell me their names; yes, I know you don't want to, but you know they're my great interest, so you must be interested in them too. I'll tell you their peasant-names in German; that will be good for you."

Again the thrilling disturbance shook Meg. And then, suddenly, she wanted her friends to be all about her: Helga, with the immovable prim braids, Rudi with his bland little smile, even tiresome Robin—she longed to hear their laughter and see their cheerful familiar faces amidst the hushed green maze of this sad wood where the birds piped and called far off and near.

But when, towards evening, they descended in the funicular cage, out of the last sunlight lingering on the mountain summit into the shadows of the valley, she was thinking how much better she had come to know Esmé during this day spent alone with him. And she liked him; yes, she liked him very much, and how impressed Rosemary, and all her friends at Tormouth, to say nothing of Derek, would be if they could see his house and his car and motor-boat, and hear him talk.

He left her at the landing-stage in the village, where Lorenz had been instructed to wait for him with *Lorelei*, apologising for not seeing her home because he must get back quickly; he had some friends from Venice coming to dinner. But she would be all right, wouldn't she? The road was not lonely and the bus would get her into Martinsdorf in twenty minutes.

The boat, piloted this evening by Lorenz, sprang away in its usual shower of foam, and Esmé sat turned towards her, with head bare to the breeze, until out of sight. The clouds had come down, and clear twilight lay over the water. The farther shore looked near and yet mysterious, with its climbing pines stained in the evening's blue; there was no light in Esmé's house, and the outlines of the Italian mountains looked like pale, delicate cardboard.

Meg walked down to the bus-stop. In spite of thinking that it would have been pleasant to go across the lake with Esmé and meet his Venetian friends, she felt more cheerful than she had done all day; the evening was cool and shut in by the ceiling of cloud, and not for the first time she was aware, as if it were a sensation pressing upon her nerves, of the sheer size of Europe, where you could take a train in Vienna and alight in India without crossing the sea; the mountains and lakes and broad fields were all on a scale calculated to make the single individual feel small and alone. And those hay manikins, looming or crouching in the gathering twilight, were really horrid; the dark streaky hay of which they were formed looked decayed. Yet she whistled softly as she walked, thinking about getting back to the *gasthaus* with its quiet welcoming air amidst the trees, and those two frocks which her mother was making for her, and supper. . . .

At the bus-stop she stood well back in the shadow of some hazel bushes, for there were the young English soldiers of the mountain-top, also waiting for the bus, and she did not want them to see her. But their behaviour was different now from what it had been some hours ago; they were subdued and anxious, and paying much attention to one of their number who was sitting by the roadside with his head in his hands. They stood round him in a group, offering awkward sympathy.

"Cheer up, Nobby, we're nearly home."

"If you can call it 'ome."

"Nice end to a day's leave, this is. Nobby poisoned."

"Shut your mucking silly mouth, can't you? Poisoned. He hasn't been sick, 'ave you, chum? You're always sick if you're poisoned."

"He still feels sick, though. Don't yer, tosh?"

"Sick and awful pain in my belly," said Nobby hoarsely.

"Prob'bly something you been eating. Foreigners—they can't cook. Give me English cooking every time. Come on, here's the mucking bus. Here, give us a hand, Chris—Eric—we'll soon be home. Up you come, chum."

They were too busy to notice Meg, who waited until they were all settled, with the sweating and chalk-faced Nobby leaning against a comrade's shoulder, before entering the bus. They got down at the railway-station at Franzendorf and went off into the dusk with Nobby half-supported by a boy on either side, while the passengers peered interestedly into the shadows after them. Meg had liked the look of their young faces and the sound of English spoken in their fresh ugly voices, and she hoped that poor Nobby had nothing serious the matter with him and would soon be well again.

CHAPTER FIFTEEN

Warning

SHE did not tell her mother about Esmé's disturbing remarks nor about his holding her hand. She felt slightly guilty about both incidents.

She knew that Mrs Lambert, were she told, would be distressed and worried. She had said more than once that she did not like Meg spending so much of her time with a man many years older than herself with whom the Lamberts had nothing in common, and Meg had always been able to retort that the others were invited too. Now she no longer had this excuse. And it was undeniable that as soon as the chaperonage of "the others" had been removed, Esmé *had* . . . well, the usual words gave quite the wrong impression, but they would have to do . . . made advances to her.

She was not annoyed with him. Men had been trying to kiss her and to hold her hand since shortly before her sixteenth birthday, so she was quite unflustered by such situations; they were merely a bore or not, according to whether one happened to like the trier. She was not annoyed; if anything she was flattered and excited, but she was also alarmed. The attentions of an extremely rich, learned and elderly man—well, perhaps elderly was too strong a word, but he was elderly compared to her—were something quite different from those of the young men of Tormouth and its surrounding villages. She had felt, ever since he had dropped that first hint about visiting Savoy, that he might be Serious.

Now so far no one had been Serious about Meg, nor had she herself been Serious about anyone, not even about Derek Jones, although she had loved him with all her poor heart. He was a shabby, thin, cheerful boy, a mere two years older than herself, interested only in aeroplanes, and flintily refusing to admit that he loved her. She had never, of course, asked him; that would have been unthinkable; but how she had thirsted, poor Meg, to hear him say it.

She was still smarting from this unhappy love when they arrived in Austria, and Esmé's attentions, Esmé's interest, had been both flattering and soothing.

But if he were going to get Serious, that was quite another matter. The mere suggestion frightened her. Better live and die in ghastly Tormouth, amidst old friends and familiar scenes, than endure such strangeness, such an upheaval! And then she remembered how unbearable Tormouth had seemed before she came away from it, and how her friendship with Esmé was enriching both her social life and her intellectual one, and felt towards him a glow of gratitude.

Later on, when they had been going about together for more than a month, she realised how unusually delightful was the life he led. The cares of every day—lack of money, lack of domestic help, minor shortages—apparently did not touch it. Her own life, as lived in Tormouth, appeared in contrast unendurably drab, and even some years hence, when she had a job, what was there to look forward to? Six pounds a week, a flat (if she were exceptionally lucky) shared with another girl, ordinary young men, ordinary pastimes—no beauty and no exquisite sense of romantic excitement. She forgot, or she had never realised, how the very stones of Tormouth Quay had glistened in perpetual moonlight while she had loved Derek Jones. She did not know that Dickens might have

created the Tormouth she saw after her love had ended, a town sunk
in dull, windless, colourless murk, peopled by ageing morons; and
when the first vague thoughts of the desirability of escape from all
this through Esmé Scarron first invaded her mind, she did not
realise that she already carried the precious means of escape within
her own skull. For under her tender young scalp was a strong
imagination, colouring, draping, gracing, piercing or illuminating
all she saw and did. But she only began to think, as the weeks went
on, how lucky any girl would be who led the life enjoyed by Esmé
Scarron.

Meanwhile, she cut no more German classes. Frau Schacht had
given her a sharp little lecture—ending on a graver note. She could
not afford to miss classes. Frau Schacht was herself too busy to make
them up to her. Also, it sets a bad example to the boys. Boys? Mr
Scott must be *thirty*. No; he is not thirty; he is only twenty-eight,
but he has seen more of the world than most young men. Do not
wander, please, Meg, from the point. Also it is not fair to your
mother, when she is working hard helping me, not to profit by
your stay here. Yes, Hans—Frau Schacht, I'm sorry. It shan't happen again.

"And soon," concluded Frau Schacht, "I shall be busier yet. The
gasthaus will be full. We are now drawing close to our busiest weeks.
And Mr Scott's *braut*—his fiancée—is coming."

"Oh? I knew he had one, but I thought she wasn't coming until
September. Is she old too?"

"I am sure I don't know, Meg, but it will be a good thing for him.
He has been rather lonely. No, it isn't funny," as Meg gave a somewhat conscious laugh, "I don't like my guests to be lonely. You
have not been friendly to him."

"He hasn't been friendly to me."

"You have not given him the opportunity. It is some silly idea
you have, I suppose. He is a very nice young man, very serious, very
clever."

"How ghastly. And all those freckles."

"Many Scottish men have freckles. It is a racial characteristic,
it means nothing. . . ."

Meg glanced down the garden, hoping to be released, but Frau Schacht was looking at her intently, and seemed to be making up her mind to speak. She waited, wondering what was the matter now.

"You are seeing much of Mr Scarron," Frau Schacht brought out at last.

Up came Meg's head.

"Yes, I am," she said. *And what's it got to do with you?* trembled on the air between them.

"Do not look like that. Your mother is troubled—worried—about it, I think. You know that he has had a wife already?"

"Yes, I do know; Mummy told me. I suppose *you* told *her?*"

"I told her, yes. And you—you think it nice for a girl not yet nineteen to go about alone with a man who is divorced?"

"I don't think about it at all, and I don't think about his wife either. Mummy hasn't said anything; she lets me go about with him."

"Meg, your mother is absolutely—I can't think of the English word—yes, that's it—besotted with you. She lets you do exactly as you please because she is afraid to spoil your pleasure. But I have known you since you were a little child. And now I speak to you for your own good. I don't want to speak to you like this; I am busy; I have many worries, and why should I trouble myself about you? But your parents were kind to me. Perhaps that's why I want to help you."

Meg was silent, listening with bent head and scarlet face. Bringing in her childhood and her parents—honestly, it was too sickening.

"Mr Scarron isn't a good man. I can't say any more, but he is not a good man. You don't want to get . . . too fond of him," said Frau Schacht.

"I'm *not* getting too fond of him. We're friends, that's all. Ask Robin—ask Mummy. He's been very kind to me and we're friends. Fondness, as you call it, doesn't come into it."

"But you like him very much——"

"I don't know about 'very' much. But I like him, yes. And I think it's unfair to say things against him. Because he speaks very well of you. I've often heard him." On reflection, hurriedly indulged in while she faced her lecturer, Meg did not recall more than one occasion on which she had heard him, and then it had been only a reference to Frau Schacht's making her guests comfortable. But there was no need for details.

Frau Schacht nodded. "Yes, so I should suppose. I have never done any harm to him."

"Then I suppose he's done harm to you—since you're so mysterious. . . . I beg your pardon, but absolutely *nothing* makes me angrier than having people run down my friends."

Frau Schacht said nothing for a minute. Then she said: "He was a collaborator in the war."

"Oh, I've heard all about that. Robin ferreted out a lot of gossip . . . I didn't believe half of it. Besides, in a war everything is in such a muddle that it's impossible to find out what's true and what isn't or who was on which side——"

"There was no doubt, I believe, about your Mr Churchill."

"I meant ordinary people. Besides, Esmé was in America for most of the war; he told me. He's a scholar; his life's work is studying Paracelsus; and he didn't see why his life's work should be upset because of the war . . . it wasn't anything to do with him . . . that's why he went to America."

Frau Schacht had been nodding her head throughout this speech. "Perfectly logical, perfectly sensible," she said, when Meg stopped speaking, "but it doesn't explain why he was on such good terms with the German commanders here before he went."

"I don't know anything about that. Besides, it all happened years ago, anyway——"

"And things that happened years ago don't matter, of course?"

"I must say they don't matter much to me. And I think it's filthily disloyal to listen to things about people behind their backs."

"So. And at Tormouth do all those ladies still say to each other exactly what they think of each other, as they used to do when I am living there? Meg, it's time, it's certainly time, for you to become a woman. The world is a terrible place and you should know that it is. You should grow up."

Meg now controlled her anger and answered in a less heated tone:

"Of course I know people don't always say everything to each other's faces. One can't, it would hurt too much. But usually it's only little unimportant things that one says behind their backs, things that don't matter. You're saying something that does matter. I don't believe it, of course, but it's awfully strong to call someone 'a bad man'.

"I suppose you mean he's had a lot—affairs?" she said, as Frau Schacht remained silent, and added, as she still did not answer, "Well, that's nothing to do with me. He behaves himself with me and that's all I care about."

"You love him," said Frau Schacht; her face had become convulsed with a kind of sick misery.

"Of course I don't, Hansi, how *can* you be such—so—oh, it's all so *silly*. I suppose you mean well, but *honestly*—and I can tell you one thing: all this—what you've been saying—has made me like him even more. I feel sorry for him now. Having enemies behind his back. *Nothing* will make me believe anything against him now. So if you meant to warn me off him you've done just the opposite, and if you meant it kindly thank you very much and I don't mean to be rude, but in spite of your opinion of me I'm quite able to look after myself."

Frau Schacht made a helpless gesture and turned away, and Meg went straight to find her mother.

"Mummy, is Hansi in—in love or something with Esmé? (here, give me the cloth, I'll clean the bath, you oughtn't to be stooping— I thought Maria was supposed to do this—well, couldn't she do it when she comes back?) Hansi's just been going on in the most peculiar way, trying to warn me against him and accusing *me* of being in love with him. It's absolutely revolting when one thinks about that poor little skinny Franz, but do you think she could possibly be?"

While she talked Meg was cleaning the bath with furious long sweeps.

"*Do* keep your voice down for heaven's sake, she's only just outside——"

"I don't care . . . *do* you think she is?"

"Of course not. I'm really surprised, Meg, that you should think of such a thing . . . you must *not* let your imagination run away with you like this——"

"I didn't. It was her. She went such a peculiar colour when she said *I* was in love with him. And she kept on calling him *a bad man.* . . ."

"(*Please* keep your voice *down.*) She doesn't like him. I know that, because she told me. He was too friendly with the German commanders during the war or something. . . ."

"Yes. She said that to me too. But I felt there was something else as well, that she was keeping to herself. And then going that awful yellow colour. . . ."

"Meg, I'm afraid she doesn't like you either. I'm sorry, darling" (as Meg lifted an indignant and incredulous face). "I don't know why—perhaps it's a kind of jealousy . . . but haven't you felt she didn't like you?"

"I always feel everybody likes me. But if she doesn't like me, why does she want to scare me off poor Esmé? You'd think she'd be glad I was going to have an awful time with him."

"She may feel it's her duty to warn you about him even though she doesn't like you. She isn't a frivolous, casual person, you know. She was brought up a strict Roman Catholic, and though she isn't what the French call *pratiquante*, she is *croyante*; that is, she still believes it all—she told me so only the other day. If she knows something bad that he once did, she won't want to see you getting mixed up with him. And she wouldn't want me to be hurt. I think she's fond of me."

"Mummy, she's simply ghastly to you—making you carry those terrific shopping bags and clean the bath—here, it's done now," and Meg stood up and absently held out the cloth.

"(Thank you, darling.) All the same, I'm sure she is fond of me in her own peculiar way. She was fond of Daddy, too, and grateful to us both. And that's why she's trying to keep an eye on you."

"Well, I wish she wouldn't. Especially as she doesn't like me. It's bad enough to have eyes kept on you by people who do like you.

And I hate all this mystery about Esmé. Why can't she say straight out what he's supposed to have done?"

"Collaborating——" Mrs Lambert murmured.

"Oh, rubbish, Mummy. They all collaborated like mad, I expect. You know how Robin adores poking about and finding out what goes on *under the surface* in places—like that book he's so mad about, *Drayneflete Revealed?*—well, he's always hinting at what he's found out about people here during the war. Awful things. I wouldn't let him tell me. Not everybody, I suppose, but . . . they had to, I expect. It may have been like that for Esmé."

"Yes, perhaps. Except that he was in America for most of the war, wasn't he?"

"Yes, I suppose he was. Oh, well. So far as I can make out all he did was to be too friendly with the German officers. Well, why shouldn't he? He's only half-English. Besides, the Austrians weren't *conquered* by the Nazis. They were on the same side. They asked them to come in. It isn't like the Norwegians or the French. It's absolute nonsense to say that Esmé 'collaborated'. They *all* did—the whole of Austria. I shall say that to Hansi the next time she starts accusing him."

"I hope you won't. We can't afford to quarrel with Hansi. And please pay attention to what she says. Because I really don't believe she would keep on about his—his general undesirability like this unless she knew something that we don't."

Meg looked sulky. Then she said sharply:

"Yes, and another thing, Mummy. She said you'd been worried about my going about with him so much. You haven't been *talking* to her about it, have you?"

"No, Meg, I have not. And don't take that tone with me, dear, please. I am beginning to be a little worried. I know he's been kind to you and I believe that he—well, he doesn't mean you any harm. But I still can't quite make out what he *sees* in all you young people —even in you, my darling, lovely as you are. (Meg, *don't* pull that face, it makes you look really *common*.) And—dearest—hasn't it struck you that a man so much older than yourself, who has been through a divorce, and travelled all over the world, might have done things in his past that make him an—unsuitable friend for you? things that might shock and upset you if you knew about them?"

Meg was silent.

"But that wouldn't matter—or of course it would *matter*, but not so *much*—except that I—I have a sort of feeling he may be getting Serious about you."

This time Meg looked up, and their eyes met in a long, solemn and rather apprehensive stare.

"Why, Mummy?" Meg said at length; her tone was subdued.

"I don't know, dear. I simply feel it. And I'm not one of those silly mothers who imagine every man their daughter knows is getting Serious. . . ."

Meg looked down again at the floor.

"So that's why, if Hansi *does* know something about his past——"

"I don't care about his past!"

Meg gave a cross and naughty laugh; her eyes sparkled, colour flew into her face, and she darted out of the room.

Her mother continued with the tidying; the small window admitted only dim light into the little, wooden-walled cell, and whenever she glanced at the hushed, cloudy afternoon outside, her eyes seemed to fall upon shadows, shadows under the thick foliage of the orchard trees where hornets crawled and darted, shadows lying in the half-veiled folds of the mountains, shadows cast across the unstirring surface of the lake. Subdued by the stillness and silence of the day, she did her work mechanically while her thoughts wandered uncertainly in apprehensive gloom, and when there came a tap at the door she started violently. The young postmaster stood there, holding out a letter.

CHAPTER SIXTEEN

Invitation

"Oh—thank you. Who is it for? Oh—me. I see—thank you," taking it from him with nods and smiles to which he responded with only the curtest jerk of his head. Since the English fräulein, who had danced so sweetly at first with himself and his friends, had been going about with Herr Scarron, he did not want to be friendly with her or polite to her mother. He hated Herr Scarron for having spent the war comfortably in America, and he hated having to bring his messages to the *Venedig*. He had been told by telephone to take this letter, which had arrived by the late post, up to the *gasthaus* so that the English lady might get it to-day instead of to-morrow, and he had sulkily obeyed.

When he had gone—Frau Schacht had as usual left the front door ajar and that was how he had arrived at the bathroom—Mrs Lambert looked at the thick silvery envelope and her own name written in a small, black, constricted hand, and then, trembling she knew not why, opened it.

The signature was Esmé Scarron's; he asked if she would have luncheon with him to-morrow—Thursday—alone. The launch would be at the landing-stage at a quarter to one, and he hoped that she would honour him by coming. He wanted to talk to her about something.

Mrs Lambert sat down on the edge of the bath because her legs were trembling, and she was still sitting there and staring at the letter when she heard a distant commotion. Faintly she heard it, as if from far away, because of the confusion of her thoughts—"Maria! Maria! *Eine hornisse!*" and then the bathroom door flew open and Frau Schacht marched in and slammed it behind her.

"Oh, you're here, Eve," she said shortly, "how well and clean the bath looks. An enormous hornet, the biggest one of this summer, their king, perhaps—in the *salon*, ugh. But Maria will soon liquidate him."

"Hansi," Mrs Lambert said, looking up slowly, "this letter is from Esmé Scarron asking me to lunch with him to-morrow. He wants me to come alone because he wants to talk to me about something."

Frau Schacht stood still, looking at her. Mrs Lambert received an impression from her face of extreme repugnance, of shrinking that almost betrayed itself in twitching, flinching skin, and wonderingly, through her own disturbed state of mind, she saw Frau Schacht drive herself on to speak.

"Well, that will be very pleasant for you, won't it? Beautiful house and delicious food and a charming host. You will not want anything more."

"Hansi, I really want your advice. Shall I tell Meg about this? The fact is, I've got a strong feeling that he—he wants to talk about her. I've been expecting it for some time, but now that it may have come . . . I don't know what to think or say. . . ."

"You think he wants to marry her?"

Mrs Lambert nodded. "I expect it sounds silly to you, as if I were counting my chickens before they're hatched, but——"

"Chickens? Ah—yes, the English idiom. No, Eve, I don't think it sounds silly. I too think perhaps he wants this. I have thought it ever since he began to make attentions to her." The words seemed to be forced with great reluctance from Frau Schacht, but without irritation, while looked at Mrs. Lambert steadily and with deep sadness. Suddenly she said impatiently, "But why are we talking here in this horrible little bathroom? Let us go into the *salon*, the hornet must be dead by now," and swept out of the door. Mrs Lambert, following her almost without realising she was doing so, received a triumphant nod from Maria on her way downstairs with the fish slice.

"I should be staking the tomatoes . . ." Frau Schacht muttered, as she sat down, then went on at once, "do you want them to marry?"

"No, of *course* not—what a question! He's more than twice her age, he isn't English, he doesn't belong to our world, and I simply can't stand him. . . . And yet, Meg does like him, and I've always thought she needed an older man, and he seems kind——"

Frau Schacht laughed. The "bitter laugh" of fiction has become a joke during the past thirty years; this did not prevent Frau Schacht's laugh from sounding shocking in the ears of Mrs Lambert. She stared at her, for the moment silenced.

"So you think he's kind? But shall I tell you who is truly kind, kind as the blessed angels we were told about when we were children? Franz is, my poor old Franz. He is truly kind. He loves the hungry dogs and cats in the street." She buried her face in her hands.

Mrs Lambert said nothing, waiting with mingled impatience and sympathy for the spasm to pass so that she could bring her back to the point. But soon Frau Schacht dropped her hands, and looked at her.

"You want Meg to marry an older man. Yes—well?"

"But not so *much* older, Hansi, and of course she must have love as well—and when I think of that I imagine someone much younger——"

"And virgin," nodded Frau Schacht with a return to her usual manner, "virgin, of course. And English, if possible."

"Yes—both, certainly—if it's possible, as you say," Mrs Lambert said defiantly, colouring, "why not? And then there's his having been married before. Hansi, can't you help me *at all*? Don't you know anything about his other marriage? Was it his fault?"

"Eve! Eve, you are such a fool, you make me so angry; how can I help you when you are such a fool?" Frau Schacht had actually jumped up, and stood there with every curl above her sallow face seeming to quiver with exasperation, " 'Was it his fault?' " (mimicking a prim English voice). "How should I know? Why do you ask me? Yes, it was his fault, I will swear on the name of God it was; no woman could bear him or live with him. Don't ask me how I know this—I can't tell you—I won't; but if things get worse—if Meg becomes truly to love him—God help the poor, stupid little girl—then I will tell you what I know. Or what I think I know. You see, it is so terrible, Eve, because I am not exactly sure, and if I tell you and it is not true after all——"

"I wish you wouldn't be so mysterious, Hansi," calmly said Mrs Lambert, now very alarmed. "Just tell me quietly, please, if you know something about him that makes it quite impossible for me even to consider him as a husband for Meg. I assure you I should be very glad to hear it."

Frau Schacht shook her head. "I am not sure. I only—suspect him of something. I don't know if he did it. And I don't want to tell you about it, because I must tell about myself, too. Perhaps he didn't do what I think. Perhaps he wants to settle down. He may be tired of doing without a wife." She hesitated. "He is not bad, you know, in *that* way. I mean, his reputation with women is not bad. He has been like other men, that is all, no worse and no better."

"But there is something very bad that you do know?" Mrs Lambert insisted, now feeling that if Harry's spirit were to appear at this instant, telling her to let Meg marry Esmé Scarron, she would refuse.

"I don't know, I tell you. I only think——"

"It isn't fair, of course—I suppose—to tell me something that may not be true——" Mrs Lambert said.

" 'Not fair!' In another moment we are playing at cricket. This is not the reason I don't tell you. It is because it would only make trouble. But I shan't tell you. You go there to-morrow, and hear what he will say. Perhaps it is all nothing, and he does not want to marry her at all. But if he does, you will have a terrible time, my poor Eve, if Meg is in love with him: what can you do? Nothing."

Mrs Lambert was silent. She stared through the flowery balcony at the lake.

Frau Schacht stood up and smoothed her dress with one of those elderly gestures that added twenty years to her thirty-seven. Her face was waxen and damp-looking. "Now I must go to tie up those tomatoes." She straightened her shoulders and went quickly out of the room.

She is quite right, Mrs Lambert thought; if Meg does care for him, I can do nothing. Am I being selfish, and just hating the thought of losing her, or do I truly mistrust him? I certainly dislike him. But suppose Hansi and I are both mistaken, and he really is as nice as he seems? Surely Meg would have noticed anything unpleasant in his character by this time, if it is there? And does she care for him, or is she only flattered by the idea of his caring for her?

She had decided, before evening came, that she would ask Hansi to help her keep to-morrow's appointment without Meg knowing about it. She did not want to set out for the visit with Meg's questions and threats and excited comments buzzing in her ears like so many hornets; she wished to confront Esmé Scarron calmly, and try to see him with detachment. She would, in pursuit of this wish, even try to forget the mysterious remarks made by Hansi.

She had so many times imagined an ideal husband for Meg, and, equally often, she had reminded herself that Meg would probably choose someone very different, even someone whom Mrs Lambert could not like. But now that perhaps the moment of choice had come, it was being harder than she had ever, in her most self-abjuring moments, imagined.

CHAPTER SEVENTEEN

Spellbinder

HE was waiting for her at the open door of his house; he came towards her as soon as he saw her coming down the path under the trees with Lorenz, holding out his hands and saying, "How very good of you to come at such short notice, and on such a heavy day. We seem to be unfortunate in our weather, don't we? But it is not going to rain, the wireless tells me. That always seems a kind of magic, don't you think?—to foretell the weather accurately eight times out of ten. Now if you would like to go with Janka she will look after you . . . and then shall we talk while we are having our sherry? I thought you might like to get our talk over. I have really spread myself over luncheon to-day; I found out from our Meg all about roast guinea-fowl and ice pudding . . . and I have been busy telephoning to Vienna—I want you to enjoy your visit," he ended, relinquishing the two hands he had been holding. His bright eyes looked into hers, his hands were warm and dry as hers were cold and moist. He wore a suit of rough, white silky material with an un-familiar pink flower in its buttonhole, and his creased skin was burned by the sun to a dark brown. Mrs Lambert smiled ner-vously and followed Janka up the stairs. She had said something conventional in reply; she could not remember what.

This museum of a house! How she disliked its spice-like scent and its shadows and the absence of air in the low-ceilinged shining rooms. Her own long face looked back at her from the dim depths of a Venetian mirror framed in pallid glass flowers and its expression gave her no confidence. She attended absently to her hair, then turned to Janka saying that she was ready.

He had had two chairs and a low table arranged at the entrance to the conservatory, and was awaiting her there. The room was extremely hot, in spite of the glass doors opening directly on to the garden, and she found the rows of books in their dark bindings oppressive, but she could not but be soothed by his manner, which was consideration itself yet not effusive or overdone. The trace of mockery which she had formerly detected had quite gone. He would, naturally, make himself pleasant to her if the circumstances were what she supposed, but she found it agreeable—and was slightly ashamed of herself—to be fussed over and waited upon. The sherry —about which they had a little discussion, because she had never before tasted Tio Pepe and at first refused to believe that it was sherry—mounted agreeably to her head and lulled her fears. She had not realised how weary she was, until she reclined in the chair into which he had put her, with the warm silent air and the subdued light soothing her senses, and her ears lulled by the faint trickling of a fountain amidst the plants outside. He sat opposite, in the one shaft of sun finding its way into the room, and all the light seemed concentrated upon his clothes and his bright smiling eyes. There was a bamboo table near to him, with some letters and photographs lying upon it, and she wondered why they were there; perhaps, while thinking about beginning a new life with Meg—("our Meg"

—oh dear, there was no doubt at all that he had said it)— he had turned to remembering the old?

"I shall go to sleep in a moment, Mr Scarron," she said languidly, lifting drooping lids, "you have made me so luxurious. I'm not used to it."

"I want you to be comfortable while you listen," he said, "because I am going to tell you about myself. It won't take long—and then we can have our roast guinea-fowl—but you must listen carefully and ask questions, and at the end you must tell me exactly how you feel . . . and then I shall ask you a question, and you must answer."

"It sounds like Portia and the Caskets . . . or something out of Hans Andersen . . . very romantic, anyway. How do I know that I shall give the right answer? Or isn't there a right answer—oh dear" concealing a yawn—"please don't think that's due to anything but this comfortable chair. . . ." She tried to go on, in a light teasing tone, but found herself unable. She was conscious of nothing but comfort and warmth and the brilliant power of his eyes.

"If you fall asleep I'll wake you up," he answered, and now, for the first time, she heard faintly the hateful note of mockery. But she was too drowsy to resent it.

"Mrs Lambert"— (there it was again; that repetition of her name like a child's mocking-song—Mrs—Lambert, Mrs *Lam*-bert)— "did you know that I have been married?"

"Yes. Yes—I—had heard it," she answered with slight confusion which her sleepiness prevented from becoming embarrassment, "for—for the minute I can't remember who told me——"

She could remember not to betray Hansi.

"It doesn't matter." The shining eyes were fixed on her own. "I want to talk to you about my marriage and why it was a failure. It ended in hatred."

"How terrible," Mrs Lambert said quietly, and no longer in a voice made languid by sleep; she had been shocked awake.

"It was not my fault," he said at once. "You may think I am trying to win your sympathy. I can't help that. It wasn't my fault. I am a lover of peace; of peace and quiet. All I ask is my studies and the mountains and quiet in which to work. But she—my wife——"

He turned and searched among the papers on the bamboo table.

"Look, this is she, this is Hella. Beautiful, isn't she?" and he held out a small coloured photograph. Dark chestnut hair fell about a dark and troubled face, and the eyes were wide open to the sunlight in a garden of stone and shrubs and water. She lay back in a deck chair, looking into the camera, with her hand resting on the head of a large dog.

"Isn't that Melchior?" Mrs Lambert asked.

"Yes—yes, it is," he replied at once, almost eagerly, "and do you know why he is so bad-tempered?"

Mrs Lambert, feeling a slight anticipatory sickness, shook her head.

"She used to beat him. She beat him until she made him as savage as herself: she liked beating him. Can you imagine, Mrs Lambert, what it was to be married to Hella?"

"Was it bad from the first?" Mrs Lambert asked, resolutely putting aside an overwhelming desire for the sights and sounds and faces of Tormouth.

He shook his head. "Not quite at first, although she always had the temper, quite simply, of a devil. Peace was the one thing she would never let me have."

"Didn't—do forgive me, but you said that I must ask questions— didn't you suspect before you married her that she might be difficult?"

He was looking at the photograph, which she had given back to him. Now a peculiar expression, which she failed to translate, came about his mouth.

"Of course. But I was young. I was twenty-six. I wanted to tame her. The 'difficultness' added——" He broke off. "I give you my word of honour that I tried with all the means in my power to hold things together. But I failed."

"Mr Scarron, had you any children?"

The question was out before Mrs Lambert realised it was coming. Now, having uttered it, she saw how greatly the answer might affect Meg's future life. Grown-up stepchildren. It simply hadn't occurred to her.

"I lost a son on the Russian front," he said.

She kept her eyes downwards and said nothing. A crushing blow; she knew people who had not recovered from that. A flood of sympathy overcame her—until she looked up, and saw him again, and then to her shame she found her dislike as strong as ever. And she could not help being relieved that there were no grown-up children.

"I had had no news for months. Then, when I came back to this house in 1946, I heard of his death. It was at Stalingrad."

Mrs Lambert nodded.

"It hadn't been possible, you see, to get news through before."

"No."

A silence, which to her seemed uneasy, followed her murmured word. He kept his gaze fixed upon the mass of papers but without any effect of relaxation or musing; she felt as if, behind his lowered lids, his eyes were watching her. And she could not fix her own eyes comfortably upon any point in the room; not upon a deep pink leather cover amongst the sombre backs of the books, nor on the white porcelain stove with its green tiles, nor on the miniature grove where the fountain dripped. It was such a depressing room, for all its luxury; it made one long for the open air.

She began to argue against her dislike of him; accusing herself of prejudice. He had been kind, courteous, attentive, apparently frank. Why must this almost physical dislike, this shrinking from him as if he were infectious, persist? No one else seemed to feel it. Even Hansi had thought that she must find him agreeable and charming. And she herself did not usually take unaccountable dislikes to people. Couldn't it be that she simply dreaded losing Meg? To anyone? Weren't all her arguments about difference in age and income merely a disguise for maternal possessiveness? And then, her wandering gaze happening to stray back to him where he sat motionless in the sunlight, she found herself confronting, full-blown, the thought that he was only a puppet, a simulacrum of a man going deftly through the motions which animate human beings. Shocked at the strength of her own dislike—and what a strange thought to have, she was so seldom inclined to fantasy—she sat up in her chair and drew a sharp, swift sigh.

"This is all very difficult for you, isn't it!" he said smilingly, making the words a statement, not a question, and again she thought she detected mockery.

"It isn't—well, divorces aren't usual in the town we live in," she said briskly, "I was going to say 'they aren't what I'm accustomed to.' But I know there are times when one has to have them, of course." She wondered whether to add a rider about not being narrow-minded, and decided against it. After all, why should she justify herself and her opinions to him?

"I am not on bad terms with Hella, you know," he said, "I see her occasionally, when I go to Venice; she lives there now. But her temper has got worse with age——"

"But surely she can't be so very old? She must only be in the early forties—unless of course she is older than yourself?"

"No, no, she is a year or so younger, and hardly middle-aged yet," he said hastily. "I only meant that time hasn't sweetened her. Fortunately her new husband comes in for the hysteria and the scenes now."

"She married again, then?"

"Almost immediately—the youngest of her many lovers."

Mrs Lambert was silent again, this time from extreme distaste. She was aware of a strong sense of *contrast*; between the world into which Meg had been born and in which she had grown up, where the family was the social unit, and the jungle hinted at in the words of Scarron, where fierce individual natures tore one another in selfish conflict. Previously, she had only dreaded a match between Meg and this man because she herself disliked him so much and because of his age and different background. Now she realised just how different, and how alarming, that background was.

There sounded a slight click, and they both glanced towards the door. It was opening slowly and the dark pallor of Janka's face appeared for an instant; then the cat Iliaster came slowly into the room and the door closed behind her. With lithely waving tail she walked down the length of the room, and as she passed her master she turned upon him her turquoise eyes and uttered a raucous cry, but she did not pause on her way to the conservatory, where she squatted in the shadow of a great drooping bronze leaf, keeping her gaze fixed upon some object, invisible to everyone but herself, in the corner of the room.

"Iliaster, lovely puss," Mr Scarron said absently, watching her.

The silence had now continued until it was embarrassing. That is, Mrs Lambert felt it so. She did not know what Mr Scarron was thinking or feeling. *She* was embarrassed, and worried, and quite extraordinarily depressed. Sadness lay upon her like a heavy load; it was apart from her anxiety; it was almost physical. And her confusion and her apprehension grew stronger, and still she did not know what to say.

But gradually, as if the idea were growing in her mind, she began to feel that she must make the first move. Perhaps he felt that as he had put so many of his cards on the table it was her turn to comment upon them. Not that she cared what he felt, but it was impossible to go on sitting here in this wretched silence. She suddenly plunged into speech.

"I know why you've told me all this, don't I?" she said, so abruptly that she was horrified even as she spoke. "Isn't it because of Meg?"

At once his head jerked up, and there he was, staring full at her with his face alight with mockery and triumph; yes, it was that, though he wiped the look off at once and replaced it with one more restrained. I've done what he wanted me to; he's won, she thought; I ought to have let him speak first, I've been a fool.

And now he was nodding his big head with the light striking back from its bald brown skin.

"Yes, Mrs Lambert. It is; that is the reason. And this is my question: Do you think I can make her care for me?"

The cautious humility of the request was so different from the bold demand which she had expected that she was completely taken aback. Extreme surprise was her strongest feeling, and then she felt thankful that she had not even hinted at the possibility of marriage. How angry, how *furious*, Meg would have been if she had! And then, suddenly, and as unexpected in its arrival as his question, anger swept over her. She felt herself out-manœuvred, at a loss, and afraid to ask him plainly what he meant in case he had meant nothing more than what he had said.

She leant back in her chair, looking at him, and her thoughts raced so swiftly that her outward expression was merely blank. Her lips remained slightly parted.

She did not lack a modest self-confidence, nor was she without experience of manœuvring and intrigue, for she had spent sixteen years in the classrooms and staffrooms of girls' schools, but at this moment, for the first time in her life, she wished herself what is known as a woman of the world. She simply knew that she was not his equal in cleverness and subtlety and ruthlessness. And she was just as simply convinced that she must fight him. She must fight him for possession of Meg, because he meant, honestly or dishonestly, to get her, and because Mrs Lambert knew that if he did, he would make her beloved child wretched.

She knew it. Not one obvious flaw could she detect in his manner, or in the story he had told her, and he appeared, apart from the difference between his years and Meg's, to possess many qualities that would make a desirable husband, and yet here was she, Meg's natural and legal protector, unshakably certain that he must never have her. O God, prayed Mrs Lambert, looking vacantly at Esmé Scarron, I'm being silly, perhaps I'm imagining things and exaggerating, but please help me save Meg. Don't, please dear God, let her love him.

"What do you think about it?" Esmé Scarron repeated gently. Not even the eyes of angry, frightened motherhood could now detect in his expression any trace of mockery and triumph.

Her hands were cold and her heart was thudding; an awful load of anxiety, the same which tortured her when Meg was late in returning home at night, or ill, had settled upon her, yet she answered with spirit:

"Oh, but I'm sure she likes you already. She is affectionate, you know, and she has such heaps of friends—and you have been so kind about everything——" she ended confusedly.

Hansi was right, she was right. I ought to have gone with them when he asked me, I ought to have been there all the time so that I could stop him winning Meg's confidence. I daren't ask him what he means by "care for", in case he only means what he says. . . .

"Thank you. I'm glad to hear you say that. I know she has many friends—it's natural, with anyone so lovely and so young."

And silly, thought Mrs Lambert tartly, I don't expect you've any idea how silly, and at the picture of this dear silliness tears came into her eyes. She got up quickly; she could endure no more.

"I'm being dreadfully rude, I know, but do you think we could have lunch?—if there isn't anything else that we—perhaps ought to talk about? I've just remembered Frau Schacht has some new people coming this afternoon and she particularly wants me to be there when they arrive—so if you don't mind——"

"Of course. And you must be starving. Isn't it curious how hungry one always is after a really important talk?"

She could only manage a faint smile in answer.

It would not be true to say *how she got through luncheon she never knew*, because she did remember afterwards that the food was tasteless and the wine—about which he fussed—seemed only sour and heating, while she was unusually conscious of the movements she made in eating. And his voice, usually so agreeable, began to grate upon her nerves, and by the end of the meal his attentions—the re-filling of her glass, the enquiries about whether she found the room too warm or her chair comfortable—seemed to her actually sickening. He must know how much I love Meg, she thought miserably, and surely he's intelligent enough to realise that I *can't* want her to marry someone so much older (not that I would object to his age so much if only his background were different)—but he simply doesn't care. He means to get her, and I'm just an old fool who can't stop him and who doesn't matter. As luncheon drew towards its end, she was not too bemused to notice that mockery had entered into his expression again, while he discussed with exaggerated deference his plans for amusing Meg during the coming weeks. He no longer in-cluded herself in these arrangements, and she felt that he was show-ing her, as plainly as he dared, that he was not afraid of her opposi-tion, and that he had only invited her here and gone through this farce of asking her opinion because Meg loved her, and because, if he wished to keep in with Meg, he must make some gesture towards her mother.

And she knew that if he married Meg she would lose her. She must fight him, and fight hard, and she had no one to help her, and if she begged Meg to come home at once, to leave Austria and frankly run away from him, would she consent? That would depend upon how much she cared for him, and Mrs Lambert swore to herself that she would lose no time in finding that out.

She managed to say good-bye to him at the edge of his garden, whither he had escorted her before putting her into the care of Lorenz, without (she hoped) betraying her agitation; but although she held her head high while he bowed low over the hand which she shudderingly hoped he would not kiss, his expression was openly mocking, and she could not comfort herself by thinking she had deceived him. And he charged her with affectionate messages for Meg! She walked away through the woods, ahead of Lorenz, with her eyes spilling over with tears.

The space and light and fresh watery scents of the lake blessedly dispelled the oppressiveness of the house, but she felt no lightening of her load as the launch drew near to Martinsdorf, looking reassuringly peaceful in the mid-afternoon light; and almost at once she would have to meet these new arrivals of Hansi's, and she realised that for the last hour her head had been aching abominably.

She heard the noise of the launch's departure. The day was cloudy and still, and the voices of bathers and children came up softly yet distinctly from the shore. She looked at her watch and saw that she had almost an hour before the new guests arrived, and, turning aside from the road, hardly knowing what she was doing, she wandered up one of the many narrow paths leading into the tamed and placid alp. She could not return to the guest-house until she had wept. The sight of its roof emerging from the orchard actually sickened her with threats of talk, action, bustle, and she walked quickly and unseeingly in the opposite direction.

CHAPTER EIGHTEEN

Knight-errant

PRESENTLY she stopped and looked about her, recalled to herself by her quick breathing and heavily beating heart, for the ascent was steep. All around was a green meadow of long grass, surrounded on two sides by woods mingling beech and larch and on the third by a field of tall and pink-tasselled maize; the fourth side sloped steeply into woods above the lake. The air was sweet and heavy and still; there was no wind in the trees and no sound. She heard footsteps, and looked round to see Humphrey Scott coming quickly down the path towards her.

"Hullo, Mrs Lambert. Are you getting in training for Everest?"

Words and smile and the English voice were too much for her; she gulped, and began to cry.

Humphrey's admiration for self-controlled women was not so strong as to make him embarrassed when they broke down. Gently putting his arm about her, he made her sit upon a convenient log, opened her handbag for her, and waited patiently while she mopped her eyes and blew her nose—which she did almost at once, for she was ashamed of herself—and when, with composure slightly restored, she looked up at him woefully, he asked in the kindest tone possible:

"What's the matter? Or would you rather not tell me?"

He was not hoping for a hasty assurance that she would prefer not to talk. He had encountered plenty of suffering in the lives of others, even if his own had been spared it, and he was prepared to listen and if possible to help. He sat down on the log beside her and lit a cigarette, to give her time. If it were money, he had about forty pounds in Austrian *schillings* and could lend her ten; say twelve, if her need were desperate. But it was much more likely to be Meg. A kind of colour, a shaking and disturbance of his detachment, entered his mind with the thought, and he turned away from it. He smiled at Mrs Lambert.

"Better?"

"Yes, thank you. I'm sorry to be such a fool."

He said nothing, but continued to look at her encouragingly.

"It would be a comfort to talk to someone—if you're sure you don't mind. I have tried to discuss things with Hansi—Frau Schacht —but she's always so busy, and besides, I don't know why, but she doesn't want to talk about what's worrying me. It isn't anything very terrible—nothing's happened yet and perhaps won't at all— sometimes I feel I'm being an idiot to worry so over nothing—and then I start thinking and I get terrified—it's Meg and Mr Scarron— you know, that middle-aged man she is always about with. Oh, I'm *so* afraid he wants to marry her."

"But he's old enough to be her father!"

The tone was satisfyingly surprised, even indignant. It raised Mrs Lambert's spirits by many degrees: *here* was the natural response to this idea which seemed to her so monstrous; and Humphrey Scott hardly knew Meg; in fact, now that she came to think of it, they seemed to avoid one another than otherwise—so he could not be prejudiced in her favour or jealous, as Robin might have been; his was the voice of common sense, and how welcome it was.

Humphrey, meanwhile, was suffering from feelings inflamed by anger and pain, and not in the least realising it.

"Well, hardly her father—I believe he's in the early forties—but that *is* much older, of course—not that I would mind it so much if it weren't for other things—naturally, I would prefer Meg to marry someone younger—but it's his *background*, Mr Scott—he's been married to the most terrible neurotic woman whom he had to divorce—and besides—oh, I can't express myself properly—but quite the worst thing about it is that there's nothing *definitely* wrong with him—it's simply this very strong feeling I've got——"

The soft plaintive voice hurried on, mournful and monotonous as a dove's without the amorous under-note, and Humphrey listened. Did Meg love the man? That was what he must know. It was the only thing that mattered, he thought, over and over again, with unwonted heat and confusion; how could he advise the poor mother when he didn't know the most important fact in the whole situation?

"Does she care for him?" he interrupted suddenly; his voice was as quiet as usual, but the question had simply slipped out like a breath; he had to know.

She turned to him fully and distractedly.

"That's just what I don't know, Mr Scott. I'm afraid to ask her. I don't think she does. At least, she isn't behaving as she used to last year when she thought she was in love with someone——"

"Eighteen," he said, as if to himself.

"Yes . . . oh, that was only a silly boy-and-girl affair . . . but this is different, this may be serious. You see, he is rich, and I'm certain he means to marry her—he invited me there, to his house across the lake—to lunch today—I've just come back, in fact——"

She began to tell him about her visit.

He listened, gathering a picture of the house and the host from what she said, and it did sound an unsatisfactory set-up. Divorce and scenes and dog-beating. Would Meg Lambert fit happily into such a setting?

Her mother thought not, but he did not know, because he did not know Meg. He could have drawn every detail of her face from memory—except that sometimes he puzzlingly could not picture it at all—and her voice echoed in his inward ear as an unusually individual voice sometimes will, but she, the girl herself, he did not know. Their first coolness had passed over into a slightly reserved amiability, but he had never talked alone with her; their conversation was limited to commonplace remarks exchanged within the group. She did not look as if she would enjoy being Mrs Scarron, but perhaps a girl like that, with light impatient movements, usually laughing, with a face which changed its expression every few seconds, perhaps this girl who was entirely unlike the only girl whom he knew well, might take to Scarron's life like a duck to water. He thought of Ruth with a sensation of relief and peace, and then he had the idea for which he had been searching, with the practical three-quarters of his mind, while Mrs Lambert's agitated voice had been talking on and on. He let her finish, then said:

"I agree with you; it all sounds thoroughly unsatisfactory. And I don't like the look of Scarron. A bad type, I should say." He remembered how he had disliked the man when they met in the *weinstube*, and how offensive were those distant glimpses of him in his ridiculous youthful clothes, driving with her and walking with her and splashing about in that pretentious launch with her. . . . "But I don't see what I can do to help you—no, that's all right," as she murmured something about its being so good of him to let her talk to him, "but I know someone who can. Ruth, my fiancée. She'll be here at the end of next week. She's a grand girl, and she's got her head screwed on the right way, and I know she'd like to help you."

"That's very kind—how?" Mrs Lambert asked meekly.

"By being a friend to your—to Meg," Humphrey answered, his enthusiasm for the plan growing as he unfolded it, "a sort of . . . elder sister to her. She can advise her . . . and put her off Scarron, perhaps, if they get thoroughly thick and you tell Ruth all about it . . . I know she'll want to help. She's so sensible; people are always telling her their troubles."

"She sounds a dear," Mrs Lambert said doubtfully.

"She is." There was a pause. "But, you know," he said, looking at her with his honest and slightly sorrowful dark blue eyes, "she can't do much if . . . Meg . . . cares for Scarron. I mean, if she does —you wouldn't want to stop . . . things, would you?"

"Yes, I would," and the mother's tone was unhesitating and strong, "because I'm sure he'd make her unhappy. If she loves him the sooner she gets over it the better. No good can ever come of it."

"Then—you think she does?"

"I don't know," Mrs Lambert's voice was weary again, and she was sitting with her chin propped in her hand, staring at the ground. "I really don't know. It seems unlikely, because she's such a romantic child. . . ."

"Romantic?" It was the first time in his twenty-seven years that he had heard the word used without a sneering or condemnatory intonation.

"Oh yes, very romantic. Poetry, music, anything out of this world . . . Meg can't resist them . . . or anything beautiful. And though Mr Scarron could give her a very romantic *life*—he owns a palace in Venice, you know, and a house in Savoy, as well as that awful place on the other side of the lake—at least, it's awful to me— I . . . shouldn't call him a romantic *person*, would you?"

He shook his head. He was not conscious of anything but pain, welling up within him from some place once hurt but long sealed, and yet the pain was also sweet. He looked down at his clasped hands and kept silent.

"But then that boy she was so devoted to last year wasn't what I should call a romantic type either," the brooding mother-voice went on. "Sensitive, I've realised that now—but hard as well. He hurt my poor Meg very much, I'm afraid. Perhaps that's why she isn't so ready to talk about things now."

"She would tell you, I suppose, if you asked her if she cares for Scarron?" Humphrey asked, after a pause.

"Oh yes, I think so."

"Then I think you should ask her" (the "you" was almost "ye". She realised that a Scots accent had come into his voice), "and if she does, I don't think we ought to interfere (Ruth and I, that is. Of course you have the right to; you're her mother). She'd be furious with us for poking our noses in. It would be an impairrtinance. But if she doesn't think of him in that way, that's another matter and we'll be glad to help. At least, Ruth will. I'd better keep out of it," and he smiled.

Mrs Lambert returned the smile with a grateful heart. If only she had had a son! Meg was just the girl to have benefited from the authority of an elder brother. Suddenly she glanced at her watch.

"Heavens—it's nearly four—I must go. Thank you so much for being so kind. You don't know what a relief it's been, just to talk about it to someone normal—yes, I know that sounds amusing, but poor Frau Schacht is *not* normal. She's very unhappy."

"You don't regarrd unhappiness as normal, then?" He had risen when she did and was now standing looking down at her.

"Certainly not. Oh, I know that we all have to bear our share of suffering—sometimes it seems more than our share—but surely happiness is the normal thing?—or content, perhaps. It is where I come from—a small town on the coast of Devonshire; I should say we're all pretty contented."

"I come from a small town, too. But it's an industrial town in Scotland. There's a lot of unhappiness there, I'd say. We Scots are more serious than you people over the Border." But he smiled again, as if he wanted to lift the conversation.

"Yes . . . but one feels safer with serious people. . . . You think I ought to ask Meg outright what her feelings are, then?"

"I do. And then will you tell me? And if she doesn't care for him in that way, I'll tell Ruth and we'll work out a plan."

"I can't thank you enough. You've been so kind. I'll ask her this evening. Oh—I must hurry or Frau Schacht will be cross. Good-bye for now."

"Mrs Lambert"—he called to her when she had gone a few yards. She turned, with a questioning look, and he came towards her, saying, "You won't tell your daughter that you've told me all this, will you? I'm sure she wouldn't like it."

"Of course she wouldn't, the little goose," her mother said tartly, "but I have to talk to *someone*. She should behave more sensibly. . . . No, I won't tell her."

She hastened down the path, still feeling extremely worried but no longer seeing the landscape and the situation in quite such an ominous light; even the hay-manikins seemed to droop less grotesquely. She now had a friend at the *Venedig*, and when Ruth came perhaps she would have two. She suffered a pang of disloyalty at having discussed Meg's affairs with a comparative stranger, but excused herself with the thought that she had hardly been able to help herself, and that she had no close friend or relative near at hand to whom she could turn. (Not that these excuses would carry any weight with Meg if ever she found out.) Yes, Mrs Lambert was feeling better, although she was sure that neither Mr Scott nor his Ruth would be able to dissuade Meg from marrying Esmé Scarron if she made up her mind to. Her mother could only pray whole-heartedly that this might not be the case.

Humphrey was not feeling better. He remained seated upon the log for some time after she had disappeared amidst the orchards, for he had been returning from a long walk over exceedingly rough ground when they had met, and without actually being tired was ready to sit still. But he was not liking it there much; the sky laden with clouds and the hushed and heavy air depressed him, and pain was still throbbing. He sat on, musing dully about nothing in particular, and presently found depression concentrating into the thought that it was shameful for someone like Meg Lambert to be in the position she was, with her own mother not knowing whether she wanted to marry a rich old man. There ought not even to be a question of it; a lovely girl like that. Yes, she was lovely. The pain lessened slightly, as if he had drawn a relieving breath, or turned cautiously to look at something of which he had been afraid, and found it harmless. She did not look like the sort of girl who cared for money. She looked as if she cared for poetry or music, as her mother had said. Poor woman, what a state she had been in; and again the thought just touched his mind, as it had once before, that to love anyone so much as that must be a burden. He wished that Ruth were coming sooner; but she would not arrive at Martinsdorf until the end of the following week, and it would be useless to write giving her an outline of the Lamberts' problems, because she would have left England before a letter could reach her. But the situation was a simple one, and would be easy to explain to her when she did arrive. She would be willing to do what she could, he was certain, even if it were only listening to Mrs Lambert . . . that is, of course, if Meg didn't care for the man.

The bewildering sensation of pain returning, he got up quickly, and, thinking that the lake was the only place in this muffled and stifling weather, went down to it and there swam about, without pause for rest, during the next hour and a half.

CHAPTER NINETEEN

Duologues

"WHAT have you been up to, Mummy? Klara at the swimming place told me you've been out in *Lorelei* this afternoon—did you go to see Esmé?"

"Darling, I can't now—these people have just come and I must go down and help Hansi. Come up to my room after supper."

"Oh, *Mummy*—is it something awful? I'm dashing out immediately after supper with Cam and Robin, we're going to dance at some new low place he's found, and I can*not* wait to hear until we get back, it may be the Small Hours."

"I *can't* stop now, Meg. You come up to my room the minute supper's over."

In spite of a black look from Frau Schacht, Mrs Lambert slipped away during the post-prandial transformation of the dining-room, when she was supposed to be entertaining the new visitors. Meg was already in the bedroom, seriously placing and re-placing a lock of hair over her forehead in front of the glass.

"I'm in a frantic hurry, Mummy, I can't stop a second. Now what's it all about?"

Mrs Lambert, whose legs were trembling, sat down on the bed.

"Meg, I think Mr Scarron wants to marry you. Do you love him?"

"*Mummy!* Has he asked your permission? Is that why you went?"

"No, no, he hasn't asked me. But he told me all about *his* marriage and—oh, Meg, I'm so worried. Do say you don't love him, please, *please*."

"Mummy, don't *cry*. What on earth's the matter? There, let me comfort you," sitting on the bed and putting a firm young arm about her, "are you very tired?"

"No, not tired at all—at least, yes, I am; but it isn't that—oh, Meg, you don't love him, do you?"

After a torturing pause the answer came, in a doubtful tone that brought no comfort.

"No-o-o, I suppose not. At least, if I was in love with D.—and you say I wasn't—then I'm not in love with Esmé. But you're always saying friendship is three-quarters of love and I'm certainly friends with Esmé. I like him very much. I like his *mind*."

"But enough to think of marrying him, Meg?"

There followed another and longer pause. Mrs Lambert had read of hope dying within one; now she experienced it. Where was the quick and firm denial she longed for?

"I don't know," Meg said at last. She had withdrawn her arm, and was sitting slightly apart from her mother on the bed. Her hair was dressed this evening in a style different from that she usually affected: by revealing her ears, and the curve of her jaw, it made her appear older; and suddenly her mother found herself looking at an unknown young woman, solidly formed and mature, whose secretive expression might conceal any thoughts or feelings. It was a shock, but the next instant she saw Meg again and then she made an effort, and pulled herself together. She reminded herself that nothing had happened yet, not even a proposal, that Meg was still two years off twenty-one and therefore still legally a minor, that they could go home at once, and risk quarrelling with Hansi, that Meg was not the kind of girl to marry a man she merely liked. . . .

"I can imagine myself married to him," Meg said, turning to her, "which is more than I could with all my other young men . . . he's kind and he knows his own mind and he's never unkind to me, like D. was. Besides, Mummy, he has such a wonderful life. Three houses, and all in marvellously romantic places. And I could help him with his work. (I am a trained secretary, you know.) Sometimes when I think how dull my life is going to be compared with his——"

"But, darling Meg, if you married him for those reasons, can't you see that it would be all wrong? Those aren't reasons to marry a man for—not when you're someone like you. You need to love——"

"And I shouldn't marry him unless I did love," Meg interrupted, colouring, but using an uncharacteristically sedate tone which for some reason increased Mrs Lambert's apprehensions, "only he hasn't asked me to—yet."

"But he has said something that made you think he might?"

Meg nodded, and suddenly laughed, pressing her cool and scented cheek against her mother's. "He hinted," she said, getting up from the bed, "and I was simply terrified. But now I'm not. I suppose every time I see him I get to know him better. But what about this afternoon? (I really must fly, the others will be waiting.) I suppose you arranged with Hansi to pack us off on that picnic so I shouldn't see you weren't at lunch . . . what did he *say*, Mummy?"

"He told me all about his marriage and why it failed (she seems to have been a dreadful, neurotic woman) and showed me a snap of her, and then—after a lot of warning and fuss—he asked me if I thought he could make you care for him."

"But I *do* care for him; how sweet. So then what?"

"I said I thought you did. And he said he was very glad and then —then——"

"Mummy, don't cry. What *is* the matter?"

"—then I couldn't stand any more, and I got up and asked if we could have lunch because I had to get back early."

"And that was all?"

Mrs Lambert, mopping her eyes, nodded.

"Well. *How* peculiar. How—how *formal*. And then not to say anything definite after all. Extraordinary Esmé. (Not that I wish he had; not just yet, anyway. I have to *get used to the idea*.) I suppose he wanted to see how the land lay with you. Did you mind awfully? (I must go, I really must.)"

"Of course I mind, Meg, I mind terribly, I can't stand the man. The thought of you loving him—married to him—simply—I can't bear it."

"Mummy, don't be silly." Meg was now standing by the door and her expression had become sulky and cold. "Surely you aren't going to be like Hansi? Why can't you stand him? He's always charming to you."

"I know he is, that's got nothing to do with it."

"Then *why*?"

"I don't know. I don't know. But I don't trust him. Oh, why did we have to meet him? Things were going so well, we were so happy——"

"*I've* been a darned sight happier since we did meet him, anyway; he's given me a marvellous time, so don't say anything against him. *He's my friend.* You know I never allow anyone to run down my friends."

Mrs Lambert looked at her miserably.

"I'm not running him down, dear. I'm not saying anything against him; I'm only saying that *I* don't like him, *I* don't trust him. He may be very nice. But I can't *feel* he is, and I shouldn't be doing my duty if I kept my feelings about him to myself—besides, that would be impossible—I'm too worked up about it—and I've got no one to talk to——"

"Poor Mummy," but the tone was perfunctory and Meg stayed where she was by the door, "don't you think you're taking it too seriously?"

"How can I, when it may be a question of your whole future happiness?"

"You didn't take Derek seriously," said Meg, suddenly crimsoning, "and you wouldn't let me—you told me I wasn't properly in love—you *teased* me. I'll never forget it. I know you didn't mean to be unkind. But you didn't understand. You said he was an ordinary tough little boy. Well, perhaps he was, but he didn't seem like that to me, and when I found you simply didn't understand how I felt about it I shut up. I didn't *want* to talk to you very much, because parents never do understand how their children feel about love— all my friends say the same thing, even your beloved Pat who can't put a foot wrong says so—but I would have told you a lot more if you hadn't been so—so *lovingly superior*. You didn't see that it was very serious for me. You—you got so *mothery* about it, instead of being a slightly helpful friend. Now you're being mothery again, but I don't mind so much this time because—well, because I don't. My feelings are different. Besides, *with my reason* I can see it's your duty to be. Only don't run Esmé down, *please*. It's so *extraordinary* to say you're 'terrified' of him. And don't fuss, *please*. I'm not going to do anything in a hurry. But I've got very *hard* since the Derek affair, very hard indeed. I *frighten* myself sometimes, I'm so hard. And if Esmé does ask me later on to marry him, and I've thought about it carefully and worked out all the advantages and disadvantages, I may say yes. But I don't know. The only thing I want now is not to be *fussed* and *worried*. If I'm fussed and worried I may go and do something fatal like saying yes or no without thinking it over properly, so please remember that whenever you *start* fussing and worrying. And now I really must go or Robin will drag Cam off without me—he's properly got his foot on the poor child's neck, she's crazy about him, silly her—so do cheer up, Mummy"—here she swooped across the room and bestowed a cross peck on Mrs Lambert's cheek—"and for goodness' sake no hard feelings."

The door slammed and the mother heard the light steps race down the wooden stairs and die away.

She sat, crying, on the bed, at one moment thinking how foolish she was being, and at the next overcome once more with *unbearable* fears.

Meg's remarks had not upset her so much as one unaccustomed to the ways of young girls might have supposed: her hardness existed, Mrs Lambert suspected, largely in her imagination as the result of histrionic wishful thinking; and the attack on her mother's attitude during the Derek Jones affair had only confirmed Mrs Lambert's own suspicion that she herself had not behaved as wisely as she might have done while it was in progress. She *had* been mothery rather than slightly-helpful-friendly. She admitted it. She had been too distressed by Meg's unhappiness to see clearly, and had acted from common sense and experience rather than from imagination, and, as she had proved again and again during nearly nineteen years, in dealing successfully with Meg imagination was the master-key.

But none of that mattered . . . it was a pity, but it was past and could not be altered . . . and much of what Meg had said was just youth and hot air . . . but what stood out from that speech of hers, what could not be ignored or dismissed or explained away however much the mother wanted to ignore or dismiss or explain it away, was the fact that Meg was prepared, in certain circumstances, to marry Esmé Scarron.

Terrifying, but true; she had said so, and she had also said that she would not marry him without loving him. It was not so bad as hearing that she did love him, but it was worse than anything Mrs Lambert had expected, because, all the time, she had been hoping for an exceedingly emphatic denial, which should make the very suggestion into a good joke.

It had not come; and the thing had been said; and here she sat, trying to think what to do next.

But she could not think; she was too old, too tired, and too worried; she could only sit there silently in the rapidly falling dusk, staring at the pale distant mountains that seemed a barrier shutting her away from all familiar things.

*   *   *   *   *

"Well, are you better?"

"Yes. I've been asleep a lot. I seem to sleep all day as well as all night."

"Good. And you've been taking the stuff I gave you?"

"Yes. Oh yes. Every morning and every evening. I swear I have."

"There, you see. I promised it would make you better. And now you can go to your mother. Hullo? Are you there?"

"Yes . . . I'm sorry . . . I got the flex-thing tangled with my heel, I'm wearing my lovely new Perugia shoes . . . oh, you said I can go to Mother . . . how soon? Please when can I go?"

"To-night, if you like. Yes—telephone her and tell her you're coming to-night. Get a gondola and go as soon as you're packed. What's the matter now?"

"It's my lovely new gauze nylon dress with the red and gold stripes. Can I pack it without crushing it? I could get some tissue-paper——"

"Get the servants to help you. Where's Constanza? Isn't she there? I've just been speaking to her——"

"Yes, I'll ask Constanza, and can I ask her for some money to give Andrea, to get a gondola——"

"Yes, yes, I don't care what you do or arrange, but get away as quickly as you can."

"You know when we heard that opera in Philadelphia. The Queen of the Night had a lovely dress. Mine's just like hers, only short, not long, like the one she had. Have you told Mother I'm coming?"

"Andrea has. I told him to telephone her at once."

"Is she quite well now? Not ill any more, poor Mother?"

"Yes, she's well again."

"It's such a lovely dress. I hope they won't——"

"Go and get ready *now*. I don't care what you do, but you're to go as quickly as possible."

"I suppose . . . there isn't a letter from America, is there?"

"Don't begin on that all over again. Hurry up and get out—or I shan't let you go."

"I'll go and see if my dress will be all right . . . and I'll ask Andrea to get a gondola——"

"Yes, yes, but hurry. Get away as quickly as you can, I don't want you staying there."

"Are you coming down for the Festival?"

"Not this year, no. And I don't want you there either . . . the house needs cleaning . . . there are repairs to be done . . . it won't be fit to live in. Now go, can't you? Hurry—get away."

CHAPTER TWENTY

High Osterwitz

THE following morning, Humphrey lingered behind when most of the guests were leaving the *speisesaal* after breakfast, and Mrs Lambert, wearing a most abstracted look, was beginning to help Maria with clearing the tables. He read his two letters and smoked, defying a bright remark from Frau Schacht that it was a pity not to get out at once on such a fine day, and when Mrs Lambert reached his table, he got up.

"Oh, don't let me disturb you, please—I can clear round you——"

"It's all right, I was just going. Er—are you feeling any better to-day?"

He was unused to situations caused by, and filled with, complex emotions, and he did not know what was the best thing to say in this one, but neither had he any thoughts of going back on his commitments made yesterday. During the night it had occurred to him more than once that it would be best if the wretched little girl did love Scarron, because that would save them all a lot of trouble, but this idea had brought about such an onset of the peculiar bewildering pain, half-mental and half-emotional, which he had experienced during his previous conversation with Mrs Lambert that he had seriously wondered if he were sickening for something? The restless night had left him this morning with one overriding feeling: he called it curiosity. Did she love Scarron? He had to know. That was why he had lingered over his breakfast.

Mrs Lambert looked at him vacantly for a moment.

"Oh! No, thank you, not much, I'm afraid. It's nice of you . . . but I've been thinking things over and I really don't see why you should be bothered with my troubles——"

"That's all right. Did you ask her?"

It was an interruption, in an abrupt tone. It occurred to Mrs Lambert, looking gently at him, that his background must be humbler than she had supposed.

"Yes. And she doesn't know yet. Isn't it dreadful? I would almost sooner have heard the worst. To go on like this perhaps for weeks——"

"What did she say?"

Another interruption. And he looked quite pale; perhaps he was annoyed at being drawn into the difficulties of a comparative stranger.

"Sh'sh——" Mrs Lambert glanced down into the garden where Meg and another girl stood talking to Robin Gascoine, then told him very briefly what Meg had said.

"So there's nothing to be done, I'm afraid," she concluded in a depressed tone, while she shook and folded the cloth, "except to wait, and not fuss her, as she said." She glanced at him; he was staring down at the table, with an expression about his mouth which she had not seen there during the six weeks or so of their acquaintanceship. He is hurt, she thought in great surprise, and said quickly:

"It was good of you to suggest asking your—your dear girl to help me. I appreciated it so much. But I don't think it's fair on her. She's coming out here for a holiday; why should she be burdened with other people's troubles? I expect she works hard, like most girls nowadays——"

"She's receptionist to a doctor. Yes, she does work hard. Of course, she won't work after we're married."

"No." Mrs Lambert looked at him approvingly. "I think you are very wise. So many young couples . . . but she mustn't be bothered with Meg. I'll manage somehow."

"Don't you mind about it any more?" he demanded, so rudely that she gaped at him in astonishment, and at that moment Frau Schacht approached.

"Now, Mr Scott, about to-morrow. Are you going with the others? I am planning an excursion to Osterwitz, the famous castle where the Turkish armies were turned back from Europe in the sixteenth century; it is a wonderful sight; the Tommies stationed out here call it Snow-White's Castle, and I believe Disney did use it for his film. Or perhaps you would prefer to wait until Miss Courtney comes and go with her?—though of course the castle is well worth a second visit—but to-morrow the weather is sure to be good. Meg is going, and Robin, and Camilla Seton, and the French boy, I cannot remember his name, and Mitzi——"

"All right. I'd like to go," Humphrey said in his usual tone, "thank you, Frau Schacht."

"Robin is conducting the party, as his German is the best and he has been there before."

"So has Meg," put in Mrs Lambert, "but she is longing to see it again. She says it's quite out of this world."

"You will not like the plumbing there," Frau Schacht said darkly, "it also is out of this world; it is of the sixteenth-century world. However, that is unimportant. Good, then. I will make packed lunches for six people. Eve, can you spare me a moment?" and she walked springily off.

There was silence for a minute, then Humphrey said:

"I'm sorry, Mrs Lambert. I'm a bit off-colour this morning; liver, I expect. Now don't worry any more about it. I know Ruth will want to help you. She's a great family girl; there are seven of them, and she keeps an eye on all the younger sisters. I'll tell her about it and we'll do what we can."

"It *is* kind of you. I'm so worried. I've never known Meg be quite like this before. She frightens me. She seems so much older."

There's room for that, Humphrey thought dourly.

"It's really a question, I feel, of preventing things from coming to a head in the next weeks, before we go home," she went on, in that soft and hesitating voice which seemed incapable of firmly announcing a decision. "We go down to Venice in a fortnight, and we shall be there for two weeks, seeing what we can of the sights, and then we come back here for a week to pack up and say good-bye. If only I can stop him proposing before then, or upsetting our plans——"

"We ought to try to keep her from seeing so much of him," said Humphrey, with the strongest feeling that this was desirable.

"I quite agree, but it's so difficult. . . ."

They talked for a little while, making suggestions and dropping them. Neither felt at ease, for Mrs Lambert thought that he was handicapped in his attempts to help her by knowing so little about Meg, and by the fact that he did not share her irrational fear of Scarron; and Humphrey was now seriously disturbed and alarmed. He seemed to have become a different person, with no control over the unfamiliar feelings which were continually overwhelming him. Most of them were too vague to be identified; all were uncomfortable; and he was also convinced, over and above them all, that sooner or later something disastrous was going to happen. At mid-morning he went upstairs and took two tablets of aspirin.

★   ★   ★   ★   ★

"I do like the theory that this is a *shady* road. Has Frau Schacht Bedouin blood, does anyone know?"

They were creeping over the long, white dusty approach to Osterwitz, in the midst of a still, rich and silent landscape that might have been the background in a mediæval miniature. The sky lacked even the thinnest shred of cloud and was coloured the dark clear blue of a sapphire, and in it flashed and flamed the merciless sun. There were no cars on the smooth hedgeless roads; no walkers; no peasants at work in the widely spreading fields. The neat white village into which the train had deposited them half an hour ago, after two hours' slow travelling on wooden seats, had seemed asleep. Now, three miles away across the plain whence round, wooded mountains soared abruptly into the sky, it looked lonely and small and lost amidst the majestic land. And tantalisingly far-off still, winding its grey wall round the steepest of the mountains and crowning the summit with fantastic turrets, High Osterwitz seemed to look down haughtily upon their slow approach.

The question had come from Robin.

"Without doubt she has said this to encourage us to make the excursion. For me, I do not care. I am of the South."

"For me, I do not care either, Marcel. I am of the Gloucestershire and I like the heat. But I detest, I really detest, walking."

"Let me have my sandwiches back." It was a murmur from the unusually small girl, dressed in white shorts and blouse, who was walking lightly at his side.

"Mammy Gascoine *like* carry Missy Camilla's sandwiches. But her po' feet done give her gyp (whatever gyp may be. So disturbing to realise how little our generation understands of its parents' slang? Necking, hefty, bung-ho, ripping, gyp. Gibberish, isn't it?)."

Camilla Seton turned upon him her large ice-blue eyes brimming with admiration, but said nothing. Her silence, which she seldom broke and then only to murmur pleasingly, was one of the qualities he found charming in her, but he never told her so, for it was not his habit to reward his girl friends with compliments or praise.

Humphrey glanced at Meg, who was also walking in silence, her face partly hidden by a coolie hat whose exaggeratedly severe line cut the soft lines of her profile. Beneath it, he knew, her expression was mysterious and remote. He knew this expression well; he had seen it visit her face again and again during the past weeks, and always it gave him the same wish: to break its calm, and bring her out of her secret retreat to look at him.

"Are you tired?" he asked now.

She shook the absurd and beautiful hat. "Only thirsty," came a murmur out of it.

"Nebber mind, chillun. Soon we all be dere—and den what high-jinks. ('Jinks'—there we go again. What are, or was, a jink?) Clam picnics, fish-frys . . . I hope no one will ask me to eat anything fried, in this heat." He turned suddenly and addressed Humphrey, whose disturbed state he maliciously suspected. "Does it remind you of Malaya?"

"It was hotter than this in Malaya," Humphrey said mildly.

He was hardly observant of the discomfort, being so intent upon keeping the place next to Meg which he had taken, apparently without design, almost from their departure. He had had some idea of asking her about Scarron; now he had realised that the plan had been absurd, and was forgetful of everything but that he was walking beside her. He still felt peculiar. He was unreasonably happy, for instance, and if he did happen to glance at the mountains, or at one of the majestic white barns with their window screens of pierced and fretted grey woodwork which graced the roadside farmyards, they appeared to him as beautiful, which was a word he never used. Meg had spoken only a few sentences to him, but her manner had lost its coolness, and several times they had laughed together; he was carrying her sandwiches.

"*V'la!* The shades!" Marcel exclaimed, as they turned round the corner formed by some lofty farm buildings on either side of the road, and found themselves confronting an ascending avenue of beeches.

"Have we got to sweat up there?" demanded Mitzi, a plain and plump Viennese who wore her silly clothes with immense dash. Her English was as idiomatic and expressive as Robin's own.

"We have," he now said resignedly. "Would you like a rest first?"

to Camilla, who shook her blonde head and went on up the sloping track, from which projected worn and polished stones.

"Then come on, all you Fascist dogs," as he followed her, "if that fragile little woman can do it, you can."

"Has there a *restaurant* at the sommet?"

"There has, with waitresses flitting about in sixteenth-century velvets. Ask Meg; she's had it all before."

"Yes, poor things. Imagine, in this weather," and Meg turned to Humphrey, who only nodded.

She was slightly surprised at his remaining attached to herself, but did not think much about it because the heat was making her drowsy and disinclined for conversation, while the landscape, this flat green and golden plain studded with round blue mountains and enclosed as if in a wall by loftier grey ones, was imposing upon her its pure and romantic spell. Although the Middle Ages, with their attendant panoply of knights, armour, castles and chivalry, usually did not enter her imagination, a fairy-tale version of all these things, softened by fancy, had presented itself to her from her first sight of Hochosterwitz. Now, as they ascended the crudely paved slope which in a very short time seemed to have carried them high above the plain, she began to feel the spell strongly once more and to wish to share it with someone, and when they were approaching the first of the lofty archways that pierced at intervals the thick walls, she turned to Humphrey with enthusiasm.

"Look—isn't it thrilling? I don't know who that is—some old Austrian lordling—but it says that this castle is where the Turks were halted on their invasion of Europe. Can you read Latin?"

They had paused beneath the arch, and were looking up at the carved inscription high above their heads with the portrait in stone, both newly restored to their original freshness, of a nobleman in ruff and armour; the rest of the party had drawn ahead of them and were out of sight, though their voices and laughter were audible.

"Well—*read* it—no. I've learnt it. I dropped it when I went to Edinburgh and started specialising. Can you?"

"Not really. I did do it for my General Certificate, but I failed. I can remember some, though——"

They stood there for ten minutes or so, spelling out the inscription and translating. The sounds made by the others receded, and nothing broke the hot, still silence except their own hesitant voices and occasionally Meg's laughter. Humphrey felt no inclination to laugh. The haunting beauty of the place and the strangeness of being alone with her weighed upon his spirits. He began to have a fierce longing that this day should go on for ever, but he saw no signs of similar agitation in her, and when they resumed the ascent he felt almost angry with her for being unmoved.

The slope wound on, past platforms of stone that had once served the castle's garrison as look-out posts whence to scan the mighty plain beneath; past low crenellated battlements standing above sheer and dizzying drops into space filled with green boughs and leaves and darting birds; and always there was the sensation of being lifted high in the clear blue air; high, high above the plain, so that one was master of it; the yellow, green and blue plain whose miniature mountains must so often have hidden the troop of knights and men-at-arms that crept out slow and glittering from concealment, raising the tocsin and the shout of alarm on the battlements of High Osterwitz a thousand feet above. And the turbaned Turk . . . strange, how strange, to imagine scimitars and dark-skinned faces and the headgear shaped like a tulip amidst these pines and the cool meadows of Europe. . . .

"They must be at the top by now," he observed at last, when their leisurely journey, broken by frequent pauses to inspect inscriptions or admire the view, had brought them on to an expanse of turf, sweeping up to a high wall with turrets showing above it.

"And drinking *apfelsaft* probably. How few people there are to-day; it's the heat, I expect; when we came the other time, with Kristin and Helga and those Austrian boys, there were masses of tourists. But hardly any English. This really is too off the beaten track for them . . . but isn't it a lovely place? And aren't you glad you came?"

He nodded, with a strained smile, and Meg emerged for a moment from her dreamy and poetic satisfaction to feel sorry for him. She would not have asked such a candid and ingenuous question of Robin, fearing a cutting reply, but she had discovered, even in the brief time they had been alone together, that Humphrey seemed more approachable than Robin, and she had not hesitated to ask him indirectly whether all were well with him. He did not look happy. Perhaps he was wishing that his girl were here; Meg could readily understand that such surroundings might make one long for one's beloved, although she had gradually formed the impression— it would be difficult to explain why—that the engagement was not a romantic one. Perhaps it was because both the parties were past what she and Rosemary called their first youth? But *he* was far nicer than she had at first supposed; he was neither condescending nor snooty when one came to talk with him alone, and she found his company agreeable.

"Meg," said Camilla in her soft debbish voice, drawing her aside as soon as they emerged into the high-walled courtyard crowning the summit, "the bog . . . it's quite unutterable." (Camilla, sister to five brothers, commanded a vocabulary strikingly at variance with her appearance.) "We waited for you. If two of us pass out cold, the other can give the alarm."

When they emerged looking somewhat green a little later, they found the young men seated at one of the long benches arranged beneath the chestnut trees that made agreeable shade in the yard, and were told that refreshments had already been ordered. They sat quietly, enjoying the coolness and shadow of the trees after the toil of the ascent, and looking about them.

This was the central point of the castle, around which its numerous stone halls and cells were clustered, and here the view of the plain—which was never out of the mind of one who stood in the castle, just as the castle could not be ignored by one standing in the plain—was shut out by the colonnaded, white-washed buildings surrounding the courtyard on three sides; on the fourth, a high wall approached by wooden steps led the unwary beholder to such a view as stopped the breath, though at this height, and, as it were, deliberately set and produced, the plain did not appear so mysteriously romantic as when seen through some ragged gap in the walls lower down. There stood in one corner an old well, with massive iron winding-wheel and wooden roof; beech and chestnut cast green shadows upon the white dusty ground, and on one side of the yard there had been constructed a buffet, where bread and butter, cold meats and cooling drinks were served by the waitresses whose dusty velvets and hair worn in long plaits had been described by Robin. They also, inevitably, sold postcards and a little guide-book.

"Now what else is there to see, Meg?" demanded Mitzi, putting *salami* into her mouth at a great rate, "you have been here before. Don't let us waste our money on seeing a lot of rubbish."

"I think your uncle is so rich," said Marcel.

"So he is, but that's no reason for wasting the money he gives me. What is there, Meg?"

"Oh . . . a lot of rooms with armour in and one huge suit of it that belonged to a giant . . . rather horrid, really . . . armour always makes me feel bad when I see it close, I don't know why. I'd much rather imagine it——"

"You are too delicate for this world, my floweret, that's the explanation. Fill yourself up with another great grey-green greasy slab of liver sausage—here," and Robin passed her the plate.

"Armour—yes—what else?"

"The chapel is simply beautiful. There's a wall-painting of the Last Supper. You ought really to see that."

"All right. Anything else?"

"Various weapons and things. I forget; very boring."

"You needn't see them again if you don't want to. Marcel—are you coming?—Robin?—and you?" turning to Humphrey.

"Calm yourself, my dear Mitzi. No one is going to move for another hour yet. And look—here comes the Amalgamated Wood Carvers Union, out on its annual beanfeast (why bean? I ask myself), and they will all have to be fed and watered before they make the rounds. Let's go when they go. You're so exhaustingly energetic. Relax," Robin said.

Mitzi's broad face smiled at him with some vexation and she shook back her crop of black curls, but the peace in the courtyard won the day, and she remained there without protest for the next half-hour, while a few tourists made their way in from the hot pathway from time to time, panting and mopping their brows, and the twenty or so men in dark suits, whom Robin had guessed to be woodworkers, sat in a group at one table, refreshing themselves and chatting. Their pale faces, high cheekbones and light blue eyes, together with the blond hue of their hair, gave them the appearance of belonging to one family, but presently it appeared that they were united only by music. Their leader, a stout man in late middle-life, mounted a bench and announced to the handful of tourists, the waitresses and the two castle guides who were waiting under the colonnade, that this was the choir of—he named what Mitzi said was a small town near Salzburg—and would now sing; their song would be about Austria.

So they stood up, with bared light heads under the shade of the chestnuts, and rolled forth a yearning yet stirring ballad with a moving refrain—*Homeland, homeland*—while their stern faces, resembling mediæval images carved in pale wood, were irradiated by a pure passion. Heard in this place that was an epitome of Austria's past, with the still and lovely plain extending its richness even to the distant mountains, the song could not fail to stir its hearers, and when it ceased, and the choir stood at attention as if hearing the last echo winging its way across the fields and villages and woods, and scattering a blessing upon them as it went, there was enthusiastic clapping.

"So touching," observed Marcel, who had not joined in it, "and what a dangerous people. Moved so easily."

Mitzi turned to him, and her expression had the quality of a comment, but she did not speak.

"Myself, I find all this—*la patrie, la gloire* and so on—*ennuyant*. And difficult. I do not know it—understand it. No one at home talked like this now. If you are talking like this about the homeland, soon you are fighting with somebody. And no one now has this energy to fight." Marcel buried his large clever nose in his tankard of lager while his supercilious eyelids almost closed over his eyes.

"But it was so beautiful!" Meg leant forward earnestly. "I'm sure they weren't thinking about fighting anybody, they were only thinking about singing well and loving Austria."

"You are idealist, mademoiselle," Marcel said pleasantly.

"Mitzi, come off the boil and let's have it," said Robin, tapping the table for silence.

"Well, nationalism is poison, of course, like Fascism," she began in a sensible tone. "It'll have to be rooted out of human nature before we can have the brotherhood of man——"

"Communism is poison, too," Robin interrupted, "and what's worse, it's a bore. But go on."

"And the sentimental love of one's own country is a disguised form of nationalism. I suffer from this myself, as a matter of fact. I'm struggling with it all the time. I've only got to hear an Austrian name when I'm abroad and I go all mushy. While they were singing just now I had tears in my eyes and a lump in my throat (I shall have to take my contact lenses out, they're getting uncomfortable——)"

"Oh, Mitzi, do you wear contact lenses? Do let me look—I've never seen anyone wearing them before. . . ."

Mitzi leaned across the table, and with an abstracted expression submitted her large brown eyes to Meg's interested inspection while she continued:

"Do you know what the Fascists did to my parents? You needn't mind hearing, I don't remember anything about it because I was only two years old when it happened. We lived in one of the flats in those blocks for workers that the Socialists built in Vienna; they were the first of their kind in Europe and the Socialists were so proud of them . . . I've read about it. Well, I was staying with my uncle in 1933, my father's brother, because he and my aunt hadn't any children and loved to have me with them, and while I was away civil war broke out in Vienna, and the Fascists bombarded the workers' flats with guns and both my parents were killed. I never went back there again, my uncle adopted me, and as he's always been rich—even in the war he managed somehow, though he is half-Jewish (I'm one-quarter Jewish, I expect you'd guessed?)—I've always lived on the fat of the land. We were in Sweden all through the war. Every comfort. But I'm an internationalist. I may get lumpy in the throat about Austria, but I believe so passionately in the brotherhood of man that it dries all my tears up. I feel too much, and when I think about *that* I can't cry. And if Austria has to be swallowed up because we're all going to be brothers and no more war, then I shan't mind in the very least. I want some more lager," and she turned and beckoned fiercely to the waitress.

"Isn't it going to be rather dull when we're all dressed in sage-green kilts and talking Esperanto?" Robin asked in an exaggerated drawl, and Camilla giggled.

"You British are so frivolous. It's heart-rending," Mitzi said. "I'm not such a fool as to think you're really decadent, I know you only like to give that impression, but *why* do you like to give it? It's so . . . so . . . *frivolous.* Now the French," rounding upon Marcel, "really *are* decadent."

He contented himself with a silent and mocking bow, and Robin said, "Oh, come. And if we are frivolous and Marcel is decadent, you're tediously serious, Mitzi dear. I *do* think the b. of m. is going to be dull; very dull. *I* intend to take a stab at propping up the tottering British Commonwealth, and in my spare time I shall do something quite too ornately useless like collecting old lace or those snowstorm-things you get in paper-weights, and when I'm not do-ing that I shall be secretly Saving the Situation, probably ending up by doing a Burgess-Maclean on you all. . . . So that's going to be my line. What's yours, Marcel?"

"Please? Ah, my job. Well, I am to go into the business of my father who make motor-cars."

"How very scriptural. But that wasn't quite what I meant. What do you want from life?"

"Girls. I like this *very* much." When the laughter had ceased, Robin turned to Camilla.

"Cam?"

"Horses, I suppose. A riding-school in Somerset. But dancing is heaven, too." Faint colour had come into her face, because it was a question which, answered frankly, would have had at the head of the list Robin himself.

"I hope to cure you of liking those unattractive animals. Meg?"

"I want a wonderful life," she answered at once, putting her elbows on the table and settling her chin upon her hands while she looked smilingly round. "I would like to work in an interesting job for a few years, and then I would like to meet someone who suited me exactly and who I suited. I would like to be their best friend, and to love them as well, and after we were married, I would like to stay in love with them, and they with me, until we were both old. I'd like three children: two boys and a girl. I want my husband never to love anyone but me, and I would be the same with him, because that's my idea of what's truly romantic. And that's what I want from life."

A silence had grown up while she was speaking. The leaves of the chestnut tree swayed in a passing breeze, sending their shadows over her as she talked, and Humphrey listened. This was the most beautiful moment of his life; he was back in the country of his lost fairy-tales, and yet the simple words belonged to every day, and what kept him motionless, what even subdued his breathing, was the knowledge that what she described was within reach. Hers was the voice of incarnate womanhood, uttering without mockery or pretence or fear its heart's desire, and that desire was what the ancient poets had called married bliss. The next instant he thought, *she doesn't care for Scarron or she couldn't talk like that*, and then with a leap forward of his thoughts that came upon him with the effect of actual and recognisable light—*I could give her that. I could give her what she wants.*

Nobody spoke for a moment after Meg had ceased. Then Robin said:

"That's very sweet, Meg. No, I mean it. Victorian, of course, but sweet. Only you won't get it, you know. Men aren't like that."

Three pairs of eyes were turned upon him, not so much wistfully, as doubtfully. How far was he in a position to know?

"Some of them are," Humphrey said, speaking for the first time in half an hour, and his voice sounded deeper and calmer than those of the two younger men, "and some of them feel that way about women. So stick to your ideas."

Meg turned to him in surprise, and the confrontation of her face to face, the meeting of her large, soft, shining eyes, seemed to kindle within him a blaze, mingling sweetness and pain.

"Are you that sort of man?" It was Mitzi, of course, leaning towards him with the liveliest interest, but Robin, getting up from the table, said:

"Now, now—none of your Viennese analysis here, please; this is a beanfeast. Come on, the Wood Carvers Union is about to receive the works," and he led the way to the colonnade, where the guides were beginning to usher their audience into the castle.

During the tour of the rooms Meg loitered on the edge of the crowd, sometimes amusing herself by seeing how much she could understand of the guide's recital and sometimes watching the faces of her friends as they listened (how Robin's changed, when he was using his brain! bones seemed to emerge from its somewhat amorphous structure and his cleverness was made plain). Mitzi kept close to the guide and continually asked questions, some of which caused him to shake his head with a bewildered smile; Marcel studied the exhibits with an expression implying that these things were ordered better in France, and Camilla looked at Robin. Humphrey Scott looked at the guide, but as if he were not listening, and as the procession moved slowly through the long bare rooms, with walls of white-washed stone and floors of dusty wood beams, Meg found herself slightly bored, and studying Humphrey because she had begun to think about him. He was much more agreeable than she had supposed, and she regretted not having discovered this earlier; also, she suspected that he liked to be with her, and this could not but recommend him. She wondered what Ruth looked like, and whether she would fit in with the crowd after she had spent the first few days of her visit alone with Humphrey, and then, being full of lager and fresh air and mildly depressed by the barbarous implements arrayed on every side, she yawned, and heard with relief the guide saying that they would now view the chapel.

When they emerged from that small, gilded baroque casket, the shadows were beginning to lengthen and there was a general consulting of watches and arguing about trains. Meg walked away from the group and, mounting the wooden steps below the crenellated wall, leaned upon it and gazed out across the plain. In the solemn evening light it appeared even more beautiful than at midday. The woods covering its mountains were now blue and veiled in delicate mist, and the stupendous shadows that lay across it so dwarfed the villages that the eye overlooked them. The sky overhead was blue, but towards the west it deepened into a peach-like yellow that coloured the distant peaks, and the entire landscape seemed to breathe forth a kind of pride in its own beauty, a slumbrous menacing pride—but there were no words to catch that spirit in.

"Have you any preference about getting the seven-fifteen or the eight-ten?" It was Humphrey, coming up the steps towards her.

"No, I don't think so," looking at him vaguely. "Why? What is it—trains?"

"I've been sent to ask your opinion. Some of them want to stay a bit later."

"Oh yes. The eight-whatever-it-was, the later one," she said, smiling, and turned away once more.

"Beautiful . . ." he said, lingering, half-ready to descend; he spoke in a low tone, almost cautiously, looking sideways towards the plain.

Meg nodded. "It's like—(do you know that poem?)

> It is a beauteous evening, calm and free,
> The holy time is quiet as a Nun
> Breathless with adoration . . .

but then it goes on about the sea; the sun going down over the sea; and I never saw a place so—so *far* from the sea as this, did you? It looks like the heart of the earth."

She was turning back to the plain once more, as if unable to withdraw her eyes from it, when the stillness of his position arrested her attention, and she paused, looking at him. As she looked, he turned slowly from his contemplation of the landscape, and looked up at her. At once she was afraid. She had never before seen helplessness in a young man's eyes. She turned quickly away, pressing herself more closely against the stone wall and trying to lose herself again in the awe-inspiring splendour of the plain, and after a moment, during which he saw her profile outlined against the sky and coloured by the glow of evening, he turned and went back to the others.

Meg remained there, feeling disturbed, and with her pleasure in the hour and the place somewhat marred. She did not consciously wonder whether he were becoming attracted to her; apprehension took the form of remembering, persistently, and without pause during the homeward journey, that he was engaged to someone else.

CHAPTER TWENTY-ONE

Carnation

"But you don't look as fit as I expected."

The dreaded words, which Humphrey had been anticipating since his first glimpse of Ruth on Villach station half an hour ago, were not spoken until the evening bus, overladen as usual with talkative peasants, had carried himself and Ruth and her luggage as far as the head of the lake. He ought to have had time enough to think of a soothing reply. As it was, he looked down at the tickets he held and said, "Don't I?"

"No." Sparkling eyes of light hazel surveyed him affectionately. "You've lost weight and you're drawn-looking. Have you been sitting up all night learning German?"

"No; I'm usually in bed by half-past ten. This air makes one sleepy. I can't imagine why I should look 'drawn'—if I do."

There was an edge on his voice. He knew that it was most imprudent to let it sound, but he could not control it. It was bad enough to have her sitting next to him; arrived; here; safely set down in Austria for the next three weeks, when he was in the state of mind that he was, without having her commenting on his appearance.

She herself looked, as usual, the picture of trimness and health, in a linen suit that had successfully avoided getting crushed on the journey, with that vivid colour in her cheeks suggesting a carnation that has just played—and won—a hard game of tennis. Her large eyes (they were the flat kind, whose size suggests that it is merely a physical accident and has nothing to do with an emotional temperament) were as usual china-blue in the whites. Her head, to which the short brown hair sat closely, was the best-dressed in the bus. He told himself that it was grand to have her here at last, dear old Ruthie, and felt himself a kind of murderer.

"Poor old boy," she said after a pause, "I'll soon cheer you up now I'm here," and put her capable hand in its tan glove over his and squeezed it. It was rather a rough squeeze, and all he could give in response was a smile which seemed to him the epitome of falseness. He made an effort.

"It's grand to have you here."

"It's grand to be here. Dear old Cat," she said in a quieter tone. Then, slipping her arm through his, she looked out of the window, noticing everything with interest, and commenting, breaking off her remarks occasionally to answer his questions about the health and welfare of her family. Humphrey had seized upon this topic with a relief which alarmed himself: was he not going to be able to talk to her, as well as not wanting her to be here? Poor Ruth, poor girl, who had got herself engaged to the blackest swine unhung.

And the questions that he had dreaded were all asked; retribution did not spare him a single one. What were the people in the house like? Anybody nice? Oh, mostly very young, just now. Nice kids, were they? A decent bunch? Would they leave them to themselves or would they be inclined to tag on? He had not said much, in his recent letters, about his fellow-guests.

He answered without embarrassment; that is, he concluded he must have, because she made no unusual comment upon anything that he said. He managed to mention the baby of the party, a rather pretty girl of nineteen. He wished the journey were over and Ruth safely introduced to the *Venedig*'s guests; he wished that she need never meet them; he wished that she had never come, and that he were still tracking Reds in Malaya, and then he began wondering— as the bus drew to a halt outside the *weinstube*, and as he had been wondering since that day at Osterwitz which had revealed to him what was the matter with him—what, in heaven or on earth, he was going to do about the situation in which he found himself?

Ruth was pleased with her first sight of the guest-house, standing amidst orchard trees now covered with the dark green foliage of late August, and surrounded by winding paths of white chalk; she liked her large airy bedroom with the balcony, sheltered by a heart-shaped eave, that looked out upon the lake; she did not like the look, at first sight, of Frau Schacht, over whom her tall height towered, and who had to look up at her when they shook hands; but she hoped to like her better, and she did like the look of Herr Schacht, whose story she knew. As for the kids, they seemed a nice crowd and not too noisy. Mrs Lambert seemed nice, too, but nervy.

"What a dear girl; such a friendly manner; I took to her at once. Meg, didn't you think Miss Courtney charming?" Mrs Lambert was performing the evening metamorphosis of the *speisesaal*, with the others rather languidly assisting.

It must be recorded with regret that Meg made a face. She was reclining in a deck-chair, half in the room and half on the balcony, waiting for Esmé Scarron to call for her; they were going to dine with some of his American friends at St Maria-am-Ossiachersee. It struck her mother, nervously regarding her, that she had begun to bloom dangerously during the last few days. So did girls sometimes look who were about to get engaged.

"The Head Pre.," murmured Robin, folding tablecloths. "We shall all have to pull up our socks."

"I can't stand that sensible type," Meg said, "it makes me feel such a fool."

"Very sporty type, no?" said Marcel, where he knelt by the *armoire* putting away the bread.

"Spor*ting*, not sporty. 'Tisn't the same thing at all," said Robin, and Camilla, who was sitting on the floor idly twisting the ends of her savagely short hair, uttered her childish giggle.

"Meg, you look nice to-night," Robin went on.

Meg glanced down absently at the black taffeta dress, sleeveless, and shaped like a chemise, which set off the beauty of her arms and throat. "It's one of Mummy's efforts; she's made me a pink one like it, too. Do I look nice?"

"Yes. Quite by accident, of course. Mitzi, isn't Meg the worst-dressed girl you know?"

"Yes, but she's such a charmer it doesn't matter," and when Meg's scream of resentment had died away, they heard the luxurious noise made by Esmé Scarron's car, coming up to the gate at the end of the garden.

"I'm off. Cam, give me my stole ... thanks ... no, Mummy darling, I *don't* know what time, but Esmé will take care of me ... good-bye, everyone."

But she did not hurry from the room, and they all noticed it. She walked, even slowly, as if reluctant to go, and in the garden they saw her pause and take a long, dreamy look up at the half-moon floating above the wooded peaks before making her way down the path.

There followed a little silence. Then Robin said: "Don't yo' trouble yo'self, Mis' Lambert. All us niggers can't 'bide Mus' Scarron, can we, black trash?" and he appealed to the others.

Mrs Lambert's nerves had not grown any stronger under the pressure of the past week, and when she saw three heads decidedly shaken, and three thumbs, as if by arrangement, turned downwards in silent condemnation, the unexpected support touched her to tears.

"Don't worry. I'm sure it's going to be all right," said Mitzi, "and soon you'll be in Venice, and have a whole fortnight without him."

"Does he not make to show you his *palazzo* there?" Marcel asked.

Mrs Lambert shook her head. "It's being repaired or having water pumped out of the cellars or something. Anyway, he apologised to Meg for not showing it to us. I'm very relieved, of course."

"I marvel that he doesn't intend to show you all the other sights, though, including what I once heard an American call 'the dogie's palace'," Robin said.

"He says he is too busy with his book on Paracelsus to spare the time, much as he would like to."

"Such a sad disappointment. Camilla, would *you* like to come for a walk?"

Camilla scrambled up, her face expressing none of the pleasure she felt, and as they went out of the room Robin said, "We must avoid the path by the church. The Head Pre. has taken her man along it."

Humphrey and Ruth were, at that moment, walking arm-in-arm down the winding way that led, through meadows and under thick shadowy trees, to the lonelier part of the alp. The air was warm; the stars were out; a mingling of afterglow, twilight, and faint moonlight gave to the darkening slopes of grass and the little wooden houses with their glowing windows a look of unreality, or of reality belonging to some other world than this, and Humphrey was wondering just how miserable a human being can be. Ruth was enjoying the sweet scents and listening to some local gossip, which interested her but which she found difficulty in extracting from Humphrey.

"Is he all that much older than she is? I didn't see him clearly, but he didn't look very ancient."

"Early forties, I believe."

"And she's nineteen . . . of course, it is a big difference but not too big, if they hit it off together. Is there anything between them, do you think?"

This expression, in the vocabulary of Ruth and her friends, meant, *are they in love*. It met with no response but a shrug.

"Of course there are all sorts of advantages apart from the obvious one" (another synonym for *love*, which these young women would go to any lengths of euphemism rather than name). "He's wealthy; you can't run a car that size on four pounds a week. But she doesn't look the sort of kid to marry for money."

"No," he said, with a sensation of gratitude towards her for the kindly judgment . . . but then Ruth was kind; always had been, she was the salt of the earth . . . and again he suffered inwardly. "Her mother is a nice woman," he added.

"Oh, she's a dear . . . and Meg's pretty, although she could afford to get rid of some of that puppy-fat, and her hair's a mess."

s.s.—6*

There was no reply; and for twelve years their relationship had been so satisfactory to Ruth and, she thought, so well understood by her, that now it did not occur to her to suspect him of disagreeing with what she said. At that moment, they came upon the log where Humphrey had found Mrs Lambert crying a week ago (at least by the calendar it was a week; in every other way it belonged to a lost life). "Now I *am* beginning to feel sleepy," Ruth said, "let's sit down a bit, shall we?"

He felt no guilt as he put his arm round her waist, or almost none. She was his dear good friend, and he liked her none the less because of the disaster that had happened to him. Once or twice, indeed, he had even felt the impulse to confide in her, ask her advice, as if she were a stranger who would not be hurt by what he confessed. . . .

"Oh, it's good to be here," she said softly, and turned her head towards him. "Dear old Cat. . . ."

But he only kissed her again without speaking.

"Didn't you get any sleep on the 'plane?" he asked presently. He thought that speech—conversation—any kind of noise between them might take his wretched thoughts off Meg and Scarron. Where were they, on this lovely night, and what were they doing?

"Not much. I dozed, on and off." She put up her hand to her mouth. "I'm sorry to keep on yawning, but I *am* so sleepy. What shall we do to-morrow? Go swimming?"

"If you like. I thought you'd want to rest."

"Oh, I shall be all right after a good night's sleep; I was pretty tired when I left home, but I feel better after being here just a few hours . . . and seeing you."

He pressed her waist in silence. He saw his chance this evening of asking her to befriend Meg growing steadily less. How could he re-introduce the subject, when it had already been dealt with and dropped? Would not Ruth think his interest in the Lamberts' problem suspicious?

He forgot that suspicion does not occur to the injured and innocent so easily as the guilty suppose.

And now, of course, he did not want to talk about Meg to Ruth; Meg was the last person he wanted to mention; but during supper

Mrs Lambert's eyes had once or twice met his own with a meaning look which, he supposed, meant that she expected him to keep his promise, and he could see that she had "taken" to Ruth. As he sat there in the moonlight, with his arm round his girl, staring down at the placid lake, he felt for the first time in his life that it was by the mercy of Providence that *this kind of thing*—by which he meant indecision, jealousy, remorse and passionate concern with feelings— was usually undergone by women. A week of it—and because he was a male he had not been in such a state *all* the time—had brought him low indeed. Thank Heaven, next week the Lamberts were going down to Venice. That would give him a fortnight alone with Ruth, and perhaps he would get better. It was all that he had to hope for.

They strolled homeward still entwined. Her active spirit had been soothed by the pensive beauty of her surroundings and by his presence, and they spoke little. She asked if he had heard of any job that might suit him, and he replied that he had not really been look- ing for anything, although his mother posted *The Times* to him in a bundle at the end of every week. He would begin looking for one seriously when they returned to England. "And then we can be married," he ended firmly, as if defying the moonlight and the scenery to do its romantic worst, while his heart felt like lead.

Ruth pressed his arm. In a moment she remarked that in that case there would be plenty to do.

"You are going to bed early, Miss Courtney; that's right," said Frau Schacht, meeting them at the foot of the stairs. "Mrs Lambert and I are going to listen to a beautiful concert from Milan. It is a pity you cannot listen too. But perhaps some other night."

When Humphrey had said good night to Ruth, and retired to his room to sit staring at an open book, Mrs Lambert and Frau Schacht established themselves in the *speisesaal*. There were a few minutes before the concert began.

"You are very sad, Eve," Frau Schacht said rather sharply, as she turned on the light and closed the shutters against hornets, "it is Meg, as usual, I suppose."

Mrs Lambert nodded dejectedly. "I've got such a feeling he's go- ing to propose to her to-night."

"Then why let her go out with him?"

"Oh really, Hansi! . . . I don't mean to be unkind, but you have no children of your own and you don't know the first thing about it. I can't order Meg about as if she were a little girl."

"Why not? She is a little girl; she is immature."

"Well, she doesn't think so. Besides, she has grown up a lot in the last weeks; I've noticed it. That's why I'm so worried."

"It is time for this to happen. You would not wish to be a possessive mother."

"Of course not, Hansi. And I don't think I am. I'm not thinking of anything except her happiness."

"We deceive ourselves," Frau Schacht said in a low tone. Then, as she went across to the wireless and began to tune in for the concert, "What do you think of Miss Courtney?"

"A dear, bright girl. I hope Meg will get friendly with her, but even if she does, I expect it's too late now; she couldn't do anything."

"Do anything?"

"It was Humphrey's idea. I got very worked up that day I'd been to lunch on the island, and when I met him by accident I told him all about it. He said he'd ask her—Ruth—to help."

"How could she 'help'?"

"By persuading Meg . . . showing her how unsuitable it would be . . . how unwise. . . ."

Frau Schacht had been standing with her back to her friend, twisting the knobs on the cabinet and adjusting the station. Suddenly she turned round, revealing a face wearing a highly sardonic expression.

"I see. What a nice idea. But lately he has not spoken about this, I think?"

"No, but then she only arrived to-day, didn't she? I mean——"

"I mean that he will not ask her now. Never mind!" holding up a finger as the opening strains of the overture to *The Magic Flute*, with their fairy-like energy, swelled dancingly into the room, "the concert is beginning. Really, my poor Eve, you are so . . . so. . . . It is you, I think, who are the little girl. But now let us listen, and forget our troubles."

Although she obeyed the suggestion, Mrs Lambert was far from forgetting her troubles. Beneath the majestic Pagan solemnity of the hymn *O Isis and Osiris*, and the gay sweetness of the bird-lovers' songs, foreboding refused to be silenced, and the apparent relaxation of her pose was quite misleading. Round and round and round went her anxiety, increased by Hansi's mysterious hints; it had become an acute alarm, rather than the general fear of Meg's marrying Scarron at some future date. Now, this evening, she was sure that something had happened. She felt certain that Meg would come back engaged.

CHAPTER TWENTY-TWO

Proposal

SHORTLY after nine o'clock that evening, Esmé Scarron's car was climbing a long, smooth and winding road leading up into the wilderness of mountains lying to the north. The light of moonset, surely the ghostliest and dreariest that shines upon the earth, veiled the rolling ridges and the forests fringing their crests. The nearer thickets of pine were filled with deep shadow. Thin autumn haze lingered in the hollows; the stars looked small and pale; the lake that was sometimes revealed at a turn in the road lying far below gleamed pale and sad, and over all the vast, dim, melancholy landscape sighed a chilling wind. "We'll go home a new way," Scarron had said, "over the mountains. I'll show you some country that will make up for our disappointment."

For when they had arrived at the village *weinstube*, famed for its trout and fine cooking, there had awaited them a telegram from his American friends, regretting that they could not come, and promising to telephone their explanation to him later. So he and Meg had dined more quickly than they had intended, and come away.

The car was now climbing, with some strain upon even that

powerful engine, a road running between wooded rocky walls sweeping steeply back from it. The shadows were gloomy and thick; only the summits caught the fading moonlight, summits so high and remote that they seemed to have no concern with the dim road winding below; yet here was none of the impressiveness of bare rock soaring into starlit air, for these mountains were muffled in woods to their very crests, and the crowding trees, standing motionless or rocking slowly in the wind under the weird light, weighed upon the senses. And how lonely it was; the valleys with their houses and people seemed a million miles away.

"We might be on the moon," Meg said presently, with candid dislike.

"Don't you like it?" and he laughed a little.

"No, I do not. I think it's dreary."

"This is one of my favourite places. Look, we're coming out on to the summit . . ." and he accelerated the speed of the car.

The next moment a low, impressed exclamation came from Meg, for the mountain walls had dropped away, and the road had emerged upon a wide expanse of rough grass. It extended apparently for many miles into the distance, where it was lost in misty moonlight and what looked like a gulf. The abrupt drop was filled with mountains. Their jagged peaks shut off the horizon. And they were *below* this plateau, and her eye caught the far-off, lunar gleam of great snows. Nearer, below the uncouth meadows rolling steeply downwards, there was spread a stupendous valley filled with vapour, and out of this silveriness, like the humps of monsters wallowing silently in a river, projected the round and tufted heads of more mountains.

"It's wonderful," she said at length, whispering, "where are we?"

"You wouldn't know if I told you. A high place."

He had stopped the engine, and was sitting with his hands resting upon the wheel. Meg turned to speak again, and was arrested by his stillness, even as she had been by Humphrey's at Osterwitz a week ago. His eyes were fixed upon the distance and, as she looked at him, pity stole into her heart; it was as if she grieved for him, yet without a reason. She looked at his strange head, with its air of belonging to an intellectual Punchinello, and studied it: it was as if she were seeing it—but truly seeing it—for the first time, as one will sometimes unexpectedly see oneself, unprepared, in a mirror; or catch, on returning from holiday, that glimpse of the familiar home-rooms seen by arriving visitors.

Meg got no pleasure from looking at this Portrait of a Friend. She quietly realised, while she was looking at it, that she did get pleasure from looking at Humphrey Scott. She also realised that she had been doing this increasingly of late and that Ruth Courtney would think it very peculiar and that it must stop. When she was not look-ing at Humphrey she could feel him looking at her. She thought that his head was drawable; she would like to sketch it. She did not know why he looked at her. It was at this point that, still quietly, she turned off her thoughts as if they were a tap.

How miserable it was up here in the dying moonlight. The silence, filled with the sighing wind, seemed as if it had been un-broken since the beginning of time. Sunlight and the calling of birds and human voices were unimaginable.

Scarron moved, and slowly turned towards her.

"I brought you up here to ask you to marry me. Will you?" he said.

Meg's heart gave a sickening plunge. The idea that this might happen to-night had not once occurred to her. She stared at him, wondering what on earth to say and wanting nothing but time; a respite; a reprieve from having here and now to make up her mind.

"Oh . . ." she said in a low, confused tone, and turned away her head, muttering, "I don't know. . . ."

He made no attempt to touch her, and she was immensely re-lieved. When he began to speak, as he did in a moment, she noticed as never before the chillness of his voice; its sound was thin and clear like the tone of the glacier water; and underneath it her thoughts, like fish, darted frantically in search of escape.

For weeks I've been telling myself how delightful his life is, she thought, and how lucky any girl would be to share it. Now if I just say yes I can share it. And now I don't want to, not at all; poor Esmé.

He was talking carefully; that was the impression she received when, the confusion of her thoughts and feelings beginning to recede, she heard his tone without fully understanding what he was saying. It was the voice of someone exploring, testing the ground, and at the same time honestly attempting to explain exactly how, and what, he felt. The note of urgency and feeling was completely absent, a fact for which Meg thanked Heaven. She sat very still, listening intently now, and praying that it would not come into his voice.

"I'm asking you because I've come to the conclusion you can fill an emptiness in my life. I've been getting more and more conscious of this for the last year or so; it's odd, but the deeper I go into my studies, especially my studies directly concerned with Paracelsus's character and nature, the more I'm conscious of this lack in myself." He paused. "I'm hanged if I know what it is. I feel it most when I'm with certain people. You, for instance." He laughed again.

"Perhaps—do you think it might be loneliness?" she was beginning with some timidity but he interrupted at once—"Good heavens, I'm never alone except when I'm working or out plant-hunting or distilling—and then I often get Lorenz in to give me a hand, just for company. I can't stand being alone. I don't suppose" —he paused again—"someone like you can possibly imagine just how alone I am, when I *am* alone. That's why Iliaster's always with me."

"Is she?" Meg turned to him, smiling and relieved at the introduction of the commonplace in the shape of a cat. "I didn't know you were so crazy about her."

"She sleeps on my bed—when I go to bed."

"Do you often sit up all night? That can't be good for you"—she nearly said "at your age," but saved herself by adding firmly, "Lack of sleep is very depressing." She felt very depressed herself; it might be the result of recent late nights.

"I can do without sleep almost indefinitely. I'm like Kundry. And almost every night, you know, I have friends and followers over at the house. We sit up all hours."

Meg was beginning cautiously to hope that this very casual proposal might have been side-tracked. She also wondered who Kundry might be, and why he called his guests followers—what a funny expression—and what he and they did when they sat up all hours. Probably they had wonderful, witty, brilliant conversations. She could imagine the women in richly heavy brocades or in floating silks, the glint of jewels in the dim room, the charm of personalities completely free and ruthless. She suddenly had a very strange thought: how tiring it was always to remember to be kind and to behave properly. And her depression was almost unbearable.

"So it isn't loneliness," she heard him say, and realised with sinking heart that after all he had his objective in view.

"No, it's nothing that can be put right by adding something to my *life*, my way of living. I've done all that. I've got all I want. This is something I need."

Meg was silent. The next instant he said:

"No, I don't think it's that."

"*What?*" She turned quickly, with a laugh that had some of the gasping quality heard when the audience's control snaps at the tensest moment of a thriller.

"A wife and children. That was what you said, wasn't it?"

"I was *thinking* that, yes. I didn't say anything." Meg was still laughing, more naturally now, as she met the quiet gaze of his luminous eyes. The moon had lifted itself free of cloud and was sailing gold and clear; a bitterly cold wind was blowing.

"You're always doing that," she added, "almost reading my thoughts. Haven't you noticed? It happens two or three times every time we're out together. But you never *heard* me thinking before!"

He smiled but did not answer. Then in a moment he said:

"I have had both, as you know. A wife and a child—a boy. My son was killed in the fighting in Russia."

"I know. Mummy told me. You didn't mind? I was . . . awfully sorry."

"Why should I mind? And you know too, I suppose, that Hella, my wife, was difficult. She was rebellious and ungrateful. I ransacked the remotest places of the earth for presents for her: rare living plants, jewels, ancient and priceless things that most men couldn't have imagined, much less given, to the woman they married. If that wasn't love, I don't know what love is."

Meg was silent. She remembered that all the young men who had said (or rather implied, for most of them were inarticulate) that they loved her, had given her things. Love, one always heard, wanted to give. If it merely wanted to take, it was not true love. But what sort of things should it want to give?

She could not pay full attention to the matter because he was speaking again.

"If I could tell you of some of the things I found for her . . . things that are only sometimes referred to, obliquely or symbolically, in very rare books . . . but I found them. It was a kind of challenge to my power, to seek them out . . . but all that doesn't matter now . . . perhaps I'll tell you more about it some other time. This other thing, the thing I need, isn't something that can be traced and bought, as the presents for Hella were."

"Perhaps——" Meg began, and he turned towards her eagerly, saying, "Yes; yes, tell me what you think about it, I want you to, I'm sure you can help me. I knew you could, that first time I saw you looking at his portrait in Villach."

"In *Villach*? But I picked you up in the *weinstube*. Mummy was horrified," and Meg tried a weak laugh.

"No, I saw you before then. But go on, tell me what you were going to say."

"I was only wondering—you know about the pearl of great price—I was wondering if what you want could be that."

Her tone was blunt yet shy. She felt herself being both "high-minded", in the slighting contemporary sense, and impertinent. He was more than twice her age, and learned, and rich (being rich did make a difference, people could say what they liked)—and was she so sure herself of possessing the pearl that she could assume another lacked it? *Of course* I'm not sure at all, she thought in confusion and shame. I only *know* that it *is* priceless. And it's such a beautiful name, like a line of poetry.

"In the New Testament?" His tone was disappointed. "Yes, of course I've read that—incidentally, if it's read by someone who understands magic, many puzzling things are made plain—but we can't be sure what the pearl is, can we? Wisdom, God, immortality?"

"No, I suppose we can't—not quite sure. But don't you think it might be—to believe in God? What you want, I mean?"

He shook his head. The luminousness had faded from his eyes and they appeared small and dull.

"Mummy doesn't know how she would ever have stood things—the war, and losing Daddy and everything—if she hadn't believed in God," Meg said with more confidence.

"And do you believe in God too?"

Meg nodded.

"The Ancient of Days—the Old Nobodaddy of Blake?"

Again she nodded. At that moment her state of mind was all that the severest member of the Rationalist Association could have desired. Faith withered beneath the huge dim sky, the ceaseless bite of the wind, and his mocking gaze.

"And I believe—that lightning and the earthquake—got itself into a human body—and carpentered tables and doors—and ate bread—and fish?" he intoned, as if it were the Creed.

"It wasn't like that——" she began, but then was silent. She was shivering with cold and she could have wept.

He shook his head. "The Force I believe in isn't measurable or comprehendable, nor can it comprehend, and it dwarfs all religions into insignificance. But I can use it. It comes into me"—he looked slowly around, moving his head so that the moonlight shone into his eyes, as if he were searching the dark hollows and the bushes that cast their shade—"and it gives me my power." He looked at her. "I can heal people, you know."

"Heal people?"

"Yes. Hadn't you wondered what happens to all my distillations? I prescribe them for people who are ill. But that isn't what I meant. I can heal people by . . . but you're shivering! It has got very cold; we're so high here that it's always cold, of course, but to-night I can smell the autumn. Even up here there is the reek of decay . . . here, put this round you; you'll soon be warm."

"Won't you be cold?" Meg said through chattering teeth, as he wrapped round her his thick coat of pale wool, but he shook his head. And almost at once she began to lose the deadly chill and soon she was glowing. The sadness, however, stayed with her.

"It has been a great satisfaction, that power," he said presently. "But now it isn't enough. I'm . . . empty. Or thirsty. I don't know which. But I must . . . eat and drink." He laughed.

"Doesn't it make you happy to be able to heal people? Do tell me about it. Is it like the 'laying on of hands' one reads about? I've never met anyone before who could do it . . . is it like water-divining, the same kind of thing, I mean. . . ."

She thought it an excellent idea to prolong this digression.

"No, it isn't like the laying on of hands or water-divining . . . and I don't want to talk about it now . . . do you know where I first saw you? Looking at Paracelsus's house. I came and stood behind you for a moment. My shadow fell across yours."

"Did it? I didn't notice."

"You were too absorbed by Paracelsus. I liked that. I thought it was a good omen and I knew that you were the one."

She gasped and he laughed.

"So I followed you back to Martinsdorf and found out . . . where you were staying." His voice changed slightly. "And then, after that, I followed you about."

"Followed me *about*?"

"Almost every day. Once I watched you when you were reading alone in the woods. Are you angry?" He was laughing. He had made no attempt to touch her; there was the space of a seat between them in the great car.

"Not really, I suppose, though it was beastly at the time. I knew there was someone or something there, I thought it was a de-serter——"

"Oh, I wasn't actually *there* . . . sorry, I'm expressing myself badly. I mean I wasn't there for very long. And you mustn't be angry, Meg. I knew you were the right person, you see. It was the greatest luck for me, your coming to Martinsdorf this summer, just when I have come to feel my lack so strongly. When I saw you, that first time, I was almost sure that you were the right one, and then when I had talked to you and seen you with animals and plants—do you remember looking at the growing plants in my study and bending over the leaves without wanting to touch them? To me that was a revealing sign. You felt unconsciously in harmony, at one with them, and so there was no need for you to touch them. Those silvery furry leaves would have been irresistible to most women— ordinary women—they would have stroked them."

"I'm *absolutely* ordinary." Meg would not have believed, a few hours earlier, that she could have made this protest at all, much less with such frightened earnestness.

"No; you are unusually closely in touch with all the world of Nature."

" 'Rocks and stones and trees,' " she said, on a half-sigh. She felt a longing for sunlight and humanity that was like thirst. And he— what did he thirst for?

"Yes. But I . . . am not in that kind of harmony with living objects," he said. "I observe them and use them. I'm interested in them too, of course; I enjoy their variety and beauty, but that isn't the same thing. I'm—separated from them. You aren't."

"You know, I really don't know what you mean," she said after a pause.

"It is difficult to explain in words. You must just accept the fact that I know you are in harmony with the living world. And if you were always with me, as my wife, I could learn from you, perhaps, to be in harmony with it too. Perhaps that's what I lack."

She did not say anything. Certain phrases he used had frightened her very much—*always with me . . . my wife . . .* and this knowledge about her, which he assumed and which she had never suspected, why should he be able to detect in her what no one else had? He must realise that all this was very disturbing and alarming.

"Can't you tell me what it is I haven't got?" he demanded suddenly, leaning towards her. "There are strong mystic powers in women."

"I haven't the faintest idea, Esmé—if you're really sure it *isn't* the —the 'pearl of great price'."

He made a movement of impatience.

"I thought you might be able to tell me."

"I'm very sorry." It was a dejected whisper, but if she had hoped it would convey a rejection of his proposal, as well as regret for her inability to tell him, she was disappointed.

"I feel I *could* learn from you, Meg. You could teach me how to live in a new way, how to look at the earth and herbs and animals——"

"Oh," she interrupted with a note of desperate impatience, "I don't know anything, I truly don't."

"Don't you like me?" he demanded again; "aren't we friends?"

"Yes, oh yes. But——"

"Then won't you try to help me? I'm weary of standing alone; I never thought I should be, but I am, and I must have help and I'm sure you can give it me. Listen; we get on well together, don't we? Well, then," as she nodded, "—but of course you want to hear that I love you, I understand that, it's natural enough at your age—and I do love you. I love you as—as someone who's lost loves the light that will lead him home. I'll make you happy. You shall have a delightful life . . . everything you can possibly want . . . beautiful clothes (I'll take you to Dior) . . . you shall fill the house with young friends . . . but no, I suppose you won't think of marrying me if you don't love me. . . ."

He looked at her broodingly.

"Do you love someone else?" he said.

Meg shook her head. She shook it rather violently. The odd thing was that just for an instant she could not be sure whether she loved someone else or not. She did not think of Derek, and yet as she made the negative motion she had a feeling of guilt as if she were lying. Afterwards, she thought that her confusion had been caused by how he put his question; had he said *anyone else*, she would not have felt this hypothetical figure so much embodied as by *someone*.

"That's one obstacle out of the way . . ." he said, as if to himself.

Meg now began to be seriously alarmed. She had shown, as plainly as she could, that she did not want to marry him. She did not want to be forced to use the word "no". She had a youthful feeling that to do so bluntly, in face of all his kindness and his superior years and advantages, would be rude. Yet it looked as if he were going to compel her to.

"I don't see what you've got against the plan," he said, and she felt a flash of anger. That's because you're a man, she thought, absurdly. She murmured something about being sorry.

"I'm *begging* you to help me, Meg," he said suddenly, and she saw that his face had become anxious and haggard, "you're the only person who can, and I'm throwing myself on your mercy. You must say 'yes'. You've *got* to."

"But it wouldn't work," she cried, becoming more and more frightened, "can't you see it wouldn't? When I don't love you, and, well, there's a—a difference in age, and I've been brought up in such a different world? We haven't really much in common, except that we—we like each other——"

"You would learn. Women are adaptable," he said.

This frightened her almost more, for some reason, than anything he had said so far. Adaptable? To what?

"I *can't*," she said loudly. "I *can't*."

"Meg, don't say it so finally. *Think* it over. Don't force me to——"

He was looking at her steadily, with head lifted and drawn slightly backwards, and for an instant her senses went into a slow black swirl. When she saw him again he was looking down; for a moment she thought his eyes were closed. Then he looked up; they were small and clear as a snake's.

"Won't you think it over, please?" he said.

Meg had been thinking: that she might be forced to stay in this dreary spot, suffering the faint light and the icy wind and his pleading until midnight if she did not do something to get them away. Her head was steady again now; she must have been overcome for an instant by the thin air of the heights.

"It won't do any good, but I will think it over, if you like. We're going down to Venice the day after to-morrow, as you know. Can we talk about it again when I come back?" she asked.

He looked at her searchingly, and she returned his look quietly enough. She knew that what she had just asked was perfectly reasonable in the circumstances; even conventional; and she also knew that, uncannily clever though he was at guessing her thoughts, he could not guess at her feelings. *They* were too simple and—in spite of his given opinion of her—too ordinary for him.

"Haven't you any idea at all whether you'll change your mind?" he said.

Meg shook her head, with a most unsuccessful attempt at a wilful smile. There was a silence that seemed to last for a long time. Then he slowly reached out and took her hand. His own was astoundingly hot and dry; she almost exclaimed with surprise as it touched her. He might have been suffering from a fever. He clasped her hand gently and held it, and somehow this drew them closer together than they had been throughout the evening.

"Marry me, Meg dear, and save me——"

His voice was so soft that she was not sure what he had said. *Save my soul* or *save me a soul?* In any case, it was something playful about a soul, but never did Meg feel less amused. For yearning pity was going out from her towards him; great waves of sympathy, a kind of weakening sorrow that blended with the pressing, surrounding melancholy of the night.

"I'm sorry . . ." she stammered, "I'm so sorry. . . ." In another moment she would have been weeping. She made an effort and said faintly: "*Can* we go home now, please? It's getting late and I'm so awfully tired."

He slowly withdrew his hand. "Tired? You have no more right to be tired than a young larch has." But he put the engine in gear, and began to turn the car round.

On the homeward journey they were both silent. They sped down into deep, clear shadow between mountains silhouetted against the afterglow of the moon, and presently there were the lights of a village in the valley far below, and Meg saw them with something like a passion of love and relief; she thought of quiet supper tables and sleeping children, and dozing cats before the fire, ordinary voices talking of simple everyday things, water being drawn from taps, beds turned down for weary people. How darling the world is, she thought, and soon I shall be home with Mummy. They came out on to a bridge with white water rushing dimly beneath, and the slope ended here; they were in the valley again.

She had spoken the truth; she was tired; even exhausted, and she could hardly keep awake. She almost drowsed, conscious only of having shed the burden of depression, and of vague pleasure in the houses and fields moving past her in the darkness. Suddenly she heard him saying, as if from the air above her head:

"Very well, then. You'll give me your decision when you get back from Venice."

"Yes. Yes, I will." She roused herself, peering out from the great collar of his coat. "Oh, we're nearly home. . . ." Her murmur died away in sheer relief. She would have ten days in which she need not think about the affair. She glanced at him. He looked serene, even cheerful, and she was pleased that her refusal had not hurt him. But —and her heart sank—was that because he did not take it as a refusal?

When they stopped at the gate, and he was helping her to lift the coat from her shoulders, and re-arranging it on his own, he told her that he would not see her on the following day.

"I have to go to a remote part of the country," he said.

"How exciting. What for—or is that inquisitive?" Much restored by this piece of news, she tried to keep blitheness from her voice.

"I'm going to look for the Wulfenia."

"The blue flower? The *unique* one that only grows in Carinthia and the Himalayas?"

He nodded. They were standing beside the car, and he was looking down at her.

"Are you going to distil something from it?"

"No. I just want to have some of the dried flowers and leaves and roots. I'm taking Lorenz for company."

"Oh . . . well . . . I hope you—you'll have a good trip. And I'll send you a postcard from Venice, and your *palazzo* is called Palazzo Tedeschi and it's on a canal called Rio San Stefano near the Bridge of Sighs."

"Quite right."

Meg hesitated. She had been speaking more gaily than she felt prudent; he might begin to accuse her of lack of feeling. She would dearly have liked to see inside a Venetian palace, but she thought it wiser not to add to the list of her obligations to him; and, sure enough, in a moment he said in a quietly cheerful tone:

"I hope to show you my palace one day. It's quite small, you know, and falling to pieces. But it's one of the loveliest in that part of the city."

It was enough to alarm her again. She smiled and quickly said good night, and was hurrying up the path under the trees before he had time to add more. She left him there, silent and staring after her. She was gasping, as she came round the corner of the house and ran up the two steps to the open front door, with relief and agitation and causeless fear. She welcomed the dimly lit entrance and its meek green plants as the most beautiful sight she had seen that evening.

CHAPTER TWENTY-THREE

Rich Franz

"How nice to see you so early, darling," Mrs Lambert said, looking up with a smile of pleasure as she came into the *speisesaal*.

"It's nice to *be* back so early—if you call this early," Meg said darkly. She leant across the length of the couch, where she had seated herself, and gave her mother a hearty kiss. "It feels as if I've been out for three weeks."

"Why? Didn't you have a nice time?" Mrs Lambert was trying not to look too closely at her pale face and exhausted expression.

"Yes. At least, I suppose we did, at first," and she explained about the Americans and their telegram.

"Ah, that was a plan of his," Frau Schacht said in an unruffled voice from where she sat in a dark corner, "he wanted to have you to himself."

Meg looked across at her without irritation, although this was the sort of Hansi-special that usually goaded her into an imprudent answer. The dimly lit room with its shabby painted furniture looked blessedly homely, after the *Götterdämmerung* scenes through which she had been driving, and the two faded women were Mummy and Hansi, with all dear old Tormouth spread out behind them.

"Come along, Meg," Frau Schacht continued, "your mother has been worrying about you all the evening, she has hardly heard the concert. I think you ought to tell us what has happened."

"Please, Hansi," Mrs Lambert murmured, in trepidation. But Meg only said mildly, as she leant back in a relaxed position:

"All right. Only I'll probably fall asleep in the middle. Well, he asked me to marry him—no"—as both women exclaimed and sat upright—"it's all right, Mummy. I said I couldn't. But he kept on so about it that I've promised to talk to him again about it when we get back from Venice."

Frau Schacht sat still and rigid, with arms extended upon her chair, looking across the room at her. Mrs Lambert said agitatedly:

"Oh, darling, that *was* silly. Now he'll think he's still got a chance. Why didn't you make it absolutely clear that you can't marry him, under any circumstances *whatsoever*, and refuse absolutely to discuss the matter again?"

Meg did not reply for a moment. When she did, it was in an altered tone. Her voice had been rather surprisingly cheerful, in contrast to her weary expression, when she came in. Now it was subdued and sad.

"I know, Mummy. I did try to tell him. But I keep on feeling so *sorry* for him. It comes over me, in sort-of waves. I've got one now. And when I feel like that I almost *could* marry him, out of pity."

Mrs Lambert was shaking her head distractedly.

"Not if you don't love him, it's out of the question. I can't think how you can even hesitate . . . does he love you?"

"He hasn't said so. I don't think he does, really." Meg hesitated. "He talked in rather an odd way. He said there's something lacking in him that I might be able to give him, but he doesn't know what it is. I think he's in a muddle *psychologically*."

"It is much simpler than that. He is wicked." It was Frau Schacht's voice, coming strainedly and harshly from where she sat in the shadows. "He is wicked like a tiger, or a snake, because he's made that way. In the eyes of God, perhaps, the tiger isn't wicked, because He made it and He knows all about it, but when it kills our children, loving to kill, loving to eat flesh, to us it seems wicked.— So you are sorry for the tiger?" turning sharply towards Meg.

"Terribly sorry. I can hardly bear it, I'm so sorry. But I don't know why. And I don't always feel like that."

"Nor do I know why you are sorry." Frau Schacht got up, as though she could not endure to keep still, and went across to a side table for a cigarette. "I think you are a little fool, to speak plainly, and conceited too, imagining you can redeem a man old enough to be your father, and rich and clever as well. But you must not try to do it; you must be prevented. It would not work. I will tell you why. Listen."

She came forward into the circle of light, where it cast its weak glow upon the couch, and sat down next to Meg, looking at her with an expression at once sorrowful and severe. "I am going to tell you something which may make you change your mind about things." She glanced at Mrs Lambert. "Your mother knows that I know something very bad about him. I've spoken about it to her before, but never told her what it is. I can't bear to think about it, and as for speaking . . . I can't ever forget it, this thing that I believe he did, because it was my fault, and my sin, and though I've prayed and prayed about it, it doesn't get any better." She paused, gazing withdrawnly into some region of wretchedness within herself. Meg's impulse to declare crossly that she would not listen had passed, and she was looking at her with an expression touched by awe.

"Don't, Hansi, if it's too painful for you," Mrs Lambert said, but Frau Schacht shook her head.

"It won't take long," she said in a brusque, quick voice. "Before the war I used to know him. I met him when I came here for my holidays from Linz, where I lived with my parents and taught in a school, a good school. I was a proud and clever girl and I was flattered by his notice." She turned to Meg and looked her in the face. "You are thinking, perhaps, that he seduced me; that we became lovers. There was nothing like that at all. There were not even kisses; nothing. But I used to visit his house over there and talk—Jesu Maria! how we talked, and I became infatuated with his intellect and I lost my faith. Yes, I stopped going to Mass and Confession because he persuaded me that there was no merciful God in Heaven Who made us all and Who came into our world to share our pain and die for us, but only a Force, something like the lightning, that is neither good nor evil but only irresistibly strong. He said that some people could use this force, letting it run through them . . . I don't know. I have now forgotten so much what he said, but at that time, I was already betrothed to Franz"—she pressed her lips together to stop their trembling—"he lived at Klagenfurt, where he had a miserable little job in a firm that exported minerals. I was not pretty, you know, and as I wanted a husband I thought it wise to take Franz who loved and admired me—Jesu! how he admired my cleverness and my teaching and the big books I read—'my clever girl', he used to call me. His clever girl! He didn't know that I saw Esmé Scarron so often, nor that I had lost my faith. All he thought about was the time when we could be married and come to live in this house that his uncle had promised us for a wedding present. Poor Franz. I was ashamed of his stupidity and his mean little job, and bored with his devotions. I wanted to marry Esmé—whom I did not love, I swear it before our Blessed Lady—and share his life of learning and luxury. As for him, I believe it amused and flattered him to have a follower—a disciple—who believed everything he said and whom he could influence."

Followers, thought Meg. That was what he called them to-night. Friends and followers. She kept her eyes fixed upon Hansi's face.

"I managed it so that they should never meet. I was here only in the long school holidays, staying with the family of Franz's uncle, and Franz was not with me for all of the time because—his job was so poor, he has never been a money-earner, poor Franz—he had only a very short holiday. And usually I went to Esmé's house across the lake, so that the villagers shouldn't know about our friend-

ship, but some of them did know: Anna Trauber, at the *weinstube*,
knew, but she does not gossip; she is religious. But one day we,
Franz and I, met Esmé and his servant, that man Lorenz, when we
were out walking together, and Esmé said good morning to us—it
was a lonely part of the mountains, where strangers would naturally
do this—and—you know what a strange-looking man Esmé is—
Franz burst out laughing." She covered her forehead with her hand
for a moment. "I shall not forget how Esmé looked at him until the
day I die. Perhaps it will be the last thing I see in my memory before
I do die. We walked on, and I felt faint, but Franz was still laughing
about Esmé's funny face, as he called it. Then, when we had gone
about fifty metres, Franz cried out that he had a terrible pain in his
back. I made him sit down and I massaged him—we supposed that
he had torn his muscles in walking. I looked round for the other
two, but they had gone. I managed to help Franz home, with much
difficulty, because he was in such pain, and next day he was better
and he thought no more about it."

She paused while she dragged deeply on her cigarette. Meg had
been listening uneasily. She suspected Hansi of trying to discredit
Esmé, and was on her guard, yet the story, so far, disturbed her. It
reminded her of something, but she could not trace the memory.

"When I spoke about this to Esmé the next time that I saw him,
he seemed amused about it all and said that if Franz laughed at his
face he must be allowed to laugh at Franz's back. And I was
frightened. There was something about all this which frightened
me very much, and from that moment I made up my mind to escape
from Esmé, and put him out of my life."

She sighed painfully, and looked across the room to where an old
clock, supported in a rickety frame of gilded wood, ticked on the
armoire.

"I must hurry, Franz will be here at any minute—his train is in—
didn't you hear it just now? Mitzi has left her room in confusion
and—well, this is the worst part, coming now. Esmé pretended not
to care that I had escaped from him, but I knew that he was very
angry. I saw him once or twice from a distance, with his friends, and
I knew that he hated me and hated poor Franz. And when the

Anschluss came, Franz and I were married at once, because we did not know what was going to happen and we thought it best to become man and wife. All went on as before, except that I no longer taught in school, but started my School of Languages here with a few pupils, and I kept house for Franz, who went each day to Klagenfurt. Esmé had gone away, because it was now winter. I was not happy, because I was discontented and, God forgive me, I despised Franz for his contentment with our life, but I did my duty like a heart of stone. And then—you know how it happened—they began taking people away to camps who had done nothing, they came at night, we lay awake, we all began to lie awake, with our hearts banging and banging inside us so that it shook our beds— and it got worse all the time. They took people from villages near, though not so many as from the towns, and always it got nearer to us. And one night they came for Franz. No"—she held up her hand as Mrs Lambert started forward—"I have him back and we sleep in the same room, and when he coughs in the night I can look after him and God knows that Franz has won his war. We have all lost our war, but not Franz, because he still loves me and enjoys to bring me presents from Klagenfurt. Isn't that victory? I tell you that it is. But on that night, when I opened the door and saw them standing there, I felt that it was my fault. This was the punishment, because I had despised him and not been content with our life. They took him away in his pyjamas, and I saw there was a button missing from the coat—poor Franz, poor Franz—and I didn't see him again for six years. And do you know what one of them said to me, when I was screaming 'Why? Why?' (he was sorry for me, I think). He said, as he went out of the door, *Ask your rich boy-friend across the lake. . . .* That's what he said. And it was Esmé who had got Franz to be sent away to that place, because Franz had laughed at him and I had escaped from his power. But it was my fault that he did it."

She had not finished speaking the last words when they heard the front door open. She put her finger against her lips and dropped it again.

Then Franz came into the *speisesaal*, carrying his hat in one hand and something cumbersome wrapped in brown paper in the other.

He stood smiling round on the three silent figures, and speaking a mixture of German and broken English.

"Here I am again, see you. *Hansi, my love, you shouldn't have sat up for me, you work so hard, I like you to get a long night's rest.* Good evening, *gnädige* Frau, good evening, Fräulein. It is not very hot to-night, no? *Hansi, this 'week-end' I have brought something I am sure you will like, something useful for our home and it will last a long time, too.* Gnädige Frau, Fräulein, you excuse if—open?" and he held up the parcel.

"You should have your soup first, Franz. Come into the kitchen; it is keeping hot, and we will see the present afterwards," Frau Schacht said in German, getting up.

"Can't we see the present, please, Herr Schacht?" Meg asked, also speaking German; at the same time she carelessly passed her handkerchief over her eyes.

"Oh yes, do show it to us," said her mother.

"So? All right. *Hansi, they want to see the present. You women are all alike, you can't resist a parcel; no, you must see what is inside; very well, then, I shall open it.*"

Coughing a little now, from his climb up to the house, he slowly —and with a patience that would usually have irritated his watchers but now only moved them almost to tears—untied the knots of the string, which he carefully rolled up and put away in his pocket, with the remark that nothing must be wasted nowadays. Then he un-wrapped from its papers, and held up, a large shining tin saucepan.

"What a useful size."

"And so strongly made. It will last for ever."

"Thank you, Franzchen. It's beautiful. You certainly do think of the most useful things." Frau Schacht kissed his cheek, but he flung his arm about her waist and, holding her close, covered her face with kisses, while he kept his moist, joyful, modest eyes fixed upon Mrs Lambert and Meg. He also winked.

"There. Now I am really home. Now let us come down to the kitchen to see how this soup tastes," he said.

When, good nights having been exchanged, the Lamberts were alone, Meg broke a long silence.

"It may not be true. She doesn't know it for certain. It isn't fair to believe it without knowing more about it. And I'm too absolutely worn out to think or talk about it to-night. I'm going to give him the benefit of the doubt."

Mrs Lambert was too disturbed to answer.

CHAPTER TWENTY-FOUR

Italy !

MEG went to her bed exhausted, yet with feelings so disturbed that she felt certain she would lie long awake. She was also teased by the feeling of having heard something in Hansi's story before; there was an element or an incident or an atmosphere there that was familiar, but it lay tantalisingly below the levels of conscious memory and, search as she would, lying with arms locked behind her head and all her nerves strained and tense, she could not bring it to the surface. But then, suddenly, she fell asleep; drifting off into that state at once commonplace, and vital to our race, and mysterious as the sea or another and unexplored planet.

She slept; with hair tangled upon the pillow; in the immemorial pose; and at once what had been temporary and personal in the room became timeless and linked to all humanity. The shadows veiled all anxiety, and muted the tick of the clock, even as plain daylight (when we allow it) will calm us with the presentation of its quiet background. And then, while she was still lying dreamless *in the first sweet sleep of night*, sadness began to flow in and to oppress her rest. It rose like a tide, but without the sea's healthful challenge; it resembled more the stealthy approach of some dreary underground lake, whose waters slide up the wall of rock that has never seen the light, only to slip downwards again in response to the pull of far-off streams running under the open sky. It welled sluggishly across her spirit, and she was disturbed, and flung over heavily and muttered in her sleep. Then, as if breaking through the sadness, a dream began. She saw Scarron, imprisoned in a cell of stone by chains that bound him to the floor, and around him, but just out of his reach, floated a great butterfly, so gorgeous that even through her stifling sadness she felt delight in the velvety violet and crimson wings. He was trying to catch it, but always it fluttered from his grasp. I must help him, she thought miserably, I must help him to catch it. He *must* have it or he will be lost. And then she awoke, crying bitterly, and saying still, "I must, I must. Oh poor, poor——"

She dried the tears away, and afterwards lay for some time looking at the dim stars visible through the uncurtained window. She felt nothing any more but this compelling pity. It seemed to be gently, remorselessly pressing her towards helping him; it seemed like a cloud so huge that it crowded out all other feelings, including her objections to marrying him. These now seemed small and unreal; even the causeless fear which she had felt earlier in the evening had shrunk to a mood that did not matter. And as she lay there, not thinking, but staring with wide and solemn eyes at the darkness of the dead of night, she felt the sadness returning; rolling in waves across the lake, sighing in on the low wind, and as it came, so her pity for him grew stronger. She could think of nothing else. But she was not so lost in this dream-like experience as to take it for granted. She did think it very awesome, very strange. Well has Reason been called divine; it had not relinquished its calm control of her mind when at last she fell asleep, still *contemplating* her own sadness and her pity, not yet swept helplessly away before its power.

In the morning she awoke cheerful and restored, and when her mother asked her if she had been kept awake by "everything", she firmly answered no, and refused to discuss the matter.

"Don't worry, Mummy. Everything's under control. I'm not going to think about what Hansi told us, I'm not going to think about *anything*. I'm just going to enjoy Venice. And you jolly well enjoy it too."

"Meg, you are naughty, you are unkind, you're so selfish, you've changed, I can't make you out; how can I enjoy anything when you may be going to marry someone who does things like that?"

Meg made an impatient kissing-mouth at her. "There's no *question* of my marrying him, Mummy."

"Even if he hasn't done anything, I hate there being any *question* of it. I want you to marry someone with no *mysteries*. All this fuss——"

Meg, catching from the corner of her eye a glimpse of someone approaching, made another kissing-mouth and ran downstairs.

Humphrey Scott, just coming out of his room, saw her back as she disappeared. Mrs Lambert, who was looking very pale, waited in the corridor until he came up to her.

"Oh, Mr Scott—I must tell you—he proposed to her last night. She said no, but he won't take it as a refusal, and she's had to promise to talk about it again when we get back from Venice. Have you talked to your fiancée yet?" Her anxious eyes searched his.

"Er—no. No, I haven't. There hasn't been much time."

"Oh, I know—and such a shame, bothering her when she's on holiday. (What a bonny thing she is, such a graceful figure; I love that athletic type.) But if you could just tell her—put her in the picture, as you soldiers say . . . I can't stand much more of this."

"All right. I will," he said after a pause.

"It is kind of you." She stood looking at him for a moment, wishing she could say that Meg had taken such a fancy to Ruth, while Humphrey was wishing he could say that Ruth had taken a fancy to Meg. Neither, however, was much good at lying.

"Very kind," she repeated. She was now wishing that she could tell him what Hansi had told them on the previous night, but that was impossible; before going to bed, Hansi had made them both solemnly promise never to tell anyone.

"I'll speak to Ruth this morning," he said. He looked at her in silence for a moment. He had hardly slept. He found it unbearable to be near Meg, and equally unbearable not to be near her, and to Ruth he could scarcely be civil, and this made him feel worse than all. And now, in two days, Meg would be going away, which was quite the best thing that could happen, and he did not know how he was going to bear that either.

"You look tired, Mr Scott," Mrs Lambert said gently.

"Oh, I'm all right," rather boorishly, looking away from her. "There's the breakfast-bell. Hope you'll get weather like this in Venice."

Frau Schacht did not usually appear at this meal, being busy making her arrangements for the day with the two maids. After breakfast was over, and Ruth had strolled into the garden to write letters until Humphrey should join her, Frau Schacht emerged, apparently from the middle of an enormous clump of coreopsis flowers which she was tying up, and addressed him as he was on his way there:

"Mr Scott, I have a suggestion to make. Why don't you and Miss Courtney go down to Venice with the Lamberts and the three young people on Wednesday?"

"Are Robin and the other two going?" he asked, to gain time. Frau Schacht's stout yet not inelegant form, in dark dirndl and blouse of navy cotton sprinkled with small red buds, appeared to him as a nice blend of tempting devil and relieving angel. Instantly, against the shocked clamour of conscience, he knew that he was going to say yes.

"It's all arranged," Frau Schacht went on, "I am only sorry that Mitzi has had to join her uncle in Spain. Three is not company, and Robin and Camilla get on so well together that poor Marcel's nose is outjointed. Well, what do you say? Would you like to go?"

"I would. I don't know about Ruth. We were going down at the end of her stay here, as you know, but——"

"There are advantages if you go now, and in a party. The weather will not be quite so hot as later on, and I can perhaps get for you reduced terms at the pensione."

"I'll ask her now, and let you know," he said and went quickly away.

"Do you want to go down to Venice on Wednesday with the Lamberts?" he called, as he approached Ruth where she sat under the nut tree; "Robin and Camilla are going, and the French boy, and Frau Schacht thought it might be more fun for you if we went in a crowd."

"Yes, I'd love it," she answered after a moment's thought, during which he had been so afraid of hearing her reject the suggestion that he hardly noticed her expression. "It is rather short notice, but the journey isn't long, is it?"

"About six hours, I believe."

"Oh, that won't be tiring . . . yes, it'll be great fun. Do you like the idea of going in a crowd?"

The tone was not flirtatious, though she had a right to make it so, because they had planned to go to Venice together at the end of her visit and to return to England from there, but she saw no point in flirting with the man she was to marry.

"Yes, on the whole—if you're sure it won't tire you so soon after the journey out here?"

"Good lord, no, I'm not tired now."

She looked completely rested, and her smooth carnation skin had begun to tan. She smiled at him; happy, kind and trustful Ruth.

"You're sure . . . you wouldn't rather come just with me?"

"Quite sure; I shall have enough of you, my dear old Cat, and so will you of me, later on."

"No, I shan't," he said steadily, and went away to find Frau Schacht. He was wondering how long this was going on. Until he and Ruth were married, probably; then affection, duty and habit would cure him.

"Ruth thinks that's a good idea, Frau Schacht; we'd like to join the party," he said; if there is such an emotion as miserable joy, he was experiencing it at that moment. He had given in to temptation, and if his guilt was strong, so was his relief from pain.

"Good," and she gave him a dry look which he did not see, "then I will make the reservations. For how long do you want to stay there?"

"Oh—the whole fortnight; we may as well do it thoroughly. Then—then we'll come back here for a week before we go home. Er—you'll keep our rooms for us, won't you?"

"At half-pension terms," nodded Frau Schacht.

"That's very nice of you. I'll tell Ruth."

Ruth remained under the nut tree, with her writing materials and paper and postcards spread around her. She was thinking about currency, about what clothes she could wear in Venice to mitigate the heat, and about the Lamberts. She wished that they were not going to be in the party; it would, to her mind, have been pleasanter if it had consisted of herself and Humphrey, Robin and Camilla, because she liked those two kids; they were quite mad but sweet. Meg Lambert, on the other hand, annoyed her. Meg reminded her of her youngest sister, Barbara, whose flirtatiousness and excitability and lack of common sense had caused the family much wear and tear during the last year, and whom, Ruth thought, hardly deserved to have got herself engaged at eighteen to a likeable young man with an unusually well-paid job. Meg Lambert, another troubler of the peace, with the same attractiveness, looked like securing a rich husband. Ruth had gathered from casual remarks dropped by the inhabitants of the *gasthaus* that Mrs Lambert was worried about the situation, and Humphrey looked browned-off when it was mentioned. This cast a little shadow over the holiday, because no one liked to see a mere kid—however silly and selfish—upsetting her mother by marrying the wrong type, and Ruth often wished to give Meg Lambert some good advice.

"All fixed up," Humphrey called, as he came across the grass, "we're going for the fortnight."

"The whole *fortnight*? But, Cat, we'll hardly see anything of Austria, and I wanted to go over that Home in Carinthia run by the S.C.F., and——"

"You can't begin to see Venice in less than two weeks. As it is, we shan't see a quarter of what we ought to."

"I thought you didn't like sight-seeing." Her tone was a little short. First Meg Lambert, now this high-handed arrangement of almost the entire holiday—she began to wonder if she wanted to see Venice so much after all.

"I don't, as a rule. But Venice is something special; everybody says so. Besides," he sat down beside her and put his arm along the back of the seat, "we needn't trail round sight-seeing all the time. We can sit in the sun and be lazy."

"I don't like being lazy and neither do you," but she was smiling again.

"I like it more than I did. Austria's a lazy place. We get such a lot of cloudy weather here."

"What's that got to do with being lazy?"

"Nothing." Thoughts about the pale grey clouds, that muffled the peaks and made the very air sedative, floated through his mind, but he had no words for them, because they belonged to the lost land of fairy-tales. At High Osterwitz, because she had visited the castle before, Meg had seemed to be leading him back again into that country; and throughout the long blissful day he had been aware of states of mind and feeling lost to him since childhood. Now the surface of his mind seemed like land heaved by a gentle earthquake, and through the cracks in its dry soil arose the scent of hidden water.

"Well, I expect we shall enjoy it," Ruth said, "you're the boss," and she smiled at him. He said hesitatingly:

"Ruthie, I wish you'd have a word with Meg. I half-promised her mother I'd ask you."

"I'd like to have a word with her very much indeed," said his betrothed vigorously; "I've been bursting to, in fact. She needs taking in hand—clothes, hair, figure, character—everything. If ever I saw a kid on the brink of making a complete mucker of her life, it's Miss Meg Lambert."

"Don't you like her?" he exclaimed, aghast at the success of his request. He felt as if he had been prospecting for a mineral and it had jumped out of the earth to meet him.

"In a way I do. She's such a baby and of course her mother's hopeless with her. She needs an elder sister who's been through it all. But she reminds me awfully of Barbara in some ways, and you know how maddening *she* can be."

"I think it's about her marrying Scarron that her mother wants you to talk to her, not—er—clothes or that sort of thing."

"It's all part of the same trouble—being in a mess. If she weren't in a mess she wouldn't want to marry him."

"I don't know that she does want to marry him," Humphrey said, feeling a constriction in his breast, "he's asked her and she's refused him. But Mrs Lambert says she—Meg—is going to talk to him again about it when they get back from Venice."

"Pretty cool, keeping him on a string like that. She'll be lucky if he doesn't back out. It isn't like playing around with someone of twenty. Is he so keen on her, then?"

"I suppose so, or he wouldn't have asked her. . . ." Humphrey got up from the garden seat. "All right, you'll have a word with her. You might point out the difference in—in age. That sort of thing. And he's half-Austrian as well. I agree with her mother that it would be most unlikely to work." He paused. "It would be very kind of you, dear."

"Oh, I don't mind. It will be a good work done, if you ask me. But, Hump, you'll have to be prepared for Meg to fly off the handle, you know. It's pretty good cheek, our butting in like this. After all, she has refused him. Or didn't you just say so?"

"Yes. Yes, she has. Her mother told me so this morning." Yet he did not feel as relieved by this news as he would have expected. *She* was so young, such a little idiot, a refusal from a girl like that did not mean much. And Scarron, twice her age, experienced, probably persistent . . . no, it meant almost nothing.

"I don't think I'll say anything until we get to Venice. We don't want her sulking for the whole fortnight. She *does*," Ruth added gently, "get sulky. I've noticed."

"Yes; I've noticed it too. She's . . . a maddening brat, if you ask me," he said with real bitterness, and poor Ruth was pleased to hear him say it; she liked them to agree about things and people, and of course, because Hump rightly disapproved of the way Meg Lambert "went on", it did not mean that he disliked her or would not try to help her, for he was as kind as he was sensible.

The kind and sensible one went off to collect his bathing-gear, feeling himself a blot upon the fair and smiling day.

*   *   *   *   *

During the next forty-eight hours, while the party was making its preparations for Venice, Frau Schacht dropped more than one remark about a lack of that excitement which ought to animate people who were going to the most exciting city in Europe. Her own sorrows had had the commonplace effect of making her less, not

more, sympathetic to those of others; perhaps the wilfulness, dis-
loyalties, worries and forebodings of most people seemed petty beside her own never-forgiven or forgotten sin; and while she perfectly realised that Humphrey had betrayed Ruth's trust, that Mrs
Lambert's happiness might, for a second time, be blighted, while
Meg might be contemplating the useless ruin of her own, none of
these facts seemed, to her, to excuse pensive faces and absent
answers. She felt impatient with everybody.

Nevertheless, she could not dismiss Meg's danger with an irritable
shrug. It was too like what her own had been seventeen years ago.
She had been unwillingly disturbed about it ever since hearing that
Scarron was paying the girl attentions; and even after she had made
her sacrifice and told her story, and heard from Eve Lambert that
Meg had decided to give Scarron the benefit of the doubt, she did
not decide to concern herself no more with the affair. She suggested
to Humphrey Scott that he should go with the Lamberts to Venice.

Ruth Courtney would have to go too, of course, but that made
no difference to Frau Schacht's plan. If Ruth lost her *braut*, that
would be a pity, but no doubt, thought Frau Schacht, she would
not much care. English girls were hard, in a curious, unfeminine
way; not hard like avaricious tarts—Frau Schacht could understand
those while condemning them—but hard like boys still at school, or
priests. None of these Englishwomen, not even Eve Lambert, whom
Frau Schacht knew to be full of feeling, was capable of the torrents
of emotion that had poured through her own veins and directed her
every action, when she was young. She despised them all as creatures
filled with milk-and-water.

But the truth was that the Lamberts as a family—and Ruth
Courtney too, because she suspected Ruth of belonging to the same
world—had won from her that unwilling admiration which un-
worldly types occasionally do win from worldly people who themselves possess streaks of nobility.

Frau Schacht had been clever at her books as a girl, but she had
wanted to use her learning to achieve money and fame, seeing herself as a populariser of literature or history with some practical
philosophy thrown in; a female Lin-Yutang or Doctor Joad or

Abbé Maigret, broadcasting and televising to the vast audiences of America. It had been a kind of perversion, a debasement, of the true teaching passion, but because, even so, there had still been in it much that was fine, it had remained uncondemned by her friends and fellow-workers in the teaching world. And she herself had not, for a long time, realised its baseness. But when she had come to live with the Lamberts; when she saw Eve Lambert's gentle eagerness to teach the stupidest child in her class as well as she taught the brightest; when she heard Harry Lambert grumbling cheerfully over his tedious and heavy war-work and saw the scrupulous care with which he did it; then at first scornfully, later wonderingly—against her will, because this behaviour reminded her of Franz and her sin —she had been charmed and won. What fools they were! And the streak of nobility in her own nature went out to greet them.

So, because the Lamberts were her good angels, it was impossible for her to stand passively by while Meg drifted into marrying Esmé Scarron. Let him be lost, in whatever way God saw fit to punish him, but Meg must be saved from a useless sacrifice. It would have seemed to Frau Schacht like destroying the better elements in herself to let Meg become, in time, corrupted by him, for she did not believe that Meg possessed enough strength of character either to make him a better man or to resist the contagion of his constant companionship and that of his friends. Enough people, Frau Schacht thought, had gone his way already, and he was no better because of them. He was not going to have Meg.

Frau Schacht knew the look of a young man in love and she knew Venice. She hoped that a combination of the two might save Meg at the eleventh hour.

She felt only a trace of regret, rather than remorse, on observing that Ruth Courtney's first good spirits appeared to have waned slightly. *So*, thought Frau Schacht, *now we are not so keen upon a massacre of the hornets. We feel less like a "bachfisch" and more like a woman. Now, perhaps, we shall grow up.*

Ruth did feel a little under the weather. She suspected that Cat was worrying about something; he had apparently given up talking; he simply hardly ever uttered, and when she teased him about his silence he snapped. It was very odd; she had seen him through moods of worry before now, when work or his family had been troublesome, but she had never known him in a mood like this. She began to worry slightly herself, wondering if there were some serious problem he were keeping from her or if he were secretly ill. It might be a duodenal; although he was young to have one, the loss of weight seemed to indicate it. But he became so irritable if she questioned him about his health that she gave up asking.

It was a pity, when the country was so gorgeous and the weather matched it. Perhaps he would be better when they got to Venice. Ruth tried to dismiss the matter, with her usual good sense; and all the time within herself, in the vast dim area beyond the rather unusually small range of her consciousness, lay the knowledge of what was the matter with her old Cat. But she did not know why she continued to disapprove so strongly of Meg Lambert.

The object of her disapproval was being sorely tried by these last two days before leaving for Venice, and began to count the hours until the party should go. She was exceedingly depressed, not with that vague, obscure, muffling sadness that sometimes came over her without cause in pensive and cloudy Martinsdorf while she was with Scarron, but with a new kind of sadness, one more directly associated with him. It was this overwhelming, weakening pity! which she had first experienced on the evening of his proposal. She did not always feel it, and while she was free from it she found difficulty in remembering how strong it was, but when it had her in its grip— and it seemed to overcome her several times a day—she would be unable to drive him from her thoughts, and on several occasions had thought that she could marry him out of pity. And then, when the mood had passed, she knew that no sympathy could overcome her lack of love for him and the fear which she felt when she imagined herself taken into his life; established as mistress of his three houses, *Lorelei*, the Cadillac, Iliaster, Lorenz, Janka and Melchior—and also, no doubt, of numerous French and Italian servants and animals at the Palazzo Tedeschi in Venice and at Lesvignes in the hills of Savoy. There was nothing to be afraid of, except the fact that she did not love him. She liked him very much; she did not shrink from the touch of his warm dry hand. Yet when she thought of being his wife she was afraid.

But there was no need to be afraid, she continued to tell herself, because she had refused his proposal. When they spoke about it again, after her return from Venice, it would only be to repeat what she had said that evening on the mountain top. It was ridiculous to be overcome by this pity for him, and to dream—as she did again, and more than once—of the great velvet butterfly that always eluded his grasping hands. And she continued to be afraid, and to dream, and to be overcome by these waves of pity. It was as if she were being attacked, bombarded!

She did not talk to her mother about her moods. Although she had made up her mind of her own accord to refuse Scarron, and had done so, she did not want to hear him criticised or abused, and, if encouraged, her mother would do both. And Meg kept more or less faithfully to her decision to keep an open mind about Hansi's accusations. She knew Hansi; had lived with her under the same roof for the three years from seven to ten, almost unconsciously learning the outline of her character as an intelligent child will, and she knew her to be both excitable and malicious. It was at least not unlikely that malice and melodrama were conspiring to accuse Esmé.

Meg was also handicapped by her upbringing. In carefully preparing her to resist evil, her parents had so surrounded her with evil's opposites that she had real difficulty in realising evil as a fact. She "simply could not believe" that anyone could "deliberately" get someone else sent to a concentration camp. The story must be an exaggeration or a mistake.

Yet there was that element of familiarity in it, which she still had not traced, and in *that* there was also fear. It linked itself to the inexplicable fear which she felt for Scarron's life and background.

She could not look forward to seeing Venice, the city about which she had been reading and dreaming for five years; she seemed lost in a sad, vague mood, heavy with mysterious pain, from which she could not rouse herself, and she was also troubled by her own lack of control about Humphrey Scott; they had "got into this silly habit" of looking at one another, and she had decided that it had got to stop, and it hadn't. Their eyes continued to meet, across the garden or the length of a room, for long moments before each looked away.

> They could not in the self-same mansion dwell
> Without some stir of heart, some malady . . .

When the lines came into her thoughts, while she was still looking down, unseeingly, with pale cheeks, after one of these silent encounters, she thrust them away as if they were deadly dangerous.

She tried to wish that he were not coming to Venice, but that was no use either. There was no difficulty about wishing it of Ruth—but there was another line of thought that was best not pursued.

None of these feelings and thoughts were clear. They drifted over her like the summer clouds that hung over the mountains before the arrival of the Carinthian autumn; faint, pale, laden with mystery and hiding what was to come.

Three members of the party, however, were cheerfully looking forward to the visit. Marcel expected to return from a tour of the galleries and churches and restaurants convinced of the superiority of French painting, architecture and cooking, while Robin and Camilla, having casually filled two exiguous suitcases with their slender clothes, lay side by side on the last evening before the party's departure, sun-bathing with hearts at ease.

"Why do you think she calls him Cat?" Camilla asked presently, after a long silence devoted to thought.

"The Head Pre.?" rousing himself to squint at her. "The Cat-that-Walks-by-Itself, I imagine. Just-So Stories."

"Yes, I've read them."

"So I should hope," shutting his eyes again.

"The boys made me. I liked Enid Blyton."

"I look forward to meeting your brothers. You have been very fortunate in them. Again and again I hear of them hauling you past appalling pitfalls."

"Yes. What shall we do in Venice?"

"No sight-seeing, for a start. It's so snobbish . . . there are thousands of superb things to be seen at home, first, before one starts on the foreign things. I'll take you to Hampton Court and Knole when we get back. In Venice Mammy Gascoine and Missy Camilla sit in de sun and drink a bery little and watch de world go by."

Camilla said nothing but an expression of pleasure appeared on her small face. Presently he said, without opening his eyes:

"Mammy Gascoine 'ticipate a tur'ble fight soon wid de Head Pre. an' her man. He not walkin' by himself no more. He not walkin' wid her. He want walk wid *de wrong pusson*. But you and I are not being drawn into it, arguing and taking sides and so forth. Nothing could be more tedious. So remember, Camilla."

"All right."

★ ★ ★ ★ ★

Towards noon on the next day the long heavy train was running under a burning sun across the plains that lead to Venice. It had wound its way down from Austria through canyons of pale, yellow-grey limestone, across light green rivers, and over wastes of white pebbles covered in spring with torrent-water, and each time that the hot and sweating passengers jammed in the corridors beheld one of the stony expanses, which were sometimes a mile wide, those unfamiliar with the journey cried eagerly, "Is this Venice? Is that a lagoon?" and the knowledgeable ones shook their heads. Being Italians, they shook their heads smilingly and sympathetically; no, it was not Venezia yet; Venezia was still many miles away; soon you will see the lagoons; but first we must reach Mestre; when you see Mestre you will know that Venezia is near.

Meg had been eagerly yet dreamily watching the changing landscape from the moment when, emerging from a tunnel still in the Austrian highlands, the train stopped at a station which appeared, to the travellers, as different; surrounded by mountains less pensive and covered by a sky more blue, while on the platforms the laughing people stood with folded arms and there was no doubt that a sense of immense leisure had come into the scene. She turned to her mother, with eyes sparkling—"Italy!"—and although she heard the Customs official with the plume of feathers in his hat sigh "Bellissima inglese", as he edged his way past her, she did not notice how casually he and his companions inspected the luggage for contraband. This was the beautiful, poor and passionate country where the almost lost art of living was still practised, the land lying behind the mountains that she had watched at morning and evening for so many weeks. She was not troubled by the increasing heat and discomfort as passengers crowded aboard at every station and the luggage gradually accumulated in the corridors until it was touching their ceilings, being intent upon the plain beyond the windows. Secretive thickets of green acacia came down to the railway's edge. Beyond them were fields of maize, with pink tassels growing atop of their broad leaves. Never was a country covered so densely with foliage; the soil itself was almost hidden, except for shady grass rides that now and then ran down between the bushes to the line. Pink houses painted with blue or yellow wreaths stood up in all this leafiness. The sky was a pale and brilliant blue and curved itself in a recognisable arch above the immense plain. The eye began to long for the sight of water.

This continued for what seemed hours. The rapid voices chattered ceaselessly around her and the busy brown hands gesticulated and the laughter was unceasing. She was separated from the rest of the party by the crowd, and presently the isolation began to extend itself to her feelings. The anxieties that had been troubling her seemed to have been left behind in Austria, and she thought of them no more.

As the hours passed, and the heat increased, the Italians grew livelier and the travellers from northern countries more silent. The sun looked steadily, with an effect of jubilation, upon the light, bright land; and the air, the foliage, the white stations where historic names last heard in some play by Shakespeare were inscribed upon the direction boards, all appeared to shimmer. Meg turned from the window only once, drawn she knew not why to look back into the mass of chattering, laughing people packed closely behind her, and saw through a gap in the crowd Humphrey's face. He was looking at her with an expression of pleasure, and when their eyes met he smiled. Her heart lifted, and she turned away.

Presently she heard the cry "Mestre—Mestre." She leaned far out of the window and felt a burning air touch her face. After a time the train rolled ponderously on.

Suddenly she exclaimed, gripping the window frame. The train had launched out on to a low and immensely long bridge. It was travelling over shallow greenish water, whence projected dark poles, tall, and of an unmistakable and familiar shape. She leaned farther out of the window, while behind her heads crowded closer and voices were exclaiming loudly, and looked to the right. Half a mile away across the lagoon a low barrier, coloured rust and brown and white, rose out of the pale water, and beyond were houses black and olive and grey, and farther off yet, soaring out of the reef of buildings that might have been formed through the ages from dim broken seashells, was a pink tower with, floating beside it, a dome. The air felt like warm cream. And all was adorably unimpressive, even slightly shabby, and marred by the erections and transactions of that commerce by which the city had once lived; there was no need for the solemn emotions to assert themselves. In a mysterious way the approach resembled a homecoming. When the train stopped at last, in that station which might belong to any small coastal town in Europe, Meg moved down the platform lost to all feelings save those of soft and delighted pleasure; she went straight through the station and on to the top of the steps that dive into the city's dazzling depths, and looked downwards. Below ran a broad green canal and over it sprang a bridge. She walked quickly down the steps and across the street and went up the bridge's rise until she stood on its summit, and then once more looked down. There, growing from stone piers, were long strands of dark green seaweed, waving slowly in the transparent water to the movement of the tide. She saw either shore crowded with pale ornate houses and thronged with people lifting laughing faces to the sun; she saw narrow streets sharp with black shadow and a vista of houses coloured ochre, and cinnamon, and grey, and rose. She looked down again at the floating seaweed—and suddenly a long black thing shot out from under the bridge with a man riding on it bent almost double, and she heard a loud, strange cry.

"*It is Venice.*"

CHAPTER TWENTY-FIVE

Bombshell

"It is lovely. It's beautiful. I don't deny any of that. But *you* can't deny that it's dirty."

"I don't mind it being dirty. It's so beautiful it doesn't matter."

"All right then, so long as you do realise it. And *don't*"—shooting out a hand and arresting Meg's on its way to her mouth—"eat *unwashed* fruit! Heavens, child, you must be crackers!"

"What shall I eat, then?" crossly.

"Peel them, of course. Here's a paper napkin—and some more bread—I wish Camilla wouldn't hang over those poor miserable cats, I know she'll get some frightful disease."

Ruth turned round in her chair to look at the third member of the party, who was stooping over a cat in the last stages of emaciation at some distance from the table where their picnic was spread. It was the third day of their stay, and the three girls had spent the morning in shopping for the elegant inexpensive glass jewellery which is one of Venice's minor prides. The young men had gone by themselves to see the Arsenal and Murano, and Mrs Lambert was spending the morning sitting in the Public Gardens, for after only three days in Venice she was missing grass and trees. The city had knocked the breath out of her, and she was not yet sure if she liked it.

"Do have some sausage . . ." Camilla was saying earnestly, "come on then, ducky, eat up—poor, poor pussy."

"It's quite spoiling her holiday, all these starving cats," Meg said, watching the scene.

"It is a disgrace. The municipal authorities ought to go into action. Can you imagine it going on in England? Cam," raising her voice, "your wine will be boiling hot, it's stood in the sun for ten minutes."

"Move it, then," was the uninterested reply as Camilla, stooping encouragingly, followed the languid cat towards a far corner of the small paved square, shut in by ancient houses, where the party had settled itself for lunch. She was surrounded by a dozen of the starving animals, hissing and fighting over the fragments of salami which she had distributed.

"Heavenly. They're just the same colour as the walls of that wineshop," Meg said, and held up a bunch of clear tawny grapes to the sun.

"You really love it here, don't you?" said Ruth, and Meg, with her mouth full, nodded.

"Better than Austria?"

"Heavens, yes. It's just my . . . glass of wine," and she laughed. Ruth looked at her, sitting in the sunlight, in that pink dress that left bare her plump golden arms and a good share of shoulder, wearing that conspicuous hat. . . .

"Yes, I'd noticed you were more cheerful," she said.

"Was I so dreary in Austria? Dear, dear." It was said with Robin's airiest intonation, and Ruth found it irritating.

In fact, she had been steadily irritated by Meg ever since the party had left Martinsdorf; it had begun on the train, when Meg had hung out of the window literally for hours and did not seem to notice the misery of a journey which had reduced older travellers to headachy silence; then in Venice she had persistently gone about with an expression of rapture that looked really half-witted, and she *would* loiter. The party was always finding itself unable to see some sight which it had planned to include in a morning's programme because they had been held up by Meg, dawdling, gazing, wandering off down a dark *rio*, or stopping to coo over a baby. Ruth too loved the Italian babies, but after one had been cooed over there was no need to do it again over the next one. Humphrey found all this amusing (or said he did, although he had now stopped laughing, as well as talking), but it irritated Ruth. It was so childish. And it was also selfish, for although Venice was beautiful it was also full of dirt, smells and appalling unemployment. No one had the *right* to drift about ignoring such things.

"Of course, if you only look at one side of Venice——" Ruth was beginning, when Meg interrupted vehemently with:

"I *adore* it. I'd like to live here for ever."

But then she became suddenly silent, and sat looking at her glass, which she turned slowly about in her fingers, with a conscious expression. Ruth probably knew that she had the opportunity to live in Venice if she wanted to, and most earnestly did she want to avoid discussing that opportunity with Ruth, whom she believed to be a kind, good and sensible girl. She did not want to advance one step farther in intimacy with Ruth. She avoided looking at Ruth whenever possible, because, when she did, she saw another cheek close to hers . . . and then she had to seize that thought and that picture, and choke it; as if, like the lines from *Isabella*, it were deadly dangerous. But all this was happening to her almost without her knowledge, because the glitter and light and astonishing vitality of Venice had acted upon her spirit like strong wine, and if she found herself in a strange state of mind and heart, strangeness was only to be expected in this city.

Ruth saw the conscious look and guessed the thought that had produced it. She glanced round once more at Camilla, who showed no sign of returning to the table, and decided that here was her opportunity to have that "word" with Meg which she had undertaken, at Humphrey's request, to have with her. She also felt in the mood for giving good advice; especially good advice to Meg.

"Well, you could live here if you wanted to, couldn't you? Or so I've been given to understand," she began lightly.

"Dear me, has that got around on the grape vine?" Meg's tone was quite the silliest in her repertoire, and as she spoke she twisted herself sideways to examine her sandal. "Damn, this thing is giving way."

"I did hear something—through your mother, actually. She's been awfully worried."

The tone was intended to be that of an elder sister, and it was only Ruth's unconscious dislike of Meg that gave to it another ring. Meg stopped examining her sandal, and looked up.

Whew! Sulks and a bit more, thought Ruth, and just for a second she had the curious impression that she was meeting the eyes of a much older woman. It was because of Meg's capacity to experience feelings that Ruth would never have. A time would be, not many years hence, when both would be married, but Ruth's outlook on life would still largely be that of a girl.

She tried to adopt a friendlier tone; she knew enough about being nineteen to guess how Meg was feeling, although she thought her very silly to take it like that.

"I know this must seem like frightful cheek, but you know I don't mean it that way. I've got a young sister round about your age and in some ways you remind me of her. We had a lot of fuss and bother at home with young Ba last year, and I was able to get her out of a jam she'd got herself into. I'd like to help you, too."

"Oh? What sort of a jam?" Meg's mood was a mixture of furious annoyance and passionate sympathy with young Ba.

"The usual thing. Wanting to marry someone wildly unsuitable, whom we could none of us stand at home."

"And did you rescue her?" politely.

"I did," Ruth answered cheerfully. "I talked to her like a Dutch aunt. And after it was all over and she was engaged to someone else, she had the decency to admit I'd been right about the other type all along."

"What a cowardly, false-hearted little traitor she must be," observed Meg, and finished her wine with a flourish.

"Hey, hey! Strong language! My sister, if you please!"

"I meant it. She shouldn't have let you persuade her."

"I didn't 'persuade' her. I just made her see what a fool she was being. She's very happy now."

"How nice for her."

"Which I'm pretty sure you won't be if you marry Esmé Scarron." She brought out the name with assurance, having obtained it from Humphrey.

"How do you know?" Meg's calm voice did not match her expression, "and how do you know I'm going to marry him, anyway?"

"Well, aren't you?"

"I've turned him down once. Didn't the grape vine get around to telling you that?"

"Yes, as a matter of fact it did, but people don't usually suggest 'talking things over' unless they're thinking about changing their mind, and I'd also heard you're going to see him again about it when you get back from Venice."

"You seem to have heard a lot," Meg said, in a rather dejected tone, and leant forward and rested her elbows amidst the bread and grapes and wine-glasses on the table. Could Mummy have told her all this? Impossible; not so much, anyway. Then who was it? Hansi?

Ruth, thinking that her quieter manner implied more willingness to listen, perhaps even a reluctant desire for advice, leant forward in her turn.

"Meg, I know you're annoyed and I do sympathise. I hate butting in like this, but I'm thinking about your mother. Don't you know how worried she is? And she's absolutely certain he's the wrong person for you."

"Mummy fusses." Meg had grown pale, and her eyes were fixed steadily upon Ruth's face. It no longer possessed youthful bloom, and Meg was glad of this, and ashamed of herself for being so.

"Not more than anybody's mother would be in the circumstances. Honestly, Meg, even an outsider can see how long the odds are against your making a go of it with someone like that—twice your age, and a foreigner——"

"He's only half Austrian. His father was English."

"But he's lived abroad all his life and he *looks* so foreign. Of course I know he's rich and could give you a glamorous life——"

"I don't care about that now," Meg interrupted; "I did at first, but not now." She spoke in a low tone without a trace of anger, keeping her eyes fixed on the table. She was remembering her dream of Scarron and the butterfly, and although it seemed remote, as she sat here in the warmth and brilliant light of Venice, yet even here the memory could reach out to touch her with a shadowy chill.

"Are you—keen on him now, then?" Ruth asked, with mingled embarrassment and bluntness.

Meg shook her head. "I'm sorry for him, that's all," she answered in the same low, quiet tone, "sometimes I'm so sorry for him I can hardly bear it. And he says I could help him."

Ruth did not know what to say. She could not quite dismiss Meg as a sillier and more obstinate edition of Ba, because there was a quality in Meg which she did not understand; had she been asked to define it, she would have said that Meg was "deeper" than her sister. In a moment, as she studied the downcast childish face, there also occurred to her the word *sly*.

"Well, of course, that's a decent enough reason for marrying someone: wanting to help them. But it doesn't get over the big difference in age, and his being foreign. And hasn't he been divorced?"

"Yes. But he divorced her, not the other way about."

"Still, it's all rather squalid, isn't it? Wouldn't you rather have someone with—a clean licence?"

Meg, who had forgotten during the last few remarks that she possessed a temper, suddenly rediscovered it. But only to lose it.

"Would you?" she asked, leaning across the table.

"Keep calm," Ruth said good-naturedly, "I have; I'm Hump's first and only. And before you fly *quite* off the handle I'd better tell you it was he who asked me to have a word with you. Your mother told him all about it, and how worried she was. I'm not so fond of interfering in other people's affairs, I can assure you."

Meg drew slowly back, with the movement of one pulling a sword out of their breast.

"I'm sorry," she said in a moment, "I didn't mean to be rude."

"That's all right. Forget it. But do think things over—*hard*—before you decide to have him after all."

Meg did not answer.

"You didn't know so many people were interested in your future, did you?" Ruth went on cheerfully; she was not annoyed; Meg had behaved just as she had expected. "Doesn't it strike you, now, that if so many people are getting *agitato* about your marrying that man, he's probably the wrong one for you? Total strangers don't usually take all this trouble over a girl who's thinking about getting tied up."

"Yes. I see. Thank you," Meg said after a pause.

"You're livid with us all; don't think you can fool me. I do understand how you feel, honestly, but you'll just have to believe that we—Hump and I—mean it well. We're a team, you see, and we always work together."

She did not know quite why she finished her sentence with this statement. Perhaps she wanted to assure Meg that, if blame were to be apportioned, she and Humphrey stood to receive equal shares. Or perhaps she only wanted Meg to realise that they were a team.

She turned away, apparently to see what Camilla was doing but actually to allow the kid to get some control over her face. She looked quite ill. What a fuss, thought Ruth, about a bit of advice. And probably half of it was temper.

"Hullo—had enough?" she called to Camilla, who now approached.

"It's hellish," said the animal-worshipper briefly, before putting her nose into her glass. "But I've left that old hag a thousand lire to buy food for them. And I'm writing to the Italian Government. Boiling wine—how beastly."

The remainder of the picnic luncheon passed rather silently. The three girls sat at the small iron table, with the carafe and the thick tumblers half full of yellow wine, and finished eating their grapes and sausage, while the life of the shabby little square flowed indifferently around them. Women came and went at the stall which sold vegetables larger, brighter in colour and surely more knotted and rugose than those displayed at home: bulbous purple eggplants like miniature airships, giant scarlet knobbed tomatoes, nameless roots twisted and brown. They looked like a gardening catalogue that had taken to witchcraft.

Pigeons sailed and fluttered about the ancient cinnamon walls of the church at one end of the square, whose flaking and faceless stone angels looked up at the light. Old women crept about in black shawls. Thin youths in open-necked shirts stood in groups gesticulating and talking at a terrific pace, where unemployed English ones would have lounged silently against a wall. The hot blue sky poured sunlight on to the crumbling brown and olive roofs, and wandering puffs of wind brought garlic and synthetic scents from the open door of the hairdresser's shop and the stench of stagnant water to the three who sat at the table, examining the jewellery bought that morning.

"This is really the prettiest"—Ruth held up a necklace made of green glass leaves, milky white berries and tiny foolish-faced doves —"don't you agree?" to Meg. She was pleasantly determined not to allow any sulking.

"Oh yes . . . but this is darling too. . . ." Meg swung a heavy circlet of beads resembling cloudy golden sugar. "It's more *Venetian*. If someone showed me this, I would think—Venice. . . ."

"I like mine best."

"It *is* too old for you, Cam. Grey mother-o'-pearl—and all those points. It's lovely, but it's *dowagery*."

"It's in good taste," Camilla said. They did not look at one another; both were thinking that the doves and berries were too young for Ruth.

"I think on second thoughts I'll give this to Alix . . . she's the baby of the family, just twelve . . ." Ruth said in a moment, competently re-packing the doves in their tissue-paper, "it's a bit youthful for me."

Camilla, who knew from Meg's face that something awful had happened while she was with the cats, self-sacrificingly summoned her social training and asked three or four interested questions about Ruth's little sister, the answering of which put Ruth into an even better temper and gave Meg time to struggle with what was hurting her. Camilla thought that she looked like a puppy with a thorn in its paw. It's something to do with H. S., she thought; I'll rally round.

Meg could hardly breathe for the pain in her heart. Her thoughts threshed now this way, now that, trying to find relief. The only way out that seemed to be offered to her was endurance: ten more days of seeing him with Ruth, and knowing that what he had told her with his eyes was a lie, and that she had got herself into an agonising situation, and that he only felt for her the "sensible" kindness of an elder brother. Yes, the only way offered to her was the way of endurance, but it was also the way that her temperament was least fitted to follow. She needed action, and she needed to hurt him. When she remembered the looks exchanged across the flowers, or down the dimly-lit length of the *speisesaal* in the evenings, she felt capable of doing *anything* that would hurt him. And he had asked Ruth to advise her against marrying Esmé. Because her mother was worried, and because he truly had her welfare at heart—but what *business* was it of his?—or because he did not want her to become engaged to someone while she was living in the same house with him? Because he had let himself become attracted . . . and he was a coward . . . oh, what shall I do? What *can* I do, to stop feeling like this? . . .

"If we're going to be there by three o'clock we ought to be pushing along," Ruth said.

They gathered their possessions together, paid their bill at the wine shop, and set off through the crowded narrow streets for the Grand Canal.

They were bound for the Lido. Three days of gazing at pictures and palaces had given them all a desire for simpler, out-of-door pleasures, and this afternoon they were to meet at the bus station on the island and have a bathing-party.

"I'm shopping for a waxen image to-morrow," Camilla observed in an undertone to Meg, while they were waiting at the riva degli Schiavoni for Ruth to buy their tickets.

Meg's answer was a smile whose misery she did not attempt to hide.

"Break its ankle. Lay the Head Pre. low," Camilla continued. "What in hell has she been saying?"

"Nothing. Oh, well—something. But it's all my fault. Can't bear to talk."

Camilla put a hand like a small cool leaf for an instant on hers. "Bear up." Then they hurried to join Ruth on the solid, heavy deck of the *vaporetto*.

The *vaporetto*, which is the Venetian water-bus, and which looks like an infant channel steamer, zigzagged its way down the Grand Canal, now drawing in to a landing-stage on one shore, now on the other, and each time that it stopped it hit the floating landing-stage such a tremendous whang that tourists who were interested in such things wondered how long the average life of a *vaporetto* and a landing-stage might be, and which one succumbed first. The English ones also wondered what a London bus-driver would have said about the steering. Soon the vessel got past the Punta della Salute and made out across the Bacino di San Marco for the open lagoon.

Meg stood near the rail and felt the sweet warm wind blow against her face. The pain and confusion of her feelings had not subsided, and she had realised that in a few minutes she must confront Humphrey. She concentrated all her self-control upon looking interested and serene, while she struggled with a temptation which had presented itself as *another way out*, and a way, also, in which she could hurt Humphrey. It would help to give her back her self-respect, and so painful were her anger and humiliation at the moment that they were far more powerful than a faint sensation of fear, touching her nerves at the thought of what she might within the next hour do.

After all, she need not say anything definite. Or she could back out of it afterwards. And again, as once on the summit of the high mountain with Scarron, she experienced that sense of impatience with the moral necessity, that longing for a life devoted to the indulgence of self.

She looked across the expanse of water, rapidly growing narrower as the *vaporetto* drew in to the landing-stage, and suddenly she saw Humphrey's head and shoulders, next to those of Robin, amidst the waiting crowd. He was looking steadily and directly at her; at her, not at Ruth. Anger rushed over her, destroying every other feeling, and she quickly turned away her head.

The wide dove-coloured sands of the Lido were almost deserted that afternoon; the warm Adriatic rolled its purple shells gently into the pools where a few Italian children splashed and played, and on the horizon lay long, motionless white clouds. Leaving behind the expensive hotels, with their Riviera architecture and their palms, the bus travelled the short distance across the island and finally set down its passengers, including the *Venedig* party, at the entrance to the public bathing-station amidst small white and green cabins and sandy enclosures planted with pink oleander.

"How peaceful . . ." Mrs Lambert said, looking along the expanse of what has been called, and not only by travel agencies, one of the finest beaches in Europe, "and before they built here it must have been better still . . . nothing but sands and sea and sky . . . Meg," turning round, "what's that poem . . . where *is* Meg?" in surprise.

"She's gone to make a telephone call," Robin said; they were all making their way slowly over the sands now, straying in groups and looking for somewhere suitable to sit down.

"A telephone call? But who to?"

"She didn't say. She said she wouldn't be long and not to worry. Camilla," turning to her, "are you coming to bathe?"

It was nearly an hour later, when they were all seated in a small café drinking tea and resting after the bathe, and Mrs Lambert had ceased trying to hide her anxiety, that Meg came towards them over the sands. The afterglow fell gently upon her pink dress and golden arms and hair, and with the hat that might have belonged to the Ancient World, and the calm, sedate manner of her approach, she suggested some minor goddess, a patroness of clay pipkins or braided baskets, newly stepped out of an Etruscan temple.

"Darling, where *have* you been?" her mother uncontrollably called.

Meg smiled and gave a reassuring wave, but did not speak until she came right up to where they were sitting. Then she put a hand on her mother's shoulder and bent down and gave her a kiss.

"Only telephoning. It took ages to get through at the hotel. I'm sorry." She straightened up, and stood looking pleasantly at no one in particular. Humphrey's mouth had become dry.

"Now," Meg said steadily, "we must all have some more tea, partly because I'm gasping for it but chiefly to celebrate. We'll have some more cakes, too. And you must all drink to—to Esmé and me. We've just got engaged. We fixed it up ten minutes ago on the telephone."

CHAPTER TWENTY-SIX

Poor Ruth

THE tea was brought, and with it a plate of cakes which came in for much unnecessary comment, and both were consumed while congratulations, after the first silence that had followed her announcement, were offered to Meg. No one looked at anybody else while they were being made, and everyone avoided looking at Mrs Lambert, who appeared stunned; she sat with her hands lying in her lap and stared at her daughter without speaking a word. Deep colour burned in Ruth's face, Humphrey was as pale as Meg herself, and everyone felt grateful to Robin and Marcel, who occupied the end of the wretched party with a lively argument about the climate of southern France and that of Venice. Everyone was anxious to get away, leaving the two who had the most to say to one another to say it in privacy, but it was realised that they must all travel back by the bus, leaving at an hour which would get them back to their *pensione* in time for the evening meal, and no one cared to make any other suggestion. They lingered on; the afterglow gradually faded and the sea darkened to amethyst, while a few last bathers sauntered up from the waves wrapped in white towelling robes that glimmered through the evening. Now they could hear the sea splashing languidly; it was the only sound except their own infrequent voices. Meg had not once looked at Humphrey. And still the air was warm—warm as it never is in England even on summer nights; it lay gently against the skin, with an indescribable softness that might have belonged to an unknown element, and the scene, the hour, the tender dying sunset, the distant flashing lights with their promise of gaiety and pleasure, drew the young heart irresistibly towards love.

"Don't let's go back to the *pensione*," Humphrey said suddenly in an undertone to Ruth, "let's stay on and get something here." The words were framed as a suggestion, but had the ring of a command.

"All right," she said doubtfully after a pause, "but isn't it rather a pity to miss dinner when we've so little currency? They'll charge us, anyway."

In answer he stood up and began to help her into her coat.

A few moments later they were all in the bus; rattling through the evening, past the ornamental gardens planted with palms and dark red lilies, and the white houses along the Gran Viale, to Santa Maria Elizabetta. Meg had taken her mother's arm and held her hand within her own and Mrs Lambert was trying not to cry. At the landing-stage there was such a crowd pressing on to the *vaporetto* that it was easy for Ruth and Humphrey to lose the Lamberts in the throng, and there was only time for them to wave to the other three before the *vaporetto*, after a final collision with the landing-stage that made both ring again, swung out into the smooth pale orange water of the lagoon and made off for the sparkling distant lights of Venice.

"Where to?" Ruth asked, thrusting her arm through his.

"Anywhere. No, I saw a place down there that looked all right, just now, from the bus; let's cross."

His arm felt unresponsive against her own, but she held on to it calmly. He was annoyed, she supposed, because her "word" with that little idiot had driven her into accepting the man; it looked as if that was what had happened. But what a little firework, what a handful! Her poor mother could never know where she was with a kid like that, and it was awfully irritating of Hump to take the engagement so to heart; it wasn't his fault, any more than it was Ruth's own, and, come to that, it wasn't really his business either. It was not as if he had known the Lamberts for years.

They found a restaurant at the beginning of the town's main avenue, whose white shutters and palm and chestnut trees shading expensive little shops had a look more of France than of Italy; the place they chose was not quiet, but economy compelled them there rather than to somewhere more expensive. They ate in the open air, and Ruth did not object to the groups at the other tables, feeling the need of noise and cheerfulness after the late tea-party.

"Do cheer up, Cat," she said briskly, after they had eaten in silence for longer than she considered either desirable or sensible, "it's no one's fault and it can't be helped. After all, she isn't going to be eaten alive. She's only getting married." And as if an instinct of which she was unaware warned her to assert her claim upon him, she added with a laugh, "I think she's rather lucky. I wish it was us."

She was looking down at her plate with a slight lingering smile when he said something in answer, and she did not hear what it was. She glanced up enquiringly and saw him looking so strange that she exclaimed:

"Darling, are you all right? You look awfully pale."

He shook his head, realising with a sick feeling that she had not heard, and said slowly:

"I'm all right. That is—Ruthie, you must help me. We've got to have this out."

"What out? What do you mean?" staring.

"I'm sorry. Ruthie, I am sorry. You must believe that."

"Sorry? What about? I don't know what the heck you're talking about, Cat. Are you *sure* you're all right? You've been in the sun all day. . . ."

He shook his head again. "No, I'm all right. But—och, this is awful" (the l was barely sounded). "I've got to tell you. We can't be married."

She stared at him with her knife and fork suspended.

"Can't be *married*? But why not? What on earth do you mean? What's happened?"

Thoughts about illness and family troubles and jobs in places impossible for the most devoted of wives to go to were running through her mind, while a deep sense of dismay and alarm had come down upon her, more because of his manner than because of what he was saying; indeed, she had not yet taken that in.

"Nothing's happened," he said after a pause, "at least, nothing . . . it isn't your . . . it isn't anything you've done, Ruthie, but I'm asking you to let me go."

"Let you *go*?" She was still completely bewildered, but at this the colour came into her face; did he feel he was being kept against his will? What *was* all this? They had never had such a "deep" conversa-

tion, with unspoken thoughts whirling underneath it, in all the
twelve years of their friendship.

"Och—I'm sorry, I didn't mean to put it like that. When you—
you won't want to go on with things when I've told you—only
there isn't anything to tell. Not really. Except that now I can't ask
you to marry me."

"But, Hump, *why* not? Don't be so fearfully mysterious. What
on earth's it all *about*? What do you mean—you can't *ask* me to
marry you? If it comes to that"—she tried a troubled little laugh;
it was a miserable effort, but as she remembered the long years of
comradeship lying behind them and the tender friendliness and
shared interests, she felt a rush of confidence which reflected itself
in her expression. She also felt that all this simply could not be true
—"you never *have* 'asked' me. Not in so many words. We—we've
always just *known* we should make a go of things, haven't we?"

He said nothing.

"Is it because you're afraid you won't get a decent-enough job?"

"I'm not afraid of anything," he said surlily.

"Yes—I know—but you have said over and over again that we
shall have to live very uncomfortably and miles away from anywhere, and you do know I shall mind leaving the Family—I'm not
making a martyr of myself—you know that too—only I've never
pretended I wouldn't *mind* leaving them . . . have you got cold feet
about that?"

He did not answer.

"Hump, can't you *tell* me what it is? Oh, please. Do try." She
gave one twist of her capable long hands, locked together on her
lap. "Can't you see . . . it's awful for me, not *knowing* why you're
going on like this? Is it something I've done? Because if it is, do tell
me. I promise I won't go off the deep end. I'll be a good girl and say
I'm sorry." She tried another laugh.

He looked up slowly.

" 'Tisn't anything you've done. My God . . . no. It's me."

"Something you've done?"

He nodded.

"Well—it can't be anything so awful. I know my old Cat. Come on—True Confession. Tell Auntie Ruth and she'll . . . kiss the place and make it well."

But he only shook his head, and she was quiet for a moment, struggling with the lump in her throat brought there by one word in her last sentence.

"It isn't fair, you know," she said, when she could speak.

"Of course it isn't." He looked up quickly and spoke almost indignantly. "Of course it isn't fair. Nothing ever is . . . in . . . in this kind of . . . och, I'm all mixed up. I'm not fit . . . Ruthie, let's not talk about it any more."

"You mean—you didn't mean what you said about us not . . . not——" Her face was alight with hope, she leant towards him so eagerly, she would forget everything, take him back as if nothing had happened . . . and it wasn't any temptation at all. He would sooner go on, now that he had taken the plunge.

"No, I didna mean that. I meant I can't tell you why . . . so let me go, like a dear . . . I'm not worth it, honest to God I'm not, and one day you'll be thankful. . . ."

But she slowly shook her head. She was beginning to experience a frightful emotion: it would not last long: training and control and character would reassert themselves; but for the moment it was despair. She tried once more.

"Hump . . ." she began slowly to lose her colour, "you needn't mind telling me. I do know . . . men are different from us (I took that series of lectures, do you remember? and they taught me quite a lot) . . . I do know there are these dangerous blondes——"

She stopped, appalled. The vulgar little joke had been slipped in to conceal embarrassment, but both at once saw Meg, as they had seen her only an hour ago: pale, looking out defiantly from the cavern of her great hat; with beautiful hair spread upon her shoulders. Ruth stared at him, almost realising the truth.

But she had been resisting realisation for so long that now resistance refused to break down. In a moment she said, in a new and harder tone:

"Is it someone else?"

"I'm not thinking of marrying anyone else, if that's what you're meaning." Guilt made him feel anger towards her; and why must she *keep on*? Why couldn't she just tell him to go to hell, and then they could both be quiet.

"I should hope not, considering you're still engaged to me!" But then she looked down at her ring and suddenly her eyes filled. "Oh, Hump . . . this is ghastly. I can't believe it's us," and out came a rather large handkerchief patterned with sporting checks. He glanced hastily at the nearest table, but the occupants, being Italian and accustomed to love in a warm climate, had taken one frank stare and were now going on eating unperturbed.

". . . simply can't believe it. . . ."

"Don't, Ruthie. Och, don't . . . dear. Better now than later on."

"If only you'd tell me what it is. . . ."

He did not even trouble to shake his head, and she looked at his haggard face over the top of her handkerchief with a feeling like hatred. Stubborn, obstinate, pig-headed . . . but she had always known he was that, and they had often joked about it. Now it was not a matter for joking any more.

Presently, when she had used the handkerchief a good deal, and made those movements of the shoulders and mouth which she had associated from childhood with "pulling oneself together", she looked across at him again. Her expression was neither mournful nor lost; she seemed to be preparing herself for a last effort.

"Hump, I've got to ask you something."

"Well?" He met her eyes with defiance, but his heart plunged with alarm.

"You needn't look at me like that. I've done nothing—that I know of. But you've got to tell me if this is our last chance—if you're going to—to finish things here and now, or if you want me to—to let you think it over. I will, if you ask me to. But I—I think it's only fair to me to—sorry. I'm not putting it clearly. What I mean is, I want to know where I stand."

In a moment he said slowly, without looking at her:

"I'm sorry, Ruth. I want it finished here and now."

"All right, then," she said after a pause. "All right," and began slowly drawing off the modest ring of gold and pearls.

"Oh, for God's sake—can't you keep it? I want you to; I'd—I'd feel better if you would. I shall only throw the damned thing into the canal if you give it to me."

"I'll keep it if you want me to," she said quietly, and they sat in silence while she removed it from the place of honour and fitted it on to a lesser finger. Then she began to go on with her dinner, remarking that this place was so expensive that it seemed a pity to waste the food. They were both reminded of their mutual economies, with a mutual end in view, spread over the last year, and felt, if possible, even more wretched.

Presently, however, Ruth began to feel that it was an outrage upon the social scene to keep up this sullen and miserable silence, and she had also detected one or two stares from neighbouring tables—not the embarrassed half-glances that would have been given in England, dear, blessed old place where somehow she felt her engagement would have stayed safe and unbroken, but frank, warm, interested, sympathetic *stares*. Dreadful! So she tried to make conversation, but so deep were her bitterness and pain that she could not keep them out of what she said, nor could she avoid the one subject which, she knew half-consciously she ought, for the sake of what peace of mind was left to her, to avoid.

"It's been quite a day for engagements, hasn't it . . . that silly little ass . . . I did speak to her about looking before she leapt; I had a word with her just before we met you, actually, but it can't have done much good, considering she sailed in like that an hour afterwards saying it was all fixed up."

He made some vague mutter in reply. So she had goaded that wild little idiot into doing it. And if he had not suggested she should speak to her, the wild little idiot would be free at this moment. But in that case, of course, *he* would still be tied up. Oh, it was a nice mess. But he was beginning, in spite of misery, to feel a stealing relief at not being tied up any more. At least he was free to *look* at her and *think* about her and *want* her. He need not struggle with loyalty to Ruth, and he was also beginning to suspect that what he had done was the right, though it was apparently the cruel, thing. It would have been downright wickedly unfair to marry Ruth feeling as he did about the other. *That* was the strongest thing he had ever felt, in all his life. It made everything else seem flat, unimportant and dull. Perhaps, in time, other things would become important again, but the staggering point was that he did not want them to. Now, he wanted to go on feeling like this about Meg. With every hour in which he opened his heart to loving, the sense of emptiness that had been with him since childhood grew less; or rather, emptiness was filled. Now, if only he need not feel such painful pity for Ruth, he would be able to see the beginning of a kind of peace. But he was feeling worse about Ruth, not better; poor old Ruthie, finishing her dinner, with her red eyelids and nose, and she had dropped a speck of food on her dress; she must be feeling very bad. It had grown quite dark, and over distant sparkling Venice floated a moon like a pearl.

Ruth had gone on talking about the Lamberts; sympathising with the mother; he did not hear half of what she said. She didn't understand, that was all. She had never been lovely or silly or selfish; she had always been a grand sensible type and this was her reward. It did not occur to him that Ruth might have had to struggle with the temptations which beset a grand sensible type; the temptation to be hard, to be bossy, to neglect the sacramental side of church-going in favour of good works, to think that she knew everything. But, from this night onwards, nothing much was going to occur to him about Ruth again. Remorselessly she was moving along the surface of Time, on her way out.

She was silent again now, busy with knife and fork, forcing the food past the painful lump in her throat.

"I don't think I'll stay the rest of the time here," she said presently. "It'll make things so awkward, and I'd like to . . . get home." Her face twitched unbecomingly, and he interrupted:

"Need you tell anyone here what's happened?"

"Oh, *well!*" she said uncontrollably, "I'm pretty tough, but I don't think I *can* stand going around with everybody, sight-seeing and—and—— Besides, I don't see why I *should*."

"No, no, of course not. I was only thinking . . . what will you do, then? Och, it seems a pity to cut short your stay in Venice——"

"Oh, Hump—don't—I don't want to laugh or I shall——" Out came the handkerchief again and she blew her nose, while he stared at her uneasily. "No," she said, when she had put the handkerchief away again, "I'm sorry, I was a bit hysterical for a minute, that's all . . . the idea of its being a pity . . . I can't stick Venice, anyway," she ended more hardly. "It's dirty and full of unemployment and it's cruel. I shan't be at all sorry to say good-bye to the Grand Canal, quite apart from . . . other things. But I *do* think it would be a pity not to see a bit more of Austria while I've got the chance, so I think I'll 'phone up Joan Masters—remember her? We were at the Coll. together—she's staying in Salzburg and I've got her address. I can get in touch with her to-morrow morning and suggest we spend the rest of the time together."

He nodded. He did not care what plans she made, *so long as he could be rid of her.* The sight of her good, honest, not-quite-handsome face was rapidly becoming unendurable.

"Tell her *you* broke it off," he said suddenly.

"Oh—I'll have to see about that. I don't know. It depends how I feel later on. . . . Hump, *can't* you tell me what it is?"

"Ruth, I don't . . . I don't know. Can't ye be content with that? I don't know why, but I just can't go through with things. That's a'."

"All right," she said in a moment, on a long defeated sigh. She almost believed him.

"You could say the sort of life I was offering you wasn't good enough," he suggested, while they were waiting in depressed silence for the bill.

"That wouldn't be true," she said instantly. "It would have been a pretty awful wrench leaving Mother and all of them, but I would have done it."

"You'll have to marry someone who lives near to them," he said, almost at the end of his tether, only longing to see the last of her, counting the hours until she should be on the train and travelling away from him into the past.

Ruth held out her arms, with her back to him, while he helped her into her coat.

"No, I just want someone who'll know his own mind and stick to me," she said.

It was the one truly bitter-scented flower that she allowed herself to drop on the grave of her engagement.

They walked away from the little courtyard shaded by chestnut trees, and crossed the road to the waiting *vaporetto*, and all the way back to Venice the moon cast her blazing melancholy splendour upon the lagoon, and on disembarking they made their way homewards, side by side and in silence, through narrow streets enclosed by tall frail houses whose stones were saturated in the amorous air of three centuries. Closely entwined figures walked slowly in the soft light of the shop-windows, murmuring to one another and laughing, while brilliant eyes of glass and china, jewels and silk, leather and steel, glittered out from the shops into the streets; it was like strolling through a marvellous museum in which a banquet was being held, sometimes through a waft of scent and sometimes through the wicked smell of stagnating water gleaming below silent houses. The glittering shadowy city, with its ornate stonework and colours like those of pebbles washed and cast up by the sea, appeared as no more than a background for the murmuring, drifting, low-laughing crowds swirling through its streets and eddying over its bridges, and always the dream-like light and tremulous quivering movement seemed to be drawn upwards into the air, and to hover there, like an immense golden moth, above the Square of Saint Mark's.

So they walked back to the *pensione* through the most exciting city in Europe, with aching hearts and feet, and Humphrey was now so tired that he felt nothing more. He was exhausted. He had no immediate plans and hardly any thoughts; he had nothing but the determination to finish out his holiday in Venice, and to see Meg bestow herself upon Esmé Scarron. Then, he thought, he would know he had finally lost that which he had never had, and he could set about getting himself a job at the uttermost ends of the earth. He looked forward to going there.

CHAPTER TWENTY-SEVEN

Rosalba

"BUT I still can't *understand why*, darling. You told me, you said over and over again, that you weren't going to do anything in a hurry. And then, absolutely without any warning, without even——"

"Oh, Mummy, do let's stop it. I'm so tired, I'm worn out, and so are you. Do let's go to sleep . . . it's nearly three o'clock. I shall look like death to-morrow."

"Meg, I don't know what's come over you in the last few hours. You've completely changed. I don't know you. You aren't my baby any more . . . yes, I know I oughtn't to talk like that, all the psychologists tell mothers they've got to 'let their children go'—and get over the idea that they ever *were* babies . . . I don't think I *have* kept you as a baby . . . or been too possessive . . . but surely we've always been *friends*, haven't we? And when you *know* how I feel about . . . him . . . and I know so much *more* about life than you do, darling . . . how can you be so . . . so——"

There was no answer from the other bed, separated from her own by a few feet of dim warm air. The room was not completely dark because of the lamps in the narrow street outside, which were still burning; the large black shapes of old-fashioned furniture loomed against the pale walls; the window was a square of faint light divided by the slats of a Venetian blind. The city was not asleep; voices, tolling bells, laughter, far-away cries, came up out of it and floated away in the darkness. It was, as Meg had said, almost three in the morning, but the dreary timelessness of the small hours hung over the room. They had not been quarrelling—that was a word which could never have been used about them, ever since Meg's birth—but there had been a series of painful exchanges, beginning after an early retirement and continuing with intervals of uneasy sleep until now. It had developed into a struggle, with the mother trying to make the daughter give the reasons for her sudden action, and Meg steadfastly and coldly refusing. As Mrs Lambert was not accustomed to either of these qualities in her volatile, passionate and warm-hearted one, except quite recently and at rare intervals, bewilderment was added to her misery. Was this Meg? Would she be like this when she was grown-up, twenty-four, or twenty-five? She might have been a stranger.

"You aren't happy, anyway, You can't say you are," Mrs Lambert said, after a long and dreary silence.

"I'm all right. I only want to get some sleep so that I shan't look too ghastly when I see him to-morrow."

"I don't think I'll come, after all, Meg. I don't think I'll be able to stand it——"

"Mummy!" Meg turned over in the bed, and Mrs Lambert, startled by the note in her voice, looked quickly across and saw the white mask that was her face turned towards her in the darkness, "you've *got* to come. I *can't* go by myself."

"That's all very well, but why should I, when you know how I feel about the whole thing?——"

"Mummy, you must come. I'm frightened." It was the voice of a child who has been taught that it is silly to be frightened, and cowardly to admit to it.

"*Frightened?* Then you *do* know how I feel. And why, in the name of all that's extraordinary, you want to marry a man you're frightened of——"

"My feet are simply burning, it's cramp or something, I'm going to put them on the floor . . ." Meg muttered, and flounced out of bed. For a few minutes her mother watched the dim figure in its white nightgown, which gave to eyes hot and smarting with lack of sleep a delicate suggestion of coolness, moving slowly and with downbent head to and fro in the space between window and door. The floor was mosaic: a silent comment upon the nature of the Venetian climate.

"Do come, Mummy," Meg said presently, as she got back into bed again. She drew the thin coverlets over her shoulders. "Can't you just love me, like you always have? Please don't be angry. I'm so tired and miserable and I don't want to talk any more. Just say you'll come."

"All right," Mrs Lambert said, in a voice almost extinguished by fatigue, after another long pause, "I'll come. But there's another thing that's worrying me—we don't know the way there."

"I can find it. I've got the map."

There was a silence, so long that it might have been thought that both were at last asleep. Presently Meg said drowsily:

"Mummy, I do love you. You're always *there*."

"Oh, Meg, I love you too. I'm sorry I was cross, but——"

"Mummy, we simply must *not* talk any more. Good night."

The silence gradually deepened, and soon was made more peaceful by regular breathing. They had fallen asleep before their sense of dreariness, and foreboding of what was to come, had been increased by the stealing light of the dawn, which now grew rapidly in the room; the hectic, warm, unfresh dawn of a southern city; not the "frightened girl" of Wilde's poem, but a decadent Venetian flushed after a night of pleasure. And presently, as the light glowed down over her, Meg moved uneasily in her sleep, and that old sadness which had crept across the lake at Martinsdorf began to seep into her dreams, filling her with its burden of pity. Now it came down from the mountains, where a car was driving fast towards Italy through the increasing light; into her spirit where fear and anger and revenge had given it a foothold; and across the dark air of her dreams drifted again in its pansy colours and texture the uncapturable butterfly.

*   *   *   *   *

"Couldn't you sleep, either?"

Humphrey lifted his arms from the parapet of the bridge on which he was leaning, and turned with sinking heart to face Mrs Lambert. It was still early in the morning; the canal ran rose-colour with the reflection of the sky, and the stones of Venice, visible now that the thronging crowds were absent, could be seen as coated with a thin,

blackish dust which might have been all that remained, after four
centuries, of a myriad crumbled masks of carnival.

"I've been seeing Ruth off," he said, thinking it best to get the
announcement over, "she's gone back to Villach. We—er—our—
the engagement's off——"

Impatiently he waited for the low exclamation of sympathy. It
did not come. She looked at him silently for a minute, then turned
away and stared down into the water. Just across the Canal from
where they stood, the Santa Maria della Salute was dark and
beautiful against the sky, with, in the foreground, light against the
dome, a white stone angel floating up in the clear air. An old beg-
gar limped up to them, whining and smiling, and Humphrey
thrust some lira notes into his dirty hand and he crept away.

Mrs Lambert looked very ill; her pallor was greenish and her
eyes reddened. He thought that absorption in her own misery
had prevented her from taking in his news, and presently she
said:

"I've been up nearly all night with Meg, talking. It was so hot . . .
we couldn't sleep, anyway. It was *insufferably* hot. I hate this place.
It's cruel and dirty."

She turned away once more and looked at the Grand Canal:
sweeping before them in its splendid curve and lined with grey,
olive and dun-coloured palaces in whose gardens grew bushes of
pink oleander; all asleep, all dreaming in the warm light. "Dirty
and cruel," she repeated. She turned to him.

"He's coming here to-day. You know—that man. We're to meet
him in his wretched *palace*, at three o'clock. I'm dreading it so much
. . . I can't tell you. And Meg's behaving so strangely. She doesn't
seem in the least happy . . . I can't believe it's all happening. I keep
thinking that it's some terrible dream and I'll wake up."

Humphrey muttered something that sounded sympathetic. He
did not want to talk, and for once he did not want to hear about
Meg. For the moment he could think only of Ruth; settling into
that corner seat, upon which she had congratulated herself exactly as
if it really mattered, for the seven-hour journey back to Villach;
Ruth, shaking his hand and wishing him good luck—God knew, he

would need it—Ruth, with all her goodness shining in a face showing no traces of what he had done to her on the previous night;
Ruth, telling him at the last moment as the train drew out of the
station that he mustn't mind, that she would get over it, and would
always wish him well and think of him as a friend. Ruth, the grand
person, the wonderful wife for someone else.

"She made up her mind very suddenly," he heard his own voice
saying, and was surprised: he had been certain of not wanting to
discuss Meg and her affairs.

Mrs Lambert looked round. "I know. I believe something happened, but I can't get her to tell me . . . did your *fiancée—oh*! Oh,
Mr Scott, I am so sorry . . . I didn't take in what you said, I'm in
such a state. How dreadful for you—how selfish of me, going on
about my own affairs——"

"That's all right . . . I don't know if Ruth got a chance to talk to
Meg . . . I forgot to ask her."

"Yes, of course you did. I don't wonder." She paused, not wishing to seem inquisitive and not knowing quite what to say. What
an odd thing to happen so suddenly, she thought confusedly,
pressing her fingers against her burning eyes; they had seemed so
devoted, and the news would certainly cast a new gloom upon the
party, already depressed by yesterday evening's bombshell. Oh,
why did these horrible, puzzling, painful things have to happen?

"Will you do me a favour, Mrs Lambert?"

"Of course—anything. You've been so kind. . . ."

"Will you tell the others? I'm going to have breakfast by myself
somewhere and then go off to the Lido for the day."

"I think you're very wise . . . don't worry. I'll tell them."

Soon afterwards he went off. She leaned upon the bridge and
watched him moving down the now crowded street beside the
canal until he disappeared; then, sighing, turned back towards the
pensione. The sun was well up and the faded colours of the *palazzi*
glowed in its light. Eight o'clock . . . twelve . . . three. Seven hours.
The muscles of Mrs Lambert's stomach constricted themselves and
she shuddered.

*   *   *   *   *

"Broken *off*?"

"Dear, oh dear," murmured Robin, looking demurely over his coffee-cup. Camilla's face assumed a blank expression; she was remembering the waxen image.

"He asked me to tell you about it," Mrs Lambert said, sitting down at the table, "because . . . I think he feels it very badly. . . ."

"I don't," Robin muttered.

". . . and he doesn't want to talk about it, of course. I don't," glancing mildly and enquiringly round at the three young faces, "*really* think we ought to talk about it either. Of course, one can't help wondering . . . but it isn't our business . . . poor young things."

"Mammy Gascoine tell 'bout dis 'fore it happen. De doomsday-rabbits done tell her, didn't dey, Missy Camilla?"

"Gosh," was all Camilla said, "poor old Head Pre."

And they were all silent for a moment; even Marcel paid tribute with a pensive gaze down his long nose, thinking of Ruth Courtney travelling back across the plain which they had crossed so cheerfully three days ago. The least imaginative of the party followed her in thought; seeing the resolute climb through the noonday heat up to the *Venedig* accompanied by the local brat with the suitcases, her arrival in the quiet, shady, shabby house, the meeting with Frau Schacht, and the fixing of that dry grey eye upon her, the brief explanation . . . and everybody felt a sense of awed relief that it was not their fate to have been banished and broken by Romantic Love. For they all knew perfectly well that it was Humphrey who had broken the engagement, and why he had done it; and for the space of a few moments a great scented shadow swept with rustling wings across the commonplace dining-room filled with busily eating tourists; Eros himself, the god in person.

It was during those moments that Robin made up his mind.

"Camilla," he said, breaking the silence, "let's go and look at the horses on Saint Mark's this morning."

"But we saw them yesterday."

"You can bear to see them again, I presume?"

"Yes, of course, Robin, I'd love to."

Presently Mrs Lambert said in a low rapid tone, "Here's Meg—

better not tell her until later—I don't want her upset to-day."

So Meg sat down to her breakfast in a peaceful silence broken only by morning greetings, and drank her coffee with heavy eyes fixed upon nothing. She did, however, notice the absence of Humphrey and Ruth, and a feeling of relief was followed by a pang at their having "gone off somewhere together". But why shouldn't they? And at least he would never look at her *like that* again. When they next met . . . but now she was afraid of what she had done yesterday, and afraid of what was going to happen to-day, and so weary after the almost sleepless night that everything—from the smallest details of the breakfast table to the glowing, moving scene just visible through the windows—seemed feverishly unreal. And passions and fears and thoughts rushed through her nineteen-year-old body even as the hot breezes swept across the crumbling palaces and the canals which were a fitting background for her confusion.

She was tender this morning with her poor mother, who seemed —in that cliché which can be true of someone in late middle-age— to have grown old overnight; Mrs Lambert was just at that stage when sleep or the lack of it can make the greatest difference to a woman's looks, and this morning there was no doubt in anybody's mind of her being fifty-five. However, she did not allow her headache to prevent her from joining in the conversation, and even ate a little, while she enquired about other people's plans for the day and commented upon them as if her heart were not about to be broken a second time.

After breakfast they all prepared to go out into the city. Mrs Lambert had gone up to their room for a moment, and Meg was lingering in the *pensione*'s entrance, looking restlessly out into the narrow sunlit street thronged with people, as if wild to be off.

"So this afternoon," said Robin, suddenly appearing at her side, "you're meeting Pal Scarron at his *palazzo* to receive his ring. And are you a silly girl!"

She turned and looked at him gravely. She felt too tired to be annoyed with him, and she was trying to fight down her fears about the afternoon, which were of more than one kind and increasing with every hour that passed, by telling herself that she was grown-up at last, that Esmé needed her even if no one else did, and that there were *solid advantages* in marrying him. She was repeating this phrase over to herself as if it were an incantation to dispel her fears, although with each repetition she experienced a feeling of disgust. She had not been brought up to think about *solid advantages* in marriage, nor was it in her nature to do so without coercing herself.

She was also assuring herself that she could always back out at the last minute, and that the hat she wore this morning, the great Roman Shepherd, was quite the most becoming she possessed: it was Mrs Lambert who had got past thinking about hats.

Robin, however, met her grave eyes without awe. His face had, so to speak, gathered its bones together and wore its clever look.

"I am about to do you a piece of good, dear Meg. My oar is going *right* in. Splash! Humphrey has broken off his engagement."

"*What?*" Brilliant rose colour rushed over her face and neck. "Who told you?"

"Your Mum. At breakfast, before you came down."

"But it *can't* be true—they were so—oh, Robin—it isn't a joke?"

"*She's* gone back to Villach. Went this morning by the early train. I've been pumping the reception-desk."

"But where's—has—he—gone too?"

"No, of course not, you clot; that's the whole point; *he's* gone off to the Lido; he told your mother; I've been judiciously eliciting information from her. So it's all bust up, *kaput*, and mind you remember that when you're bestowing your heart and hand this afternoon."

"How frightful," Meg said in a low tone after a pause.

"Nonsense, how frightful. You know why he did it, or if you don't you ought to. We all do. Marcel and I have had a bet on it ever since she came, and now he owes me five bob. I'm taking it in lire; very convenient."

"How disgustingly heartless boys are!" Meg's grave composure vanished abruptly.

"Too true, Miss Dale. Well, I didn't mean to interfere. I told Camilla so, and I said she wasn't to, either. We weren't going to get involved. But Mammy Gascoine got a great *big* heart, and she not like to see Young Missy and Young Massa pining away like a couple ob hants. She want put a spoke in Mus' Scarron's wheel, too, 'cause she not like dat man." He paused, and moved back with one finger the hair flopping over his forehead. "I shall now leave you; I'm taking Camilla into the Piazza San Marco to propose to her."

She did not hear what he said. She was staring down at her sandals with deep colour in her face, and, after a dry, smiling glance at her, he went away.

Meg did not move. Her strongest feeling was embarrassment that he and the rest of them should know how she felt about Humphrey (but that was *dreadful*; she made an uncontrollable movement of shame)—and should have talked about Humphrey's feelings for her; they had noticed those long silent looks, they had put two and two together, they—and *they* thought that he liked her. She was not alone in thinking so, or mistaken—yet perhaps they were *all* mistaken, and he only—liked her looks.

She had had that happen to her, more than once.

But he had broken his engagement! *He* had broken it; Robin had said that *he* had; and the wonderful, sensible, beastly Ruth had gone away. . . . Oh, poor Ruth. How cruel; how awful for her. How awful of *him*. And why had he done it? Her heart seemed to stop. And when? Yesterday evening? While she and her mother were in the *vaporetto* crossing back to Venice, and she was trying to stop her mother's tears, with her heart full of miserable and torturing jealousy? Why break it off, then, an hour after she had announced her own engagement?

Oh, she had been afraid, after what she had done yesterday, but after all perhaps it was a good thing that she had done it, because it had forced him to break his engagement, and now he was free. He was *free*.

She looked up slowly, and the sunlight fell into her eyes and warmed her skin. Such a soaring of her spirits followed that she actually began to smile. All the colours in the street brightened; every shape, every thing, looked beautiful.

Then the warmth and light and beauty faded. It *seemed* as if he had broken his engagement because she had announced her own, but why should he? Why make himself free an hour after she had made herself a prisoner? (She felt like one now; there was not one solitary reason that she could find in favour of marrying Esmé Scarron.) If only she could find him; go out to the Lido this morning; make some excuse to her mother; find him. . . .

"Sorry to have been so long, darling. Where do you want to go first?"

Meg looked at her, and all other feelings were banished by another kind of shame. It was she, the beloved and loving daughter, who had made her mother look ten years older and given that greenish-white hue to her face. Slowly the last trace of happiness faded.

"Go?" she said vaguely.

"Your dress, darling."

There had been some talk, arising from a miserable attempt on Meg's part to be *sensible* and *hard*, of spending the morning in buying a dress that should present her in the most attractive light to Esmé Scarron. It was what a great many mothers and daughters, all over the world, would have done in similar circumstances, but it was not, as a suggestion, being of any help now to the unhappy Lamberts.

"Oh . . . I don't think I want one, do I?" Meg was realising how absurd her idea had been; how could she even have *imagined* going out alone to the Lido to look for him? What could she *say*? What would he *think*? And suppose he did only like her looks? She must have been mad. . . .

"Oh, all right, dear. That pink looks very nice . . ."—Mrs Lambert gulped; when she embarked upon making the pink she had not known that she was happy—"and after all, we've got to save our currency—though I suppose if you—we're—going to stay on here, he will——"

Meg slowly slipped an arm through hers.

"Let's go and sit somewhere cool, Mummy, and watch the people and not talk. And I'll buy you a lovely ice. You must be worn out. Let me carry your things." She hesitated. "Mummy——" she began, then checked herself. Mrs Lambert looked at her in dim and mournful attention. "Nothing," Meg said, and they began to move slowly down the street—between the girls with tanned bare shoulders, the Americans, the Germans in dark glasses with their gentle fair hair and steel jaws, the little old women in black slippers and shawls, the stunning ageing beauties in white suits, the eclipsed, everyday Venetians.

Meg kept a close clasp upon her mother's arm, but had retreated into the great cavern of her hat. She had been tempted for an instant to relieve a little of Mrs Lambert's misery. It could have been done, although throughout the painful, wearying night she had stead-fastly resisted the impulse to do so, as if it had been an evil tempta-tion. Now, when she saw by sunlight the havoc of her mother's face, she felt the impulse even more strongly. But to speak *now* would mean explaining—confessing—why she had acted as she had. And that would mean telling about Humphrey. And that was the one thing she could not talk about to her mother. She could not. Her mother would have to go on suffering. She would have to suffer until three o'clock that afternoon, when they would meet Esmé. And then—and Meg's spirits stirred faintly beneath their load—perhaps she would find the courage to—to stand up to him. She hoped so; at least, she tried to hope so. She felt so sad, in the midst of all the brilliance and bustle and sunlight and heat, and sorrier for poor Esmé than *ever*, so that she forgot to be sorry for poor Ruth. Her sadness and her pity for him were exactly in the mood of Martinsdorf; coming to her in waves, as if they were roll-ing across the lake, as if she were being invaded.

*   *   *   *   *

Robin and Camilla were sitting beneath one of the Four Horses on the façade of Saint Mark's.

Although they are about two thousand years old and are superb works of art, these horses share, with the back-door entrance into Venice previously described, a sort of homeliness. To sit under them is very comfortable and peaceful, because they are not so large as to inspire awe; and because the green with which the years have coated their bronze is a gentle colour, like that of the canals which thread the city lying below; and because the gallery of alabaster, yellowed by time, which must be traversed to reach them is narrow, and small, and worn to silky smoothness by the passing of countless millions of people. There is about these four sturdy, sensible-looking horses a strong flavour of belonging to the people. They can be imagined as coming alive in the small hours and picking their way deftly, without fuss, along that little gallery and down into the Square, where, under moonlight as green as their own skins, they would usefully pull a phantom fish-cart or give rides to ghostly holidaymakers. They came to Venice from the Hippodrome at Byzantium, where the roaring *aficionados* once went mad for the Green faction or the Blue, so they are accustomed to crowds and noise, and the façade of Saint Mark's, overlooking the Square, is the right place for them.

"Darlings; I do love them; this one is actually my favourite," Camilla said at unwonted length, gazing up contentedly at the one above her head.

"He has the most amiable expression of the four," said Robin. He did not appear quite so much at ease as usual; had more than once shifted his position on the plinth; and was gazing now down into the Square, blazing white in the sunlight and thronged with crowds and a-flutter with pigeons, and now at the improbable height of the Watch Tower shooting solidly up into the blue; then back again at Camilla's snub nose or her spikes of hair glittering in the sun. The light and the heat were blinding and dreamlike and delicious, and the noise of the crowd drifting over the vast pavement beneath came up as if from some strange-voiced sea.

"Camilla," he said presently.

She looked at him attentively. He put back his shelf of hair with a finger and tried again.

"Camilla, why do you think I brought you here?"

Camilla, screwing up her ice-blue eyes against the sun and wondering why he used her name so often, answered, "To see the horses."

"Yes, partly that. But I also brought you . . . you see, I thought it would be nice for you to be able to say to people when we're both old, *My husband proposed to me under one of the horses on Saint Mark's.*"

"You mean you're asking me to marry you?" she said, after her usual pause for thought.

"That was my intention—my general intention," and this time he blinked rapidly two or three times.

"I'd absolutely adore to marry you, Robin. It was an absolutely wizard idea to ask me under the horse and I'll always remember it and I think it's marvellous of you," said Camilla, becoming lobster-red in the face.

"Oh, good. Well, how very agreeable. I must say it's a weight off my mind . . . we're so well-suited that I quite imagined something would prevent it at the last minute—your accepting me, I mean—we'd turn out to be brother and sister or you'd go mad before my very eyes . . . I should adore to kiss you . . . may I?"

The party emerging at this moment from the Cathedral on to the gallery consisted chiefly of Americans, and they saw nothing un-usual in a Boy and a Girl kissing in the sunlight under one of the Four Horses of Saint Mark's. They stood smiling and approving, and one of them, preferring the scene to many of the historic build-ings in Venice, commemorated it with his camera.

* * * * *

"That must be it," Meg said in a low and weary tone, "the one with the red shutters."

They stood upon a little bridge in the heat and hush of early after-noon, looking into a square courtyard whose floor was of black, rippling, evil-smelling water, and which was shut in by tall narrow palaces, painted yellow and rust, that seemed to sleep. They had come by wandering ways far from the Ponte dei Sospiri, across bridges of crumbling brickwork and rusting iron, through tiny courts where the sun blazed down upon closed shutters and tattered washing, deep into the heart of the city, leaving behind the thoroughfares thronged by tourists and the shops selling souvenirs; and the air about them had grown quieter as they wandered, until the subdued roar of voices in the markets and on the *rios* bordering the Grand Canal had died off into a silence, so deep that they could hear the leisurely splash of approaching oars as some boat laden with firewood or fruit came down the canal, and the *whish* of air through the wings of a flight of settling pigeons high on some sloping roof. A hidden belfry struck out each quarter on a thin-toned sweet old bell, as they crept from street to court, and the sky was of a thin warm blue that seemed to give the sound its colour; these two things, the bell and the sky, had been with them for the half of an hour, and now made a kind of home, a familiarity, in a foreign place.

"Yes . . ."—Meg had been consulting the map—"this is right. Here's the bridge, and the palaces on each side . . . look, if we go across here we can get round to those steps . . ." and she led the way.

Mrs Lambert followed slowly. The silence and heat and the beauty of these mouldering courts and alleys had been soothing to her, and she had walked as if in a dream, wishing that the journey might never end, but now, being forced to face the moment of awakening, she looked about her. The dreadful poverty of the worst courts was not to be seen here; the houses were faded by sun-light, and their walls flaked and peeling, but some had flowering plants on their balconies, and small, carefully tended gardens, and their open windows revealed elegant shady rooms.

Esmé Scarron's tall yellow palace had two ogee windows, set one above the other, in its narrow face. They had balconies of scrolled ironwork below, and their twisted white stonework above; a flight of steps, the lowest sunk below the canal and covered thickly with dark green seaweed, led up to his door. At one side of them was a small courtyard, with an iron gate leading into the street that was no more than a narrow bank above the canal. A window overlooked this garden, with faded red shutters standing half-open.

"We ought to have come by gondola," Meg said—"our first visit to a private Venetian house."

She had become exceedingly pale, and in spite of the heat, her hands were very cold. They stood side by side, in front of the little garden, staring up at the *palazzo*; awed by the drowsy silence, and the atmosphere of an ancient past brooding over this backwater; putting off the moment when they must mount the steps leading to the door; break the hush; stir the house into life.

"What's that? I've never seen it before," Meg said.

Mrs Lambert shook her head over the satiny brown flowers, shaped like trumpets, covering a bush in the little garden. "Nor have I . . . I think they're dead, as a matter of fact."

Meg gave a low hysterical laugh. "I'm sure they are . . . they would be. Mummy," suddenly bending towards her and speaking in the softest possible whisper, "don't be angry with me—but I'm not actually *engaged* to him yet—s'sh!—yes, I *know* I did, but it wasn't true. I only asked him to come down here. I said I'd made up my mind and I'd tell him when he came, and I suppose he thought —well, I could tell from his voice on the telephone he did—that I was going to accept him. So you see, darling, things aren't quite so awful as you thought. . . . I nearly told you, *so* many times last night when you were so upset, only—s'sh!—you see, now I can always back out if I want to—only I'm *terrified* of what he'll say— s'sh, Mummy. Oh, I don't know—yes, I do, but I can't ever tell you, not *ever*. So do cheer up, darling—and now I'm going to try to wake up the house."

She went up to the window, and, putting her head between the shutters, looked in. Mrs Lambert, still trembling with a mixture of incredulous indignation and reviving hope (how *could* Meg have been so cruel to her?—and *lying* like that), watched her anxiously from beyond the iron gate. She heard her call, and in a moment she spoke to someone.

"Oh, who is it?" she almost whispered.

"It's an old woman," Meg said, withdrawing from between the shutters. "I think she's going to let us in."

In a moment, there was a movement and a gleam of white behind the bush with the brown flowers, and through its foliage they saw a door standing open, with an ancient creature in black dress and coloured headscarf standing beside it, motioning them to enter.

"He can't be here yet. We'll have time to get cool," said Meg.

The door led directly into a large, low room, whose air, after that of the burning streets outside, struck chill; and at once Mrs Lambert recognised the scent of hidden spices that she had first encountered in the house in the Austrian mountains, and felt the familiar oppression of spirit. The beauty of this great apartment was of a different kind from that of the rooms in Scarron's other home: lighter, more sensuous, more worldly; but equally daunting to the eye of Tormouth, and she sat down gingerly in the midst of terra-cotta walls, a floor covered in mosaic of black and yellow stars, gilt bergère couch and chairs, and curtains of light, rust-red silk. The reflections of the water outside rippled and spread ceaselessly across the naked goddesses tumbling on the ceiling, and the Loves who were binding them in chains of flowers.

"It's like the Sleeping Beauty," she said very softly, when they had sat in silence for a little while, with nothing moving save those ripples, with their curious effect of illusion; something that could not be caught or pinned down, something continually coming towards one on the chill, aromatic air. . . .

"All his houses are; I expect the one in Savoy is just the same."

Meg's heart was beating fast and she was becoming increasingly afraid. There was no question, now, of doing anything but tell him that she could not marry him. But she feared his anger, and her conscience was pricking. She looked out between the shutters at the rich evil water sleeping in the sun, the graceful red and white spring of the bridge, the palaces coloured like zinnias, and over all the joyous and unmodest blue of the sky. It was difficult to imagine the Christian heaven in such a sky. She glanced at her watch.

"He's late," she said.

"Meg, what are you going to—do?" It was the quietest imaginable murmur. Her mother's eyes were fixed upon her with, for the first time for many hours, an expression of hope.

"Don't worry, Mummy darling," Meg answered, a little absently. It was easy to think of telling him "no" when she could think clearly, but while this mood of pity was upon her she could not think clearly. And the house had brought back the mood. Perhaps the scent of spices recalled it to her nerves, with memories of that other house, in Austria; perhaps the ripples on the ceiling recalled the lake there; perhaps it returned to her because of the chill air of the room, contrasting so strangely with the light burning colours and the creamy flesh of the egg-faced goddesses. It was the sad, water-scented air of some cloister beside a river. She remembered, now, that he had told her the house was being repaired, or had recently been; and perhaps the cellars were still damp.

A clock, with a charming gilt shepherd-boy lounging against it, struck the half-hour, and the door of the room opened slowly. The old woman stood there, accompanied by an even older manservant wearing a black apron, who balanced a laden tray.

Mrs Lambert sat up. "Tea! Oh, how delicious."

The old woman, glancing quickly at her, came across the room and paused beside a low table, and the man followed. While they were setting out the silver spirit lamp and the jugs, and the china thickly banded with gold and looped with flowers, and arranging covers, and adjusting plates filled with tiny sugar cakes that did not, to a Tormouth eye, appear to be of the best quality—the door opened again and a ghost drifted quickly into the room.

That is, at the first startled glance they gave her, the word *ghost* came into the minds of both Mrs Lambert and Meg, but then, at the same moment, they recognised her. Mrs Lambert stood up, hesitatingly, with her eyes fixed on her, and Meg did the same.

But at first she took no notice of them. For all the quickness of her entrance, there had been something stealthy about it, and now she paused, half-way down the great room, as if undecided whether to go on or turn back, while she looked mischievously towards the servants, shaking back her fleece of silver hair. At the same instant they looked up and saw her.

At once the old woman came energetically towards her, chattering in Italian and making gestures that were almost threatening, while behind his wife the old man, still bending over the tea-tray, joined in with even more menacing words, keeping his head lowered and turned towards the new-comer. A smile of contempt was on his old olive-coloured face.

The tall woman listened to what the two were saying for a

moment, then snatched off the little black hat she wore and threw it on to the couch.

"I'm staying for tea—now," she said, in a cooing pettish voice, "I just came in for the hell of it, but now I'm staying." She turned to the Lamberts, and somehow they knew that she had all along been aware of their presence. "Hullo. Haven't we met before?" she said, and now it was the careless voice of a normal, rather insolent well-bred woman.

"Yes . . ." Meg said carefully. "Mummy, don't you remember? At Mr Scarron's house in Austria, that time we went there to tea? I'm afraid," addressing the apparition, "I don't really know your name. Mr Scarron called you Rosalba."

"I'm Mrs Charles Putnam," she said lightly, and went across to the bergère and sat down on it. Her black cotton coat slid apart, showing a dress of silk nylon printed with great pale roses that fascinated Meg, for a bemused second, by their likeness to skulls. "Aren't you going to have some tea?" she went on, while her white hands, with their slipping, glittering rings, moved amongst the cups. "I'm staying for some, now. *You heard what I said*. If Mein Papa comes in and catches Rosalba here he'll be very angry, but I don't care. He won't do anything to me while you're here." She bit into a sugar cake, looking steadily at Meg as she did so. "He doesn't want you to know about me. That's what Mamma says, and *I* think she's right." She gave a sudden ringing laugh. "Do have some tea, won't you?" she said charmingly, turning to Mrs Lambert, and rapidly filled a cup. "Milk—or lemon? Oh, there isn't any—I'm *so* sorry. Papa only has these two old things to do everything for him now and they're almost past it, as you can see. Constanza!" in a high soft scream. The old woman, who had been standing with her husband near the door, looking sullenly down at the floor, came forward, and Mrs Putnam spoke to her in Italian and sent her out of the room.

"Do you like my shoes?" she continued, extending her little feet towards Meg, "aren't they darling? Perugia made them; he's madly expensive, but there's no one like him. They cost sixty pounds English, but Charles sends me a lot, of course." Her blue bloodshot eyes suddenly spilled over with tears. "He likes me to look 'nice'. That's what he calls it—oh, my God, 'nice'. In that Back Bay voice of his—you know. We were married for eighteen months and it was absolutely *heaven*. But you couldn't expect it to last, of course; I didn't. At least, not really."

"Are you staying here, Mrs Putnam?" Meg said gently, in a moment.

"My dear, of course not. I'm with Mamma again. But she doesn't live far from here and we'd been shopping and—I'm afraid Rosalba was naughty—I gave her the slip and came on a *vaporetto*. Terrific fun. (I'm not allowed out alone, you know, because I fall about and faint. Such a fool and such a bore, aren't I?) Oh, I just thought it would be . . . *grazie*; Constanza," as the old woman silently thrust at her a little dish of thinly sliced lemon, "my dress was here, that red and gold one, they wouldn't pack it up properly for me, so—it *was* partly that." She suddenly turned on Meg, and leant forward, staring at her.

"You didn't really take it, did you?" she said softly, and Meg slowly shook her head. She had not expected to wish that Esmé would come, but now she wished it, exceedingly, and so did Mrs Lambert. The latter had succeeded in catching the eye of the old woman—with what purpose, it was true, she hardly knew—but had received only a blank stare and a shake of the head. The nibbling of indifferent cakes and sipping of Earl Grey tea continued for some time, without conversation. Meg still felt a grue down her spine from Rosalba's question, and avoided the glance of the eyes that every now and again slid slyly towards her. The poor thing's intrusion (both Lamberts had by now deduced uneasily that it was an intrusion) had had the unexpected effect of warming Meg's feelings towards Scarron. Kind Esmé, allowing his afflicted friend to wander in and out of his houses as her pathetic whim suggested; establishing a relationship between them which justified the mocking-affectionate use of "Mein Papa"; and putting up with the rages and accusations of a damaged mind. "Very angry" with her! Meg would be very surprised if he were; but she did begin to hope that Rosalba's presence might make her own task easier; perhaps

Rosalba might refuse to leave when good-naturedly invited to do so, and then Meg could slip in some remark, in an undertone, to Esmé about having nothing to say, really, except that she had decided it was "no". She could add an apology for having brought him on a nine-hour car journey to hear her say it.

She hoped that things might turn out like this. But suddenly, without warning or reason, she saw such a clear mental picture of the drawing-room at Tormouth (on Sunday afternoon, as was proved by the presence of a large cake and two or three old family friends) that she realised, for the first time, precisely how exotic, and how unpromising, her present situation and company were. The chances of her getting away without, at the best, considerable embarrassment, were small. If Esmé really had forbidden Rosalba the house this afternoon, it was because he had wanted—naturally enough—to have his interview with Meg in private, and he must have telephoned to his poor friend on his way down from Austria. Rosalba had deliberately, not unknowingly, disobeyed Mein Papa. He was certain to be a *little* annoyed. He might even be annoyed to see Mrs Lambert. And he might also be slightly irritated to find that all his kindness to his protégée was made plain. He had been hiding his light under a bushel, as truly kind people often did, and that was why "he doesn't want you to know about me".

But there did seem to be quite a number of reasons why he should be angry to find Rosalba here, and Meg began to feel frightened. It was the effect of the atmosphere of the room, and her sleepless night, and the fantastic fragility of Rosalba's appearance. *A skeleton in party dress.* The phrase jumped into her head, and would not leave it.

Her mother began to speak quietly, looking at the floor.

"Meg, don't you think we ought to be going? Mr Scarron is so late that I'm afraid something must have held him up indefinitely, and you know we promised to meet those people early this evening. . . ."

So Mummy was beginning to feel frightened, too. Meg was just about to agree to the plan, but suggest delaying their departure by ten more minutes to give Esmé a chance to arrive, when they heard unmistakable sounds of an arrival outside; the swish and strike of an oar, a man's rough voice speaking in Italian; and then, a moment later, the loud excited speech of Constanza, who, with the old man, had almost run out through a second door at the far end of the room, on hearing the sounds by the water-steps.

The Lamberts' stomachs plunged, and they stared at each other with widened eyes. Too late. But Rosalba turned her head to one side, as if listening, and remarked, before drinking some tea:

"I think that's my mother."

When the door opened, as it did almost immediately, to admit Constanza and the old man, both chattering agitatedly and accompanied by a woman, Rosalba got up so quickly that she knocked against the tray, sending a cup to the floor and breaking it. The woman came across to her rather slowly, walking as if she had been hurrying but could now relax; and jerking away from her throat, which was wreathed with many strings of pearls, a gauzy black scarf. She was all in airy black, from her small jet-sewn hat to the improbably fragile straps that formed her shoes, and the stockings thinner than a breath on a mirror. She did not look at the Lamberts, but said something in an exasperated tone in Italian to Rosalba, who laughed and shook back her fleece, then ran to her and buried her face on her shoulder. They were both unusually tall women, and the height of their slender heels gave to each a few more inches. They stood for a moment, while Rosalba made hysterical sounds, and her mother, with a bored and irritated, yet somehow relieved, look on her saffron monkey's face, held and rocked her slowly with an arm thick and white as marble; Meg and *her* mother, who had begun quickly to gather together their possessions for departure, could see it gleaming through a transparent black sleeve. They saw also rose-hued lace and narrow ribbon and embroidery, veiling the body of one who ignored the advance of old age. For the hair cut short to the big shapely head was silver, and the neck was corded and slack.

The Lamberts were feeling like housemaids, and housemaids in disgrace at that. The new arrival had not once looked at them, and Constanza and her husband were creeping about with the tea-tray

and the broken cup, muttering to one another, hurrying in and out
of the room, and occasionally pausing to address indignant remarks,
obviously about Rosalba, to Rosalba's mother. The former suddenly slipped her arm about her daughter with a decisive movement,
and led her to the bergère and made her sit down. Then she seated
herself beside her, and, putting down the huge envelope of black
straw that was her bag, looked for the first time at the Lamberts.

"Oh—how do you do," she said, in English with hardly any accent. Her tone was strikingly uncordial. Rosalba lifted her head
long enough to say, "The Princess Molina. She's my mother," then
dropped it again.

"I am Mrs Lambert. This is my daughter, Meg," Mrs Lambert
said, "how do you do."

She was so anxious to get away, out of this frightful house, that
she was hardly aware any more of feeling like a disgraced house-
maid. She *was* aware of the Princess's personality, because it filled
the room like a Kleig light, but she felt it almost absently. It was
overwhelming but not important. In a few moments she and Meg
would be out of its way.

"Are you going?" The Princess leant back on the bergère and
crossed her still-wonderful ankles. "Oh, don't go yet. Stay and have
some more tea. Or would you like coffee better? I've told Constanza to make some. I've never acquired this English tea-habit.
Weren't you supposed to meet Esmé here?"

"Yes, at just after three. But something must have happened; it's
nearly four," Meg said, trying not to sound pert, trying not to
sound awed. It was all very well, but no one could speak naturally to
a woman like this; a woman plainly immensely *wealthy*, with
clothes of an elegance never even imagined; and with melancholy
huge eyes that, most disconcertingly, seemed interested in herself.
They did not stare; those eyes could never mirror an ill-bred feeling; but they did not leave her face.

"I'm afraid we can't wait any longer. We have to meet some
friends at five o'clock on the other side of Venice," said Mrs Lambert decisively. She was sitting upright on the edge of her chair
with bag and gloves held upon her knees.

"He'll be furious if you go," said Rosalba, "won't he, Mamma?"

"He'll be furious anyway."

"Because *we're* here, you see." Rosalba gave her ringing laugh. "He *implored* us not to come here to-day, you know, Mamma. *Both* of us."

"I should not be here, if you hadn't gone off in that quite extraordinary way." Constanza came in with the coffee at this moment, and the Princess said something to her in Italian in which Meg caught the words *il signor*, and Constanza answered as if receiving an order. "Now . . ." to Mrs Lambert. "You will have some coffee, I'm sure."

She sounded *so* sure that the remark was not framed as a question. Mrs Lambert's voice was louder than she could have wished as she answered, "No, *thank* you, *really*. We must *go*."

Rosalba was leaning forward, glancing from one to another with glittering amused eyes and cheeks flushed with excitement. It was extraordinarily disagreeable, and the Lamberts were also hampered by their own embarrassment at the attitude of the other two, who might have been waiting for the curtain to go up at a good play. The Princess was pouring out coffee now, but she kept darting side glances from under eyelids that almost touched her lower lashes. It looked like a mannerism which years of intrigue had made uncontrollable, perhaps unconscious. It did not match her excessively sophisticated manner and dress, and it set the *comble* on Mrs Lambert's alarm. She suddenly stood up, and Meg did the same. The Princess looked up at them, smiling, with the coffee-pot suspended in one long and palely freckled hand.

"It's all right," she said soothingly, "here he is."

Now, standing in arrested movement with eyes fastened on the door that led into the garden, the Lamberts heard a repetition of the sounds of arrival; the splash of disturbed water and the dry scrape of oar against rowlock, voices—two voices: the gondolier's and another's. Constanza exclaimed, and ran to the garden door, but the old man had got there before her and was tremulously working at the catch. Rosalba's breathing could be heard throughout the room, and suddenly she slid along the bergère to her mother's side and tried to nestle there. The Princess pushed her away with decision; then, changing her mind or her plan, put that thick arm of marble about her, and drew her close. So they were sitting, not looking towards the door but down at the ground, when the old man opened it and stood aside to admit his master. Mrs Lambert sat down as suddenly as she had got up. Meg had already taken her former place on the edge of her chair.

Scarron seemed to bring in with him the heat of the streets. He wore light clothes, as usual, and an orange rose was pinned in his coat, and he was very pale, with a kind of white glare on his skin. He came into the room quickly, and the old servant shut the door after him, and went out with a bag and overcoat which his master had thrust at him. The bridegroom had come for the bride, but something had gone very wrong.

Mrs Lambert said, a long time afterwards, that it was sheer panic-stricken embarrassment that pushed her into speaking—at once, before the very slight pause, which she knew the Princess to be enjoying, had had time to become *silence*.

"Where on earth have you been, Mr Scarron?" she demanded loudly and cheerfully, even as she might have enquired of some Joan or Sheila late for the Senior English class, "we thought you were lost."

Look for an instant into the divided and piteous mind. Yes, he is almost lost, and he knows it. Now close again; let darkness resume.

"I'm terribly sorry, I've been trying to get here for the last hour. The car broke down some way outside Mestre and I didn't get into the city until after three, and then someone who shall be cursed for ever took the last gondola at the *stazione* just ahead of me. But here I am"—he smiled with an effort at Meg, who smiled timidly, solemnly, back—"and only so very sorry to have kept you waiting. Darling," turning to the Princess, "you've seen that they've had tea and everything, I'm sure." His eyes moved on slowly to Rosalba. "Naughty, naughty one," he said gently, "when you were so much better. You promised me you would stay in every afternoon and rest." She looked at him, without answering, trying to smile, and Mrs Lambert saw with a prophetic sickness that it was exactly the same kind of smile as Meg's.

"Yes, we've had tea, thank you," she said briskly, "and I was just saying to the Princess that we must be going. We have to meet some friends at the other side of Venice at five o'clock and it must be after four now."

"No, it is not quite four," he said, glancing at his wrist, "I have told the gondolier to wait and I will send you off in good time, don't worry. And I'm sending *you* off now, my sweets," he added lightly, but turning to the other two so quickly, with such a swooping movement, that he seemed to turn *on* them, "I'm really very cross with you both; you've been ill, the pair—the *precious* pair—of you, and you ought both to be at home resting after your morning's shopping. . . . So off you go, darlings. I know Mrs Lambert will understand."

Mrs Lambert was hoping, with all her frightened heart and soul, that his command (it *was* that, in spite of the gay sweet tone) would be disobeyed.

"Oh surely, Esmé," the Princess said, leaning back and crossing her ankles again and putting her arm, not gently, about the shaking Rosalba, whose eyes did not leave Scarron's face, "we need not go until Andrea has gone out and found us a gondola?" She paused, then went on playfully, "And what will you do, darling, if we—we go on strike and refuse to go at all? Dose us with some more distillations? But this poor poppet"—cuddling Rosalba with a sort of mechanical savagery, as if she were using the caress merely to emphasise what she was saying—"has had enough of your medicines." She did not look at the Lamberts as she spoke, but, when she had finished, darted her under-glance at them to see how they were taking what she had said.

"Oh, I think they've done her good," he answered, showing his teeth; what he did with his face, where the sweat now glistened, could not be called smiling. He turned to Meg—and here it may be said that he had taken notice of Mrs Lambert for the last time; he never looked at or spoke to her again—"Rosalba has been taking my medicines," he said. "I do prescribe for my friends sometimes. You see all that—that lovely thick hair of hers—well——"

"For your friends; yes; if one or two of them die or go crazy that's their affair; they shouldn't be such fools as to let you prescribe for them." The Princess's voice was deep and dull-sounding, like that of some angry common old man. "But your daughter—that *is* what the English call 'a bit thick'."

He said something very quickly in Italian and she laughed. "No, I think we'll talk English; I like to practise my English. Yes," with mocking cheeriness, looking now at Meg, who was sitting quite still, with parted lips, staring at Rosalba, "this big girl is his. You wouldn't think she was thirty-five. . . ."

"Mamma, need you tell them?" Rosalba whispered. "I don't look as old as that when I've got one of my really lovely dresses on; I've been told I look *twenty*-five, I wish you hadn't——"

The Princess whispered something in Italian, and although her eyes had begun to swim with tears, Rosalba giggled, turning her head slyly to look at Scarron.

"But *he's* sixty," she said softly, almost coyly. "Aren't you, Mein Papa?"

Meg looked quickly at the floor. Its black and yellow mosaic stars were blurred to her eyes by the intensity with which the crimson blood had rushed into her cheeks. She felt aware of an unforgivable indelicacy. She did not think; she did not even condemn; she realised nothing but the burning sense of shame. And there followed complete silence in the room. No one moved and no one spoke. The light, old ticking of the shepherd-boy clock went on, and the ripples flowed without beginning or end over the naked women on the ceiling. Presently the Princess, who had kept her sideways gaze fixed upon the frozen Mrs Lambert, rushed into speech at precisely the instant when the latter, with a long sigh, moved in her seat.

"It really *was* naughty of us to come this afternoon. I knew you would be angry, Esmé . . . and men over sixty can't afford to get into rages. It is bad for their blood-pressure. But I'm worried about this one"—again the sharp squeeze of Rosalba's shoulders—"and I know your friends will excuse it if I speak frankly—and," the eyes turned to Meg and stayed there, "Miss Lambert *is*—in a special position, isn't she?" The Princess leant forward. "Rosalba isn't getting well as quickly as we hoped. I'm not satisfied with this new man. Of course, I know it's difficult——"

He interrupted her sharply in Italian. He was sitting forward in the chair into which he had seemed almost to collapse, so desperate was the movement, a few moments ago. His head was lowered between his shoulders and his eyes had a clouded appearance. He had not looked at Meg. The Princess ignored what he said and continued, smoothly and in a tone whose mockery was open and insolent:

"If you bring up a girl as a boy, this psychiatrist seems to think, she may develop such an obsession with femininity that no man will be able to stand living with her. He seems to think Charles Putnam behaved quite normally and excusably. He doesn't think, though, that your distillations have *helped*." She paused. Mrs Lambert was trying to catch Meg's eye. But Meg, with a deep flush burning in her cheeks, was still looking down at the floor. Her mother, almost desperate now with fear and embarrassment, cast rapid glances from one face to the other. No one looked at her. The eyes of the Princess and Scarron appeared to be locked, like wrestlers of equal strength, in a grapple that each would die before breaking.

"Basil had the best of it, really," the Princess continued, "didn't he? However, we don't want to go into that. You don't like remembering that he knocked your teeth out, and of course I understand that; I quite understand it; any mother would, and his burning the girl's clothes you had made him wear since childhood, and running away to become a common soldier. Any boy who hadn't been ruined by your interesting experiment would have done the same thing—only it was hard on me; I still think it was hard. But no doubt you felt it too. As any normal father would. And he *did* have the best of it. He died. Now *this* poor naughty one"—she turned with playful ferocity on Rosalba—"do you know what she did this afternoon? Ran away. Yes, while we were peacefully shopping. If it hadn't been for her, we should not have been here. So you had better give her an extra strong dose of your nasty medicine the next time you get the chance——"

At this point, two things happened. Rosalba burst into a frightful wailing cry, "Oh, Mamma, you *are* a liar. *She* told me to, *she* made me come"—and Mrs Lambert stood up. She stood up quickly, and said in a tremulous but loud and clear voice:

"Meg, dear, we must go," and went across the room to Meg's side. Meg looked up and, with eyes fixed on her mother's face, got slowly out of her chair. Scarron turned his head, also slowly, and looked at her.

"Don't go. Please don't go yet. *They're* just going—and then I can—perhaps I ought to explain a little," he said.

As he sat there, almost crouched in the low seat, with his dull eyes fixed upon her, Meg felt the waves of sadness beginning to come out of him, and to invade her spirit. But they were a cry for help that was no longer heard. She defeated them by merely stooping to pick up her glove that had fallen to the floor, and settling her bag under her arm, and then she shook her head.

"No...I'm sorry...no," she said in a low voice, not looking at him.

He seemed to crouch lower. He remained quite motionless, and there was something in the pose of his head and the expression of his eyes that frightened Mrs Lambert almost into fainting. She remembered afterwards that she had, absurdly, murmured something that might have been a conventional farewell of some sort to the three now-silent creatures (it was hardly possible to see them as *people*) sitting there, before she thrust her arm through that of Meg, and they almost ran to the door leading into the garden.

No one attempted to stop them. No one spoke. Old Constanza was nowhere about, nor was her husband. A moment more, an instant's horrifying struggle with the complicated ancient handle, and the door opened. The burning light of afternoon streamed into their eyes, they caught the musky scent of the bush with brown flowers, mingled with the smell of canal water. Mrs Lambert pulled the door violently, and it shut with a slam. And, oh, there was the canal, leading *away* under the bridge, and the gondola, the gondola that Scarron had told to wait, moored to the striped post by the steps. The gondolier looked round at the sound of the closing door.

Behind them, in the room, there was silence. The shutters were still half open and they could have seen, even amidst their distracted progress towards the water-steps, any movement that might have been made within. But no one, nothing, moved. Only, in a moment, there came a kind of scream of pain.

"For God's sake, *quick* . . ." Mrs Lambert said.

They almost slipped into the water as they got somehow down the steps. They repeated the name of the *stazione* nearest to their hotel over and over again, imploring the man, offering him fistfuls of notes, weeping now, in their passion to get away. He looked at them suspiciously for an awful moment, then suddenly—perhaps because he had heard the sound from behind the shutters, perhaps because as a man experienced in touristry he knew that English ladies do not become agitated over nothing, perhaps merely because of the lire notes—he suddenly became active and helpful, nodded emphatic agreement, and quickly assisted them into his craft.

It rocked beneath their feet. They almost fell into the seat, clinging together, gasping, comforting one another, while the gondolier bent to his oar. Then they felt the boat move forward, a faint breeze from its gathering motion began to blow against their faces, and they passed under the bridge and away.

Away; between the sleeping yellow palaces and through the reflected red and white arc of the bridge, down a long evilly scented canal where mats of dying flowers hung down over blind blank walls; over water now changing from a dark murkiness to a lighter and more healthful green; while they sat close together, murmuring to one another, comforting one another, telling one another not to be frightened any more, that it was over, that they were free, and going home. . . .

Voices calling from windows across the canals, children playing on the narrow spaces between water and ancient, flaking flower-decked palaces; lovers strolling and laughing in the light of the sun; shops and cafés and Americans with their cameras again. Onwards; towards the strong sunny light quivering at the end of one last long narrow *calle* lined by grey palaces and dimmed by thin cold shadows, and so, passing under the Bridge of Sighs, out at last into the movement and colour and splendour of the Grand Canal glittering in the radiance of late afternoon.

CHAPTER TWENTY-EIGHT

Himmelblau

WHEN the gondola reached the landing-station nearest to the *pensione*, Meg got up unsteadily, and with the gondolier's aid helped her mother to disembark. She was now more frightened by Mrs Lambert's pallor and look of exhaustion than by what had happened, and she was thankful when the man accepted the sum marked upon his tariff-card, and a small *pourboire*, without argument, and at once, having made one or two pitying remarks and shaken his head over Mrs Lambert, proceeded to get his craft away. He did not offer to help them back to their *pensione*; no doubt there were Americans waiting for him at his regular *stazione*.

They stood in the street, surrounded by the hurrying or drifting crowds, and the peace and coolness of their room at the *Pensione Loredan* seemed far-away and unattainable. Meg looked about her, with her mother's weight leaning heavily on her arm. Oh, to see Humphrey—or Robin and Camilla—even that hopeless little Marcel—but they were alone.

"Darling, can you walk? It isn't really far; you can almost see it from here."

Mrs Lambert nodded. She was trembling now, and her eyes were almost shut. She had grown suddenly silent as the gondola neared the *stazione*, and Meg was afraid that she would faint.

They moved slowly off into the brilliant colours and lively movement of the crowds. Many people looked at them with sympathy, for in the city of pleasure the citizens have time to spare; one or two of them even stopped and offered help, but Meg was haunted by the fear of pursuit and so afraid that she would not pause for an instant. Shaking her head and occasionally pointing towards the sun as if to imply a touch of it, she guided her mother slowly but steadily towards the *Calle d'Oro*, and at last, with almost tearful relief, into the *pensione*.

Fortunately, the reception clerk had left his desk for a moment. Had he been there, he would have delayed them with questions, for although people frequently become ill in the lovely aguish place, that does not make Venetian hoteliers more inclined to treat them casually when they are: agues are bad for the tourist trade. But they passed through unobserved, and then began the endless ascent of the stairs; down dark corridors with cool mosaic floors where odours of appalling plumbing lingered; across stone landings decorated with appalling hazy water-colours of Saint Mark's, and so at last to their own Number 31 near the roof, and the comforting sight, on opening the door, of their possessions lying about; the necklace of white glass flowers bought lightheartedly yesterday, the photograph of Meg's father beside her mother's bed, and their shabby suitcases.

"There, darling . . . we're safe now. Come along now; you lie down, and I'll make you comfy."

"I'm sorry to be such a fool," Mrs Lambert said faintly, as Meg gently forced her on to the bed, took off her shoes, and covered her lightly but warmly with the coat brought against the alleged chill of Venetian evenings, "I can't seem to stop shivering. . . ."

"All right, darling. They can't get at us. We're safe. *Home-again, home-again, jiggety-jig.* Do you remember how Daddy always said that to us when we came in from shopping?"

Mrs Lambert gulped and began to cry; helplessly, with cheek and nose thrust into the pillow, and her eyes shut. The tears gushed uncontrollably between the lids.

"Oh, Meg . . . Meg. I'm so frightened. Horrible, horrible people . . . and they nearly got you. . . ."

"There—there, poor Mummy. Don't, darling, don't cry. It's all over. There's nothing to be frightened of any more. S'sh . . . s'sh . . . *gosh,* wasn't it awful!" She had seated herself on the bed beside her mother, and was gently, lovingly patting her shoulder, but now she stopped, with hand suspended, and stared unseeingly into the shaded corners of the room, which was in half-darkness because of shutters drawn against the afternoon glare. Her eyes widened and suddenly she gave an uncontrollable, twisting shudder.

Mrs Lambert sat up, trembling, and seized her hand.

"You won't see him again, will you? Promise. You must promise. I'm going to make you swear. You're legally under my control until you're twenty-one, and I'm going to make you swear . . . if necessary I'll take it to court . . . I can't stand any *more* of it, I tell you. . . ."

"*All right*, Mummy darling, all right—you haven't got to. Of course I'll swear—I'll do anything you want me to if only you'll lie down and rest and not worry any more. Do you think I *want* to see him again? I'd sooner swim all down the Grand Canal," Meg interrupted herself with a tremulous giggle, "and as for m-*marrying* . . . he—he can't *do* anything, can he, Mummy? Sue me for breach or anything?"

"I shouldn't think so . . . but he might hire someone to stab you or mutilate you," her mother said faintly, "he's capable of it. They all are, I should think. What people! I could never have imagined. . . . Meg," raising herself again upon her elbow and looking at her with tear-drowned eyes, "you won't go out alone, will you? Not here; not in Venice? And when we get back to Martinsdorf we'll go home at once. We won't stay for the last week. . . . You won't, will you? Promise."

"All right, lovey. *Do* lie down. Here . . . I'll get you an Aspro." She moved about the room, opening the familiar little pink and white packet, pouring water into a glass, disengaging the faithful White Sister from its covering. Mrs Lambert lay with her eyes shut. Presently she said:

"Why do they all go on *seeing* each other? Why don't they all go as far away as *possible* from each other? They must be mad . . . they all are, I think. They look it. That wretched, wretched girl. I shall remember her face till my dying day. . . ." She swallowed the Aspro and drank some water. Meg, having refused one for herself, lay down on her bed with one hand under her cheek and her face turned towards her mother.

"Mummy," she said after a long silence, "how much of that do you suppose was true?"

Mrs Lambert, who had been drifting into an uncomfortable doze, started wide awake.

"Now that will *do*, Meg. It doesn't matter how much of it was true. That isn't the point. But I expect most of it was. Thirty years ago—in a foreign country, and with plenty of money—he could do what he liked, I expect, and no one would interfere. . . . But that isn't the *point*. The point is that she could . . . could sit there and say it . . . and you saw the girl—woman—his daughter—there must be *something* in what she said. And remember what Hansi told us. You saw how *he* looked." She shuddered. "I'll never forget that, either. It was—horrifying. That's the only word." She began to struggle up into a reclining position. "Now you promise me—you've got to *promise* me—to see what they're like. Not to believe *exactly* what she said, not all of it—it sounded like something in a madhouse to me—but that they're horrible, vile, terrible people, *all* of them. *Promise* you can see it."

Meg was frightened by her flushed face and trembling lips and most of all by her manner, from which all composure and common sense had gone. She said soothingly:

"Mummy, of *course* I can see it. I think they're *utterly* horrible."

"Very well, then. Thank God that you've got away from him. Yes, I mean it. In your prayers to-night."

"I haven't said any for ages," shamefacedly.

"Then it's a mercy that I've been saying them for you, and please get into the habit again at once." The trace of tartness was most welcome to Meg.

"Mummy," after a pause, "please—do you feel just a little better?"

Mrs Lambert opened her eyes at the sound of the flat, eight-year-old voice that had often thus besought her when she was prostrate with headache, and looked into the anxious face of a young woman. It was a young woman who had recently told her a lie, and she hardened her heart.

"Not much, I'm afraid."

"Shall I squeeze your head for you?"

"No, thank you, I'm going to try to sleep."

Meg knew then that she was in disgrace, but she felt such relief at being free, and safe with her mother, that she accepted the fact without inward sulking. She did feel slightly ashamed of having lied, but not as much, she supposed, as she should have. She thought that the agonising confusion of her feelings ever since that conversation with Ruth Courtney yesterday (yesterday!) justified everything that she had done. It was all very well, but no one, *no one*, but herself, knew how desperate she had felt . . . and still did. She sighed, and shut her eyes. At once a vision, astonishingly alive and angry-coloured, of a yellow palace in a red cloud swam there in the darkness. She opened them again quickly.

"You aren't going out, are you?" Mrs Lambert asked drowsily.

"Mummy, of *course* not. I'm going to lie here beside you, and the first thing you see when you wake up will be my beautiful old face."

There was no answer; and gradually the quietness of the room was increased by the gentle sound of regular breathing.

But Meg lay with open eyes, listening to the murmur of life coming up from the streets. She lay upon her side, looking at her mother's thin, flushed face in which the eyelids had only just ceased their nervous fluttering, and gradually penitence and remorse stole into her heart. She had behaved very badly; she had made the one she loved best in the world sick with worry, and she was a Beast. But now there was going to be an end to all this. She would henceforward devote her life to her mother.

She moved uneasily, turning upon her other side. A mile or two away, across the massive ancient roofs laden with their weight of chimneys shaped like bell-flowers, and their thick tiles, and crumbling faceless statues, the yellow palaces still slept in the waning sunlight; and, in one of them, were those three still sitting in hateful silence? or had the other two gone away—back to the life they spent together in anger and dependence, in impatient betrayals and in madness? and was *one* now raging through the rooms alone, baffled and furious and lost?

She shuddered, and slowly sat up on the bed. She did not want to think any more about Esmé Scarron. She was going to shut her mind to him; and, in pursuance of her recent vow (it was no use thinking or hoping that she would have the chance to devote her life to someone else), she decided that she would not confide to

Mrs Lambert some vague and extraordinary suspicions. She might be imagining and fancying; she had done that all her life. But whether she were or not, now was not the time to trouble her mother with her thoughts. She would keep them to herself. Later on, much later, she might perhaps confide them to somebody, and probably it would be to her mother, because it was she alone who knew what had happened; and how those three had looked, and what they had said, on this afternoon that already seemed, because of the hours in it which were so startlingly different from ordinary hours, to belong to the historic past of the Lamberts' life. The ripples on the Venetian ceiling, and that last expression which Meg, without looking at him, had seen from the corner of her eye whitely burning on Scarron's face, would take their place, reluctant though she and her mother might be to admit them, on the tablets of memory that were most deeply engraved. They would be with the look of horror and surprise on her father's dead face when the Heavy Rescue workers brought him in, and the first sight of the flower-filled hall of their new home, which her parents had had when they came back from their honeymoon. Meg had not seen all of these pictures, but some of them she had seen, and she knew, because her mother had often told her, of the others. Now this Venetian afternoon would join them. It was strange, she thought, how she already thought of Esmé almost as if he were dead.

Of course, she told herself, if she had known that he was sixty years old she would not have played, even as lightly as she had done, with the notion of marrying him. She would have placed him at once and irrevocably as a Kind Old Thing . . . though, when she thought about the matter carefully, she did not remember once having *truly* thought of him as kind. He . . . she struggled to pin down the thought, but it eluded her, even as the butterfly in her dream . . . he behaved like someone *imitating* kindness; like someone . . . her imagination began to work . . . living in a foreign country who copies the habits of the best sort of its inhabitants, because he believes that this will get him what he wants there.

But what Esmé Scarron had wanted, she now would never know.

She was not troubled any longer by a feeling of pity for him, because indignation had replaced with its healthier glow the helpless, reasonless grieving. She felt that she had been treated very badly; deceived, taken-in and generally made a fool of, in a way so skilled as to be truly alarming.

But she had escaped. That was all that really mattered; and gradually, as she lay there with the quietness and the comfort of her mother's presence beginning to act upon her with calming effect, her thoughts strayed to where she longed for them to be: following Humphrey where he sauntered along the soft strand of the Lido in the waning afternoon light, with bent head and hands in pockets, thinking. About his broken engagement? Ruth? Herself?

She could have drifted off into sleep in this mood, that was half sadness and half delicious hope, had not a quiet, persistent impulse kept her awake. Presently she slipped off the bed and knelt beside it. She was unable to still her shaken and troubled mind to her own satisfaction, but apparently the will was taken for the deed, because, after she had said the Lord's Prayer and forced herself, with an uncontrollable sensation of hypocrisy, to add a plea for Esmé Scarron, peace began to descend upon her. She explained about the hypocrisy at some length, and the peace deepened.

She lay down once more, and glanced at her mother, who was sleeping quietly. Meg shut her eyes, and almost at once drowsiness began to steal over her. She heard the voices and laughter and footsteps in the street coming up to her more distinctly yet hollowly, like sounds made by ghosts, and then she heard them no more.

*   *   *   *   *

When she awoke, the room was full of the afterglow. She looked languidly across at the other bed and met her mother's eyes.

"Hullo, Mummy darling. Had a nice sleep?"

"I had horrible dreams, and I still feel dreadfully tired."

This was true. But it was also true that she felt better than when she had lain down. However, still feeling that Meg ought to be punished a little, she suppressed the more cheerful fact—although she felt remorseful as she did so.

"I expect dinner will cheer you up."

"I don't think I want any, dear."

"Wouldn't you like it up here on a tray?" Meg suggested, now really dismayed. She was longing to go down to dinner, in case Humphrey should be there, and although she still felt too sobered and shaken to describe herself as *cheerful*, she had undoubtedly been refreshed by sleep. But if Mummy were going to be ill on top of everything else, it would be the *end*. She never had been able to bear her mother being ill.

"No, dear, of course not. They might not like it. I'll get up in a minute, and go down as usual."

They were quiet for a moment, while Mrs Lambert reflected, and Meg, sitting up shoeless on the bed with hair disordered about her flushed face, stared dreamily at the glow coming between the slats of the blind.

"That was Hella, of course," Mrs Lambert exclaimed suddenly. "Now I think about it, I can see a likeness to that photograph he showed me, but of course he took good care to choose one that didn't date her by the clothes. She looked about twenty in the one he showed me. Actually she must have been nearer thirty. . . . Oh, and I remember now—how quickly he took me up when I said something about her still being young! I suppose she's his own age —perhaps a year younger—not more. Italian women age so quickly. . . ."

"Mummy, need we talk about it? It's all so horrible. I just want to forget it."

"I dare say you do—now. You didn't think so when you lied like that about your engagement."

"I know, Mummy. It was beastly of me."

"Nearly all last night, Meg, when you saw the state I was in . . . nearly insane with worry, and you never admitted you weren't really engaged to him at all, you never even hinted at it. And it would have made all the difference to how I felt, all the difference in the world."

"I know, darling. I am most terribly sorry."

"I still *cannot* think why you did it."

Meg turned her head away quickly, so that only a sheet of bright hair and that sadly immature nose, cutting the curve of a baby's cheek, were visible.

"Oh . . . I can't tell you. I will one day, perhaps. Oh no—I won't. Ever. But I am *terribly* sorry."

She suddenly flopped off her own bed and on to her mother's, and enveloped her in a rough hug, pressing against her the crumpled cotton dress and fuzzy hair and warm skin, while bestowing on her a kiss brimming with love.

"There. All better now?"

Mrs Lambert, finding herself for a number of reasons unable to speak, replied with a dignified inclination of the head, and they proceeded to get ready for the evening meal, which would be served in a quarter of an hour, in a silence that was more tranquil than that in which they had lain down to rest.

But although Mrs Lambert felt that Meg had now been punished enough for her inexplicable behaviour, and might be forgiven, she did not intend to take her into her confidence about plans for the next few days. She would only protest and argue, the mother thought, as she washed her hands with a scented soap whose lady-like yet bracing fragrance said *Tormouth*, and Mrs Lambert felt that she could not endure any more scenes. As the hart desires the water-brooks, so did she long for peace. She briskly dried her hands and looked absently into the glass, but the face she saw there drew from her a mild murmur of dismay. If Mr Scarron was sixty and looked forty, she was fifty-five and looked seventy. The fact did not lessen her dislike of him.

She glanced across at Meg, who, with an expression of complete absorption, frowning brow and hand steady as a surgeon's, was slowly laying pink paint upon the curves of the woman's-magazine-illustration mouth. Her face was glowing like a rose (there is no other accurate comparison), and Mrs Lambert took a moment from her own preoccupation with plans for escaping as soon as possible from the continent that contained Esmé Scarron to wonder at the resilience of youth. She also wondered—for experience had taught her that Meg did not often think about what she was doing at the

moment—what were the thoughts that had brought that rose-look
to her face?

When they came into the dining-room a little later, it was
already crowded with guests eating their way steadily through the
short but substantial menu. The two German ladies, at the table
next their own, lifted dull eyes in the crimson faces bent over their
plates and nodded to the Lamberts in greeting. They were immense, these ladies. Meg had watched in awe how they seemed
visibly to add to their bulk at every meal, consuming and assimi-
lating slice after slice of bread, glass after glass of wine, in addition
to copious platefuls of spaghetti cooked in oil, piles of fried potatoes,
and slabs of *veau*. Mrs Lambert, from the depths of an unplumbable
tiredness, looked at them this evening with her usual reflection that
one of her favourite writers, dear Elizabeth-and-her-German-
Garden, had been right about the Germans both male and female;
all those seemingly unkind references in her books to their militar-
istic nonsense and their size and their greed were as true in 1954 as
they had been in 1904 . . . tiresome, troublesome creatures that they
were.

There was no one else at the table allotted to the party from the
Gasthaus Venedig, and the Lamberts began the meal in more or less
tranquil silence. Meg was not surprised to find herself enjoying the
food, because she always did, and Mrs Lambert found herself, as
she had expected, too tired to eat. The one whose life was now devoted to her own did not notice this. Meg's entire attention was
concentrated upon the door of the dining-room, and in trying not
to look towards it. Except for a lingering, strange, bruised feeling
within herself, the events of the afternoon might never have taken
place, so completely (for the moment, at least) had she forgotten
them, and all she thought about now was Humphrey. But it was
almost half-past seven, and he had not come. Perhaps—and Meg
suddenly found the forgotten afternoon revenging itself by threatening her with tears in public—he was not coming.

"How late everybody is," observed Mrs Lambert, while they
were waiting for the small saucerful of stewed fruit with which the
Loredan's evening menu customarily abruptly collapsed.

"Can we have coffee?" Meg asked.

"Well, darling, it *is* extra, and everything's so expensive——"

"Oh, do let's. To cheer ourselves up." (And to keep us fifteen minutes longer at the table.)

"All right. But you know we must save every bit of currency we can."

Though actually we shall take a little back with us to England, as we're going to leave a week earlier than we expected, Mrs Lambert reflected, as she gave their order to the waiter, but there was no point in starting an argument about this with Meg; and, besides, she felt too exhausted to talk.

While they were waiting for the coffee, her mind slid off into thoughts of peaceful, quiet and delicious things; a cup filled with primroses standing in sunlight, the last few pages of Fauré's *Requiem*, the bubbling song of birds in early spring, and—on a lower plane, certainly, but so comforting—her kitchen table on a winter morning arranged for cake-making, with the white and yellow bowl and the sugar in its packet with the pleasing label and her faithful wooden spoon. She thought, too, of the piece of linen stamped with a richly intricate design for embroidering that she had indulged herself with before leaving home; and how she had looked forward to beginning upon its first, largest and finest flower—in what colour? pleasant to hesitate over so many delightful ones, pleasant at last to make a choice—and how, thanks to Hansi and the shopping and that dreadful man and Meg, bother them all—she had never had the time or the peace of spirit even to make an expedition to buy her silks.

"Oh, there are Cam and Robin!" said Meg, in a voice of relief. (If someone came, someone else might.)

"Had a good day?" she asked, when, greetings having been exchanged, they were rather silently arranging themselves and Robin was giving their order. Camilla went red and nodded, and he answered:

"Very agreeable, thank you. And what about you? Are you now betrothed to Pal Scarron? The ring *bery* old and vallyble, Mammy Gascoine 'ticipate. May I see it?" But the glance he gave her expressed plainly that he expected to hear quite other news.

"Oh—well—no—I'm not, as a matter of fact." Meg looked across at her mother, then down at her plate. "As a matter of fact . . . well, the fact is we had a perfectly ghastly and frightening afternoon. It was *so* awful, Robin, that we'd rather not even talk about it. Do you mind?"

"Of course I mind. Who wouldn't? I could weep with baffled curiosity. But Mammy Gascoine bery pleased to hear Missy Meg gib dat man 'im marching orders at last. Mammy done put a spoke in him wheel *dis* time, heh? Prevent him ebber drivin' de one-hoss shay again, she 'ticipate."

Meg smiled, but did not answer. She was more grateful to him than she yet dared to admit—though still very embarrassed when she remembered what his remarks implied—for the "spoke" which he had manipulated, but her gratitude was tempered by the sharp thought that he had no idea, none at all, how serious things had been. He still thought of Scarron as nothing worse than "scamp", and a bounder. If he could hear what her own suspicions were, would he still find it all so amusing? But she was not going to make the mistake of telling him.

Their coffee cups were almost empty. Mrs Lambert had begun to glance round in the vague way that meant she was looking for her spectacles and bag. All right, Meg thought dully, so he isn't coming. But I'll see him to-morrow. At the moment, the knowledge did not bring much comfort.

Robin had been consulting in an undertone with their waiter, and, as the man went away, he turned to the Lamberts.

"Don't go yet, please—if you aren't in a hurry. They're just bringing some champagne. Camilla and I are engaged."

"Robin! How delightful! I *do* congratulate you—and you too, dear," Mrs Lambert said, turning to the silent and crimson Camilla.

"I thought you were joking this morning—I'm terribly pleased for you both. Oh, it *is* nice—thank goodness *something* nice has happened *at last* on this perfectly ghastly day!"

In fact, the announcement added—illogically, perhaps, but undeniably—the last touch of misery to Meg's mood, but in a moment, having scolded herself for selfishness, she was gaily toasting the pair and joining in the discussion of their plans. The atmosphere of the small party moved at once into a blither key, and somehow the fact that their usual waiter, a cheerful little man, was replaced this evening by a gaunt one who seemed to disapprove heartily of the proceedings, only added to the gaiety.

And still—Meg stole a glance, under cover of the laughter, towards the door—he did not come.

"Of course *now* I shall cherish the nicest possible memories of the Piazza San Marco," Robin said. "The last time I was there, I was four. I wanted to stay and look at the pigeons, but my strongminded aunt strode right across the Square, with screaming me in one hand and her sketching-things in the other, and slammed me into the arms of my nanny. I've often thought it can't have done us any good with Musso.; my uncle was Ambassador at the time."

"Can he help me with the Government about the cats?" demanded Camilla, moved to words at last.

"Possibly. He's pretty old now, of course. But we'll certainly try . . . hullo, here's Marcel . . . come and drink some of our frightful champagne, Marcel. We're engaged—Camilla and I are, that is, not anybody else. Can you let me have that five bob you owe me to-night, please? and if you like to double the other bet we made, I'll take you on." The last part of the sentence was spoken in French, and so rapidly that no one but Marcel, who laughed and nodded, understood what had been said. As Marcel was settling himself into his place, and offering his felicitations, someone else came up to their table, and Meg looked up, and there was Humphrey. She looked down quickly at her plate. But no one was noticing; he was not looking at her; he was looking enquiringly, and with the beginnings of a smile, round the circle. *He had seen the champagne-bucket. He thought that they were celebrating her engagement.* Oh, how could he even *begin* to smile? And down, down, *down* went her heart. But Robin was sailing, with even more than his usual assurance, into the situation—*dear* Robin, thought Meg, with her first true impulse of warmth towards him—and saying:

"Yes, you must come and drink to Camilla and me—here's a glass and he's just bringing another bottle (I shall have to swim back

to England, but don't anyone be deterred)—yes—this afternoon—
no, you need not think Meg is in on this; *she* went to see Pal Scarron
this afternoon, and it's all off. *Kaput*. Finish. Don't ask her what happened, because she won't talk. Perhaps she saw something nasty in
the gondola-shed. But we're all *terribly* pleased. It must be one of the
few occasions in social history, don't you think, that an engagement
and a non-engagement have been covered by the same celebration?
Oh, *grazie*"—to the waiter. "Now, Humphrey. Let me pour it out
for you . . . yes, it is a surprise but not to me. I've been leading up
to this for weeks. How blind you have all been! Yes, I am rather,
but it's with happiness. Now, drink up."

"Hearty congratulations to you both." It was Humphrey's most
stolid tone and his Scots accent was strong. He raised the glass and
looked smilingly at Camilla, seeing nothing but the blue glow of
Meg's dress on her far side; then he drained it, sat down next to Mrs
Lambert, and, picking up the menu, stared at it in silence. The others
kept up an unbroken chorus of talk and laughter, and Meg's voice,
he thought dourly, was the loudest of the lot.

Relief, coming at the end of the long day's torturing thoughts,
had taken the shape of anger with the object of them, even as it does
with the mother who, snatching her child almost from under the
wheels of the bus, gives it a good smack. He had only returned
for the evening meal at all because his desire to know the worst had
become unendurable when the light began to fade and the last
swimmers came up from the lonely sands; and his first glimpse of
Meg at the table, laughing and surrounded by her friends, had sent
his heart turning over. What Keats called *a wild surmise*—many of
them—had rushed through his head. He looked quickly round the
long room, but the big head and slender body in the light clothes,
which he had grown to loathe the sight of, was nowhere to be seen.
Perhaps he had been called away?—but it was most unlikely that
he would have held an engagement party in the dining-room of the
small and obscure *Pensione Loredan*; the smartest and most expensive
place in Venice was more his mark, Humphrey was thinking, as he
crossed the room to the *Venedig* party's table. But there they were,
anyway, and all grinning all over their faces except Mrs Lambert.

She looked as if her day had been about as cheerful as his own. In another moment he was standing amongst them, and that young ass Robin had broken the news.

The *way* he had broken it was increasing Humphrey's feeling of dour withdrawal, as he sat unseeingly scrutinising the scrawling purple writing on the menu; as though it didn't matter a damn to anyone; with some rubbish out of that book about a farm that he was always quoting from; as though they had all been laughing their heads off for the last hour about something which, in the past few days, had come to mean so much to Humphrey that he now attached to everything connected with it a kind of sacredness—although, he knew, it was only the muddle that a kid of nine-teen had got into with her affairs. It was not until later that he grudgingly realised, and paid tribute to, Robin's airy tact.

He had suddenly become hungry. He had eaten little all day, and now the ample early platefuls of the *Loredan* were scarcely enough for him, and he regarded with some dismay the abrupt descent into stewed apricots; but all the time he ate, he was as conscious of Meg's movements on the other side of the table as if they were sensations within his own body; he felt the forward swing of her hair when she bent towards Camilla, and her voice—it did not occur to him any more that it was too loud this evening—seemed to move within him when she spoke.

Meg was content. She was also a very little drunk on the cere-monial champagne. Longing was assuaged, and she was content to sit laughing with her friends, with cheeks burning rosy fire and eyes sparking out dark brown jewels, not looking at him and not think-ing about anything else. He was here. Let the future do what it liked.

Gradually the room began to empty and the saturnine waiter to glance in their direction.

"Each time he flic-flac with his serviette a little more near at us. I think he mean us go," said Marcel.

"Let him," said Robin, "I don't get engaged more than once a year" (Camilla glanced at him quickly), "and I shall sit here until midnight if I please."

"You ought to take Camilla somewhere glamorous for the rest of the evening " Mrs Lambert roused herself, smiling, from thoughts which had taken her far indeed from the present company. "You ought to go out in a—in a gondola."

"We can't, thanks to the dear old currency regulations . . . not that I'm complaining, mind you. Now that I have a wife to support —all right, a fiancée, then—dear me, that hasn't made things any better, has it—no one will be more slavish in their submission to Her Majesty's Government than I shall."

"But we ought to be making a move, I suppose . . . though it's such a delightful party that I don't want to. Meg"—Mrs Lambert's glance crossed the table to the young person in the blue dress— "what are you going to do, dear?"

She hoped, with all her heart and against all experience, so tired was she, that a miracle might occur and Meg suggest that they should spend what was left of the evening quietly in their room . . . so likely, with Venice glowing and murmuring and glittering outside the front door! But Meg seemed in no hurry to suggest that they should immediately rush down to the Piazza San Marco. She hesitated, looking down at her lap, then glanced across with, "Oh . . . I don't know. What would you like to do?"

"I don't really know, dear," Mrs Lambert said, controlling an impulse to reply *Go to sleep for six weeks in my bed at home*. She remembered as she spoke her plans for returning at once to England. She ought really to wire this evening to Hansi, warning her that they would be back at Martinsdorf three days earlier than they were expected. . . .

"What do you want to do?" she said patiently, as Meg remained silent. Robin and Camilla were talking to one another, and Marcel was accepting a cigarette from Humphrey while giving the latter a disparaging account of the restaurant where he had lunched. The Lamberts carried on their discussion in a kind of vacuum.

"There's a concert near the Rialto to-night, with singers and musicians on gondolas," Meg began hesitatingly, leaning forward, "and I did rather want——"

"*I* don't want you wandering about at night," her mother interrupted decisively, "and, quite frankly, I'm afraid to go with you. Yes, don't smile, I am; we might run into *him*, and then I don't know what would happen . . . the mere idea is bad enough. Why don't you have an early night for once?"

It was at this point in their conversation that Marcel, becoming aware of Humphrey's wandering attention, allowed his own share to die quietly away while he faked some business with his lighter.

"Oh . . . all right, then. And I can go through my clothes a little, perhaps; I haven't looked at them for weeks and they're chaotic."

As Meg was beginning to get up from the table, feeling sick with disappointment but remembering her vow of earlier that afternoon, Humphrey suddenly turned to Mrs Lambert.

He was smiling, but the Scots that came into his voice when he was moved ran through his words like a Highland burn.

"Will ye let her come for a walk with me? I'll take good care of her," he said.

Meg did not move. Slowly her colour changed, but she remained with eyes fixed quietly upon her mother, who hesitated.

"That is, of course, if you'd like to," Humphrey added quickly, aside, and Meg, without looking at him, answered faintly. "Oh— yes, thank you."

"It's very kind of you," said Mrs Lambert, but although she had begun her sentence with the reflection that it *was* very kind of the poor fellow, after a day spent roaming the sands brooding upon his broken engagement, when she next spoke quite another idea had entered her head. *And, oh, was there going to be more trouble? Had there been trouble going on all the time which she had never, in the midst of all the surface trouble, suspected? A sort of underground movement, or enemy submarine trouble, which was about due to surface?* It was per- haps the worst moment of her day.

But it did not last long. It was conquered by another feeling, which, from its onset, she made no attempt to resist. She suddenly felt that she must give up trying to do anything about Meg. Calm- ness swept quietly into her, and she experienced the beginnings of peace. She smiled upon them both—they were now looking at her, surprised perhaps by her long hesitation, with faces paler and more solemn than the occasion demanded—and said almost absently:

"Well, that would be very nice. It's a pity to miss any of Venice
... you run along, then." She fumbled for her bag and her spectacle-
case and found both put into her hand—shovelled was the word
which afterwards indulgently occurred to her—by Humphrey.
"Don't be too late, dears," she added, still absently, as she withdrew
herself from the table with a smile which included everybody and
thanked Robin for his party. But the words were mere routine; she
spoke them only because she had said them to Meg, with varying
degrees of anxiety, almost every night during the past two and a
half years.

When she reached her room, she sat down on the bed. She intended to give the two younger creatures time to get some distance
from the *pensione* before she cautiously descended again, and made
her arrangements for the next day's departure. But the minutes
passed, and she made no move. She sat with hands in her lap and her
usually braced shoulders drooping; it was a relaxed posture, and the
tick of the clock drew out the quietness of the room. It was an
Italian room, of course, and a room in a cheap *pensione*, and perhaps
it was both graceless and impersonal, but all the same it was about
one-third full of heavenly silence and peace. Later on, Mrs Lambert
thought vaguely, through a haze of weariness, there would be
rooms that were filled completely with peace, like cups. Like cups,
she thought, and drew her feet up on to the bed; hundreds and
thousands of cups in houses all over England (for oh, she was never,
never going abroad again), and every room, she thought, as she
stretched out, sighing, to her full length, filled gently to its brim
with peace.

Her eyes shut themselves. She began to think about her embroidery, and the large flower with which she meant to begin it,
and she imagined with drowsy enjoyment making the first stitches
in the first leaf. And what colour should it be? At once she decided,
without any hesitation at all, and as if her decision reflected some
lightening, some drifting away of heavy shadows, from the climate
of her mind, that it should be blue. The colour that the Germans
(tiresome, troublesome creatures although they were, they certainly

possessed a wonderfully poetic language) called Himmelblau or heaven-blue. A blue . . . with a great deal of white in it. A blue . . . seen only on the hottest, clearest days of summer, when the sky looks as if . . . it had never known . . . the presence of clouds . . . that could cast a shade. The blue of a turquoise . . . stone. The brightest, tenderest . . . gayest possible . . . heavenly blue. . . .

CHAPTER TWENTY-NINE

Delle Salute

WHEN Meg and Humphrey stepped across the threshold of the *pensione*, they did so in silence. In silence, too, they walked rather quickly down the narrow street, less crowded now because its inhabitants were indoors eating supper, and dramatically lit by golden light streaming from windows and doorways. He did not attempt to take her arm, and if she had taken his—which she would perhaps have been justified in doing—she would certainly have lost him. They walked side by side, awed by the weight of unspoken love; it was not embarrassment that they felt, nor even delight at being at last together, and free; it took the shape of a mutual, scarcely formed wish that they might walk on like this for ever. Each was as strongly aware of the other's presence as if it had been audible music; his very coat sleeve, near to her own bare arm, seemed to Meg charged with himself and with love, but he, although equally aware of the movement of her skirt as she walked, was thinking about Ruth, and what he felt consciously towards Meg was a kind of resentment. It was she who had forced him to behave like that towards Ruth. She had so much power over him that she could compel him to act like a swine. She had not said one word to encourage him towards acting so; she was apparently innocent; but she existed; she was there, wasn't she? and had been for two months, with her eyes and her mouth and her hair, driving him steadily towards dishonour. He did not use the old-fashioned word in his thoughts, but it was what he meant. It was as well that every wise feminine instinct which she possessed warned Meg to remain passive and silent.

In a moment they reached the end of the narrow *calle*, and came out on to the Grand Canal, running dark and ample between tall palaces whose windows glowed gently upon the darkness. Shadowy flowering bushes leaned from the gardens over the water, and all about were the murmuring, drifting, sauntering crowds, the people of Venice at home to the world, in their own city, on an autumn night.

"Let's go to the Santa Maria delle Salute, shall we?"

He did not look at her as he spoke, but she turned to him, and saw his pale, irregular features, and the thick, sand-hued lash springing from the eye that by this light looked almost black, lit by the exciting subdued glow.

"All right," she murmured.

"We'll have to go by *vaporetto*," he went on, turning sharply in the direction of the booking station.

"All right," she said again.

They found a place near the rail on board, whence, looking back on the vista sliding away from the stern, they saw with unseeing eyes spectral palaces floodlit in pearly white or softest gold, and the serpentine, curving shape of the Canal unfolding itself, with all the sparkle and glow and glitter pouring itself out from every building into the darkness; with no harshness, and never coming within any distance of conquering the night. Here, although all was illuminated, night and the shadows ruled, and it was never possible to ignore or forget their beauty.

The Salute stands upon a projecting point of land, and beyond it the Grand Canal spreads out majestically into the light and glory of the open sea. To-night the moon was hidden in cloud. From the steps of the great church, where Humphrey and Meg seated themselves, they looked across to palaces which still slightly confined the scene, but already here the expanse of water was wider, while from the left, where land ended, there blew in a warm freshness across the dark. Looking to the right, they could discern in the dimness the beautiful and winningly modest outlines of buildings constructed during the ages when man's pride in his own works was still subdued by his reverence for God.

The Salute with its colossal dome and admonishing angels soared behind them into the night, but they preferred to keep their backs to the arrogant splendour, and to sit at its feet. Here, where the sea lapped the long step and the green weed waved to the tide; here, where other lovers sat silently embracing in the dimness; and beggars wandered by; and children were carried past in their parents' arms; the tide of common life seemed to flow all about them, and all the time they were surrounded by a scene of astonishing beauty, fantastic yet solid, exotic yet fanned by the fresh breezes of the sea. The double sense of contrast added to the confusion, the troubled happiness, of the hour.

During the short voyage on the *vaporetto* they had exchanged a few remarks about the weather and the passing scene, without meeting one another's eyes. Now they sat side by side; in silence, but growing more aware, with every passing moment, of being together. The loitering people, the black gondolas each bearing a single light that went gliding over the breaking and changing lights on the water, and the crowd slowly moving along in the soft glow on the opposite bank, all seemed like phantoms, and it was as if they two were watching a marvellous show, a pageant, that existed for them, and for them alone. Humphrey was gradually coming to feel less resentful towards her, as the sweetness of having her there, subdued and quiet, grew upon him; and he remembered that not once had she—so friendly, so forthcoming to everyone—made advances, which would have led to his becoming entangled, towards himself. It was true that she had looked at him. If she had not, he would not have been moved by some confusion of hope and shame to break his engagement. But he found himself unable to blame her for those looks. How could he? when for weeks he had lived for them, and on them; and so, as the night breeze lifted and fell in soft gusts, his hostility died away.

"What's the matter?" he said, more bluntly than he intended, as she broke a long silence during which they had watched the traffic of the canal gliding by; she had stirred at his side and drawn her breath quickly.

"I'm sorry. It was silly of me . . . I'm sorry."

"Nothing to be sorry about. Are you cold?"

"Oh no," looking round quickly with a smile, then as quickly turning away, "how could I be? It's so warm, the air's like milk. . . . No, it was . . . just for a minute I thought I saw . . . you know—*him*," and she gave a nervous laugh. The last thing she wanted to do was to introduce Scarron's name during their first hour alone together under the new circumstances, but she was frightened, and instinct told her that Humphrey would not be annoyed or really think her silly. In fact, she could not have said anything that would have sooner banished the last remnants of his resentment.

"Him?" He looked amused yet grim, and she noticed, with a dawning pleasure half-fearful, how thick were the muscles of his neck and how powerful the hands hanging relaxed between his knees; she had indeed got hold of something new and delightfully difficult for herself! "He can't hurt you."

"Oh, I don't know . . . he was so *furious* this afternoon. He didn't *say* anything, but it was how he looked. I suppose I did . . . let him down rather badly."

"He asked for it," Humphrey said curtly. He did not want to talk about letting people down. But the feeling of discomfort passed instantly, because by now they were looking at one another, and by the faint diffused glow of the lamplight and the floodlighting of a palace on the opposite bank, he could see the expressions passing over her shadowy sweet face. She said timidly—urged by an impulse to discover, if possible, where she stood, if not "just" where she stood:

"Were you . . . surprised when I . . . broke it off so suddenly?"

He shook his head. He had not taken his eyes off her own, and suddenly she looked down.

"Not . . . even a little bit?" she asked.

"No," Humphrey said coolly. Later, when things were more settled, when he knew where he stood, he might tell her about those long hours of misery on the Lido sands. Or he might not. He was not a young man given to grovelling.

"Oh . . ." Meg said, but not in the deflated tone that might have been expected, while, disconcertingly, a little smile touched her lips. She was deciding that she would not tell him just yet that she had never been engaged to Scarron at all. To do so would mean confessing why she had done it—to hurt him, to revenge herself upon him for the power which he possessed over her. No, she could not yet confess that; and, feeling that the heavenly sweetness of a mutually declared love was farther off than she had supposed, she breathed a faint sigh.

But in spite of these reticences, and in spite of the pride which kept them silent before one another, and thoughtful, and unwilling to meet one another's eyes, there was above all these feelings, like some great golden cloud or like that gathering together of all the glow of Venetian light into the sky over Saint Mark's—a delight in being together. And they felt that one day, soon perhaps, all would be well with them, and so well. There was not in either of their minds, as they now strolled slowly along the bank in the dim and glowing night, one shade of disappointment. This first hour spent together, although different from what each had imagined that it would be, was wonderful. And it had changed them both. They each felt this. They were exalted, yet sobered. It was the foretaste of that "married bliss" which Humphrey had first imagined at High Osterwitz.

They wandered on, through the murmuring, glittering streets, sometimes passing over bridges above the water where long lights lay reflected, and sometimes losing all sight of the canals. He had now drawn her hand within his arm, and as they walked on, and while he felt the warmth of her side against his own, Meg began to speak hesitatingly, once more, about her fear of Scarron.

"Forget it," he said, sturdily and a little impatiently.

"I know it's silly of me . . . but you didn't see his face when I shook my head. I keep on seeing it. . . ."

"What do you think he's going to do? Lie in wait and stab you?"

"No . . . nothing so——"

"So what?" He bent his head close to her in order to hear, and Meg, looking up, received a glance that sent her eyes flying down again.

"So ordinary." She thought of confiding to him her strangest suspicions about Scarron, and decided at once against it. Better not to poison this hour with such thoughts, better to thrust them into the back of her mind, to lie beside that knowledge of the world's wickedness and misery which, for all its immovable lodgment there, troubled her so seldom. She knew—how, she did not know, but she knew it—that Scarron's power of evil was not going to be allowed to spoil her happiness, and that, truly, was all that mattered.

She was greatly comforted by the support of Humphrey's arm, and also by his quietly amused attitude towards her fears. She felt that he would not have assumed it had there been any real reason for her to be afraid; it was fatherly as well as lover-like, and she delighted in it. It promised so happily for their future.

But in fact Humphrey was disturbed by what she said. She was so dear to him, and "getting dearer every minute", as Jo March said of her Professor, that he found it too easy to imagine the feelings of the man from whom he had taken her away. If Scarron—in that palace in one of the back canals of the city that Meg had just been describing to him—if he were enduring what Humphrey himself had endured all day on the sands of the Lido, with in his case the added knowledge that there was *no hope*, then there might indeed be danger. Of what kind, Humphrey had no idea. But he pressed Meg's arm to his side and began to look carelessly into each gondola that passed—infrequently now, for the wide canals and busy streets were left behind—over the motionless, evilly scented water. It was not likely, Humphrey thought, that the man would be walking the streets. His money had got him out of the habit of associating with ordinary crowds.

Humphrey was the more protective towards his girl because—he now felt—he had indulged in resentment against her. Bless her, it wasn't her fault. She could not help being a charmer. And, his heart suddenly filling with joy at the thought that he had really got her, the face of Ruth as she had seen it this morning at dawn (this morning!) faded and was seen in his mind's eye no more.

Meg had begun to chatter, exactly as a mating bird does, and he was listening, with one half of his mind convinced that it was pretty good nonsense she was talking, while the other half listened with delight to the mere sound of her voice. It was some account of a new dress, to be bought as a souvenir of Italy and Italian fashion, for Meg, now feeling that he was her friend as well as the person she— yes, it could be said out loud in her mind—loved, had naturally begun to treat him as such. Later, she would expect him to babble to her about metallurgy and mining in the same earnest yet inconsequential style.

It was while they were strolling thus, through a little square of ancient houses whose fourth side consisted of the wide-ish water of a still, black, silent canal, the whole scene gently revealed in the moonlight now falling from a sky bare of cloud, that the gondola stole out upon the water; crept, almost silently, across Humphrey's vision as if conjured up from the black deep. Meg, who was walking on the side nearest to the houses, saw nothing.

The gondola was canopied, and the shadows within the canopy were thick; the gondolier, a silent, tall and black figure, bent to his single oar, and sent his craft forward with a faint rustling watery sound that was just audible beneath the clear chatter of Meg's voice.

Humphrey, cautiously turning his head, looked more closely into the apparition.

Piled at the feet of someone who sat beneath the canopy was a dim mass of flowers and grasses, in which he could just discern the velvety heads of bulrushes and bundles of reeds, starry white blossoms, withies, and masses of dark water-plants. Then the light of the moon glided across the canopy, and shone for a moment on a great Punch's nose, a domed brow where silver hair grew high and thick, and on sick and wretched eyes that caught the mild light like the scales of a fish in the dark as they stared from side to side, searching for what they lacked and now would never have.

Humphrey's whole body seemed to him to contract for a moment of time. It was not fear. It was the sight of the man, coming upon all that they had thought and imagined and said, and the

strangeness of his coming; so silently, over the thick black water in
the deserted place, while a sickly odour floated out on the air that
might have come from the marsh-plants.

The next instant, his muscles had relaxed, and quietness returned
to him. Scarron's thick body in its light clothes sat upright, youth-
ful-seeming as always, but the look on his face made Humphrey
sum him up as *poor old devil*. He did not know that he was pitying
Scarron for a pain of loss which the older man was not enduring.
Humphrey, an ordinary human creature, had not much conception
of spiritual appetites and privations, or of reachings-out after satis-
factions other than those of the heart and the flesh. Nevertheless, his
involuntary pity did him honour.

Now the gondola was passing on; it was gliding into the ripples
and shadows and reflected lights; and then it entered the heavy
twilight at the far end of the canal, beyond the faint light cast by a
lamp fixed high on an ancient wall, and the soft watery rush of its
passing died away. It was not possible to make out the dark shape
any longer, although Humphrey looked long into the maze of
quivering reflections. Gone, he thought, and for good.

From one of the many churches of Venice, a worn, sweet, nun-
like old bell quavered out the hour. Meg broke off her discourse
with a start.

"Heavens. Twelve," she said dreamily.

They paused, and stood still in the deserted square. She was
smiling up at the moon, but he was looking at her.

"I meant to be in early," Meg said. "I meant never to worry
Mummy again. Do you know," turning to him, "only this afternoon I made a vow to devote the entire rest of my life to her? And
now——"

"Now I've got you," he said.

"Now you've got me," in a low tone, without looking at him.

Instead, she looked round at the hushed, lonely, moon-whitened
square of crumbling houses. There was not a tree or a shrub in
sight. The paving stones were covered in a thin black dust. One
light burnt dimly behind the doors of a small and dirty café; as the
breezes of early evening had died down, the water had begun to

send forth its odour into the warm night, and now it filled the
square: the historic, unforgettable, secret soul of the city wandering
out beneath the moon.

"Are we lost?" she asked.

He shook his head.

"I suppose we ought to go home. But I don't want to. It's so"—
she drew a quivering breath—"lovely here. The canal, and everything . . . need we?"

"We can stay out a bit longer if you like. There's nothing that
can hurt you," he answered quietly.

For regular

early information

about

FORTHCOMING
NOVELS

send a postcard giving

your name and address in

block capitals to:

The Fiction Editor:

HODDER AND STOUGHTON LTD.

1, St. Paul's House

Warwick Square

London, E.C.4

No. 1 *New York Times* bestselling author **Christine Feehan** has had over   y novels published and has thrilled legions of fans with her sedu   Dark Carpathian tales. She has received numerous honours throu   out her career, including being a nominee for the Romance Writ   of America RITA and receiving a Career Achievement Awa   om *Romantic Times*, and has been published in multiple langu

Visit Christine Feehan online:

www.christinefeehan.com
www.facebook.com/christinefeehanauthor
@AuthorCFeehan

Praise for Christine Feehan:

'After   m Stoker, Anne Rice and Joss Whedon, Feehan is the
pe   most credited with popularizing the neck gripper'
Time magazine

'The queen of paranormal romance'
USA Today

'Feel   as a knack for bringing vampiric Carpathians to vivid,
virile life in her Dark Carpathian novels'
Publishers Weekly

'The   zingly prolific author's ability to create captivating and
adrenaline-raising worlds is unsurpassed'
Romantic Times

By Christine Feehan